The
Fallen Sun

David R. Grigg

ISBN: 978-0-9942566-1-4

2nd Edition

January 2019

Cover and interior design by David R. Grigg.

Typeset in Geomanist and Calendas Plus,
fine fonts from Atipo Foundry (atipofoundry.com)

Published by Rightword Enterprises,
Melbourne, Australia

www.rightword.com.au

for Daniel and Ellie,
in whom rest my hopes
for a bright future.

Measuring Time on Sunfall

Time on Sunfall is measured differently from how we do it on Earth. Here are some rough equivalents to help you understand the story.

Names for time periods

A shuttering	About 24½ hours	The equivalent of one day.
A decant	10 shutterings	About 1½ weeks
A centend	100 shutterings	About 3½ months
A millend	1000 shutterings	A bit less than 3 years
Waking	Morning to evening	The equivalent of "today"
Lastwake	Last waking	"yesterday"
Nextwake	Next waking	"tomorrow"

Character ages

Age on Sunfall	Earth equivalent	
1 millend	2¾ years	A toddler
2 millends	5½ years	A school-age child
3 millends	8½ years	Mid-primary-school child
4 millends	11¼ years	Pre-pubescent
5 millends	14 years	Early teens
6 millends	17 years	Late teens
7 to 8 millends	19¾ to 22½ years	Young adult
9 to 12 millends	22½ to 34 years	Mature adult
12 to 20 millends	34 to 56½ years	Middle-aged
20 to 30 millends	56½ to 85½ years	Senior

Cast of Characters

Clan Bellringer

Ardens	The clan head.
Lambent	Elder son of Ardens. Heir to the clan.
Candens	Younger son of Ardens, Lambent's fraternal twin, born only a few minutes after him.
Campana	Sister to Candens and Lambent, several years younger than them.
Eccua	Wife of the clan head, mother of Candens, Lambent and Campana. Born into the Horsebreeders clan.
Tinnio	An old man, an uncle of Ardens. The Pendulum Master.
Nola	Tinnio's wife. By birth, also from the Horsebreeders clan and Eccua's aunt.
Sonor	An elderly cousin of Ardens. The Book Master.

Clan Mirrormaster

Nitens	The clan head.
Lucida	Niten's wife and the mother of Adura. Born into the Stonemasons clan.
Adura	Daughter of the clan head.
Maryam	A niece of the clan, Campana's best friend.

Clan Signaller

Solus	The clan head.
Calora	Solus' wife and the mother of Hermia and Blaze. Born into the Weavers clan.
Hermia	Daughter of the clan head.
Blaze	Son of the clan head and heir to the clan.
Vivens	Cousin to Blaze and Hermia.

Clan Woodminer

Fervens   Commander of the Militia, a kind of combined standing army, police force and emergency service.

Clan Healer

Percuro   The clan head.

Medeor   Percuro's son, heir to the clan and Healer of Souls.

Radians   Percuro's great-nephew.

Doriens   Another great-nephew.

Non-Clan Members

Libeth   Campana's maid.

Jud   Officer in the Militia, raised from the ranks.

Denn   Head of "Clan Delver", living on the fringes of society.

Other Important Clans

Clan Glassmoulder

Clan Metalworker

Clan Boatbuilder

Clan Ropespinner

Clan Icebreaker

Clan Stonemason

Clan Weaver

Clan Carpenter

The Fallen Sun

1

Candens

In the freezing, eternal darkness, Candens set fire to his bow.

The tiny, hesitant flame flickered and then answered his prayers as it caught in the pile of his broken arrow-shafts and grew. It began to lick up and over the shattered pieces of the bow. Fumbling, he reached beneath his layers of clothing and pulled out the shards of frozen wood he had tried to thaw by placing them there next to his shrinking flesh. With hands so cold that he could no longer feel them, he fed the wood to the struggling fire. The logs he had stacked around might catch, or they might not.

Exhausted, he had to sleep. The logs would burn and give him warmth, or they would not. He would either awake, or he would not. There was no more that he could do.

Surely this was the lowest point of his life? How had he fallen so low? All that he could hope was that his fortunes would eventually swing upwards again, like a pendulum.

Like a pendulum...

As sleep began to claim him, all of his thoughts were of a great pendulum inside a darkened tower, swinging, swinging, swinging...

Like a great engine of time, relentless, implacable, the pendulum swung through a long, slow arc, slicing the air inside the dim tower.

Nearby, the bob of its twin hung tied out of the way, waiting for its own turn to serve.

Such light as there was within the tower came through the shutters high above where the two pendulums were

I

suspended. It streamed across the inside of the tower in narrow, horizontal beams, illuminating drifting motes of dust. The shutters here were usually kept almost fully closed to prevent any wind or rain entering, which might affect the movement of the active pendulum.

Candens' father Ardens stood watching the exact position of the pendulum bob as it swung over the marks engraved in the floor, his face grave, concentrating.

The bob swung towards him and its point reached a particular mark.

"Now!" Ardens said.

With a grin, Lambent reached up on tip-toe to yank on the signal rope. Lambent always went first; that was the rule. Candens knew that he would be next, but it wouldn't be the same. It never was.

The rope rang a bell in the tower. Not one of the big bells, of course, the ones that sounded out the great peals. This was just a small signal bell to tell the cousins in the Bell Chamber that it was time to sound the next peal.

"Now it's your turn, Candens," Ardens said.

Candens reached up as Lambent stepped aside. He pulled the rope with both hands, feeling the strong resistance of it in his arms. It was harder to pull than he had imagined. There must be a lot of rope, he thought, to run all of the way up to the top of the tower.

So, he pulled the signal bell, but he felt no thrill in doing so, even though he could now hear the loud four-tone peal crashing out from the tower and rolling over the landscape, the vibrations in the stone felt even down here in the Pendulum Chamber. No thrill. Their cousins would have reacted to Lambent's signal, had probably never even heard Candens' superfluous second signal as they worked to sound the huge bells above.

Ringing the signal bell had been a special treat for the boys. This waking was their third birth commemoration, their third millend. Three thousand Shutterings and Unshutterings since they were born.

Lambent had been born first, so the servants had told Candens many times; born a whole six hundred heartbeats before their gasping, exhausted mother had squeezed Candens out into the arms of the midwife.

Lambent went first. That had always been the way of it: born together, but unalike. Born together; but Lambent had been the first; would always be the first. And that meant everything.

⌒

Another thousand Shutterings had to pass before the boys were old enough to be allowed into the Bell Chamber itself.

Every waking of their lives, Candens and Lambent had heard the thundering peals coming from the tower standing high above the rest of the manor buildings. A dozen times each waking came the full four-bell peals and five times between each peal the solitary ring of the bell with the deepest note. That was how time was marked out in Sunfall. That was the proud work of their clan, but never before had the boys been permitted to enter the chamber where the bells hung.

Their little sister Campana, not yet three millends old, had cried angry tears when Candens and Lambent left the breakfast table, both boys visibly excited by the coming treat.

"I want to go, too!"

Campana had pouted, stamping her foot, but Ardens had been unsympathetic.

"Girls are not admitted to the secrets of their clans. You know the reason why, Campana. If not, your mother will tell you once again."

This came with a stern look at their mother Eccua, who nodded in submission and laid a trembling hand on the girl's arm.

Now, Candens was gasping for breath as he climbed, following his black-haired brother up the long wooden stairway which spiralled around inside the Pendulum Chamber. Ardens strode on ahead, now half a circuit ahead of the boys, whose short legs couldn't keep up.

Ardens was waiting for them at the closed door at the top. "Now. One more inter-peal bell remains to be rung. We'll wait for them to ring it before going in. By my tally that should be in twelve counts from now. Eleven, ten..."

Ardens counted down. At his "Zero!" there followed the slightest pause and then a single deep note rang out from behind the door. It was loud, very loud; and felt rather than heard. Candens felt the staircase—and his whole body—tremble in response to the note.

Ardens opened the door and Lambent quickly dodged in before it was completely open. Candens followed more slowly.

They were high; higher than Candens had ever been before. He had been up to the observation platform on the outside of the tower, of course, but the Bell Chamber was higher still. It was open on four sides, cold and brightly lit. Looking out over the landscape, squinting against the fierce glare of the Sun, Candens felt dizzy.

Nevertheless it was the bells which drew his attention. Four huge cylinders hung from the ceiling of the chamber, the largest of them taller than a grown man. It was still trembling from the most recent stroke and it was so close that Candens could feel the air vibrating on his skin.

Lambent looked up at the bells and reached out to touch the nearest one to him, in awe. "Are they made of—*metal*?"

Ardens nodded, a smile of satisfaction crossing his face, the smile of proud ownership.

"Yes, metal. That is a very important secret. No one must know of it outside the clan."

"But they must be worth a *fortune*." Lambent

emphasized the last word with amazement. "And the bells in all the repeater towers—"

"Yes. But only metal gives the sound we need; a sound which carries far."

Candens, too, was surprised. All his life he had imagined the great bells up here to be made of glass or pottery, like the ones the servants used. Metal was... well, it *was* money.

"Did we make the bells?" he asked now. "Our clan?"

"It is hard to say," their father said. "Our clan has certainly possessed them for many generations. These bells are ancient. The metal is archaic steel—godsteel, the Dims call it—like the ribs of the skeleton towers. No one now alive, not even Clan Metalworker, knows how to work such steel. If they did, the skeleton towers would have long ago been broken up for their metal."

At the back of the chamber, on the darkwards side, their uncle Resens was standing, with their cousin Darien beside him. Both men wore thick leather pads strapped over their ears. Resens nodded at the boys and gave a small smile. Darien appeared uninterested and to a degree unfriendly, staring out away over the landscape.

"Now, boys," Ardens said. "The peal is coming up and we must be ready. Take your stations as I've taught you. You stand over here, Lambent and you over there, Candens. Put on these ear-pads. Watch the signal bell, Lambent. You won't hear it, but you'll see it swing."

Excited, his heart beating fast, Candens held on to the rope he had been given. It reached up through a hook in the ceiling at the rear of the chamber and from there to a heavy wooden beam, pulling it high and back, the tension of its weight keeping the rope taut in Candens' hands.

They had been shown what to do with a makeshift rig in one of the work sheds below, without the great bells, of course. This, though, was the real thing and Candens was nervous.

5

David R. Grigg

The signal bell shook, but Candens could hear nothing through the pads. Ardens slapped Lambent on the back. The boy twitched his rope off the hook as he'd been taught and the heavy beam swung free. Lambent ran forward a little, pulling on the rope to help speed the movement of the beam. Down it swung through its arc, gathering speed, until at its fastest it struck the great cylinder of metal.

Even through the pads, the sound of the huge bell, so close, was extraordinary. Every particle of Candens' body seemed to vibrate and ring, making him feel weak and helpless, bewildered. So much so that when his father's hand came on his own back, all he could do for a moment was gape. Ardens shook his shoulder roughly and Candens came to his senses and twitched his own rope. It didn't come free from the hook. Frantically, he twitched it again and to his relief this time it came free and the beam began to move. He helped it swing forward as he'd been shown and in a moment the second bell of the peal rang out.

Candens couldn't hear his father's voice, but he could see his disapproval and the words form on his lips: "A little late."

Then their uncle Resens swung the next wooden hammer and the third note rang. Darien swung the last and the peal was complete. Each bell had its own distinctive sound. The order of the bells told everything. *DIN! DAN! DON! DUM!* Every person in Sunfall knew that sound. It was the Shuttering Peal, perhaps the most important peal of all; the peal which brought an end to each waking.

His ears still ringing in sympathy, Candens moved to the opening on the sunward side of the tower, rested his arms on the stone wall and looked out in fascination. Though he couldn't hear them, Candens knew that the nearby repeater towers would already be sounding their own peals; would have started the moment the cousins there heard the beginning of the peal from the manor. The towers further away still would hear those bells and begin striking their

6

own. In a short while, all of Sunfall would know that it was time for the Shuttering.

Candens still felt a little light-headed being so high. From here, he could see all across the country. The Sun was blazing at the centre of the bay, too blindingly bright to glance at for more than an instant, surrounded as always by clouds of glowing mist.

Closer to hand, down below on their own estate, the workers were moving through the fields, closing the high shadow-gates to shade the crops. In the clustered buildings of the manor the servants would be going from room to room closing the wooden shutters tight. It would be the same across the whole land.

At his father's touch, Candens took off the ear-pads.

"All right, boys." Ardens nodded his pleasure. "Well done. Now it's time for bed."

By now Candens was resigned to Lambent taking first place in their activities. Even at play, Lambent took it for granted that he would be the first to make a move in some board game, the first to aim at targets with his bow, the first to look for a place to hide. In their lessons, Lambent was the first to be asked a question by their tutors, even if he was rarely the first to give the correct answer.

There was one activity, though, where Candens took priority, and that was simply because Lambent had no interest. That was in learning the work of their elderly cousin Sonor, the Book Master.

Sonor had never married. He lived alone in a small suite of rooms on the second floor of one of the manor's secondary buildings. His workroom was unique because it had no shutters. Bright light always flooded in, illuminating the ranks and ranks of dusty books on the shelves lining the room and the high wooden tables filling the space at its centre, each always with half a dozen or more old books open.

Sonor himself seemed to have taken on the characteristics of his work: his cropped white hair like dust on his otherwise bald scalp; his wrinkled brown skin the match of the leather bindings of the books; his small spectacles glinting back the light like the windows.

"The work of the Book Master is to keep track of the count of Shutterings, and to record what has happened in the manor and in the rest of Sunfall each waking, as best we know of it." Sonor waved his arm at the thousands of books around him. "Each Shuttering, the Book Master makes an entry and numbers it. To him falls the responsibility of telling the ringers when to sound the start of each centend, the start of each millend."

Candens had been fascinated, Lambent bored. And so it was Candens who spent the most time with Sonor, reading through the ancient volumes, scanning the pages and noting the ranked numbers in the left margin. Every hundred entries came a line ruled across the page, every thousand a double line in red. The entries themselves were usually dull enough, though occasionally in the older volumes he found longer entries outlining the course of a public dispute or even an armed conflict between clans.

After a while, though, he noted something strange and asked the old man about it.

"These red dots. What do they mean? There seems to be one roughly every three and a half centends."

The old man pursed his lips in mock annoyance. "Come, Candens, that is not very exact. Count and see."

Candens bent to the work and after a while looked up. "They are 365 shutterings apart. Well, one was 366 shutterings. Was that a mistake?"

"They record an ancient measure of time, whose origin is lost in antiquity. These intervals were called 'yeres', or so they are called in the very oldest books here."

"What strange numbers, though. They aren't usefully divisible by anything. How odd."

"You are right; the division of time into hundreds and thousands of shutterings is far more sensible. Nevertheless, my father and his father before him, and I suppose every Book Master past, always recorded these old intervals, though we now have no need of them. I have kept the tradition going, however, and I hope that whoever succeeds me will do so." He looked directly at Candens as he said this. "Tradition is important. It is what holds society together."

And with that Candens had to be content.

⌒

And so the time passed until he and Lambent, two brothers alike in age but not in looks or temperament, reached and passed their fifth millend. Now they were both old enough to be pledged, when the next ceremony came around.

Candens did not suspect then how that event would change the future course of his life. How it would sever the intangible thread holding his fortune in place and let it begin its long, slow swing downwards towards disaster.

⌒

He was sound asleep, dreaming of a mechanism, a complex thing of wheels and ropes and little levers, a mechanism that once he had completed it, he knew, just knew, would solve all of his problems and make him famous across the breadth of Sunfall.

The ingenious design vanished from his mind in a flash as the shutters of his room were opened wide, flooding the room with bright sunlight. Lambent jumped onto Candens' bed and started to pummel him.

"Wake up, idiot. This waking is the Pledging, don't forget."

Outside, the bells were still sounding the Unshuttering Peal and the repeater towers had not yet begun to answer. Throughout the manor buildings, the servants would be going from room to room, opening the shutters on the sunward side and beginning the business of the waking. On any other morning, Candens would have slept in for a little until he heard the house-bells ring for breakfast. And so too would Lambent, who often had to be roused by the servants and dress in a hurry to avoid the wrath of their father, who was impatient of any lack of punctuality.

"Time is our business, our reason for being." Ardens would be sour-faced whenever either of the boys was late for some event. "If *we* of Clan Bellringer cannot respect time, who will?"

"Wake up!" Lambent thumped Candens in the chest. His blows weren't hard, not really, not quite enough to bruise, but annoying. Candens thumped back and shoved his brother away.

"All right, all right, I'm coming. What's the rush? There's two peals to go before we have to leave."

"Ah, but you need to be ready. Need to pretty yourself up for the girls. You don't want your pledge bursting into tears the moment they announce your name. Mind you," Lambent added with a mischievous grin, "in your case they'll probably cry whatever you do."

Candens surged up and rolled Lambent off the bed onto the floor.

"Don't talk so soon. It's not about how good-looking you are. Maybe Father will pledge you to that skinny, buck-toothed Glassmoulder girl. The one they were trying to get rid of at the last Pledging."

They heard a soft knock at the door and it opened part-way as the manservant Parr looked in. He was a dark-haired man approaching his tenth millend.

"Lambent, Candens." Parr gave a polite nod to each of them. "Magister Ardens has decreed that breakfast will be early today. You'll hear the house-bell in only a few score heartbeats. You'll both need to dress quickly. Casual clothes for now. I have your travel clothes ready for once breakfast is done. Come on, quickly, now!"

Lambent threw a pillow at the man, who dodged with a smile.

"I'm serious. You need to get moving."

Parr had started to close the door. Before he could complete the action, however, it was pushed fully open and their younger sister Campana ran in, her auburn hair flying out behind her.

"You're going to be late; Father will be *ang-er-ee!*"

Candens threw his other pillow at her and she shrieked and scampered off out of the door, right into the arms of her maid Libeth, who was wielding a hair-brush.

Candens was already pulling on a light shirt and black pants. "You heard, Lambent, father will be *ang-er-ee*," he said, mimicking Campana's voice.

Lambent just smiled, but Candens noted that his brother's step was quick as he headed off to his own room to get dressed.

The house-bell began to ring, summoning them to breakfast. Candens completed his preparations as swiftly as he could, but then lost considerable time hunting for his shoes. He found them at last hidden on top of the wardrobe. Lambent's work, he was sure. Shoes on, he combed his tangled brown hair and headed down the stairs to the dining hall.

The manor wasn't a single building, but many; and the families of each of his uncles and adult cousins had their own apartments and dining rooms. As clan head, of course,

Candens' father owned the grandest building on the estate and its dining hall was big enough to host a score of important visitors when required. That made it feel a little too large and cold for ordinary use by just the close family, but Ardens always insisted on it.

Despite Candens' haste as he hurried across the stone floor, it was no surprise to see Lambent already there, chatting to their father, who turned and frowned at Candens, pointing to the seat to his left in an unspoken command to sit down quickly. Lambent smirked.

It wasn't fair. He wasn't late; he was just... second!

2
Campana

"Sit up, Campana. Don't slouch. And straighten your dress, it will get crumpled. You don't want to disgrace our clan at the Pledging, do you?"

Campana suppressed a desire to stick out her tongue at Great-Aunt Nola, who was sitting opposite her in the jolting carriage. But then there would be sharper words and her mother would have to get involved. Right now her mother was leaning her head against the shuttered window, her eyes closed, though surely not asleep.

Instead of being rude to her mother's aunt, Campana sat up and dutifully straightened her bright yellow dress. In truth she didn't want to crumple it. It was new for the Pledging. She was delighted with it and proud of the clan emblem she had been allowed to embroider on its breast. Great-Aunt Nola nodded her approval. "That's better."

Campana hated travelling to the city in the carriage because the Sun's glare always obstructed her view of their destination. At least going back home she had the fun of watching the carriage's shadow stretch out, racing ahead. Still, this trip would be worthwhile, with the excitement of the Pledging to look forward to.

Just then, Great-Aunt Nola peered out of the darkwards carriage window, where a few buildings were now passing by.

"We're almost there, I think."

Campana looked out. Most of the buildings were long, low constructions, but then came a much taller one, which was a sign that they were nearing their destination. Outside of the clan manors, it was rare to see a building more than one storey high unless it was a bell tower or a signal tower. In the city centre, though, many buildings reached to two or even three storeys high, such was the demand for space. The taller the building, of course, the larger the umbra—permanent shadow—cast behind it.

"Eccua." Great-Aunt Nola turned to her niece as they pulled into one such long shadow. "Open your shutters. We're just about there. Eccua!"

Campana's mother stirred and opened her eyes. She sat up, seemed to pull her thoughts together for a moment, then sighed and opened the shutters on her side of the carriage.

Now Campana could see out on all sides. The streets were crowded with carriages and men on horses, all coming for the Pledging Ceremony and the important connections they would make for their families. Two mounted couriers threaded through the crowd, distinctive in their blue and gold, no doubt bearing last-moment important messages from the signal towers.

The Bellringer carriage joined the slow queue moving towards the Council Lodge and Campana could now see her father Ardens on his black stallion, with Lambent and Candens riding beside him.

Such was the crush of people that there was a tedious wait for their carriage to draw up to the entrance of the Hall. Campana was getting hungry and was eager to reach her clan's private quarters at the Lodge. Campana was grateful that her father was on the Clan Council. Each of the twenty clans on the Council was granted a private apartment within the building, where the Clan heads could stay before and after meetings.

At last they drew up beside the steps leading to the brightly-lit arched doorway. The carriage door was opened by a servant and Campana climbed out quickly. Without waiting for her mother and her aunt, she ran quickly over to the steps and then up towards a group of people just about to enter the building.

Too quickly.

At the top of the steps Campana stumbled and, arms flailing, toppled forward, right into the back of an older girl, knocking hard against her. Campana only just managed to stop herself from sprawling onto the stone pavement and ruining her new dress by clinging on to the other girl for a moment.

As Campana let go and straightened up, the girl whirled around to give Campana a furious look, which twisted her otherwise-lovely face. Her long hair was dark, almost black, and her dress was a deep emerald green. On her breast a clan emblem flashed out—tiny mirrors set in a square grid, reflecting back the sunlight.

Campana had never met the girl before.

"I'm sorry—" she began.

The dark girl ignored the attempted apology.

"Why..." She looked Campana over with a cold, scornful expression. "If it isn't the Bellringers' brat; racing to get to the food, no doubt."

Then she leaned towards Campana and said with emphasis, "It's about time you people learned your proper place. You're not as important as you think you are."

Campana was left open-mouthed as the older girl turned abruptly and walked quickly through the doorway into the building.

3

Candens

Ardens stopped his sons on a landing part-way down the stairs which ran from their private quarters to the Council Chamber.

They had exchanged their dusty travel clothes for freshly pressed tunics, each with the white bell-tower emblem of their clan sewn onto the breast. Ardens fixed the boys with a stern look. "Remember. All of the other clans want our secrets, just as we want theirs. There will be questions you must not answer: sly, subtle questions, which you may think harmless. They'll think you two are still callow boys—not far wrong there—and easy to fool. Don't fall for their tricks. Think carefully about everything you are asked. Say nothing to such questions. Smile and change the subject. It's a game, you understand, but a game we can't afford to lose."

They walked on into the Council Chamber. A long table ran down its centre, at a right angle to the direction of the Sun. Along the sunward wall, panels of shutters were angled so as to catch the Sun's rays and deflect them upward to the white ceiling of the chamber, providing generous but diffused lighting.

On the wall opposite the Sun were mounted the emblems of the twenty clans who currently comprised the Clan Council out of the hundred or so clans within Sunfall. So far as Candens knew, the Bellringers had always been part of the Clan Council. Not that the membership changed very often. The last change he knew of was in his grandfather's time, when the Signallers had been admitted.

16

The table took up only the centre of the room, with space on either side. Clan heads and their male kin moved about, talking. Many platters of food, with jugs of ale and water, were set out on the table. A few of the older men sat at one end, their heads together, talking in whispers, slight frowns on their faces.

With a nod to the boys, Ardens moved off to join his peers. In a moment, he too was deep in discussion.

"I'm surprised there's so much to talk about." Candens looked around. "Surely most of the pledges have been arranged already, by signal, or by meetings at the manors."

"Most of them, yes." Lambent's gaze was flicking over the representatives of the other clans, as though he were looking for someone in particular. "But Father says there can be last-moment changes. Sometimes a pledge is promised before the Pledging, but then suddenly refused just before the ceremony. It's bad form, of course, and shameful, but it happens, he says. Then they have to scramble and accept what they can get, or nothing. It's all a big game."

A splendidly-dressed older man moved towards them. His rich, deep blue tunic was well-made, but failed to disguise his substantial paunch.

"The Bellringer boys, isn't it?" he asked in a friendly, avuncular tone. "You've both grown since I saw you last."

Candens inclined his head in respect. "Magister Glassmoulder."

"No need to be so formal. Call me Nitens. Now, which of you is which? The dark-haired one, you're the heir, is that right? Pardon my forgetting your names."

Lambent nodded and smiled. "Lambent is my name, Magister. Yes, it's my good fortune to be the heir. This is Candens, my brother."

Your brother, the not-the-heir, Candens thought sourly. Lambent never seemed to consider that Candens might not be happy with his secondary position, accepting his own good luck without question. All for the sake of being born a few hundred heartbeats earlier. But Candens kept quiet and forced a smile.

"Your family provides us all with a valuable service," Nitens said. "What we would do without the regular peals, I don't know. Really remarkable how you know when the bells should be sounded. I've always wondered how you did it."

This was so transparent a ploy that Candens almost laughed. Before Lambent could say anything—Candens didn't entirely trust him not to give something away—Candens replied for them both.

"Indeed. I've always been interested in how glass is made and shaped, Magister. It would be fascinating to learn more about it."

Nitens Glassmoulder did laugh at that.

"There's a great deal to it, a great deal," he said after his chuckles had subsided. "Well, very nice to have met you both. Looking forward to the Pledging, hey? I hope your father has arranged good-looking girls for you."

He raised a hand in greeting to another clan head and moved off.

"Maybe that means you're not getting that ugly Glassmoulder niece after all," Candens said. "Try not to be too disappointed."

"Who knows? I wouldn't trust anything he says," Lambent replied, with less humour that Candens had expected. "See you later, there's someone I have to talk to."

With that he headed swiftly off, weaving through the crowd of men.

Outside, the local repeater tower sounded the third bell since the peal. Candens adjusted the count in his head, an action so familiar to him by now that he was barely aware of it: fifth peal, third bell. Three thousand and one, two, three…

As his subconscious count continued, Candens tried to follow Lambent's dark head in the crowd to see who his brother was in such a hurry to meet, but he was distracted by a heavy hand on his shoulder. He looked around into the grizzled face of a short but well-muscled man. Unlike everyone else in the chamber, he wasn't wearing a tunic bearing the emblem of a clan, but rather a leather jerkin fastened tightly around his waist with a heavy belt. The handle of a dagger showed in its sheath on the belt. For an instant, Candens felt a flash of alarm. Had he done something wrong? But the man spoke to him in a calm voice.

"You're Candens of the Bellringers, right? The one who's not the heir?"

Again? Candens gritted his teeth with irritation. Was Not-the-Heir going to be his name from now on?

"Yes, I'm Candens," he replied, with too-obvious annoyance.

"No need to get angry. I'm Fervens of the Woodminers, Commander of the Council Militia." The man gave a wry grin. "For what it's worth, I'm not the heir to my father's clan, either."

Candens relaxed a little.

"All right. How may I help you?"

"You might be able to do something for me; for the Council. Have you ever thought about joining the Militia?"

The Militia kept the peace in Sunfall, ensured that Council decrees were obeyed, kept crime under control and helped out in emergencies like fire or flood. Candens had read in Sonor's books how in the past they had even intervened to stop violent feuds between clans. Candens was aware of their work in general, but had no idea of the detail of their operations. He considered Fervens' question for a moment and then answered truthfully.

"No, not really."

"A lot of our officers are the second or third sons of their clan heads," the Commander explained. "There's not much pleasure in always hanging about at your manor just in case something happens to the heir. You need to do something with your life; make a contribution to Sunfall. If something *were* to happen to your brother that would be no problem. You're not bound to the Militia for life."

"Well, I can handle a bow, but otherwise I'm not very good with weapons." Candens had never been skilled at the martial arts other than enjoying archery as a sport. His attempts to use a club or quarter-staff had been clumsy.

"That's no problem," Fervens said. "We train our people very well. The training is hard, but by the time we're done with you you'll be an expert. And damned fit as well."

"I don't know," Candens said. "I'd have to think about it."

Commander Fervens nodded.

"Of course. You've got a lot on your mind today anyway with your Pledging. But do consider it."

"Yes." Candens nodded. "I will think about it."

In truth, he wasn't very interested, but Commander Fervens didn't seem like the kind of person who would take a simple 'no' for an answer.

Fervens slapped him on the shoulder. "Good man!"

Candens filled a beaker with water and picked up a bread-roll stuffed with slices of beef and vegetables. He took a bite and looked around, trying to identify people. The clan emblems made it easy to identify the families, of course; but he didn't know the names of many of those wearing the emblems.

Candens spotted Lambent over in a corner, deep in animated conversation with another, somewhat older man with blonde hair. Lambent was shaking his head, but the other man persevered with whatever he was saying, making eager gestures. Lambent glanced quickly about and then deliberately turned his back on the room, blocking Candens from seeing what was going on. Candens frowned. Lambent was very much his own person and Candens suspected that there was a lot that his brother didn't share with him.

Before Candens had time to think more about what he had seen, he was approached by a rotund, elderly man. The emblem on his tunic showed a pair of snakes entwined around a silver tower at the top of which blazed a golden Sun, the emblem of the Healers, the clan which looked after both the physical and spiritual needs of those living in Sunfall.

"I am Magister Percuro," the old man said. That title made him the Clan head, then. "And you are?"

"Candens of the Bellringers," Candens answered. Then, with a feeling of grim defiance, he added, "the one who's not the heir."

4

Campana

Campana felt considerably refreshed after tidying up in the Bellringers quarters at the Lodge. Her father and brothers had already left. Now she was waiting with ill-concealed impatience for her mother and her aunt to get ready so they could all go down to the Women's Chamber on the other side of the Great Hall. Great-Aunt Nola was speaking firmly and insistently to Campana's mother.

"Come now, Eccua. Your face looks fine. You don't need to talk to anyone. Just smile and nod, that's all that you need to do."

Campana's mother was always uncomfortable at big social occasions, something which Campana found inexplicable. But finally, she did stand up and nod with resignation.

Great-Aunt Nola led the way down. Campana, learning the lesson of her unpleasant encounter on the steps outside the Hall, followed demurely, but she was still fidgeting, urging the two women to go faster. Social events were rare occasions for her and she didn't want to miss a moment of this one. Besides, now she was really hungry. When they finally reached the Womens' Chamber, Campana found the trestle tables laden with food and satisfied her hunger while she looked around.

The Chamber was crowded with elegantly-dressed women moving to and fro. Around them moved their daughters, of all ages from toddlers of one millend up to young women between five and six millends old, about to be pledged. In another millend, Campana would be one of these.

She enjoyed listening to the gossip, picking up tantalising fragments of whispered conversations.

"And so she said to *him*—"

"So irresponsible of her, but of course that clan has always—"

"My dear! Such a scandal! The Militia arrested, positively *arrested* one of the Ropespinner girls. It seems that she—"

"Well, don't tell anyone, but there are times when I quite sympathise with what they are saying. Why shouldn't—"

Across the room, Campana glimpsed the girl she had bumped into on the steps, in the company of a tall, older woman with a severe face and black hair braided and tightly wound into a bun. Her mother, perhaps?

Campana quickly looked away, not wanting to renew contact with the girl. Then she heard her name being called. It was Maryam, a niece of the Mirrormasters clan. Their manor was some distance away from Campana's, but they frequently wrote to each other and enjoyed getting together whenever they could. Accompanying Maryam was an older girl, her cousin Adura, who Campana knew was the daughter of the clan head. While Maryam's face was alight with pleasure, Adura's face was set and unhappy.

After Maryam and Campana had chatted for some time, Campana looked up at the older girl, who was gazing off across the room as though bored.

"Are you being pledged today, Adura?"

"Sold off like a cow at the market, do you mean?" Adura scowled. "Yes."

Campana was dismayed at the bitter tone of Adura's reply. "I thought—"

"You thought that being pledged in marriage to someone you may never have met, someone you had no say

23

in choosing, would be a joyful occasion? You'll grow up soon, Campana, and learn better."

"But... but won't your father make sure that your pledge will be someone good? Someone you can grow to love?"

"Love? It's not about any of that." Adura's lower lip trembled for an instant before she went on. "It's all about being a bargaining piece. My father will have agreed to the pledge which offers the most benefits to our clan. My pledge could be a lame, ugly idiot with warts for all he cares, so long as it suits his purpose. It's the same with all of the clan heads. Yours will be no different when the time comes." She made an impatient gesture. "Oh, why am I wasting my time talking to you children?"

And she stalked off into the crowd.

"Don't mind her, Campana." Maryam leaned closer in sympathy. "The gossip from the servants is that she's fallen for one of our grooms and wants to marry him. I don't know if it's true. Uncle Ignis wouldn't dream of allowing it, but he's not the monster she makes him out to be. I'm sure her pledge will be a good one. I'm sure once she finds out who it is, she'll get used to the idea, well before they're married."

Despite Maryam's comforting words, Campana's excitement at attending the Pledging Ceremony had all but evaporated. First she had been humiliated by that unpleasant girl on the steps and now her joy at meeting her friend had been spoiled by Adura's bitter words. Nevertheless, she tried to remain cheerful.

"Listen," she said to Maryam. "Hear the bell? Not long now until the sixth peal. That's when the ceremony starts, isn't it?"

Even as she spoke, servants were moving through the room, quietly passing on the word to each group of chattering women that it was time to go.

"I'd better find my mother and aunt." Campana smiled at Maryam. "I'll catch up with you later."

She saw that her mother was doing her best to 'smile and nod' as she had been bidden. Campana felt sorry for her mother. For her this whole event was an ordeal to be endured rather than anything joyful.

"Come on, Mother." Campana went over and took her mother's hand. "It's time for the ceremony. We'll have to find father and the boys."

Eccua gave her daughter a wan smile, but came along willingly enough, followed by Great-Aunt Nola.

Several paces ahead, Campana saw Adura again. She was walking towards the Hall with a stony face, less like a cow brought to market, Campana thought, than a sheep to the slaughter.

~

Campana had a good view of the proceedings in the Great Hall. Her clan, like the others represented on the Clan Council, had been given seats close to the stage.

The hall was lit only through a few opened shutters high on the sunward side. For the moment, the larger shutter doors were closed. A bright beam of light surrounded the lectern where the speakers would stand, directed there by an angled mirror set into the roof of the Hall. Servants could shift the mirror to aim the light where it was most needed.

The soft murmur of voices in the hall faded away as the Healer of Souls came in through an archway leading from an adjacent chapel. He walked into the brighter pool of light on the stage and stood at the lectern. He opened the huge book already set there and looked up, his silvery robe glittering.

"Welcome all here." The Healer of Souls spoke in a loud, clear voice. "I am Medeor of Clan Healer. I am honoured to open this ceremony today."

A murmur of soft comment ran through the crowd; Campana gathered that Medeor had only recently replaced his father Percuro in this ceremonial role.

"We are gathered here to celebrate the beginning of the relationships of those being pledged today," Medeor continued. "It is appropriate, then, that I ask us to reflect on the beginning of all things; the beginnings ordained by God, our great Father, the head of all clans past, present and future. Hear then the beginning of beginnings as written in the Book of the Sun."

He cleared his throat and began, scarcely needing to glance down at the Book as he spoke the familiar words.

"In the beginning, God created the Earth and the Sky. And the Spirit of God moved over the face of the Earth. God saw that everywhere it was dark and cold. And God said, 'Let there be a Light.' And behold! There was a great light, high in the darkness of the sky. And God named it the Sun."

The Healer paused a moment and then continued. "But God saw that the Sun was far from the Earth and the creatures He had made and that the dark and the cold were but little dispelled. And God said, 'Let the Sun fall to the Earth.' And behold! It was so."

As the Healer spoke the word "behold" servants hauled on the ropes of the two huge shutter doors on the sunward wall. They rolled to the left and right until the blinding glare of the Sun poured dramatically through the gap into the hall, flooding it with light.

Campana stared for a moment at the Sun. It was considered the right thing to do to bear the Sun's intensity for at least a heartbeat or two. On the other hand, staring too long was seen as being overly pious and was a definite hazard to the eyesight. Some over-eager worshippers now had to be led about by servants because they were effectively blind. Campana looked away, blinking, as she waited for the after-image of the Sun to fade. She thought she might have caught a glimpse of the Pillar of Fire, on which it was said God had placed the Sun to prevent it descending all of the way to the Earth and burning through it.

The servants now rolled the shutter doors closed again and the Healer went on a little more, blessing the congregation and the Pledging, while Campana fidgeted.

Finally he was done and old Magister Neptus of the Boatbuilders, the current Council President, approached the lectern, limping a little. He was an elderly man with a thick thatch of white hair, contrasting markedly with the darkness of his skin.

"It is my great pleasure," the President said, in a soft, reedy voice, "to announce the Pledgings of millend one thousand one hundred and sixty-three." He looked up at the gathered clans. "All of us here wish those being pledged the greatest happiness and prosperity once they are married. I'm sure they will all do their clans great credit. Now then, let us begin. Bring forward those to be pledged. As always, the young men should stand to my left and the young women to my right."

Lambent and Candens were already down on the floor of the hall and Campana squinted, trying to see them but the shutter doors had been opened again, this time only by an arm's length. The light created a bright pathway running down the centre of the hall and, by contrast, dark lanes on either side of it where the pledgees were gathered. The glare of the light down the centre made it almost impossible to make out any faces, a deliberate theatrical effect.

When all was still, there were eighteen young people on the floor of the hall; the young men stood on one side, the young women on the other. There were to be nine pledgings then; and most would have no idea to whom they would be pledged.

Magister Neptus consulted a paper in front of him. He began calling out names, striving hard to project his weak voice into the Hall.

"Clan Woodminer pledges Lucid, son and heir of the clan. To him Clan Icebreaker pledges Glacia, niece of the clan."

David R. Grigg

Two young people stepped into the path of light, walked forward and hesitantly joined hands and stood before the lectern.

Magister Neptus continued down his list. Two more pledgings followed. Campana paid little attention, waiting impatiently for her brothers' names. Finally they came.

"Clan Bellringer pledges Candens, younger son of the clan. To him Clan Mirrormaster pledges Adura, eldest daughter of the clan."

"Oh!" Campana exclaimed. "Oh—good!"

Good? Was it? She thought of Adura's bitterness and set face as she had left the Women's Chamber. But... well, Candens was so nice a person, Adura would surely learn to love him.

Below, Candens stepped forward to take Adura's hand and walk forward. Campana wondered if Candens would be pleased to have come before Lambent for once in his life. But then, in this ceremony, precedence meant coming later, not earlier. She leaned forward, expecting Lambent to be next, but in fact it was a pledging between Clan Metalworker and Clan Weaponsmith.

Now only two young people remained unpledged. Campana looked up at her father, who was beaming with pride that his heir was gaining the highest precedence here today.

"Clan Bellringer pledges Lambent, son and heir of the clan. To him, Clan Signaller pledges Hermia, eldest daughter of the clan."

Lambent stepped forward and took the hand of a young woman wearing an emerald-green dress.

As the couple moved into the light, Campana gave a gasp, her heart sinking. It was the girl she had stumbled into on the steps; the one who had sneered and told her that the Bellringers needed to learn their place. *She* was going to be Lambent's wife!

Candens

Blinking in the bright light, Candens found it difficult to see the face of his pledge, though her delicate hand was warm in his. She had barely given him a glance and now stared forward, her gaze fixed on the Council President.

The pledgings were done and the audience applauded. Finally, the huge shutter doors were closed on the Sun and smaller side shutters opened, inclined upwards, to admit a gentler light into the Hall.

"Pledgees," the Council President said, "you may kiss your partner. Only one kiss, now! Anything more comes later once you are married."

The old man chuckled at his own witticism, echoed by the audience.

Candens turned to his pledge. Adura: that was her name; Adura of the Mirrormasters. It would be embarrassing to forget that. She had deep brown hair, cut at shoulder-length. Her face was rather narrow, with high cheekbones, her lips thin. A plain face, but pleasant enough. Adura's expression, though, was cold; as cold as the darkness beyond the reach of the Sun. As Candens leaned forward to kiss her, she turned her face away so that he could only place a chaste kiss on her cheek. She flinched a little as his lips touched her.

Baffled, he looked around. His brother Lambent was giving his future bride a passionate kiss on the lips and she was responding enthusiastically. What was her name? Hermia?

As Lambent leaned away, his arm still around the girl, Candens saw her lovely, laughing face for the first time. She

29

was entrancing, a delight. A sudden painful stab of envy ran through him.

⁓

"You seem glum, Candens." Ardens glanced over at his younger son. "Is your pledge not to your liking?"

It was early on the waking following the Pledging Ceremony. They were riding back to the manor ahead of the carriage carrying the women. Lambent, eager to get home, had spurred his horse forward when the manor came into sight. He was now well ahead and Candens was alone with his father.

"Well..." Candens hesitated in replying to the question. "It's more that she doesn't seem to find me to her liking."

Ardens reined in his horse and they came to a stop, close enough for easy speech. They were now well within the clan's estate and on either side, Dims were hard at work tending the crops and fruit trees.

Candens glanced down the slope, towards the Sun sitting over the bay. It was wreathed in flaming swirls of mist, creating the illusion of blazing towers and curving ramparts—the "Castle of the Angels" some people called it. The wind was blowing the mist in their direction; soon it would be enveloping them where they stood on the hill.

"Many women are unhappy at first with their pledges," Ardens counselled. "Many men are too, come to that. It can take a while to get used to each other and that sometimes doesn't happen for a millend after you are married."

Candens thought briefly of his mother's perennial unhappiness and wondered if she had ever become used to being married to Ardens of the Bellringers. He couldn't say that to his father, of course.

"Lambent and Hermia seem happy enough with each other." Candens changed topic slightly, trying not to sound bitter; trying also not to keep thinking of Hermia's bright, laughing face, her dark hair and full, red lips and her enthusiastic return of Lambent's embrace.

"A good pledge, that one," Ardens agreed. "A triumph, if I may say so. I wasn't sure that it would come off until the last moment. The Signallers are becoming a very important clan. Our society is more and more reliant on sending signals. An alliance with them will benefit us greatly. Your pledge, too, is a good one. The Mirrormasters are one of the great clans, though of course they are much beholden to the Glassmoulders."

"But what good..." Candens stopped.

His father looked at him gravely. "Go on. I grant you leave. Now is the time to ask such questions."

"What good do all these alliances do? The Signallers aren't going to let us in on their secrets, are they? And we're not going to tell them ours."

"No. Our deepest secrets must be protected at all costs. However, alliances created by pledges and marriages can allow clans to work on mutual goals, each bringing their own knowledge to their part of a task without actually sharing it. Sometimes that can be a delicate dance, but it works."

Unaccustomed to such open talk with his father, Candens was still hesitant to express his true thoughts. But he found the courage to go on.

"Surely, though, if everyone in society shared their secrets openly, that would be better. Everyone could profit from the shared knowledge to develop new ways of doing things. I've even got some ideas myself—"

Ardens cut him off.

"That is dangerous talk. It has been found through the bitter experience of history that unbridled knowledge in too many hands can cause serious problems. Our existence here is fragile. Everywhere beyond the light of the Sun is dark and frozen and will always be so. Too much novelty might threaten our existence."

"But..." Candens stopped again, realising that he could not pursue this line any further without incurring his father's wrath. He was silent, shivering a little as the mist drifted up from the bay and began to roll over them. A soft drizzle began to fall. After a moment, Candens tried a different tack. "All right, I understand, father. But why don't we get a choice in whom we are pledged to? Why do the pledges matter?"

A flash of impatience showed in Ardens' face.

"As I have said, they matter because alliances allow us to work on mutual goals. And there are many important questions to be decided at the Clan Council. Alliances allow us to influence the responses to those questions. A clan can do favours for an allied clan, offer better prices on its products, offer services at no cost. For example, one part of the terms of your pledge to the Mirrormaster girl provides for the supply of mirrors to us at a considerable discount. We need those mirrors so we can make productive use of that big umbra in the middle of our barley fields."

Have I been traded off, then, for the price of a few mirrors?

Candens sighed, thinking of Adura, whose expression had remained cold as she had been introduced to his family members after the ceremony. She had been polite and had responded briefly to direct questions, but volunteered nothing of her own. And never once had she smiled. Afterwards, Campana had tried to excuse Adura's behavior to him, but it hadn't made much sense. All he had picked up from Campana's chatter was that perhaps Adura had fallen in love with someone else.

Just like me—

Candens put a stop to that thought and forced himself to put Hermia's face out of his mind. The drizzle was turning into rain and Candens' face was getting wet. Drops trickled into his eyes. If he cried now, his father would never know... but he controlled the weak impulse.

"Come on." Ardens moved off slowly, expecting his son to follow. "Let's get ourselves home. The mist doesn't show much sign of shifting."

They started up the slope again, where the manor buildings were now swathed behind a curtain of mist. The huge bell-tower cast a visible shadow through the fog like an endless dark tunnel. Even when the mist was falling elsewhere, the tower's umbra reached far out across the hills and almost into the outer darkness beyond the reach of the Sun.

"How long will it be before I will be married?" Candens asked after a moment or two.

How long would it be before Lambent married Hermia? But he didn't dare voice this part of his question.

Ardens shrugged.

"That is one matter which is traditionally the choice of the bride. Within reason, of course. We consider that pledgees are too young to marry immediately. Around a millend later is typical. Much beyond a millend and a half is unusual, but not unheard of. Of course..." Ardens stopped, as though pondering whether to go on, but then continued. "Of course, should the girl fall pregnant—not a desirable state of affairs, but of course it does happen, young people being what they are—in such a case the marriage would occur as soon as convenient."

"But what if I was a Dim? I could marry anyone I wanted then, couldn't I? And marry her as soon as we both liked."

His father looked at him sharply, his face flushing. He put his hand to his horsewhip as if tempted to make use of it.

"Don't speak like that! You are a clan member, second in line to be clan head. A clan which is one of the twenty greatest in the land, a clan represented on the Council. What the Dims do is of no concern to you. Let me never hear you make such a comparison again."

"All right." Candens nodded. "All right. I'm sorry, father."

All the same, the Dims had more control over their lives than Candens did. Maybe it would be worth being poor and having to work in the fields, or as a servant, if he was free to marry the person he really loved and someone who loved him back. Candens went home with a heavy heart.

6

Campana

"Libeth." Campana looked at her maid. "Can I ask you a question?"

It was some eighteen shutterings after the Pledging Ceremony and Libeth was in the process of brushing Campana's long hair, which seemed to Campana to wilfully tangle itself far too often.

"Of course."

Campana was silent for a while. Then she said, "What if you knew someone who was going to marry someone and if you knew something about that someone, that second someone? Oh, bother!"

"It sounds very confusing," Libeth said. "Try again."

"Well, if someone, a girl, said something which was really—unpleasant. And if that girl was going to be married to a boy you knew, should you tell the boy about it?"

Libeth considered, looking into Campana's face in the small mirror propped on the dressing table.

"Did this girl say the unpleasant thing to you?"

"Yes. But I'd just knocked into her, so maybe she was just angry with me. But what if she's always like that, so horrid and rude and she marries someone—"

Campana suddenly realised that she was saying too much. She had often been warned against discussing family matters with the servants.

"Sometimes people do say harsh things they don't really mean, if they are angry," Libeth pointed out. "It's probably best not to repeat them."

"Yes, I'm sure you're right."

Campana wasn't convinced though. Ever since she had returned to the manor, she had been thinking about her first encounter with Hermia and worrying about whether she should tell Lambent about it.

After the ceremony, when the families of the pledgees had met, Hermia had for the most part simply ignored Campana, giving no sign that she had ever encountered her before. Perhaps she had been regretting her earlier outburst? But Hermia's parents, Magister Solus and Magistra Calora, had also seemed rather aloof and proud.

Lambent seemed not to have noticed. He was clearly smitten by Hermia. Even now, almost two decants later, his enthusiasm showed in his eyes and tone of voice whenever he spoke of her, which was often. So he probably wouldn't pay any attention if Campana told him what Hermia had said.

Campana sighed. Surely once she was a little older, people would take her more seriously? Then again, maybe they wouldn't. After all, she wasn't allowed to learn anything important about the clan's work. Each waking after breakfast, her father and brothers went off to their business while she was left to her female amusements: playing card games with her mother and great-aunt, practising the lute, singing, embroidery, or reading books. Sometimes there was the treat of visiting the ladies of other clans and gossiping. None of it was productive, all of it just time-filling.

Not only could she not help her brothers, she barely knew what they did inside the great tower except that it had something to do with making the bells ring on time. That seemed to be the whole heart of what the clan did. She was never permitted to ask them, let alone see the inside of the tower or the chamber, high above, where the bells were rung.

Once she was pledged and married, it would be more of the same. She wouldn't be allowed to learn the secrets of her husband's clan, whichever one it turned out to be. Nor would she be allowed to choose him or his clan.

For the first time since the Pledging, Campana began to understand Adura's bitterness… and perhaps to share it.

7
Candens

"Clear!" bellowed Great-Uncle Tinnio. "Haul it up now, quickly, quickly. Here comes the second bob!"

Candens and Lambent hauled on the ropes to pull back the bob—the heavy weight at the end of the pendulum—as that of the second pendulum was released and came swinging swiftly towards them. They had to move quickly to be out of its way.

They were in the Pendulum Chamber and they were being trained under the strict supervision of their great-uncle, the Pendulum Master. He was an old man now, having passed his twenty-fifth millend not long before. But he was still vigorous and very stern. The two young men were here to learn the Clan's craft, which could only be entrusted to direct family members, never to servants, despite its often physical nature. Above them in the dim tower, their father Ardens looked down on proceedings from the landing of the wooden stairs which spiraled up the inside of the tower.

Candens' arms were aching as he and Lambent fastened up the first bob, pulled well out of the way. The second bob was now swinging in its great arc back and forth across the chamber, its sharp pointer marking out the time to each peal as it moved over the engravings on the stone floor.

The employment of two pendulums was a clever arrangement, Candens thought, and he wondered which clan head had devised it long ago when the bell tower was built. It was vital to keep the count of swings going, even when the first pendulum had lost its energy. Resetting and restarting a single pendulum would risk losing track of time. With well-practised moves, the first pendulum could be hauled out of the way to allow the free passage of the second with no loss of time. Then the roles of the bobs were interchanged so the swinging continued without interruption, on and on, as it had done so for hundreds of millends, perhaps for thousands. The Bellringers took time very seriously.

"Uncle." Candens waited until the transfer was done. "Why does the bob move?"

"Why? A foolish question. Naturally it moves. You lift a weight, drop it, it falls. Being attached to a rope it is forced to move from one side of the room to the other."

Despite his role as tutor, Tinnio was usually annoyed by any questions, most of which came from Candens. Lambent just looked on with a smile.

"I don't mean its swing back and forth. I understand that," Candens said. "I've been wondering why the plane of the swing changes through the course of a waking. The bob doesn't return to its starting point exactly, but each swing shifts a little around the outer circle."

Tinnio's face darkened.

"What is the good of asking why? You might as well ask why a stone falls to the ground, or why the Sun shines. It is not for you to question the way of things. That is how it is and has always been in the memory of the clan. All that matters is for us to keep the pendulums swinging, count the tally of the swings and to sound the peals at the correct times."

That almost prompted another 'Why?' from Candens, but Lambent jabbed him in the ribs with an elbow and Candens decided it was wiser to stay silent. But keeping his mouth closed didn't stop the questions from swarming in Candens' head.

Once the excitement of transferring the pendulums was over, there wasn't much to do in the chamber except watch

David R. Grigg

the pendulum and mark its swings. Every swing, regardless of how much distance the bob covered, took exactly the same amount of time. This was a minor miracle which made Candens want to ask why all over again, but he knew that he would get no answer from Tinnio or anyone else. Not even from his cousin Sonor, who knew more of Sunfall's history than anybody.

Beneath these thoughts, a thread of his subconscious mind constantly kept the count. Ten counts to every swing of the pendulum; that was the way of it. His count neared five thousand. The bob reached the extreme position of its swing and poised for an instant before swinging back, its pointer aimed precisely at one of the engraved marks in the floor. At that moment, Tinnio called out "Mark! Ring the bell!"

Lambent pulled the rope for the signal bell, just as he had first done when they were only three millends old. As the bob swung back over its mid-point, the peal began overhead. The eighth peal of the waking.

As the sound of the bells died away, Candens' cousins Valend and Nitens arrived to take over their duties for the next shift and Candens and Lambent were free to go. Nitens was about the same age and responded cheerfully when Lambent slapped him on the back in gratitude for this release. Valend was older, always serious and business-like; he merely nodded at Candens as they exchanged places.

In the courtyard outside, Lambent let out a sigh of relief.

"I'm glad that's over for now. How boring it all is! I'm going out for a ride before dinner, do you want to come?"

This was an unusual offer from Lambent and Candens thought for a moment about accepting, before finally shaking his head.

"No, I have some things I want to do in my workshop."

Lambent gave him a disgusted look. "Still fiddling with those old pieces of junk? You need to start living, Candens. Wake up and enjoy life. I do!"

Candens quelled the sharp response he was tempted to make. How could he enjoy life when Lambent was going to marry Hermia? Instead, after a pause, he said, "I'm fine as I am. And I want to know how things work."

"Or fail to work, in your case. Tell you what, ride with me nextwake and I'll show you something which might change your ideas; wake you up at last."

"What do you mean?"

"It's a surprise. Wait and see."

With that, Lambent headed off for the stables.

On the following waking, Candens sat at his workbench, probing at a dirty, rusted shape with his hardened wooden tools.

The object on the bench was so broken down with age that it was hard to make out what it had originally looked like, let alone what its purpose might have been. About two handspans across, it had been brought to him by one of the Dims after it had been turned up by a plough. The field workers all knew that Candens was interested in these ancient artefacts which turned up from time to time, although Candens knew it was almost guaranteed they all laughed about it behind his back.

He had been lucky to hang onto this piece, because it was clear to Candens that beneath the dirt he was patiently scraping away, it was composed mainly of metal. His father, had he known of it, would have sold it off. Perhaps he still could, once Candens had finished examining it.

There were small wheels in the object, with prongs on them which appeared to mesh with notches in other, smaller, wheels. Candens was carefully sketching out the arrangement as he explored the device. Once, no doubt, all of these wheels had been able to turn. For each turn of the larger wheel, the smaller wheels would turn several times. Was that a clue? There was a long piece of metal here; was it some kind of lever? He gave a sigh. Perhaps he would never understand it, or the other things that had been dug up. Yet the process of wondering about them, trying to guess how many millends ago they had been created, was stimulating to his mind. He had hunted for any reference to such devices in the oldest volumes in Sonor's library, but found nothing.

He put the rusty thing aside and turned to his other current interest, far simpler to understand. It was a wooden frame from which he had suspended a small stone on a length of cord. Candens often sat and simply watched the bob swing. He had experimented with different lengths of cord and had finally found a length—about as long as his forearm—which exactly matched the mental count he had been trained to keep. This small pendulum swung ten times for each swing of the big pendulum.

Candens couldn't help thinking that if he and Lambent and the cousins in the repeater towers, had with them such a simple arrangement using this exact length of cord, they would have no need to keep the count in their heads.

When he had suggested it to his father Ardens had rejected the suggestion with contempt. His father didn't approve of Candens' hobby and had made it clear that he wasn't interested in 'frivolous innovations'. If only Candens was the heir, then when he became clan head, he could make whatever innovations he wanted. Perhaps he could persuade Lambent to listen...

Just then, Lambent himself came into the room, laughing loudly at Candens' obsessions. He made Candens put down his work and dragged him off to the stables. Candens followed with resignation. Somehow, he didn't think Lambent would be much interested in his innovations either.

8

Adura

She knew what the servants whispered about her, how they explained her discontent. The whispers had become a little more obvious after Adura had returned from her Pledging and had failed to comply with the stereotype of radiant happiness, or show any evident gratitude towards her parents for their choice of her future partner.

It was true that she had once made friends with one of the apprentice grooms in the clan's stables. But then she had been barely more than a child and that was all it had been—a simple, innocent friendship that had come and gone as she had grown towards womanhood.

She loved no one, least of all herself. Since the Pledging, she had even begun to hate the sight of herself in the mirror.

It did not help her inner turmoil that her house was full of mirrors, reflecting her own image back to herself everywhere. When she was alone in her bedroom, she sometimes turned the mirrors to the wall, or hung a dress or a blouse over them, to avoid looking at her own face. Whenever her maid Alla came in and found the room that way, she would give Adura an odd look. Perhaps she just thought Adura was being lazy and careless with her clothes.

When she could not avoid the presence of mirrors, Adura tried to turn her eyes away from them. Though her mother always called her 'pretty', Adura had long known that she was not beautiful by the standards of her society. Now, though, she saw an unattractive, unhappy young woman, her face becoming gaunt and her eyes shadowed.

To avoid the mirrors, Adura had begun to spend more time outdoors, riding endlessly around the clan's estate with Alla as her reluctant companion. On one of these occasions, Adura finally began to regain a degree of hope for her future.

Alla knew enough about Adura to disbelieve the story about the romance with the groom and to understand that there was, at least in part, a deeper cause to Adura's discontent. She rarely had much to say for herself, but during one of their rides, Alla spoke up.

The Mirrormaster estate was not a large one. It was shaped like an arrow-head, with three ridges, the longest and highest of which ran up a slope almost directly darkwards away from the Sun. "The Master's Arm" was what the common people called the longest ridge. It was good, highly-productive land and the path along its slope led through fields of corn and oil-flower.

Adura and Alla had ridden out to the highest point of the ridge that morning where there were excellent views. With one hand raised to shade her eyes from the glare of the Sun, Adura gazed down towards the bay, where in the distance they could see the fisher boats dotted on the water and the passage of a galley, tiny oars flashing rhythmically.

Alla sat quietly for a while looking at the scene with Adura, but then she spoke up.

"Mistress, you are so unhappy. Forgive me asking, but is there anything I can do to help?"

Adura tried to smile at her maid. She knew that Alla meant well.

"Not unless you can change society; change the way that we women are treated."

Alla shook her head.

"I cannot, mistress. But I heard about... Oh, I really shouldn't say."

Adura looked sharply at Alla.

"Say what? You obviously mean to tell me, don't make excuses."

Alla blushed a little.

"It's something that I heard from my cousin. She's the maid to one of the nieces of Clan Watermaster. And she says..."

"Alla, I don't want to hear your gossip."

"It's not gossip, mistress, not really. But my cousin overheard her mistress talking to a friend about a group— about some kind of organisation of women, calling themselves The Daughters. She told my cousin to keep it quiet."

"But yet your cousin, it seems, told you about it. So much for the trustworthiness of servants. I don't think I should listen to any more, Alla."

Alla blushed again.

"I wouldn't have said anything to you, mistress, if you hadn't been so unhappy. And my cousin didn't hear any details. Just that there is a group of women who are trying to make change happen in society, she said. All I wanted to say, really, was that you aren't alone, mistress. Others feel the same way that you do."

Adura was silent for a long moment. Was it true? Was there some kind of association of Bright women wanting change? Even if there was, though, wasn't it too late, now that she was pledged to that gawky boy from Clan Bellringer?

"Perhaps you can find out more from your cousin, Alla. Don't say that I was asking. But if she finds out any more about this group, perhaps she could let you know. And then you could tell me?"

Alla bobbed her head.

"Yes, mistress. I'll try."

Perhaps there is hope yet. For the whole ride back, these words ran back and forth through Adura's mind.

9

Candens

"Where are we going?" Candens tried again as their horses left the environs of the manor.

Lambent laughed.

"We're going to the signal tower at Baker's Mount. Father has an important message he wants sent and there are a couple of others. I'm writing to Hermia, too."

"But why not just wait for the courier?"

Candens was a little breathless already. Lambent was keeping his horse to a steady canter, as though he was in a hurry.

"I told you, I have a treat for you. You'll find out when we get to the signal tower."

Candens was silent after that, knowing that Lambent would be unlikely to share any more until it suited him.

The hard-packed dirt road led behind a small hill on the sunward side and into the shadow on its darkwards side. A sudden chill fell as the Sun was blocked from view and they entered the cooler shaded air. It was considerably darker here, but there was still enough diffused light from the sky to see their way. Still, other than the path ahead and a couple of stock corrals, there was not much to see. The corrals were empty now, but after the Shuttering peal they would be full once the herdsmen led their cattle there to sleep.

That was another of those facts which everyone else seemed to take for granted, but Candens always found puzzling. Why did both humans and animals need a regular period of darkness and sleep? Even the crops and fruit trees, so the field workers told him, would not flower or seed properly unless the Sun was blocked by closing the wicker shadow-gates every Shuttering. But why? With the endless sunlight available, why shouldn't creatures and plants want to make use of it all?

Behind them, they heard the bell-tower at the manor strike the third solo bell since the last peal and more faintly in the distance, a repeater tower echoed it back. Pieces of time, divided up and announced throughout the land. An important task; perhaps a vital one, and something for which Candens' clan could be proud. But if the Bellringers, their bells and their secret pendulums were to vanish utterly from the face of Sunfall, would it really matter? Surely humankind would find some other way to measure time? The dripping of water or the falling of sand, perhaps. Candens put these fruitless thoughts aside, as he so often had to do.

The brothers rode back into the light. Candens blinked against the dazzle. His horse shook his head a little and whinnied softly, not liking these sudden changes of illumination any more than Candens did.

Up ahead, finally, he could see the tall signal tower. Set on the peak of a hill, it was impressive despite being only about half the height of the bell-tower at his own manor. At its top, mirrors glittered in constant motion.

They entered a small courtyard just as a blue-and-gold uniformed courier galloped past them on the way out. In the yard, another courier was carrying his satchel out of a small stone building at the base of the tower. Lambent and Candens led their horses to the stable. Lambent dismounted, tossing his horse's reins to a servant without a second glance and immediately set off towards the tower. Candens did the same, rather more slowly and gave his bay gelding an affectionate stroke of his muzzle before he left him.

Inside the building a middle-aged man with a grey-streaked beard sat behind a desk with neatly-stacked piles of papers. In a corner, leaning against a wall with his arms crossed, was a much younger man with blonde hair and neatly trimmed beard.

"Lambent!" The younger man called out when he saw them. "You're damned late!"

Lambent smiled, full of his usual charm. "Couldn't get away. Father took forever to write up his signal. You should make your ciphers easier to use."

The blonde man laughed. "But then, Lambent, they would be easier to crack and you wouldn't want that."

"It's all nonsense anyway." Lambent took out a folded sheet of paper from the inside pocket of his jacket and handed it to the man at the desk. "I'm sure it's all just boring stuff about sheep and barley."

"You know my Uncle Clare, I think." The young man nodded in the direction of the seated man. "Who's this? Your brother?"

"Yes. Candens, meet Blaze. Blaze, meet Candens." The two shook hands. As he did so, Candens recognised Blaze as the man Lambent had been talking to so earnestly at the Pledging.

"You're not much alike, are you?" Blaze said. "I thought you were twins."

"We are." Candens nodded. "We were born at the same time, anyway. Some twins look identical, I know, but we're not like that."

"And Lambent popped out first. Lucky for him, eh? You should have been quicker off the mark."

Candens said nothing, but was starting to dislike Blaze already.

Lambent pulled another message out from his jacket.

"This one can go in the clear; it's just a silly letter from my sister to one of her friends. She's been saving her allowance to send it. And I have a letter to Hermia. Will you be seeing her?" Lambent addressed this question to Blaze.

49

"Not for a long while. I'm on a circuit of the towers, checking all is well. You'll have to send it by signal. You'd better have a coded version unless you want Clare here to know all your tender lover's secrets."

Colouring slightly, Lambent nodded.

"Yes, of course it's coded. She knows the pass-phrase."

He handed over a final piece of paper to Uncle Clare, who examined the sheets for several moments and then said, unsmiling, "Nine bronze rings."

"Nine!" Lambent exclaimed in mock horror. "Come on, Clare; I'm practically family now!"

The older man shook his head, with no flicker of a smile. "Practically is not actually. Nine. Or I'll give you change from a silver."

In the corner, Blaze laughed. Lambent shrugged, opened his purse and began counting out the annular metal tokens. The transaction done, Blaze clapped Lambent on the shoulder.

"Come on, let's go out and be about our other business. Does Candens here know about it?"

Lambent glanced at Candens with a smile. "I've told him he's in for a treat."

"Oh, it will be that, all right." Blaze gave another laugh. "Come on."

As they left the building, another courier was waiting to enter. Candens realised how busy the signal tower must always be.

Blaze led them around the tower, into an area out of sight of the buildings and courtyard. From here, across the curve of the hills, Candens could see distant bright lights flickering on and off in a confusing pattern. They were from the nearest Signaller tower, transmitting its messages to this tower.

There were a lot of similarities between the operations of the Signallers and the Bellringers, he thought. Both required repeater towers scattered across the landscape to pick up and send on their information, although the Signallers could build their towers further apart than those of the Bellringers. But then, a signal tower could be rendered useless when the wind drove the swirling mist from the bay to cover it, blocking its glittering mirrors from sight in a dense cloud of fog and rain.

For the first time, Candens began to see that there might be something in what his father said about the importance of pledges in enabling clans to work together. Perhaps if...

His thoughts were interrupted as Blaze led them into the shadow behind the tower. Its umbra stretched far away from this small peak, eventually becoming lost as it merged into the spreading shadows of the neighbouring hills and became simply a part of the outer darkness.

Blaze pulled something out from an inner pocket.

"Here's the stuff. Do you have the money? And don't pull that 'practically family' remark on me."

Blaze said it with a smile, but Candens had a feeling that Blaze was deadly serious.

Lambent took the small package and Candens heard the clink of rings as he paid for it. An alarming number of rings, he thought with a frown. Whatever 'the stuff' was, it was expensive.

"You can't smoke it around here," Blaze said. "Uncle Clare knows the smell and he'll pick it up from an amazing distance."

"That's all right," Lambent replied. "I know where we're going with it. There's a friendly girl I know, lives on the other side of Featherton, her father's a baker there. And she has a little sister—"

Blaze laughed. An unpleasant laugh. He slapped Lambent on the back. "Good luck with that! Your brother here looks like he needs cheering up."

"Yes, he's a bit down in the dumps. I don't think he likes the girl he got pledged to."

"That's not true!" Candens protested, even though it was true really. Blaze grinned. "Adura of the Mirrormasters, that right? I wouldn't worry too much. That whole family spends too much time staring into their own mirrors; sends them a bit crazy."

Candens gave a bitter laugh. "And I shouldn't worry about that?"

"No," Blaze said. "I'm sure you'll put her right once you're married. A bit of the old in-out will make her forget what she sees in her mirrors. That right, Lambent?"

"Right," said Lambent.

As if he would know, Candens thought.

⁓

They retrieved their horses from the stable and Lambent set off. Not back the way they had come, but along a road leading down the slope and towards the Sun. Like most such roads, it zig-zagged back and forth, not so much to handle the slope, which was not steep, but more to avoid the need for horses and men having to face continually towards the blinding Sun.

Along the way, they passed one of the strange skeleton towers. There were about a dozen of these towers dotting the landscape of Sunfall. Candens called a halt, ostensibly so that he could get a drink of water from his saddle bags, but in reality so that he could stare for a while at this tower. Set on a small hill, it was a mere open framework of narrow, twisted beams, but much taller than any stone building, even those in the city. Its bones and ribs were made of the archaic black godsteel no one now knew how to cut or drill. They were believed to be very ancient, regarded by the Dims— and a few Brights—with fearful superstition. Even the long spider-web shadows of the towers were usually avoided, the land there left wild and untended.

Lambent was impatient.

"Come on!" he said and started his horse down the slope again.

Ahead was a small village Candens had ridden through a few times in the past without giving it much attention. It was, after all, mainly the domain of Dims—servants, field-workers and the merchants who met their limited needs. Like any such town, it mostly consisted of a single row of shallow stone buildings. Only a few of them reached two storeys in height or were more than one room deep. The buildings were all constructed on the darkwards side of the street so that their shadows did not fall over the roadway.

A little way past the other side of the town, Lambent struck off the main road to follow a narrow path up the slope of a hill. They ducked through another small patch of shadow and Candens saw a small white peasant's cottage. Like most such dwellings, it was constructed of wattle daubed with mud then painted white, its roof made of wooden shingles. To one side was an enclosure where a dozen chickens pecked at the ground and beyond it was a small field with neatly laid-out rows of plants, in the midst of which Candens saw two young women, working with hoes and bending to pull out weeds.

Lambent pulled up and leaped down from his horse. Candens followed his example, though much more slowly. Lambent was striding off into the field, careless of where he placed his feet.

"Viala!" he called out.

One of the young women looked up and raised a hand to shade her eyes against the sun.

"Lambent..." She frowned as she recognised him.

"Come on, Viala, aren't you glad to see me? I've got a present for you. And I want you to meet my brother Candens, here."

Viala had a pretty face, darkened greatly by long exposure to the sun. Her nut-brown hair was tied tightly beneath a red scarf which protected her head. She gave

Candens a perfunctory smile and bobbed her head in greeting, before turning back to Lambent.

"I don't think..." she began, but Lambent leaned in and kissed her on the mouth, silencing her protest.

Behind the pair, the other young woman now stood, leaning on her hoe. She was younger than Viala, with a broader face and reddish hair under a blue scarf. Candens couldn't interpret the look she cast in his direction, but it wasn't particularly welcoming. He was starting to feel very uncomfortable.

Lambent was whispering intently to Viala, who was shaking her head.

"No," she said. "Not yet, anyway. Leia and I have to finish weeding the turnips. Father will be furious if it's not done by the time he gets back from the bakery."

"Come on, you told me he never gets back until just before the Shuttering. There's plenty of time."

The girl was adamant, though. "No. You and your brother go into the cottage. There's water, bread and cheese there if you want it. Leia and I will finish as quickly as we can. But it will be a couple of bells at least."

Lambent was annoyed, but controlled it. "All right. I have something that can keep us entertained until you come, anyway. I was going to share it with you, but we'll use it ourselves while we're waiting. Come on, Candens."

It was obvious that Lambent had been in the cottage before and was familiar with its layout. He led Candens confidently through the small kitchen and into a back room. Though humble, the cottage was clean and well-maintained and a good deal better than most Dim families could manage. Those who worked in towns in trades were much better off than mere field workers.

Lambent closed the door of the small room, which featured two narrow beds, one to each side of the room. Clearly this was where the sisters slept.

"Sit down," Lambent commanded and Candens reluctantly sat on the bed nearest the open window.

"Are you sure about this?" Candens asked. "I don't think we should be doing this. Father..."

Ardens had always cautioned Lambent and himself about being too friendly with Dim girls. "Not fair on them, nor on yourself," he had always said.

"Shut up," Lambent said. "First we're going to smoke this *marana*."

He reached into his jacket and pulled out the package which Blaze had sold him. Lambent opened the package. Inside was a small cube of a brownish material and two clay pipes. He pinched some of the material and stuffed it into the bowl of one of the pipes. Then he pulled out a tinder box and spent some time striking a flint to start a small flame in the powdered tinder. Finally, he used that to light the substance in the pipe. An aromatic smoke arose and Candens wrinkled his nose.

"Here." Lambent passed the first pipe to Candens. "Suck in the smoke and breathe it down. You have to keep the *marana* burning."

He prepared and lit his own pipe and began to demonstrate. Candens had seen the field-workers using clay pipes and he knew that Uncle Tinnio also used one from time to time, smoking the dried leaves of the tobacco plant grown on an estate somewhere on the other side of the Sun. He assumed that this was more of the same.

He tried to do as Lambent had directed, but found himself coughing uncontrollably. Lambent slapped him on the back. "Try again. Take it a bit more slowly this time." Clearly Lambent was familiar with this *marana* business.

It didn't take long for Candens to begin feeling very strange and the world started to whirl around him. In the corners of the room, strange patterns began to flicker and form the transient shapes of bizarre creatures. He felt very light, as if he was floating and after a while he had to lie down on the bed to stop falling over.

With a shock, he realised that he had lost track of the count, the count that he had been trained always to have at the back of his mind. Three thousand two... no, it was gone. What would his father say? But then, his father wasn't here. That was good.

It seemed an eternity after that before the door of the room opened and a female voice said, "Sun and shadow! What a stink!"

Candens tried to rise, but it was beyond him. Lambent, though, staggered to his feet and lurched towards Viala, who was standing in the doorway. She put out a hand and pushed him away, so that he stumbled back and fell on the bed. Leia stood wide-eyed behind her sister.

Through a haze, Candens heard the younger woman say, "What are we going to do? We can't have them still here when Father comes back!"

"No," Viala said. "Come on, we'll drag them out together one by one. Quick, now!"

She leaned down and began to pull on Lambent's arm. He swore and tried to pull her down onto the bed with him. But this was no soft, cossetted Bright woman who spent her time at music or embroidery. Viala was a peasant girl who worked hard with her arms and legs every day. She batted off his attempted embrace and Leia yanked on his other arm. Together, they managed to get Lambent out of the room. Candens heard him protesting in a languid voice.

"Aw, Viala, come on, sweetheart, I just—"

Candens fell asleep briefly, the room still spinning around him, before he was woken and pulled up by the two young women. He could barely stand, but they bundled him briskly out of the room and then out of the cottage.

It was impossible for him to mount his horse, quite impossible. Instead, Viala, her face sour, wrapped the reins around Candens' arm and knotted them tightly. Lambent, leaning drunkenly against his own horse, had been treated likewise.

"Now go!" Viala said. "And don't come back, either of you. Go on, get moving, or I'll take my hoe to you, I swear it. If you're anywhere near this cottage when my father comes back, I'll kill you, do you hear?"

Together, leading their horses, the brothers stumbled off down the dusty track into the glare of the Sun.

10

Campana

"They're here! They're here!"

Campana called out to Libeth from where she stood on the balcony above the entrance to the manor, shading her eyes against the Sun and looking down the long driveway of the estate to where it met the common road. She had been waiting there for bell after bell since the fourth peal, despite the maid's attempts to make her come inside and wait more decorously in the drawing room.

The Pledges of both brothers were arriving more or less together, each as fashionably late as the other. It was now a quarter of a millend since the Pledging and it was customary for the pledges to meet again formally after such an interval.

Campana had been looking forward to this social occasion for a long time. Down below, she could now see her brothers standing on the steps waiting to greet the carriages, Lambent several steps ahead of Candens, who seemed to be hanging back.

Campana frowned. Both her brothers had changed in recent times. There had been one particular waking when they had returned very late together, barely before the Shuttering peal. Both had appeared to be rather unwell and neither had said much. The next waking, Libeth had suggested delicately to Campana that the brothers might have drunk an excess of wine somewhere. Once they had reached their sixth millend, their father had begun to permit them to drink a small quantity of wine with dinner, but he kept a close control of the supply and the servants were under strict orders not to permit them more. So perhaps that was it. They had got drunk together and had been suffering the consequences. But ever since that unhappy return, the easy banter between Lambent and Candens had vanished and Candens kept even more to himself than previously.

"Come", said Libeth. "It's time to go down, or you'll seem rude."

Campana sighed. She was eager to see her friend Maryam again and had hoped that she would arrive well before the awful girl from the Signallers. But there was no helping matters, so she went down willingly enough to wait inside the entrance hall. Her father, mother and great aunt were already there. Great-Aunt Nola pursed her lips in annoyance as she watched Campana take her place, but then that was her great-aunt's usual response on seeing Campana.

Lambent and Hermia came in. Lambent's arm was around Hermia's waist, making for rather a clumsy entrance, Campana thought. Hermia, though, was all smiles and gently pushed her pledge's arm away so that she could greet Lambent's family properly. She made a curtsey to Ardens, who nodded with a slight smile; embraced Campana's mother Eccua and kissed her cheek, to which Eccua responded as though startled; curtseyed again to Great-Aunt Nola; and then came to Campana and offered her hand.

Campana hesitated and looked up with a frown at Hermia's lovely face. Hermia had never given a sign that she had ever said anything out of the way to Campana, but there was something about the look in her eyes... Campana nevertheless held out her hand and Hermia took it firmly.

"I'm sure we shall be such good friends in future, my dear." Hermia squeezed Campana's hand painfully hard. "*Shan't* we?"

Hating herself, her hand aching, Campana forced herself to nod.

11

Candens

Candens sat beside Adura during the interminable dinner, feeling uncomfortable and miserable. The food tasted of nothing but ashes in his mouth.

Adura had said very little since she had arrived and had not smiled at all. In fact, he had never seen her smile. She gave every impression of enduring a duty she could not avoid. Doubtless there would be several more similar meetings before they married and then what? A lifetime of the same for them both?

Across the table, Lambent and Hermia were chatting away. Candens avoided looking directly at them, especially at Hermia. But once, when Lambent was distracted by the need to deal with a servant delivering a platter of food, Candens was unable to help himself. Disconcertingly, Hermia met his gaze and smiled with slightly lowered eyelids, a tantalising glance. Candens turned away, feeling his face flush and forced himself to look further down the table to where his sister was describing some event to her friend Maryam, using animated movements of her hands, triggering a stern rebuke from Great-Aunt Nola, sitting on her other side. Great-Uncle Tinnio was in the midst of a conversation with Ardens, speaking a little too loudly; in fact he was becoming rather deaf.

Eccua, as always, sat quietly beside Ardens, gazing into the distance, apparently paying little attention to what Tinnio was saying to her husband. Perhaps, Candens thought, he could talk to her later about his concerns. Unlike his father, she would at least listen, even if she could do little to help.

Servants cleared away the precious steel plates used for the meat course and replaced them with beautifully-carved wooden platters laden with fruit and cheese. Glass cups were filled with an aromatic white wine—the family's own vintage, made in very small quantities. Candens seized his immediately and took a deep swallow.

Lambent hadn't offered to take Candens for any further 'treats' since the expedition to visit the Dim girls and Candens would have refused anyway. He still felt embarrassed by the visit and by the debacle of how it had ended. But he was fairly sure that Lambent had continued his experiments with smoking *marana*. He didn't seem to be sleeping well lately. Candens could see dark circles under his brother's eyes. For that matter, there was something overdone, feverish, about Lambent's laughing cheer with Hermia.

The meal at last came to an end. Candens had eaten little and Adura apparently even less. She hadn't touched the fruit or the cheese, though she had sipped at her glass of wine.

His parents stood up and left the dining hall with Nola and Tinnio following.

Lambent seized Hermia's hand. "Come on, I'll show you around."

They practically skipped off together, giggling like children with Hermia's maid Lea trailing after them.

Apart from Adura's own maid Alla, who was standing out of earshot to one side of the hall, Candens found himself alone with Adura for the first time. An uncomfortable silence followed. Adura's gaze was cast downwards as though in modesty, though Candens knew that wasn't it.

"Look..." he said after a long moment. *I know you're unhappy about our pledge*, he almost said, but stopped himself. "Are you afraid of heights?"

Startled, Adura looked up at him as though seeing him for the first time.

"No." Adura wore a puzzled expression and the faintest hint of a smile. "Why do you ask?"

"If you're up for a climb," Candens said, "there's a great view I could show you."

She considered.

"All right, then," she said at last and this time her mouth definitely twitched in the direction of a smile.

He didn't offer her his hand, but stood up from the table. "This way..."

A wooden stairway zig-zagged its way up the outside of the tall bell-tower, eventually reaching a platform which ran all around just below the level of the bell chamber. Alla, looking up, begged to be excused the climb and they left her standing at the foot of the stairs. It was a long climb and, by the time they reached the platform, Candens and Adura were both struggling for breath.

"Oh!" Adura gasped as they both collapsed onto the wooden seat set there. "That really *was* a climb!" Her face was flushed with the exertion and she was the most animated Candens had ever seen her.

As they regained their breath, Candens waved his hand at the spectacular view. They were seated with their backs to the tower. Leaning forwards, they could see the fields of the estate spread out like a map, with the field-workers crawling over it like toiling ants. To their right, the Sun blazed out from its position above the waters of the bay, with incandescent clouds of mist swirling around it. To their left, the dark shadow of the bell tower stretched, spreading far out across the landscape darkwards towards the ice-covered mountains only dimly visible in the distance.

"It's beautiful." Adura said. "Thank you for showing it to me."

Candens, as always, had been mentally keeping the count since the last peal. "Put your hands over your ears" He demonstrated to Adura with his own. "Like this. Now; now!"

Obediently, she followed his example, though with a puzzled frown. A moment later and the bells just above them began their deafening peal. Even with their hands clamped tight over their ears, the sound swept through them. The wooden platform trembled with the vibrations of the peal and Adura looked at her Pledge with alarm. He smiled and mouthed, "It's all right, you're safe."

After the bells came sweet, empty silence.

"I'm sorry that you don't like me."

Candens spoke impulsively as Adura uncovered her ears.

Her face crinkled with sadness and she looked down at her lap.

"It's not that I don't like you, Candens," she said after a while. To his astonishment, he saw tears beginning in her eyes. "I don't know you, really, but it's not you that I dislike."

"What is it then?" Candens nodded for her to go on.

Adura looked out across the splendid landscape.

"It's the whole business of being pledged against my will; of being married, of being..." She stopped and pounded her fists against her knees. "Oh, darkness take it! Of being *useless*!"

"You won't be useless." Candens was startled by her vehemence. "You'll—"

"I'll *what*?" Adura spoke fiercely, looking back at him. "I'll bear your children, who will be all looked after by servants. And I will just *sit*. Oh, I'll have things to do: I'll find things to do. But they will be meaningless things. Meanwhile you, your brother and all the other *men* will do the work of the world, learning all of their clan's secrets, talking together in the Council Chamber, directing the workers and making all of the decisions."

"But that's the way it has always been."

63

It was the worst thing Candens could have said, but he didn't realise this until Adura stood up abruptly.

"Yes, it is." Adura's face and voice were flat and cold once more. "That is the way it has always been and always will be."

With that she set off down the stairs, without him.

12

Candens

"I'm going to join the Militia."

Two decants—twenty Shutterings—had passed since the dinner with their Pledges. Candens was in Ardens' study, which was lit evenly by the sunlight reflected from the white-painted ceiling above them. Ardens sat behind a heavy wooden desk, frowning at his son, who stood before him on the elaborately-patterned woolen carpet as he made his announcement.

Ardens laid down his pen. "You are *not* joining the Militia."

Candens sighed. He had expected this.

"Yes, I am. You don't really need me here. Lambent is the heir. Uncle Tinnio is Pendulum Master. There are plenty of cousins to do the work of the clan."

"You should be here, learning the business." Ardens sat back, folding his arms.

"I *have* learned the business. I know it better than Lambent. I won't forget what I know. But I want to do something else with my life, at least for a while."

"You'll be married soon."

Candens gave a short, unhappy laugh.

"No I won't. Adura has written to say that she wants to put off our marriage for at least a millend. She'd make it later, if she could, but I don't think her family will let her."

"I see."

Ardens sat for a long while, silent, his arms still folded. Candens felt an urge to shuffle his feet where he stood, but

65

David R. Grigg

forced himself to remain still and maintain his father's gaze until Ardens finally broke the silence.

"You are determined then. You really want to do this?"

"Yes."

"You'll find it hard. The training won't be easy."

"I know. That's part of the reason why I want to do it."

"Hmmm. You might change your mind once you start. Still... I suppose it would be good for you; might teach you some additional skills."

"Yes. You'll let me do it, then?"

Ardens shrugged.

"Now that you are pledged, you are of an age to make your own decisions, I suppose. So yes, I will allow it."

"Thank you, Father. I'll send a signal to the Commander and set off as soon as I hear from him that there's a place for me."

"Oh, there'll be a place for you. They're always looking for good men."

Candens smiled. "Am I a good man, then?"

Ardens frowned.

"Don't fish for compliments, Candens. But yes, you at least have the potential to be a good man. I just wish..."

Ardens' voice trailed off and he shook his head, as if in irritation.

Candens raised an eyebrow. "You wish...?"

"I wish you were staying here," Ardens continued after a moment. "You are a good influence on Lambent. Sometimes I worry about him."

"I don't think I have much influence over him." Candens was not about to betray his brother's secrets, but he had to try and help his father. "I think he'll be right once he is married. He'll be happy with Hermia. I understand she wants to be married sooner rather than later."

66

That had been a bitter piece of knowledge and it was part of the reason he had come to his decision about the Militia.

"It will still be quite a while, perhaps the best part of a millend; several centends at least. But yes, perhaps you're right. She certainly seems to be a spirited girl. You'll take leave to attend their wedding?"

Something twisted painfully inside Candens, but he was able to reply calmly enough.

"Oh yes," he assured his father. "I wouldn't miss it for the world."

13

Adura

Adura sat at her dressing table, her mirror uncovered; she had passed through the nonsense of hating to see her own face, to the obvious relief of her maid.

In front of Adura was the signal she had received earlier that waking. It was encoded, of course, and now, pen in hand, she was slowly decoding it with the cipher and key-phrase Hermia had sent to her by carrier.

Hermia had initiated this correspondence. Touching Adura's arm as they had left the Bellringer manor a few decants ago, Hermia had drawn her aside while the grooms were fussing about something wrong with the harness on the Signaller's coach.

"You are unhappy, my dear," Hermia observed. "Please tell me about it. We are to be sisters, after all."

Adura had poured it all out in a bitter flood, spilling forth her anger and her unwillingness to fit into her chosen role.

"But *you* don't seem to mind it," she had said to Hermia with a weary sigh as she finally reached the end of her rant.

"A woman has many ways to influence men and through them, to influence events." Hermia had smiled. "We are much more powerful than men like to think. I am content, but if you cannot be content, there is a group of women I think you should talk to. Have you ever heard of The Daughters?"

Wasn't that the name Alla's cousin had overheard her mistress use? Alla hadn't been able to find out any more from her cousin, but now...

"I *may* have heard something about them."

"The full name of the group is the Daughters of the Dark. An overly dramatic name, meant to shock."

"The Daughters of the *Dark*... oh."

It *was* shocking. 'The Dark' was the embodiment of everything bad and evil in the world, surrounded as they were in this oasis of light by an endless unlit landscape which stretched out to infinity, for all anyone knew.

"As I say, it's an unfortunate name," Hermia had continued. "But like you, these women are not content with their role in Sunfall and are trying to do something about it."

A little while after she had returned to her own manor, Adura had received a packet from Hermia with the cipher and an address to send the signals to, with the mysterious name 'Raven'.

Now at last a reply had come and the letter was in her hands, fully decoded: a letter from Raven.

Reading it slowly through once, then again and again, Adura at last began to feel some hope.

14

Candens

His father had been right. The Militia training *was* hard.

Militia headquarters were in the city, but they owned a tract of rough, inhospitable land a long way Sun-leftwards around the bay. It was a place of many rocky hills and their associated dark shadows, interlaced with icy streams of water draining from a glacier half-seen in the dim darkwards. It was here that the Militia trained its men and officers to a high pitch of fitness and resourcefulness: running long distances carrying a heavy pack; learning to shoot accurately from horseback; mastering the use of a quarter-staff in close combat and overcoming an opponent without any weapons. The hard discipline of the training quickly weeded out many of the candidates, but Candens stayed with it, determined to find a place for himself among the Militia's officers.

The Militia camp was situated on a short, high ridge jutting into the bay. On its darkwards side, the hills threw deep shade into the inlet separating it from the mainland. Despite the closeness of the peninsula to the Sun, it was cold enough down in the inlet for the water to be flecked with floes of ice. The Shadow Prison lay down there in the dark and cold, a horrible place which Candens had visited only once.

One evening, six decants after he had begun his training, Candens lay on his bed in the hut to which he had been assigned, trying to sleep. Every muscle of his body was aching after the most recent exercise, which had involved racing his fellow trainees to the very top of a twisted shadow tower, climbing up the treacherous slippery godsteel beams. He had won, just, a bare few moments before the others. He suspected, though, that rather than the physical exertion involved, the real aim of the exercise had been to dispel any residual superstition the men might have had about the strange towers.

Even as tired as Candens was, it wasn't easy to sleep. The hut was hot and noisy. He shared it with three other men. Two of them—Crestor of the Icebreakers and Lux of the Metalworkers—were still sitting up, telling jokes and bantering with each other, though the Shuttering peal had sounded two bells ago. The third man, Jud, had fallen asleep long ago.

Jud was just... Jud. A Dim. Candens had at first been surprised to find himself sharing a dwelling, sharing the training, with a Dim. He had thought that the officer class would be restricted to members of the Clans. But it seemed that a hard-working, talented Dim could work his way up through the ranks. Jud was one such example.

Crestor and Lux tended to treat Jud with a degree of aristocratic disdain, mostly ignoring him. But Candens had grown to like and respect the man, who was a little older. Dark-haired and muscular, he was very strong and had proven to be clever and skilled. He didn't speak much, but what he said was always worth paying attention to. He had a sly sense of humour and his white teeth often gleamed out from within his impressive black beard. When he laughed, the earth shook. Now, though, the hut was shaking with his snores.

Candens was striving to gain the respect of his companions, particularly Jud, but he wasn't yet sure that he had done so. His body was slowly starting to harden up, his abused muscles beginning to put on mass. And he had found that with continual practice his accuracy and reach with the willow-wood bow was coming along well. At least well enough for Sergeant Stavens, the gruff older man leading their training, to acknowledge that Candens might have some talent with the weapon. Eventually.

Finally, Crestor and Lux stopped talking and Candens dropped off to sleep. It seemed only moments later that he was awoken by loud knocks and the door opening.

"Up, you lot," Stavens ordered. "We're riding out to tackle some curfew breakers."

There were groans from Crestor and Lux, who perhaps now regretted not bedding down immediately after the Shuttering peal. Candens said nothing, but sat up and started to pull on his boots. Jud had awoken in an instant and was silently doing the same.

No formal law dictated a curfew after the sounding of the Shuttering peal, but it was a well-respected custom that once the shutters were closed no one travelled or carried out business until the Unshuttering. Those breaking the rule were suspected to be about some criminal endeavour and liable to be questioned by the Militia. The Militia rostered a proportion of its men on watch-patrols who roamed the land between Shuttering and Unshuttering, calling on reinforcements as required. This made for a frequent lack of sleep for militiamen, in theory made up for by a short sleep period after the mid-waking meal, when the shutters of the men's huts were closed again. Candens was learning, with difficulty, the soldier's ability to nap at every good opportunity while still being able to snap awake, fully alert, within seconds. It was a talent that Jud at least had mastered.

Candens' horse Raya had already been saddled by one of the Dim foot-soldiers. Candens stroked her muzzle affectionately. He had always been fond of horses, but Raya was special: bred and raised to be a Militia horse, she had been quick to respond to the training alongside her new master. Now Candens trusted her implicitly.

Jud drew up alongside on his own horse, giving Candens a friendly nod.

"Where are we going, have you heard?" Candens asked him because Jud seemed to have sources of information within the ranks which never percolated up to the other officers.

Jud pointed out across the bay. "See where the mist is falling? They tell me the wind's been blowing in that direction for a dozen bells. The Healer's manor is right in the middle. I'll wager there's been something going on there."

"Mist Thieves" were a common problem for the Militia. A sustained period of fog and rain gave criminals cover to sneak in to a property unseen. Seeking help was more difficult, since the nearest signal tower to a manor under attack might also be in the mist, so they would have to send out a rider to seek help further afield.

"It's quite a distance." Candens looked where Jud was pointing. "Surely there are patrols in the city that could get there faster?"

"We'll go by galley, you'll see. As for the city patrols, who knows what they're up to? Besides, they'll want to blood us trainees."

Jud was right. Stavens led the small group of men and officers along Militia's Arm, as the narrow peninsula was called, and down to a dock where a sleek galley was waiting for them. They dismounted and led their horses on deck and the galley's oars began to sweep the moment the last horse stepped on board.

The galley sped through the water, scattering glittering spray from its oars. This close, the Sun was hot and blinding. Canvas awnings were drawn down on that side to shield those on board. Candens had to whisper soothing words to Raya, who was restive and anxious as the ship entered slightly rougher water and the deck rocked from side to side.

Sooner than Candens would have guessed, they were drawing up to another dock and riding up the slope to the Healer's estate. Jud had been right about that, too.

After a short ride, they reached the gates of the estate. The Unshuttering peal was sounding now and fieldworkers were moving down the rows and opening the wicker shadow-gates to let the Sun fall on the plants again. Everything was still dripping with water from the mist, which was now moving away with the shifting winds.

Stavens spoke with the clan head, Magister Percuro. Candens recalled meeting him at the Pledging Ceremony and nodded politely as the old man's gaze swept over him, but Percuro showed no sign that he had recognised him.

The thieves were long gone and Stavens fired a series of sharp questions at the old man, a little rudely, Candens thought. Certainly Percuro looked uncomfortable. Yes, the thieves had been seen, glimpsed through the fog riding away. Who had seen them? Percuro nodded at a tall dark-haired boy standing at his side.

"My grandson, Radians. It was he who sounded the alarm and sent for you."

Radians' face was marked with adolescent acne, but despite his youth, he appeared to be bright and gave a clear account. He had seen four riders leaving the umbra of a warehouse, headed for the darkwards fence. No, he hadn't been able to identify the men, but gave a reasonable description of their horses.

"What was stolen, Magister?" Candens asked.

The old man rubbed his white-bearded chin, hesitating for a moment, apparently unhappy to be quizzed.

"It appears that about two dozen packages of a particular medicine have been taken. That's almost our entire stock until we can grow and prepare more. It's made from the dried buds of a herb called *cammatis* and has many useful properties in healing, although it does have some side effects and can be abused." Percuro paused again. "The common people call it *marana*."

15

Adura

Underground, out of sight of the life-giving Sun, the room was dim, lit only by small flickering flames set at intervals along the stone walls. This alone was enough to fill Adura with a thrill of defiant excitement; a sense of finally having taken a bold step towards her future freedom.

She had carefully followed the instructions she had been given, conveyed to her in the coded signal which had finally arrived, decants after her first contact with Raven. Three wakings later the carrier had brought the package she had been promised, containing the disguise which had allowed her to travel unnoticed to this rendezvous.

She sat in the cool cellar, shrouded in a black cloak and wearing the black-painted wooden mask she had been given on entering. Around her sat about a dozen other figures, hooded and masked as she was. Adura had no idea who they were, except that they must be women who felt as she did. She wondered how many of those here were also attending for the first time and how many had been to such meetings before. She had no way to tell.

The hooded women had come one by one into the cellar over the period of two bells. Adura had been the second one there and had now been waiting, shivering a little, for a considerable time. No sound, no conversation, broke the boredom; the instructions Adura had received had been emphatic that she avoid speaking and she presumed the

76

others had been told the same. In any case, no one, it seemed, wanted to be the first to break that commandment.

She was beginning to become impatient when the door opened and a tall figure came in. Like those seated, this figure was hooded in a black cloak which covered her hair and concealed her figure. But unlike the others, her mask was painted a dark red.

The woman's voice, when she spoke, was strange, a little muffled and changed by passing through a wooden grill in the mask.

"I am Raven. Welcome, Daughters of the Dark." The woman looked about her. "We have two new members here today: a particular welcome to you both. I will not name you. Here we use no names. Your clans are of no importance and must not learn of your involvement. Until our society is ready; until we have *made* it ready, being known to be involved with The Daughters would be to court your utter disgrace. Remember that well. Do not seek to discover who your fellow members are, nor reveal your own identity. Speak here only in whispers, through this mask, which disguises your voice. Never remove your mask. Secrecy is our biggest strength."

Raven drew a breath and raised her voice.

"Daughters! We are the agents of change. We will no longer endure the strictures which our society tries to impose upon us. We will take bold actions, I promise you, actions which will expose and condemn the inequity with which we women are treated. We are angry and we will *not* remain silent. With your help, we shall soon be ready to strike such a blow as will be the talk of all Sunfall. A blow which no man will be able to ignore."

The thrill of joy which ran through Adura almost made her gasp.

16
Candens

Candens was on an after-Shuttering patrol in the city: four men led by Commander Fervens himself. Candens' basic training was now complete, though he knew he needed to gain a great deal of experience before he really deserved to be called an officer.

Being out in the city after the Shuttering peal was an eerie feeling. Although the main streets were as bright as ever, no one else was about. Nothing moved. The windows of every building were shuttered. No carts trundled along the cobbles, no crowds were in the square outside the Council Lodge and no beggars sat in the shade of the buildings. It was quiet, too, with only the soft sound of the patrol's boots and the occasional caw of a bird breaking the silence.

They soon moved off the wide streets and entered the maze of narrow lanes which ran behind the buildings. Here the Sun never penetrated, though some owners could afford mirrors, which threw light over locked delivery doors and through barred windows to provide an extra degree of security. The rear of most buildings, however, was in permanent shade. Here thieves could more readily exercise their trade and this was the reason for the Militia patrols. But the patrols were limited and the greed of criminals was not.

They were on foot, the better to move quietly through these confined lanes. The Militia's best strategy in the city was to move frequently and randomly around the lanes, to ensure there was no regular pattern which thieves could predict and exploit.

As they turned the corner of a lane, Candens saw a quick movement. Three figures coming out of a doorway at the far end of the lane, making a startled motion as they saw the patrol.

"There!" Candens pointed.

Commander Fervens called out: "Stop! You there! Stop!"

Instead, the figures dashed across the lane and then vanished from sight.

The patrol began to run, with Candens in the lead. He kept his gaze fixed on the door the figures had come from, so as not to mistake it for any of the many other doors and hatches giving on to the lane. He reached the door and found it swinging open. It was hard to make out in the shade here, but Candens saw that a small hole had been sawn in it, allowing the thieves to push in a rod and lift the bar.

Commander Fervens and the other men caught up with Candens.

Fervens looked around to get his bearings. "This is one of the Carpenters' workshops. There'll be valuable metal-tipped tools in there, a good target for thieves. All right. Crestor, let's have a torch."

Crestor of the Icebreakers was another man in the patrol. He knelt on the cobbles and quickly struck a flint, the sparks fiercely bright in the dimness of the lane. In a moment he had a flame going in the tinder and then used it to light a tarred cloth wrapped around a stick.

"But where did they go to?" Candens looked around the lane. "I saw them run but then they were gone."

Fervens gave a grunt and paced up the lane, followed by Crestor with the torch. He bent down to a wooden grating low in the stone wall. The cobbles here were shaped to create a shallow channel leading to the grating.

"Down here." The Commander grasped the grating and easily pulled it free. "Into the sewers. Candens, you'll ruin your uniform, but down you go. Crestor, you follow with the torch. Quick now!"

Suppressing a feeling of distaste, Candens held his unstrung bow in one hand as he slid through the narrow, slimy opening. He dropped down a couple of arm-lengths to splash into a noisome stream. He was in a stone-lined tunnel about six arm-lengths in diameter. Some distance ahead, he could see a flickering light and heard the sound of splashing. He took a moment to string his bow and pull an arrow from his pouch and then ran. Behind him, he heard Crestor drop down and then saw a flare of bright light from the torch.

From ahead came the sound of an oath and the flickering light went out, dowsed no doubt in the stream of filth. Crestor's torch, however, cast enough light now for Candens to see where to place his running feet on the uneven surface. As his eyes began to adjust to the dimness—much darker even than the shaded streets above—he started to see the dim outlines of three men ahead. Two were large, bulky men; one was thin and wiry.

The same light made Candens a perfect target. He saw the thinnest man place something in an arm-length stick. Then the man bent back and whipped the stick forward. Unseen and unheard, something came at Candens and ripped through his uniform at his right side, tearing the cloth and lightly scratching his skin. Some kind of wooden dart, he thought, sped on its way by a throwing-stick.

He saw the man fitting another dart. Instantly, Candens dropped to a squatting position to reduce his target area. Even as he did so, he was notching his arrow and drawing his bow. Behind him, Crestor was drawing closer with the torch and Candens' shadow shifted distractingly before him. Ignoring it, Candens aimed and then released. A cry of pain told him that he had shot true. The man dropped the throwing stick and ran away, an arrow lodged in his arm.

Candens stood and pulled another arrow from his pouch. As Crestor caught up with him, he shot again, at one of the bulkier thieves, who was too fat to run quickly. The thief emitted a high-pitched scream as Candens' arrow found him. Running forward, Candens saw the man slumped against the curving tunnel wall, howling with pain, an arrow through his shoulder. Candens ran past. Crestor could deal with the man.

The tunnel reached a junction ahead and the men Candens was chasing split up, one dodging to the left and the other to the right.

Candens, his breath coming hard now, paused. It would be a perfect place for an ambush by one or both men if he was foolish enough to run around the corner. The men might have lost their throwing-weapon, but they would surely have clubs. And Candens would be all too easy to see, lit by the light of Crestor's torch.

Moving softly to the right so he could aim as far as possible down the left-hand branch, Candens drew his bow to its limit, straining, then released an arrow at the far wall of the tunnel. It struck the stone with a spark of light and clattered down the side-tunnel. Casting the bow aside, he was on the run before it fell. Enough light from the torch was reflected down the passage for Candens to see the thief turning back from looking with surprise at the arrow's flight. He struck the man hard with his own club. A brief struggle in the stinking stream of water lasted until Candens got in another blow with his club and the thief was unconscious.

He looked along the other branch of the tunnel. But the man who had held the throwing stick was gone. That was puzzling. There didn't seem to be any place the man *could* have gone. Candens paced down the passage for a few steps, but couldn't see any obvious openings. Shrugging, he gave it up and returned to the thief he had caught.

With the help of the other men of the patrol, he and Crestor hauled the two thieves, their hands bound behind them, up through the grating. A clinking bag of stolen metal-tipped tools had been recovered along with the men.

"Well done." Fervens' hand rested on Candens' shoulder. "Good shooting, Crestor tells me. Not easy, in those conditions."

Candens shrugged as though it meant nothing, but he couldn't repress a smile, pleased with himself and particularly pleased that he had earned the Commander's approbation.

And so the time went by for hundreds of Shutterings. Each waking, or after the Shuttering, Candens was on patrol with his fellow officers, keeping the peace and investigating crimes. A violent quarrel among a group of drunken Dims; the murder of a female servant at the Horsebreeder's manor; a theft of rings from a delivery coach; breaking up a rowdy disturbance outside the Council Lodge: these were all part of the Militia work which kept Candens and his new friends busy. The work and the continual training were difficult, but satisfying. Candens began to feel that this was his destined role in life; that he could be content as a militiaman, if not exactly happy.

He grew in other ways, too. He met a friendly barmaid called Mara and began to regularly visit the tavern where she worked. Eventually she took him to her bed and taught him how to give and receive pleasure there. It was a happy relationship, but both of them knew that it could never become deep or permanent. She was a Dim, he a Bright, the son of a clan head. And he was already pledged.

He received communications from home from time to time, mostly letters from his sister Campana, delivered by the horse-drawn mail carriage, slower but much cheaper than sending a signal. With each letter, she sounded to be less of a silly child and more a mature young woman. She sometimes mentioned her coming Pledging from time to time, but without much enthusiasm, Candens thought.

Ardens only sent the occasional signal; rather stiff, formal notes about the business of the clan. Only trivial little messages came from Lambent. He never heard a word from Adura.

Then came the news that he had been expecting, yet dreading. Lambent and Hermia had agreed on a date for their marriage, only four decants away, forty Shutterings. So soon! He would be expected to attend, though if he could find some Militia duty which conflicted, he would gladly make his excuses.

Finally, only a decant later, came a signal from his father which shattered all of Candens' plans for his future. After decoding it, he stared at the words in dismay.

> "Great-Uncle Tinnio is dead. Come home at once. I need you as Pendulum Master.
>
> —ARDENS."

17
Candens

The manor of the Signallers had four towers and each of them was continually busy with glittering light. The estate was higher in the hills and farther from the Sun than was usual for a major clan, and the air was cool. Shivering a little, Candens rode alone towards the manor with stone in his heart, as cold as the frost which showed in the shadows of the towers. He was coming late to the wedding, his work in the Pendulum Chamber having detained him. In truth, he had delayed longer than was really necessary to brief Valend, his stand-in. He was in no hurry to arrive. No joy lay ahead for him.

Today Candens would be forced to watch his brother marry Hermia, the one woman Candens himself had ever desired. *If only*—he caught himself thinking, but suppressed the thought quickly.

He might also meet again with his own pledge, Adura of the Mirrormasters. He knew that she had been invited, but he didn't much look forward to seeing her. She was still refusing to agree to a date for their union. She must be coming under increasing pressure to do so from her own family, but so far she had managed to resist it.

He reached the Signaller manor at last and dismounted from Raya. He had grown so fond of the strong, patient creature that he had bought her from the Militia, paying a substantial price which included the value of her training.

A groom was close at hand to take Raya's reins. The man inclined his head deferentially.

"The ceremony is about to begin, sir. It is taking place in the Chapel of the Sun. You see it over there? I'm sure that if you hurry you will be in time."

Candens merely grunted in reply, but set off towards the large building that the groom had pointed out. It formed an annex on the sunwards side of the main manor building. Most clans had at least a small Healer's chapel within the manor where the family worshipped and where their health and spiritual needs were addressed. But this one was more of a full-sized church, presumably to provide for the needs of servants and field workers as well.

It appeared to be quite new and, as he stepped inside and saw how beautifully it was constructed and decorated, he realised that the Signallers must be wealthy. Candens recalled reading that in his grandfather's time, the Signallers had been simply the Messengers, a relatively lowly clan. In those days there had been no signal towers, only mounted couriers riding back and forth over the land. But then someone in the clan had come up with the method of sending coded signals via flashing mirrors, greatly speeding up the delivery. Eventually the signal towers were built and respect for the clan had grown to the point that they were admitted to the Clan Council. So progress *was* possible in Sunfall. But oh, how slow it was.

As he entered, he was met by a female servant, who curtseyed and led him quietly to his place, next to his Great-Aunt Nola, who greeted him with a weak smile. On her other side sat his sister Campana, who turned and winked at him.

Candens still hadn't become used to this new Campana, who was no longer the skinny girl he remembered from before his time in the Militia. She had grown in height and filled out in body and was now quite a good-looking young woman. But her sense of fun still appeared to be intact.

David R. Grigg

In the distance, Candens could hear the seventh peal of the waking sounding out and, barely conscious of it, he began the mental count again from zero.

As the peal came to an end, a figure clad in glittering silver emerged and came to the centre of the raised stage. The chapel's Healer, dressed to officiate as a priest. The ceremony began. After a long and tedious introduction, the priest called on the families of the two pledges to bring them forward.

From the left Candens' parents Ardens and Eccua led forward Lambent, dressed in pure white. From the right came Magister Solus and Magistra Calora of the Signallers, leading their daughter Hermia.

Candens drew a short, painful breath. Hermia had never looked so lovely to him as now, draped in red cloth which fell to her ankles, clinched around her waist with a sash of bright yellow, her hair dressed with red, orange, yellow and blue feathers creating an illusion of flame. Candens couldn't take his eyes from her and the words of the long ceremony came and went without his paying them the slightest attention. Even the ceremonial flooding of the chapel with sunlight at the climax of the ceremony barely registered.

It was over. Lambent took Hermia in his arms and kissed her eagerly, as the audience applauded.

Staring at Lambent and his new wife embracing there, Candens felt none of the simple self-aware envy that he had felt back at the Pledging Ceremony. No. Now he stared at Lambent, for the first time, with real jealousy.

She should have been mine, Candens thought. *You have wasted your energies in gambling, confused your brain with drink and marana and shown disrespect for your pledge by visiting other women.*

And then, finally, the thought that he had been trying to suppress all his life.

I hate you, Lambent. I should have been the heir, not you.

86

As the wedding guests filed out of the chapel on their way to the nuptial feast, Candens thought that Adura had not come to the wedding. Then he caught sight of her on the other side of the chapel and his heart sank a little. She could easily have made an excuse, given that she was not yet part of the Bellringer clan and had no direct connection with the Signallers. But there she was, looking towards him and half-raising a hand in greeting. She remained where she was as he weaved his way through the departing crowd to reach her side.

He hadn't seen her, nor she seen him, since he had joined the Militia. She stood looking at him, assessing him. He wondered what she thought about what she saw. He certainly felt much stronger and more confident in himself, no longer the boy who had taken her up the bell-tower to see the view.

"You've put on weight," she said at last. "I don't mean *weight*, I suppose. You're much bulkier, stronger. The Militia must have been good for you."

"Yes." He nodded. "It was. I wish I was still in it."

She had changed, too. She was more mature, a little taller, her bust a little fuller. But her face had grown leaner. Her hair was cut at shoulder-length and she wore an un-patterned light-grey gown. A single round mirror-brooch was pinned to the breast of her dress. A difficult silence fell between them as the remaining wedding guests left the chapel, until Adura spoke.

"The new millend is almost here. Your sister will be pledged, I'm sure."

"I suppose so. It's hard to think of her being pledged and then married."

Adura looked away from him for a moment. "It comes to us all, whether we want it or not."

"Have you... I mean, I wanted..."

Candens' earlier feeling of self-confidence had vanished and he felt all a boy again.

"You want to know when we will be married?" Adura looked back at him, her gaze direct and unwavering. "The answer is never, Candens. I will never be your bride. I came here to tell you so in person."

"But—but we are pledged."

"Do you think pledges are never broken? Do you? You are wrong. There may be many reasons why a couple pledged do not marry. For example…" She paused and drew breath. "For example, one of the pair may die."

Her words felt like a plunge into icy water.

"Do you mean that you would kill yourself rather than marry me? Am I so horrible?"

"No!" Adura's nostrils flared in anger. "I told you before that I have nothing against you. But I won't be locked away in marriage, denied any rights; denied my ability to make a change in the world. I won't. And I've found—"

She stopped suddenly and started to walk briskly away. Candens caught up with her and grasped her arm, forcing her to look at him. There were tears in her eyes.

"You've found what? Someone you want to marry instead of me? Who?"

Adura shook her head and bit her lip.

"No, no, that's not it, that's not it at all. I've said too much. I won't be forced to marry anyone. Not you. Not anyone."

"Listen. Why won't you let me help you? I don't want to lock you away, or stop you doing whatever you want to do. We don't have to have children, if that's the problem, if you're afraid of that."

Deep down, part of Candens wondered why he was trying so hard to win Adura round. Given that he couldn't marry Hermia, what did it matter if he never married anyone, let alone this tormented soul?

88

"Dying in childbirth doesn't frighten me. Oh, why can't you *understand*? It's being in a cage that I'm frightened of."

"I won't put you in a cage—"

Adura's face was flushed now, her tears drying up as she tried to make her pledge understand. "But will you tell me the secrets of your clan? Will you share your work with me? Tell me what you do each waking, ask me to help you with your problems?"

"Well, I..."

What she asked was impossible, she had to know that.

"No." Adura answered her own question. "You can't, can you? No man ever shares the secrets of his clan. Goodbye, Candens. I'm going back to my own manor. I don't think we'll ever meet again."

And with that she walked off and out of the chapel door.

18

Campana

Everything was different at the manor after Lambent brought home his bride. Campana grieved, but could do nothing.

And yet what had changed, really?

Certainly Lambent and Hermia had taken over the large suite of rooms where Tinnio and Nola had lived. Great-Aunt Nola had been shifted, despite her protests, to a smaller room more fitting to her status as a widow. Tinnio's death had aged her dramatically. Her hair was now almost all white and her memory was beginning to fail. Campana no longer lived in fear of her great-aunt's strictures and she saw that her mother, too, seemed more relaxed and less anxious.

No, that wasn't the problem. The problem was how Hermia's presence seemed to have radically distorted the relationships between Campana's brothers. At breakfast and dinner, Campana looked anxiously from one of her brothers to the other, seeing the new tension between them.

Lambent, on the surface, seemed deliriously happy. But she couldn't help noticing that sometimes at table his hands trembled and he always looked as though he needed more sleep. He often drank wine to excess, ignoring the occasional caution from his father.

Candens, though, Candens... he seemed to have turned to stone. He was operating as though controlled by levers and pulleys. He spoke when asked a direct question, but only rarely made a comment of his own. He always seemed absent, his mind elsewhere. He was always the first to excuse himself from the table to return to his important work in the tower (whatever that work *was*, Campana thought irritably), or else in his small amount of leisure time after dinner, he went to his workroom, or outside into the yard to exercise and maintain his archery skills.

Even her father Ardens was different when Hermia was at the table. Campana was no fool; she could see that Ardens found the young woman attractive, without being overmastered by it. Hermia, though, constantly fed his regard by her flattery, commenting often about the importance of the work of the clan. Campana's mother, seeing this, was silent, but her mouth flattened into a thin line of disapproval.

As for Campana herself, she had been given no reason to like Hermia any better. There was nothing she could point to, nothing she could complain about to her father or to Lambent. Yet always in the air between them was something unsaid, an implicit threat.

By now Campana had persuaded herself that Hermia's hurtful words at their first meeting at the Pledging Ceremony had been nothing but angry posturing by the older girl and had meant nothing. But nevertheless, Campana and Hermia were not and would never be, "such good friends".

One evening, only a few decants before the next Pledging Ceremony, Campana watched Candens at table. Since Lambent's marriage, Candens had been eating with his eyes mostly downcast towards his meal, rather than engaging in conversation with the others at the table. But this evening for some reason he looked up and Campana could see him stare down the table at Hermia, who was telling some amusing story. She saw, just for an instant, the raw pain in his eyes. Then he looked down again, as though uninterested in Hermia's tale. A few moments later, he pushed his plate aside and making a muttered apology, strode from the table.

After a moment's hesitation, Campana made her own apologies and followed him. She saw Candens was headed for his workshop.

She knew Candens' workshop well. When she had been just a little girl, Candens had often made small toys for her, little wooden carriages, a horse with moving legs and tail, a model of the main manor-house with tiny shutters that opened and closed. Back then, she had been a welcome visitor to the workshop, but Candens had now taken to locking the door. It was locked now and she tapped hard on the wood.

"Who is it?"

"Campana."

There was a long pause and then the door opened. Candens had thrown a sheet of cloth over one of the workbenches, obviously to hide whatever was there. *God forbid that a female should see anything connected with the clan's secrets*, Campana thought with heavy resignation.

She came in, swept a stool clear of wood shavings and sat down. She gazed at him a moment, considering.

"She's Lambent's wife," she said at last. "There's nothing you can do about it. You have to forget her."

Candens' face spasmed in pain and he looked away. "I don't know what you're talking about," he said, his voice hollow.

"Yes you do," she said simply. "What about Adura? When will you be married?"

Candens gave a short laugh and shook his head.

"Never, according to her. Perhaps her clan will force her to honour her pledge, I don't know. She... oh, the Dark take it!" His lip trembled and Campana could see that he was only preventing himself from weeping by sheer force of will. He drew a long breath and then said calmly enough. "It's all such a mess."

Campana was silent, her heart heavy, wishing desperately that there was something she could do to make things right again. But it was impossible.

"Look, living here in the manor, coming in contact with Lambent and Hermia every waking, it's killing you. Can't you move somewhere else, live in a house alongside one of the repeater towers?"

"No. Not now that I'm Pen... not now that I have an important job here in the Bell Tower. I need to be here." Candens sighed. "I wish to God I could have continued in the Militia."

"Then you're going to have to forget how you feel about Hermia. She's... she's not really such a nice person, you know. She has a beautiful face, but.... well, she's been very unpleasant to me a few times."

That made Candens angry. "I don't want to hear such stuff. What right do you have, anyway, to tell me what to do, how to feel? Do you want me giving *you* advice once you're pledged?"

"Yes," she said simply. "If it's good advice."

Candens shrugged and turned away, picking up one of the many pieces of rubbish which lay on his bench and starting to tinker with it. The conversation was over.

Campana left the workshop, closing the door behind her. Outside, to her alarm, she was startled to see Hermia, arm in arm with Lambent, who was unsteady on his feet, his gaze vacant. Had Hermia been listening at the door? What had she overheard?

Hermia met Campana's gaze and smiled. She looked like a cat who has just knocked over a jug of cream.

Campana shuddered and walked briskly away without a word.

~

At breakfast the next morning, Ardens was handed a folded paper by the manservant Parr. It bore the blue seal of a signal. Candens wasn't there, having left the table early to go to his work, as usual.

The signal must have been sent in the clear, because Ardens looked up only a few moments later. "Here's bad news. Medeor, the Healer of Souls, has been killed. Thrown by his horse, it seems, and hit his head on a rock."

Campana's mother gave a little gasp. "Oh, that's terrible, really terrible. I knew him... knew him a little, when we were children. And Percuro's younger son Astus died several millends ago, too, I recall. How awful for them." Her eyes filled with tears.

Lambent, who appeared to be suffering from a headache, frowned. "He was old Magister Percuro's heir, wasn't he? What will the Healers do now? As I hear it, Medeor's only child so far is a girl. Who will take over now as the heir?"

Ardens considered. "It will pass to Astus' son Radians, Percuro's grandson, I imagine. But he's probably too young to become Healer of Souls just yet. They might ask Percuro's younger brother to do that job in the interim. Lustris is his name."

Despite the sad news he had announced, Ardens was now in a surprisingly cheerful mood.

"So, Campana." Ardens addressed his daughter. "When you are pledged soon, there'll be a new Healer in charge. He'll barely have had time to be trained for the job. I hope he doesn't make any mistakes and leave you unpledged."

That was her father's feeble attempt at humour, Campana knew. She was not amused and indeed, a chill ran through her at the thought of the Pledging. It was coming upon her all too soon.

19

Candens

Candens looked down from his seat in the Great Hall at the pledgees assembled in the shadows, the two groups parted for the moment by a bright lane of sunlight from the opened shutters. Somewhere down there was his sister Campana, but he was having trouble making her out.

Exactly a millend ago, it had been he and Lambent down there, nervously awaiting the announcement of their pledge. A thousand Shutterings... in some ways it felt as though it had been a thousand millends. His whole life had changed since then and not for the better.

Lambent and Hermia were not here. Hermia had pleaded a severe headache and Lambent, little interested in formal family occasions, had elected to stay with her at the manor.

His mother was here, of course, her dislike of public occasions notwithstanding. Campana's forthcoming pledging had brightened her mood and it was she who had been shepherding an increasingly feeble Great-Aunt Nola about, rather than the reverse.

And his father, naturally, sat at Candens' side. He wondered to whom Ardens had pledged Campana. What deal would he have done, what benefits to the Bellringer Clan had he managed to obtain in return for selling off his only daughter?

My God, Candens thought, *I'm starting to think like Adura.* He shook off the idea with irritation. Campana would surely have a better pledge than his own had been,

95

there was that, at least.

The formalities of the event rolled on. They never altered.

Lustris, the new Healer of Souls, gave an awkward, hesitant reading from the Book of the Sun and then Magister Neptus, the Council President, limped up to the podium. He appeared to have aged a lot in the past millend, his back more bent, his white hair thinning. He began in a rather tremulous voice:

"Magisters and Magistras; members of the Clans. It is my honour this waking to announce the pledgings for millend one thousand and sixty-four. I am sure..."

It was at this point that the un-altering tradition of the Pledging Ceremony changed, perhaps forever.

Magister Neptus's words were choked off by an arm bent around his throat. A dark shape could just be glimpsed behind him. He was pulled backwards and at the same moment, the hall was thrown into darkness as every shutter was closed tight and the great shutter doors were slid rapidly shut. Only the pool of light reflected from the circular opening in the ceiling still fell down, spotlighting the now vacant podium.

As shouts of astonishment and outrage began to come from the audience, a tall figure stepped into that bright space. Hooded and dressed entirely in black, it wore a red mask. Despite his shock, which had brought him to his feet, Candens thought that he could see several similar black-clad figures in the shadows, only faintly illuminated by the beam around the podium.

The figure in the spotlight spoke in a loud, commanding tone and though it was distorted by the mask, it became instantly clear that it was a woman's voice.

"This ceremony is at an end!" The woman shouted. "Let it never recommence! The enslavement of women must be broken, our enforced ignorance swept away never to return! So say the Daughters of the Dark!"

Candens was already pushing past his relatives to reach the stairs. His eyes were having trouble adjusting to the sudden dark. But he could see that a couple of militiamen and other members of the audience were also on the move towards the podium.

Before any of them could reach the black-clad woman, however, there was a bright flash and a simultaneous deafening bang. A cloud of dark smoke could be seen billowing up in a pillar along the beam of light from the mirror above, but its spread must be far wider than that. Within moments, smoke had filled the hall and Candens began to cough and blink as he reached the foot of the stairs. He quickly lost all sense of where he was. He dropped down and found a layer of clear air just above the stone paving. It took him a moment or two to work out which direction the stage would be and began to crawl towards it as fast as he was able. Why didn't someone open the damn shutters? It would let out the smoke and let in some light.

A cacophony filled the hall; angry voices, screams and sobs. And a great deal of coughing.

Candens reached the edge of the stage and hauled himself up on it. Still staying low, he found his way to the sunward wall. Taking a deep breath, he stood up and fumbled his way to where the ropes controlling the movement of the shutter doors should be. But they were not where he expected. His foot knocked against something and he crouched down to feel a loose length of cut rope and one of the heavy counterweights lying on the floor. He gave a muttered curse.

Just at that moment, someone blundered against him, then crouched down to be under the layer of smoke.

"They cut the ropes, did they?"

Candens recognized the voice of his old friend Jud from the Militia. He must have been on duty in the hall.

"Jud? It's Candens of the Bellringers, here."

"Candens? Good," Jud said. "We'll need to push the doors open. Give me a hand."

Together they began to push. Without the counter-weights, it was a hard business, but others soon saw what they were doing and joined them. The welcome light of the Sun began to spill back into the room.

Others had found means of opening some of the smaller shutters, whose ropes had also been cut. In a few moments, there was enough light to see and the smoke began to drift out of the openings.

It was chaos inside the hall. Several people had been overcome by the smoke and were lying on the ranks of steps, gasping for air or completely unconscious. Others ran about, as though with no idea where they were going. Many others had escaped through the doors at the back of the hall.

Magister Neptus, the President of the Clan Council, lay in an undignified heap beneath the shutters, his hands bound behind him and his mouth gagged with a black scarf. Candens took a step towards the old man, but others were already at his side and caring for him. Candens turned back to the hall.

Ardens, his father, was at the far end, doing his best to control the panic.

Much closer stood Candens' mother Eccua. Her eyes streamed with tears, whether from the smoke or emotion he could not tell.

"Candens!" she called urgently. "Where are the girls who were to be pledged? Candens, *where is your sister Campana?*"

Startled, Candens looked around. He could see a few of the young men who had been due to be pledged. But not a single one of the eight young women was anywhere to be seen.

20

Candens

An undignified hubbub filled the Council Chamber.

Magister Solus of the Signallers was a tall, lean man with dark hair turning white at his temples. He hammered on the table for quiet. Candens didn't know him well, having met him only a few times. He had seen him last at Lambent's wedding, leading Hermia forward alongside his wife Calora.

Solus had stepped into the breach as President of the Clan Council, apparently by the simple force of his personality. The current President, Neptus Boatbuilder, was still in his private apartment, incapacitated by the shock of the recent events at the Pledging Ceremony and the rough way he had been treated.

"Gentlemen!" Solus called out in a loud, commanding voice. "Gentlemen! Come to order!"

The noise subsided and all eyes turned to him.

Candens sat next to his father on a chair which had been brought in especially for him. It was an unusual honour for someone like himself, not even the heir to a Clan, to be admitted into the deliberations of the Council. But then, these were unusual times.

Solus nodded in appreciation of the quiet. "We need to make some decisions on how to respond to this outrage: to identify these unnatural women and to destroy their organisation."

There were no compromises then, Canden noticed. No consideration would be given to whether there were real grievances that might need to be addressed.

David R. Grigg

In truth, he was angry about what had happened and deeply worried about Campana's safety, but that didn't stop him acknowledging, with his own experience in mind, that the whole business of pledging really was outdated and ripe for change.

"Magister Solus, I seek leave to speak." It was Candens' father Ardens. Receiving a nod, he went on. "Immediately after the hall was cleared, I sent my son here to the city bell tower. As you know, it commands an excellent view of the streets nearby. Our men there saw no sign of any unusual movement either before or after the incident. At the time of a peal the men are too busy to keep watch, but it still seems hardly possible these women could have entered the hall unobserved and even less possible they could have left its environs burdened with the girls they abducted."

Solus nodded. "I sought a similar assurance from the signal tower, though as it is further away it doesn't command a clear view of the streets near the hall. Nevertheless, they would surely have noticed any mysterious group entering or leaving the city. Further to that, I have had signals sent to all of the towers in our network alerting them to the news and asking them to report anything unusual. The towers currently within the mist will of course take longer to respond. Our couriers, too, have been notified and will keep their eyes open for anything out of the ordinary during their rides."

Commander Fervens of the Militia stood up, not bothering to request permission to speak. "This is useful information; thank you both. My militiamen are currently searching the buildings around the Hall for these women. Naturally we first searched the public areas of the Hall itself. But now I seek the permission of each clan head here to allow my men to search the private apartments in this building."

Instantly there were several protests. Each clan's private rooms in the Council building were considered part of their own manors, sacrosanct.

"Surely you can't be accusing any of the great clans to be supporting or shielding these women?" From the Bookbinders, Magister Valus' fat face was red with anger. "That is outrageous!"

Commander Fervens was unmoved. "I need to investigate every possibility. For example, it's possible that The Daughters have taken over a suite of apartments by force."

Candens thought it highly unlikely that Fervens really believed this suggestion. It was just a piece of diplomatic cover. *Could* one of the clans be involved with the Daughters of the Dark? Why would they do that? On the other hand, each of the women who were part of the protest had to be *someone's* daughter and surely each was a member of some clan or other. They had certainly not been Dims. Only Bright women were pledged.

Solus leaned back in his chair, rubbing his greying beard and examining the faces of the clan heads who were raising objections to Fervens' request. Candens saw that Fervens, too, was taking careful note of the same people. After a moment, Solus called for quiet again.

"I for one hereby grant the Commander permission to search the apartments of Clan Signaller. I suggest that you all do the same, lest your refusal be seen as a cause for suspicion."

A lot of grumbling arose, but one by one the clan heads gave the permission requested and Fervens left in order to direct his men. Candens itched to join them. Discussion continued for a long time after, but few useful decisions were reached; just a lot of outraged feelings vented. Solus eventually called a break and refreshments were brought in. As chatter arose, Candens leaned over to speak privately with his father.

"Father, give me leave to help Fervens in the search. Campana may be in danger."

"No."

Candens was startled by the abrupt refusal.

"But... aren't you worried about Campana?"

"Yes. But it is Lambent's role to join the search. I have sent a priority signal to fetch him. You have important duties at the manor and you need to return."

Furious, Candens felt his face flush with anger. "But *I'm* the one who is Militia-trained. Valend can continue as my stand-in at the manor."

Ardens was firm. "No. Enough. Lambent is the heir and he is Campana's eldest brother. It is his role as my deputy to amend this insult to our house."

"Lambent?" Candens' voice nearly broke with despair. "It's always Lambent, isn't it? Despite how he gets drunk almost every evening, despite..."

Candens froze in mid-sentence as Ardens shushed him with a furious growl.

"Keep your voice down. You will do as I tell you. Things are as they are. Lambent is still a little wild, I agree, but he will settle down now that he is married and even more once he has children. None of this is to the point. He will join the search and you will return to the manor. I will hear no more from you on this."

Candens bowed his head to show outward respect and obedience, but his fists were clenched so tight that his knuckles ached. He desperately wanted to hit something really hard.

21

Campana

She could see nothing. It was utterly, completely dark, something she had never experienced before in her life and it was frightening.

Everything had been a blur since the woman on the podium had shouted out her bold manifesto followed by the subsequent explosion. Hands had firmly seized Campana in the smoky confusion and led her away. She had gone willingly enough, coughing and eyes streaming, thinking that some kind person was leading her to safety. A door had opened and shut behind her. Then, before she had a chance to regain her breath and take stock of her surroundings, a bag had been thrown over her head, shutting out what little light there had been. Someone nearby screamed in a high pitch, abruptly cut off with choking sounds.

Panicking, Campana had tried to pull free from the hands which held her wrists.

"Help!" she had begun, but a moment later something was wrapped around the outside of the bag at the level of her mouth. It was tied tightly behind her head, forming an effective gag. She could now neither see nor speak. She could breathe only through her nose and it was a struggle to pull in enough air through the weave of the enclosing bag, which stank of onions. Her arms had been pulled behind her back and bound with rough twine. Then had come a push in her back, forcing her to stumble forward.

"Move!" A female voice had ordered her along. "Walk quickly, or you'll be hurt. Nod if you understand."

Campana had felt the prod of something firm at her side. A knife? She had nodded, hating herself for being so compliant; for having been so easy to capture.

Walking blindly, stumbling a little, Campana was led onto what seemed to be a slope downwards, turning to the right for a long time. Then it levelled out. The passage seemed to go on forever and Campana soon regretted the decorative shoes she had worn to the Pledging. They had looked so lovely, but were uncomfortable to walk in for any distance. She would have nasty blisters. Finally they reached another slope upwards, this time turning to her left. After a pause she heard a door open and she was pushed through it. Hands turned her through a quarter-circle before a voice had addressed her, less threateningly than before.

"There's a bench behind you. You can sit. Sit now."

It was completely dark. On either side Campana could feel the warmth of other bodies. Had they been abducted as she had? The person on her left seemed to be having a great deal of trouble breathing. There was movement as someone leant over Campana. The gag was untied and the bag pulled off. The same must be happening to the other prisoners as she heard sobs and cries of bewilderment. All of the voices were female. Even without the bag over her head, however, Campana could see nothing. The darkness felt dreadful.

"What's going on?" Her voice was steady given the circumstances. "Why have you taken us? Where are we?"

"Be quiet!" A stern female voice, strangely muffled. Campana remembered the red mask the figure on the podium had worn. Was this the same woman?

"I will explain matters soon," the voice said. "Quiet, all of you! You sound like gabbling geese."

Most voices ceased, but there were at least two girls sobbing. Frightened though she was, Campana felt mostly anger.

"Now." The woman's voice began again. "First of all, you will not be harmed."

"We have already been harmed!" Campana burst out in outrage.

"Shut up, or you will find out what harm really means," was the angry reply.

Campana had no chance of seeing the face behind the voice, no matter how hard she tried. There was no light at all. Even after the Shuttering there was always a little light sneaking through cracks in the shutters into her room. But here was so dark that her eyes had started to play tricks and create patterns which weren't really there.

"You will not be harmed," the female voice repeated. "We have taken you away from the Pledging for your own good."

Campana wanted to protest again, but forced herself to be silent.

"You will be returned to your families all in good time. But they will pay and pay well. The Daughters of the Dark will make good use of your ransoms."

"So you're just thieves, then, despite all your fine talk?" Campana was furious by now.

In the moment's silence that followed, she instinctively knew that there was a blow coming. The hard slap rocked her head and she cried out in pain. It hurt a lot.

"You talk too much for your own good. Gag this one properly."

Hands fumbled at her, but Campana clamped her mouth tight shut and moved her head from side to side to avoid the hands.

"I can't do it." This voice was different and younger. "She has her mouth closed."

Campana frowned. Was there something familiar about that voice?

"Can't we have some light?" Another voice came. Was it one of the kidnapped girls?

"No." The stern voice came back with a short answer. "Silence, both of you! You are not to speak and there will be no light. You new members need to learn to operate without light if you are to become true Daughters of the Dark. Here. *I* will gag her."

Thumbs pressed painfully into the corners of Campana's jaw, forcing her teeth open. The gag was forced in and then tied, very tightly, around the back of her head.

"There." The older voice returned, satisfied now. "It is done. You other girls need to understand that the same will happen to you if you misbehave. This foolish girl will suffer for her insolent and ignorant comments."

Suffer? Campana considered this. What more could they do to her? There was fear in that thought, but considerably more anger. For the first few moments, while the masked figure on the podium had been speaking to the stunned audience in the Great Hall, Campana had felt a certain degree of excitement. Could women really have a more important role in society? Would that be a good thing? Surely it would.

Now she only felt a considerable disillusionment. The bold manifesto which had been declared so dramatically seemed merely a flummery trick to conceal much baser motives.

"No more nonsense from any of you. Listen to me without speaking. You will each be taken from here to a separate room. The door will be locked. It will be dark, like this, with no windows." Campana heard someone whimper at that, but the voice went on. "Each of you will be permitted an oil lamp. If you haven't seen one of these before, it will be explained to you. Each room will have a bed and a chamber pot."

More murmurs of protest, but these were ignored.

"Be quiet! Many a Dim lives in much worse conditions. You will be brought your meals. You may expect these conditions to last for at most a few Shutterings while we negotiate with your clans. Then you will be returned to the care of your families. Before that occurs I shall be speaking to each of you individually to explain our campaign for the freedom of women. In the end you will be free to make your own choices. If you wish, you may go ahead with whatever pledge your clan has made for you, but I would strongly counsel you against it. If you hold firm and refuse to be pledged, your family cannot force you into marriage."

The speaker paused and her voice seemed to change marginally.

"I know that some of you feel aggrieved by what The Daughters have done today. I am sorry for the discomfort you are enduring, but it has been necessary. I hope that after reflection—and you will have plenty of time for that—you will come to understand that our mission is a true and well-meaning one. You may even decide to join us in it."

Never! Campana stiffened with impotent fury. She would never join The Daughters. If it took the rest of her life, she would find out who they were and make them pay for what they were doing.

22
Candens

The morning after the aborted Pledging Ceremony, Candens left the city, still feeling aggrieved by his father's refusal to let him help in the search. Eventually he had to put that aside and not dwell on it.

The wind was blowing strongly from sunward as Candens approached his clan's estate, so everything was surrounded by a dense, wet fog which restricted visibility to a dozen arm-lengths and Candens almost missed Lambent, who was riding in the other direction, towards the city.

Lambent, indeed, did not notice his brother until Candens had hailed him twice. At the repeated call, he drew up, blinking away the raindrops running down from his dark hair. He was at first confused, barely able to recognise Candens in the fog, but then he sat up a little straighter on his horse and wiped away the moisture from his face.

"Candens! Well met, brother, well met."

Lambent's lips moved, but his voice was insincere, a mere formula.

"Lambent." There was a long pause before Candens continued. "How is Hermia?"

"Hermia? Oh, her headache. Gone, I think. She's fine, just fine." Lambent's tone was still a little distant, as though he had had to think for a moment who Hermia was. "What's going on in the city?"

"No word about Campana. Mother's very upset, but she's holding up. The Militia are searching everywhere. It doesn't seem as though The Daughters can have left the city with the pledgees. Father wants you to help in the search."

Though what good Ardens expected from Lambent, Candens had no idea, but he didn't say this aloud.

"We'll find her, though it's a nuisance," Lambent assured him. "I hope I don't have to be away from home for too long. I'm supposed to be racing against Lux of the Icebreakers in three Shutterings. I've put a big bet on it."

"Not too big a bet, I hope." Candens tried to keep the anger out of his voice. "He was in the Militia with me and he's a damn good rider."

"Is he? Oh well, we'll have to call the race off if this business isn't over by then."

"Yes. Well, you had better get on to the city."

"The city? Oh, yes. Well, I'll see you later, then."

"Send me a signal if you hear anything. Use the family cipher. Best to keep what we know quiet. We don't want the Daughters of the Dark intercepting our signals."

Lambent was startled. "Do you think they could do that?"

Candens shrugged. "I don't know. But it pays to be cautious."

"Coding messages up is a damn nuisance. Takes me most of a peal. Wish I could get a servant to do it for me. Still, all right. I'll see you later."

Lambent started his horse forward and rode off into the fog. Watching him vanish into the mist, Candens felt only despair. When Ardens died, as he eventually must, Lambent would be clan head. Who could know what the fortunes of their family would be then? Candens didn't like their chances.

~

Back at the manor, Candens tried to put aside his worries about Campana and address his work. His cousin Valend had been acting as Pendulum Master in Candens' absence. Shortly after his return, Valend approached him with a report.

David R. Grigg

"We've got a problem in the chamber that we'll have to fix soon. It's the suspension of the Sun-left pendulum. Let's climb up and I'll show you."

Together, they climbed the winding stair until they reached the wooden gallery which ran around at the very highest level just below the Bell Chamber. Valend opened the shutters a little to give them more light to see.

"There." Valend pointed to the top of the swinging pendulum. "The rope beneath the suspension ring is becoming badly frayed. It will last for another couple of decants, perhaps, but we'll need to replace it before it breaks."

It would be a tricky business and Candens wished, not for the first time, that Great-Uncle Tinnio was still alive to give advice. Tinnio must have done this several times during his lifetime. First a new rope had to be obtained, cut a little longer than the required length and then hung for a full waking with a weighted bob to allow it to stretch. Only then could it be swapped for the old rope and the final adjustments made to the length to ensure it perfectly matched the rope being replaced. The work had to be begun and completed while the other pendulum still had enough energy to swing. It also needed to be done without interfering in any way with the movement of the active pendulum.

"Well spotted." Candens nodded at his cousin. "Do you think it can wait until my father returns?"

Valend shrugged. "How long will he be away?"

It was a reasonable question and one Candens couldn't answer. Ardens might stay in the city with his mother until Campana was located and released. Who could say how long that might take?

"Never mind," he decided. "We'll just have to go ahead and do it. When is the next transfer due?"

Candens was asking when the currently active pendulum would have slowed enough for the other to be started in its place.

"Not this waking, but the one after, probably about the third peal."

"All right. We'll do it then, if we're ready. We'll have to prepare well. We'll need Nitens and perhaps Uncle Jervens as well. Do we have a replacement rope?"

"Not yet. I put in an order to the Ropemakers as soon as I saw the problem. It should be here in time. We'll measure it out and cut it here."

"Good. Well done."

"If the rope is delayed, we can wait for the next transfer, a couple of Shutterings on. We could do an out-of-sequence transfer at any time, of course, but it's best to keep to the sequence if we can."

"Yes. Tinnio would have done it that way, I am sure."

Valend made an excellent Pendulum Master and Candens couldn't help feeling exasperated that his father had forced him to return to the manor to take up the role. Still, with this kind of problem to face, it was probably best for him to be on hand.

As Candens returned to ground level, he was full of trepidation. It was time to face his next major challenge: he had to have dinner with Hermia.

Hermia greeted him at the entrance to the dining hall. She reached out to him and rested her hand lightly on his upper arm—a compassionate rather than an affectionate gesture, he was sure—as she gazed into his eyes.

"Candens! Any word about poor dear Campana?"

Candens felt Hermia's touch through the cloth of his jerkin. So close. He could feel her breath on his face. He fought to control his surging emotions.

"No, I've heard nothing. I wish that my father had let me help in the search."

Hermia smiled. "Of course, it must be very frustrating for you. But I'm sure she'll be found soon and safe. After all, who could wish her any harm?"

Candens could only shake his head and step back away from her. Hermia dropped her hands to her side, still smiling.

"Let's put all that unpleasantness aside for the time being and have dinner. Just you and me; won't that be nice? We so rarely have the chance to talk."

"Just you, me and the servants," Candens agreed, controlling himself stiffly.

Candens was torn between feeling that it was, indeed, very nice and an agony that he would betray his desire for her.

Hermia laughed.

"Yes, the servants. Although they don't really count, do they?"

Candens only shrugged in response, adding to his despair and anger at himself. What a dull clod Hermia must think he was.

Once they were seated, Hermia took the cup of wine the servant girl Leah had poured for her and raised it in a toast.

"Here's to success in finding Campana safe and well."

Hermia drank a mouthful.

Candens lifted his own cup and downed a generous gulp. Hermia was more beautiful than ever before, with her sparkling eyes, lips painted a deep red and dark hair falling about her shoulders. Candens fought against the desire to spend the whole meal looking at her, but it was equally impossible to spend the whole time looking down at his food when it was just the two of them. He drank some more wine. Why hadn't he found some excuse to avoid this dinner? Because he couldn't resist her, no matter how hard he tried.

After a while, Hermia continued the conversation. "It was terrible what happened at the Pledging, don't you think?"

"Yes." Candens considered his response. "I can almost forgive the desire to protest. But I just don't understand what motive those women had in kidnapping the girls."

"Oh that's easy," Hermia insisted. "They had to stop the Pledging being simply reconvened at a later date."

"But... surely that's silly unless they mean to keep the girls forever or to do them some harm. They can be pledged once they are free, even if there isn't a formal ceremony."

"True, but who knows what might happen in the meantime? Perhaps one clan head or another might change his mind about a pledge already promised."

It was an intriguing thought, certainly. "Then you think the girls will be released soon?"

"I'm sure that the Daughters of the Dark won't do the girls any harm. That would sway clan sentiment deeply against the group."

"It's pretty deep already. The Clan Council was in an uproar."

"Ah, how lucky you men are to be involved in such deliberations. Or perhaps not so lucky. I'm sure such decisions would be far beyond my poor abilities."

Candens looked at Hermia sharply as her voice struck a note of false modesty. Did she really mean what she was saying? He examined her face for insincerity, but she just smiled and took another bite of food and then changed the topic.

"By the way, have you heard? Old Magister Neptus has announced his retirement as Council President. He hasn't been in good health for some time and the shock of what happened at the Pledging has prompted his decision. He's backing my father Solus to become his permanent replacement."

"Oh? Good."

Candens replied automatically, then reconsidered. Was it good? Candens wasn't at all sure. He was surprised to discover he had already finished his wine. The manservant Jenn brought over the flagon and refilled his cup.

Candens concentrated on the meal in front of him, in order to be done with it as fast as possible and escape. Hermia asked a few more questions and he gave her monosyllabic responses, feeling churlish and rude.

"Come now, Candens," Hermia said at last. "This won't do, my dear. You must make an effort. Tell me about yourself. Tell me about your time in the Militia, if that's easier. I'm sure I would find it fascinating."

Had Hermia really called him *my dear*? Surely it meant nothing. Candens took another gulp of the wine. His hand was trembling as he began an account of his training and some of the things he had seen on patrol. That was safe enough. He told her of chasing the thieves down in the sewers and how he had nearly been speared by a wooden dart. He omitted to say that one of the thieves had mysteriously escaped. Why did he do that? To make himself look better, he admitted to himself.

"How brave you must be!" Hermia's eyes glittered with secret amusement. "Poor Lambent does nothing more exciting than racing horses over level ground. I find that so boring."

Both of the servants were away from the table as she leaned forward and whispered, "Now if only *you* were my husband..."

Candens couldn't believe that he had heard her correctly. He didn't know how to respond.

"I..."

To cover his confusion, Candens reached for his cup of wine, missed his aim and knocked it off the table. It shattered on the floor and a wide red pool of wine spilled over the stone. Jenn hurried forward to clean up the mess.

Hermia sat back and laughed and continued to laugh as Candens made a clumsy excuse and left the table.

23
Candens

Lying on his bed in an agony of confusion and raging emotions, Candens barely slept between Shuttering and Unshuttering. Had he really heard Hermia correctly? Had she suggested...? No, surely not.

He couldn't have Hermia even if she were to fall into his arms. Marriage was for life and adultery, if discovered, was punished harshly by the clans. Of course it happened, but it was kept extremely discreet and never spoken of. Supporting such a clandestine relationship under the roof of a single manor would be almost impossible.

Besides, Candens' desire for Hermia was not mere lust: he wanted to have her as his life's partner; to be able to show her off proudly; to have her at his side when they attended balls and dinners. He wanted her as his *wife*. And that could never be. Unless... With an angry curse he dismissed the ugly thought which followed, but going on like this was also intolerable. Campana had been right. He would have to find a way to leave the manor, his role of Pendulum Master notwithstanding. He would have to leave and never see Hermia ever again.

Weary, he got up from bed when Parr came in to open the shutters and went down to the kitchen to grab a chunk of bread and cheese. He couldn't go in to breakfast, where he would have to sit with Hermia again. He went off to his workroom.

Just after the second peal, glancing out of the un-shuttered window, he saw one of the Signallers' blue-and-gold uniformed couriers ride up and hand over a signal at the gate. A little while later, Parr came in and handed it over to him. It was from Lambent, encoded in the family's private cipher, as Candens had instructed. Candens now began the work of decrypting the message. This was difficult: Lambent had made a mistake with the coding part way through and it took Candens considerable effort to work out what the mistake had been so he could undo it and read to the end of the message:

"No luck finding girls. Letters received from Daughters, demanding ransom and claiming girls are safe. Campana's ransom too high, father says. Trying to negotiate. Returning to manor nextwake if no further news."

To Candens' shame, his first response to this news was to be thankful he wouldn't be left alone with Hermia much longer. He didn't trust himself now. Tonight he would make some excuse and avoid having dinner with her.

Angry at himself, he forced himself away from these thoughts and back to the matter at hand: Campana. At least there had been communication and a ransom demand. From there it was just a matter of arguing over its amount. At least Campana was safe, a valuable hostage.

A knock came on the door of his workroom. Out of habit, Candens threw a sheet over the mechanisms on his bench and then went to the door.

It was Valend. "Bad news."

"About Campana?"

"No, about the replacement rope. We just received it from the Ropemakers. There is a flaw in it and I think we should demand a replacement. Come and have a look; see what you think."

Valend had taken the rope into a storage room off the Pendulum Chamber. Valend's brother Nitens was already there, slowly spooling the long rope from one coil to another, running his hands over it and examining it in the full light of the Sun coming from an un-shuttered window.

Candens examined the rope and saw that in the place Nitens was pointing to, the strands weren't perfectly twisted in and could come apart under strain.

"Yes," he agreed. "Can we wait for another, do you think? Will the existing rope last?"

"Yes, I think so," Valend said. "It's a pity and the Ropemakers may argue about replacing it. They don't really understand about our need for quality, of course, but they can take this rope back and sell it on to the Boatbuilders or someone similar."

"All right. So it may be another couple of Shutterings before we can tackle the job. One good thing is that my father and Lambent will be back nextwake. They'll be here to help when the new rope arrives."

"Good. Well, I think we should do an out-of-sequence transfer as soon as it's had time to stretch. Better that than risk a break."

"Yes. So with luck, we can do it the waking after next."

Valend nodded and Candens headed into the Pendulum Chamber to take his shift, thinking over his immediate future. Perhaps his father would have better news about Campana when he returned. In the meantime, Candens had to try and avoid Hermia.

~

Candens remained in the Pendulum Chamber until well after the normal dinner-time; but in the end it was futile. As he left the bell-tower, Hermia was waiting for him. He tried to brush past her with a brief apology, but she put a hand on his arm. Her grip was gentle, but for him it was like an iron shackle.

"Come," she said. "I told the servants you were working late. I can't possibly eat dinner by myself. I would be so lonely. Let's go now."

He couldn't refuse her. Together they went back to the dining hall and the servants brought in a meal. This time he pushed the cup of wine away from easy reach. He would *not* allow himself to become drunk.

The dinner began normally enough. Hermia made polite conversation about her activities during the waking. Again, she was dressed in what Candens thought a provocative manner; but then Hermia always dressed well. When the main course was done, Hermia beckoned the servant girl over.

"I'm a little cold, Leah. Could you bring my shawl from my room, the matching green one? I'm not sure where I left it. The green one, mind."

The girl nodded and headed off. That left only Jenn in the hall, leaning against the wall while he waited for a command.

"I've been meaning to say to you..." Candens stopped.

"Go on. What?"

"It's about Lambent. I wish... I wish you'd stop him drinking so much."

Candens was conscious of the hypocrisy when he had drunk too much himself the previous evening.

"Do you think I *could* stop him?" Hermia said. "He lives fast, my husband. He burns up a lot of energy. He says a little wine helps him build the fire back up again."

Candens frowned. "But he needs to learn to be more responsible, now that he's married. And because he's the heir..."

Candens' voice trailed off, worried he'd said too much but Hermia waved him away.

"Oh, my dear, you don't need to worry about that. I can be responsible enough for both of us." She called to the manservant Jenn and asked him to bring a bowl of fruit. "Strawberries, if you can find any. And a peach; I must have a peach, all right?"

Jenn nodded and left the hall, then Hermia turned back to Candens.

"Why are we talking of Lambent?" she said. "Tell me more about yourself, Candens. You're usually so quiet at dinner. I can't resist having you to myself and finding out more about you."

"There's nothing much more to say."

Candens blushed a little and looked down at his plate, but Hermia was not so easily swayed.

"Come now, that won't do. What do you aspire to? What are your hopes and ambitions?"

Candens shrugged, uncomfortable with this line of questioning, suddenly conscious they were alone in the hall.

"It doesn't matter what my ambitions are. I need to continue with my role here to help manage the clan's business."

Hermia's smile widened. "But there must be more than that. No man thinks only of his work. What truly lies in your heart? You must tell me."

Candens shook his head, forcing himself to remain mute.

"Come now." Hermia persisted, eyes alight with curiosity and amusement. "I can tell that you are hiding something, Candens."

Again he forced himself to remain silent, but his heart was battering against his chest as though it wanted to burst out. Hermia half-closed her eyes and teased him softly.

"Tell me. What is it you most desire, Candens?"

Candens could not resist any more. He looked at her smiling, lovely face and all the frustrations of his life boiled up in an instant.

"You. You're what I want."

It was as though a bolt of lightning had run through him. He gaped, his voice high with stress, "Oh God! I didn't mean that. I had better go."

Candens pushed away his plate and stood up.

Hermia, though, still sat calmly as though nothing had happened. If anything, her smile widened. "You didn't *mean* it, or you didn't mean to *say* it? Sit down, sit down, you don't need to panic. I've long suspected your feelings. No woman could be so unaware of a man's regard. I am flattered, Candens."

Candens stood frozen in place, feeling as though his body was on fire. He wished vainly that he would combust on the spot and turn into a pile of smoking ashes. Hermia sipped more wine and leaned back in her chair, toying with the beaker, running her finger around its rim.

"Lambent, however..." Hermia looked across at Lambent's younger brother. "Lambent doesn't suspect a thing. He likes seeing other men admire me when we're in company. But if I respond to flattery with a teasing comment, or sometimes if I so much as glance back in a way that he doesn't approve, he becomes insanely jealous. When he's still sober, of course. After that, all he sees is the wine. He's often incapable once he eventually comes to bed."

Hermia stood up and walked over to Candens, leaning in to speak softly and placing her hand on his arm. "Lambent is a great disappointment to me. But now I know how *you* feel... well that could change matters. You were right, you know. He does drink too much. Who knows, he might have an accident while he's drunk. He might trip and fall down the stairs, perhaps and then where would I be? Where would *we* be, Candens, if something like that were to happen to Lambent? If poor Lambent were to die?"

Again the direct, knowing look and a half-smile.

"You can't mean..." Candens stopped himself. Contradictory thoughts fought for control.

Hermia's expression did not waver. She went on. "I'm sure you could think of many ways such a sad accident might occur. Someone as clever as you, someone trained in the Militia."

"Do you mean...? What are you asking?" But Candens knew, really.

"I'm not *asking* you to do anything, Candens. All I'm

saying is that if you want something, really want to make it yours, you have to stretch out and *take* it. Otherwise it may forever remain out of your reach." Hermia smiled and a bolt of desire ran through him. He fought it back.

"No."

"No to what, Candens?"

"Whatever it is you're suggesting."

Hermia's smile vanished and she dropped his arm.

"Think carefully, Candens." Her face was intent, her lips tight. "Your whole future may depend on this. You've been very indiscreet with me. Do you want me to tell Lambent what you've said to me this evening? It would be very bad for you. Instead, I'm holding out the prospect of what you most desire, so you said. Are you going to just cast it away?"

He was silent, his pulse aflutter. Could he really refuse her?

"Yes," he whispered. "Yes, I am."

She paused a moment, staring at him as though incredulous.

Then strangely, she smiled, and whispered "Oh, you're going to regret that!" Then, glancing quickly about, she swung her hand and slapped him hard. He staggered back, stunned.

At that moment, he saw that Hermia's maid Leah was standing at the back of the hall, holding the shawl she had been sent for. Jenn was just returning, carrying a bowl of fruit. They both stared at Candens and Hermia, their eyes wide.

Hermia turned on her heel and ran from the room.

The Shuttering peal began.

24

Campana

Campana lay in the semi-dark in a locked room. On a small chest of drawers next to the bed a little oil-lamp flickered. It was just a shallow pottery dish containing oil, with a raised column in the centre which held a burning wick. It gave off very little light, so that the room was barely brighter than Campana's usual bedroom with the shutters closed. A small jug held more of the oil, so that she could top it up when the lamp had exhausted its supply.

She couldn't hear any bells. For the first time in her life, Campana had no idea what time it was; whether it was time to sleep or time to wake. Only her own body's rhythms meant anything. Right now, she felt hungry, so perhaps it was a meal-time?

She had eaten once already, a simple meal served on a wooden platter brought by one of the Daughters, her face concealed behind a black mask. Despite Campana's questions, the woman had said nothing but even in the dim light, Campana could tell that this was a thinner and probably younger person than the stern woman who was the leader. Campana would be very happy not to encounter *her* again.

Trying to ignore her growing hunger, Campana lay back on the bed. She wondered about the others who had been kidnapped. It seemed very likely that her friend Maryam, who had also been among the pledgees, was locked away too, probably in another room nearby. She had tried calling out to the others from her cell, but had received no answer. The door must be too thick to pass sound.

The room itself was not awful. It didn't appear to have been designed to be a prison cell, even though it seemed to be buried somewhere in the dark. A soft carpet covered the floor and the bed linen was freshly laundered. The table in the centre of the room was well-made and smooth to the touch. But the door was locked on the outside, which made it a cell nonetheless.

A rattle sounded at the door and it opened to reveal a dark-clad figure, holding a tray of food and a large pottery jug. The woman signed Campana to remain still on the bed, as she had on previous occasions. Campana nodded reluctantly and the woman entered with the food.

"How long am I going to be kept here?" Campana knew it was futile, but was unable to stop herself.

The woman in black shook her masked head but Campana persisted.

"Why won't you speak to me?" Well that was obvious, really. The Daughters didn't want to be identified. Their leader, the older woman, had been furious when two of them had spoken.

Logic didn't prevent Campana's frustration from surging up into an uncontrollable rage. Just as the woman placed the tray onto the table, Campana reached over and deliberately knocked the oil lamp off the chest of drawers and dashed it to the floor. Oil spilled wide over the carpet and the burning wick set it alight. Blue flame ran across the pool of oil, which now ran towards the dark-clad woman's feet. She stepped back in alarm, gasping in shock and with both hands lifted her long dress above the flame.

Campana took instant advantage and launched herself from the bed, grabbing hold of the woman's wooden mask and pulling. It was tied tightly by a cord, however, and did not come free. The woman grasped Campana's wrists and began to fight back, kicking and striking Campana with her knees. Blue flames flickered around their legs. Struggling, the two twisted around each other, gasping and cursing. Finally, Campana realised that the woman had bumped up against the frame of the bed. She pushed as hard as she could and the woman fell back onto the bedding, releasing one of Campana's wrists. Campana grabbed again at the mask and this time pushed it upwards, away from the woman's face.

"No, no!" the woman cried. But it was too late. The mask was free and the flickering flame from the floor lit up her face.

Campana released her with an exclamation, turned and threw a blanket over the burning oil to smother it, casting them both into utter darkness.

Campana had already seen enough, however. "Adura! I know it's you."

A long, long silence ensued. Then Adura's voice came in a whisper.

"You mustn't tell. You mustn't!" She sounded terrified.

Campana considered finding the open door in the dark and trying to get out before Adura could stop her. But there were doubtless other locked doors between her and freedom and it might well be futile. No, there had to be a better way.

"I won't tell," she told Adura. "Not if you'll help me."

"I can't, I can't," Adura whispered. "Not now. Not after what I've done. If my father... if my clan find out... I didn't realise it would be like this. I thought it would help break up the old system and free us women. But now, I don't know. After the way she treated *you*... I'm so sorry."

"Who is your leader? Tell me that, at least."

"I don't know, I really don't, Campana. I've never seen her face, she keeps it behind her mask and it distorts her voice. She calls herself Raven. That's all I know. We all have to wear masks when we meet."

"Raven?"

"It's not her real name, I'm sure. Now, let me up, please. I have to feed the other girls and Raven might come back any moment."

Adura's voice was still only a whisper, but it was intense in its pleading.

"Only if you'll promise to talk to me again and think of a way to get me out. Oh and bring me another lamp."

"I promise. Please, Campana, please let me up."

Reluctantly, Campana let Adura get to her feet. The burned area of carpet smelled foul.

"Where is this place, then?" Campana asked. "What kind of place is built underground, with no shutters?"

Adura gave a hollow laugh.

"It was an old shadow house. A place... oh, you're too young to understand. Men have places like this to drink, to gamble and perhaps to... to meet with women who aren't their wives."

"I'm not a child any more. To have sex, you mean."

"Yes."

"But where is it?"

"Under one of the city buildings. Under a warehouse, I think. There's a secret passage leading here from under the Council Lodge. I imagine the Councillors must have used it to get to the shadow house, but it's been forgotten. Raven somehow found out about it, about how to get to the passage. Now please let me go. I'll bring you another lamp after I give the other girls their meals."

"One more thing..."

"No, no!"

Campana heard Adura close the door and turn the key in the lock. All she could do now was wait in the darkness and figure out how she could force Adura to help her escape.

25

Candens

"It's outrageous," Ardens said. "We can't possibly agree."

Candens and Lambent were in their father's study, seated at a small round table, talking over the ransom demand they had received lastwake. Candens was doing his best to react normally and had forced himself to meet Lambent's gaze without showing any guilt. Lambent, on the other hand, was his usual casual self. Clearly Hermia hadn't yet carried out her implied threat to tell her husband of what Candens had said during their recent dinner alone. Candens firmly pushed these thoughts aside.

"What are they asking for?"

"Five hundred steels."

It was a small fortune; almost a quarter of their income for a millend. The Bellringers' income was unusual among the clans; since they offered their time-keeping services to society as a whole, each of the other clans paid them a fee every centend at a rate set by the Clan Council. Other than that, their only income was the profit they made from selling their agricultural produce.

"We *could* pay it, though," Lambent suggested. "I guess it would hurt for a bit, but it's only money."

Ardens' face grew red with anger.

"Only money? I begrudge giving those damned women a single ring, a single bronze ring. If we give in now, all of this will just happen again. We can't agree to this kind of extortion. The Militia will find them eventually and Campana will be freed."

David R. Grigg

Just then came a hard rap on the door of the study. Ardens looked up, surprised. Before he could respond, the door opened by itself. Candens' mother Eccua stood outside. She looked paler than ever and there were dark smudges beneath her eyes.

"What is happening?" she demanded.

"My dear, we are discussing clan matters." Ardens spoke with an acid edge to his voice. "I will speak to you later about those matters which concern you. Now…"

"No." Eccua took a step into the room. "If you are discussing Campana, *my daughter*, then I want to know what you are deciding. I won't be shut out from this. I want to have a say."

Ardens flushed and stood up. "As I told the boys, you aren't well, Eccua. The stress has been too much for you. Go back to your room. Lie down."

"No." Eccua held her ground firmly. "I won't be excluded. Not any more. Not about this. It's not a clan matter, it's a *family* matter. Tell me what you are deciding about Campana."

"Father…" Candens intervened. "Mother is right. We need to hear her voice." And, in the face of his father's obvious displeasure, he stood up and went to fetch a chair for his mother, drawing it close to the table. "Please sit with us, Mother. Sit down."

Obviously starting to feel the reaction from her uncharacteristic outburst, Eccua fumbled with a trembling hand for the arm of the chair, pulled it closer to the table and sat.

Ardens took a deep breath and resumed his seat. Candens leaned over to his mother and softly gave her a quick summary of the ransom demand. He omitted his father's refusal to pay anything, merely told her that the sum demanded would be a great strain on the clan. She nodded, but said nothing.

Turning back to his father, Candens asked, "What about the other kidnapped girls? What do the other clans say about their ransoms?"

That just made Ardens even angrier.

"I don't know what ransoms are being asked for the other girls. It wouldn't be honourable to ask. Perhaps the same as us, but I doubt it. That Mirrormaster girl has been freed already, what's her name, Campana's friend?"

"Maryam," Eccua said in a soft voice.

"Yes and the Bookbinder's daughter. The Bookbinders aren't rich, but she's free."

"What do those girls say about where they were kept?" Candens asked.

"Nothing useful. From what I hear, it was dark, underground perhaps, and they were made to walk there. They went down a slope and then walked. A long walk, they said."

Lambent slouched lazily back in his chair. "It could be anywhere. Lots of the city buildings have wine cellars or cool-rooms underground."

"The Militia will be searching those, surely," Candens said. "It can't be anywhere as obvious as that. I'm more interested in how they got there. Some kind of underground tunnel? There are the sewers, of course... I've been in them. But surely the released girls would have mentioned the stench; they can't have missed that."

"I suppose not."

Ardens stared through the opened shutters across the fields and orchards of the estate, his fingers drumming on the table.

"Ardens, we can't rely on the Militia finding Campana." Eccua spoke up. "We need to be sure..." She stopped for an instant. "We need to be *certain* that she is safe. I know the cost is awful, but she's our child. *My* child. We can't leave her unransomed."

Tears started to well in her eyes. Ardens did not reply, as

a frown etched deep twin vertical lines through the centre of his forehead.

"Perhaps you could offer half the amount they are asking for and see if they'll agree?" Candens suggested. "That will hurt, of course, but we could manage."

Ardens hesitated, then made a brief, sharp nod.

"It burns me to offer even that, but I suppose we must. Your mother is right; we can't let Campana come to any harm. The pledge I'd arranged for her was a good one."

Candens winced at that. Did his father have no other concern for his only daughter?

"And what if they refuse that, Ardens? What then?" Eccua asked. "Will you agree to the full amount?"

"Let's wait and see," Ardens counselled. "No point in speculating. And now, my dear, I really do think you had better go back to bed."

Eccua sighed, but nodded and stood up without argument.

"All right. But promise me that you'll keep me informed? I want to know what is going on."

Ardens gave a curt nod.

"Yes, yes. I'll let you know. Now…"

Eccua put a hand on Candens' shoulder and gave it an affectionate squeeze. Then she turned and left the study.

"Well then." Lambent yawned as the door closed behind his mother. "That's agreed. Can I go now?"

"No," Candens said. "I need to talk to you both about the Pendulum Chamber."

He quickly outlined the need to replace the fraying pendulum rope.

Ardens nodded his approval. "So, you'll do it nextwake?"

"If the new rope is back and passes our checks this time," Candens nodded. "We'll need you both to help; it's a tricky process to get right."

"Damn. Do you really need me?" Lambent grimaced. "I was going to meet up with Blaze. He's on another tour of the signal towers."

"It's past time you did the same for our repeater towers," said Ardens. "I've been asking you to do it for long enough. Your meeting with Blaze will have to be put off. This is much more important."

It was obvious that Lambent was deeply unhappy, but he did not protest further.

Their father dismissed them and they left his study. But once they were on the gallery outside, Lambent said, "Come on, Candens, you can manage without me nextwake. What with you, father, Valend and Nitens, you can cope. I'll just be in the way. You tell Father I'm sick and I'll sneak off to see Blaze. How about it?"

Angry, Candens stopped walking and reached out to halt Lambent too.

"No, I'm not going to do that. We do need your help. Now tell me why you really want to meet with Blaze? Are you buying more *marana*?"

Lambent pulled roughly away from his brother's grip and stared at Candens in angry surprise. "I don't see what business it is of yours. And no, it's not *marana*. I've given up that stuff."

Candens caught the ambiguity in this reply at once. "If it's not *marana* you're buying from Blaze, then what is it? You're not desperate to meet him just for the pleasure of his conversation. I don't believe that for a moment."

Lambent shoved him away, hard. Candens was pushed against the railing of the gallery. For an instant, Candens thought he would topple over and down into the dining hall two floors below, but he grabbed the rail and regained his balance.

"I told you." Lambent kept his voice low with obvious effort, in case their father should hear. "It's none of your business what I do, where I go, or what I choose to buy."

"You're a fool." Candens was now furious. "Your wife is a beautiful woman, you have important responsibilities and eventually you'll run this place. Why do you have any need to find pleasure elsewhere? No, damn that! You have no *right* to seek such pleasure. *You are the heir!*"

"And that's what it's really about, isn't it?" Lambent wore a cold expression on his face. "You jealous prick. Well, to the dark with you."

As he stalked off Candens fought to regain his composure. Jealous? Yes, he was jealous, but he could bear it if Lambent was a better man. But in his heart he knew that wasn't true. He would never be able to bear it.

26

Campana

In the stories she had read as a child, it had seemed exciting; thrilling even, when the heroine was kidnapped by mist-riders or other miscreants. The handsome heir to one of the big clans always sneaked through the umbra to find the camp of the villains and made a thrilling rescue of the girl, to whom it turned out he had been secretly pledged all along.

She was finding the reality of being kidnapped very different. It was both uncomfortable and very, very boring. She had nothing to do except lie on her bed and stare up at the ceiling, watching the dim patterns of flickering light from the oil lamp. And there was no rescue in prospect, let alone by a handsome young heir.

According to the only measure of time that she had, her stomach, it was nearly time for one of the Daughters to bring her the mid-waking meal. Campana was careful never to speak to the person serving her until she could be sure that it was Adura. She had grown to recognise Adura's way of walking, the tilt of her head behind the wooden mask and the way she held the tray. These were as identifiable as a face, when that was all you had to go on.

Adura didn't come very often; perhaps once every three or four meals. Campana could only suppose that there was a roster and the Daughters were returning to their own clans in the intervening time, making some excuse to their families when they needed to be absent. Surely that couldn't be kept up for too long? Their families would surely begin to wonder about it.

It had been several Shutterings now, Campana thought. She had been keeping a rough tally each time she had been fed, by means of tying knots in a ribbon she had pulled from her Pledging dress. She would never wear that dress again, she thought sadly. It was filthy and scuffed now, the hem of the skirt blackened in places by the flames from the burning oil she'd spilled on the floor.

How long was all of this going to take? What was her family doing? Would her clan pay the ransom being demanded for her? Surely her kidnappers couldn't keep her here forever?

These thoughts were interrupted by a rattle at the door as it was unlocked. It opened to reveal two figures. The first one was rather stouter than the one behind and wore a red mask. It had to be Raven. Was the other one Adura? Yes; Campana thought it was.

"Now." Campana recognized the familiar, half-muffled voice of the woman leading the kidnapping. "Perhaps you have had time to consider our aims. We took you away from the Pledging for your own good."

Why did anyone think they had the right to decide for Campana what was for her own good? Campana was angered by this, but she stayed silent. With Raven, the less she spoke the better.

"I can tell you who you were to be pledged to, you know," Raven added.

"How do you know?" Campana was curious despite herself. A moment later, it came to her. Clearly they had taken the paper which the Council President had been about to read from... stolen it, more like.

"We have our ways of finding these things out. Don't you want to know?" Raven adopted an air of superiority that made Campana want to laugh.

"No, not really," she said, quite honestly. It really didn't seem to matter now. Would the pledging go ahead? Not if she were never released, that was certain.

Raven was clearly annoyed by this response, which was the way Campana wanted it.

"I shall tell you anyway," Raven decided. "You were to be pledged to Radians of the Healers. Do you know him? He's an awkward, gawky lad; not well-favoured. Has pimples."

Campana considered. She might have met him once, as a boy. In any case, she couldn't bring his face to mind.

"So?"

"So?" Raven's tone was incredulous. "You are content to be married off to this half-stranger, bound forever to another clan but prevented from learning any of their knowledge?"

Raven was straining for effect, Campana thought. For the first time, she wondered if the woman was being sincere in her outrage. If not—if she was putting it on—then what did that mean?

"Perhaps not content," Campana acknowledged. "But I would have accepted it, yes. One has to endure many things one might not desire. Being locked away in a dark cell for many Shutterings and then being lectured to, for example."

Raven began a furious response, but then stopped herself. It took her a moment before she could go on.

"Very well. I see that I can do nothing with you. Your clan is being difficult about your ransom. Perhaps they don't consider you to be of any great value."

"Perhaps not," Campana agreed. "In which case there doesn't seem to be much point in your holding on to me, does there?"

"You have a stubborn nature, Campana. But so do I. You will be kept here until your clan agrees to your ransom, however long that might take."

With that, Raven turned and marched out of the door. Somewhere outside, another door opened and closed. The other figure remained standing in the room. Campana couldn't speak Adura's name, just in case it wasn't her, even though she was reasonably confident of her identity.

"I'm hungry," she said instead.

The masked figure nodded and left the room, closing and locking the door of Campana's cell behind her. After a short while, she returned with the familiar tray. She put it down on the table.

"Will you speak to me?" Campana asked, still being cautious.

The figure reached up and lifted the mask from her face.

"Yes," Adura whispered. "It's time that we talked. But keep your voice down. I don't think Raven will return, but the other two prisoners mustn't know that I've been speaking to you."

"Only two?"

"Yes, the others have been ransomed. Campana, your ransom has been set very high, much higher than for the others. I don't know why."

"Nor do I. Excuse me a moment, I really am very hungry."

Campana reached over to the tray, picked up a piece of bread and bit into it. Adura waited a moment before speaking again.

"This is all so wrong. It's not how I imagined it would be at all. My beliefs haven't changed. Pledging young people to each other without their consent is wrong. And I still hate how we women are kept in ignorance. But what Raven has made us do here... this isn't the right way to bring about change. I don't understand her thinking."

Campana leant forward. "So, then..."

"So I *will* help you to escape, Campana. But... oh, I'm so afraid. Raven has threatened that if any of us don't do exactly what she wants us to do, then our families—and the Militia—will receive messages exposing us as members of the Daughters of the Dark. I can't risk that, Campana; I just can't."

"But nevertheless you'll still help me?"

Adura nodded and Campana felt a wave of relief which made her dizzy for a moment. "Oh, thank you, thank you!"

"But if you get away..."

"Yes, I understand. I'll keep your name out of it. What do you tell your family when you leave to come here?"

"I have a friend who tutors me in music at her manor. She's agreed not to let anyone know that I haven't been coming to lessons recently. She believes that I have a lover who I meet in the city."

Campana laughed for the first time since she had been captured. "That's wonderful. Now, how are we going to do this? Where are we in the city? Do you come and go down that passage from the Council Lodge?"

"No, there's a much quicker way. Up a flight of spiral stairs outside there's an old door which leads to a narrow lane which runs behind the Signal Tower. I suppose it was the old entrance to the shadow house, but now it just looks like the entrance to some cellar. The whole lane is narrow and in deep shade. We put on these black dresses and masks once we're inside."

"Why is there a passage to here from the Council Lodge as well?"

Adura laughed. "So that Council members using the shadow house weren't seen by anyone else coming and going, of course, particularly not by their wives. I'm not sure how the passage was ever forgotten, men being what they are. But perhaps the shadow house was closed a long time ago and so the way here wasn't needed any more. Perhaps some virtuous Council President in the past had the shadow house shut and the passage sealed. I don't know."

"And you have a key to the door upstairs?"

"That's the problem. No. Raven always meets me. She is here, waiting for my knock. I presume it's the same for the other Daughters. She lets us in and then leaves and returns several peals later and takes over until the next Daughter turns up. I imagine she must go away to sleep somewhere nearby, even though it's in the middle of the waking. That way there's always at least one person here with you. She lets me in, but then locks the door behind us as she leaves."

"You mean..."

"Yes. Right now, I'm as much a prisoner as you are."

Campana groaned in frustration, but Adura went on.

"Don't worry. I have a plan..."

27

Candens

"Carefully, carefully, now!" Ardens' voice came up to them from the floor of the chamber, many arm-lengths below.

Valend and Candens were on the top-most gallery again, nearest the suspension point of the two pendulums. They had cautiously extended a hook on a long pole to catch the top section of the frayed rope so they could pull it closer to them. Every move was taken slowly. It was vital not to interfere in the slightest with the motion of the active pendulum.

The next task was for Candens to stand on the railing, lean over to where the rope was connected to the suspension ring and untie the complex knot. To make this procedure less hazardous, he was wearing a leather harness around his chest with a rope connected at its back. Valend had wound its loose end around the gallery railing and was now bracing with all his strength so that Candens could lean out safely over the frightening drop.

Even as he worked on this delicate task, Candens couldn't help thinking about how they could improve this arrangement. Surely they could fix a hook above, between the nearest pendulum suspension point and the gallery, from which a harness or even a small platform could be suspended? They could do the same on the other side of the gallery for the further pendulum. Once this waking's work was done, he would take steps towards achieving that, ready for the next time they needed to replace a rope or examine the suspension points.

Lambent hadn't turned up to help. Ardens' scowl when this became clear had been ferocious and he had sent off Parr to find him. Candens suspected that the servant wouldn't find him; that Lambent had ridden off to see Blaze regardless of his father's orders.

Dinner last evening had been stiff and awkward. Ardens was preoccupied with denunciations of the Daughters of the Dark and their extortionate ransom demand for Campana. His mother, only partially recovered, had sat pale and still, saying little. Hermia... well, she had been unusually quiet, too, with little of her usual vivacity, her eyes mostly downcast. Candens wondered what she was thinking and worried that Lambent would see the obvious change in her demeanour. But Lambent, still furious with Candens' attempted interference in his life, had largely ignored his wife, instead glaring across the table at his brother as he drank heavily, even more than usual.

Candens forced his attention back to the task at hand. He couldn't allow himself to be distracted at this perilous moment. It was slow going. Even though the pendulum bob had been removed so the rope was now slack, the knot had been tightened by the rope's lengthy suspension over many millends and the free end was almost impossible to move. He would probably have to cut the rope. He felt at his waist for the knife there in its sheath, but left it there for now. Great-Uncle Tinnio would have perservered and undone the knot.

Then he saw movement below. It was Lambent, running up the spiral staircase. Candens was pleased that his brother had finally turned up, though he could have done without the distraction. He stopped what he was doing and waited.

Once he heard Lambent's gasping breath as he arrived at the gallery level, Candens gratefully resumed his work, assuming that Lambent would keep quiet once he realised what was going on and how delicate it was.

The next moment, though, he found that he was being yanked roughly backwards by the harness. He exclaimed in surprise and was forced to let go of the pendulum rope. He tumbled backwards to sprawl on the floor of the gallery and Lambent kicked him, hard, in the ribs.

"You bastard!" Lambent said. "I called you a jealous prick lastwake and I was right, wasn't I? But it's not just my being the heir that makes you jealous, is it? You want Hermia too!"

Lambent kicked again. Candens grabbed at Lambent's foot in defence, throwing him back, out of balance. Valend grabbed Lambent's arm and Candens slowly got back to his feet.

"I don't know what you're talking about." His voice was flat.

But of course Candens did know. Hermia must have carried out her threat and told Lambent what he had said to her.

Lambent clenched his fists. "She said you wanted her, that you've been leering at her when I'm not there; sending servants out of the room. Trying to get her to help you to… to…"

Lambent couldn't complete the sentence, but swung at Candens' jaw. Candens, with his long militia training, moved his head quickly to one side and grabbed Lambent's arm. Lambent pulled away, struggling and pummelling Candens with his free hand. Valend pulled at him, finally breaking him away. Lambent's face was flushed and his eyes were wild. Candens realised that his brother was drunk. Valend held Lambent's arms tightly to keep him from attacking Candens again.

Ardens' furious, alarmed voice came up from down below.

"What's going on up there? What are you doing?"

Facing Lambent, Candens spoke as calmly as he could, though his body was shaking with emotion and reaction.

"That's not how it was."

He felt sure that at most, Hermia would have warned Lambent about Candens' declaration of love for her. Lambent was just putting his own lurid interpretation on what she had said. The alcohol he had obviously been drinking wasn't helping his brother be rational. Lambent took a long, deep breath and appeared to calm down. When he spoke after a moment his voice was like ice.

"Valend, let me go. It's all right; I won't hurt him. Let me go."

Valend reluctantly released Lambent and took a step back. He was obviously uncertain what to do, now that he had some idea what this was about. A smile twisted across Lambent's face. It should have been a warning to Candens, but he missed its meaning.

"I won't hurt him," Lambent repeated. "I'll damn well *kill* him!"

Before Valend could react, Lambent launched himself at Candens and grabbed his throat, pushing him back against the gallery railing, which gave an ominous creak.

"You'd like to kill me, wouldn't you, Candens? That's what Hermia says. Take my place? Take my wife. Well, to the dark with you. I'll see *you* dead first!"

Lambent's fingers tightened on Candens' throat but Candens hadn't been in the Militia for nothing. He easily broke Lambent's grip and tried to knee him in the groin, but his brother turned and deflected the blow. Candens held onto Lambent's wrists and forced his hands away. Lambent twisted his body this way and that, spitting and cursing. Candens was the stronger, but his side was afire with pain and he wasn't sure he could overpower Lambent and keep him quiet. Besides, he felt a growing despair: it was all over now anyway. He would have to leave. This despair gave way to a swelling rage. It wasn't fair, never had been and never would be.

He let go of Lambent's arm and felt quickly for his knife, intending to threaten his brother with it, force him to stop fighting and listen to reason, but Lambent immediately began to smash his freed fist into Candens' face. Candens had the knife out and was raising it when Lambent twisted and pulled away to avoid it, crashing back hard into the railing. With a scream of shattering wood it gave way. Lambent, on the brink, grabbed Candens with terror gripping his entire face. Out of balance, with Lambent's weight dragging him, Candens couldn't prevent both of them toppling forward and over the edge.

Lambent screamed.

An awful moment of vertigo shot through Candens and then, suddenly and unexpectedly, he came to an abrupt halt, the harness cutting painfully into his chest as Lambent dropped further, his right arm held by Candens' left hand. He went on screaming, dangling there but Candens couldn't continue to hold his weight. It was impossible.

"The rope!" He gasped to Lambent, unable to gesture. "The pendulum rope!"

Lambent looked wildly around and then stretched out towards the rope of the inactive pendulum, only an arm's length away. He grasped it with his free hand and held it tightly. With a gasp of relief, Candens let go of his brother's other hand.

For one precious moment, all was well. Lambent swung back and forth, like some human pendulum himself. Candens could hear their father yelling out in a horrified tone. But now the rope, already frayed and weak, was bearing more than its usual load. It broke and Lambent fell again.

By miraculous good fortune, the rope had snapped just as Lambent had been swinging towards the centre of the chamber. A dozen arm-lengths down, he struck the rope of the active pendulum and was able to grab it with both hands. But by then he was falling too fast to stop and could only use the rope to slow himself a little. He slid down the rope, struck the bob with his feet and crashed backwards onto the floor.

An awful silence followed, spreading out to engulf the entire space. Still dangling above the void, Candens heard his father curse with utter fury. Then a jerk came from Candens' back, followed by another. He was slowly being hauled upwards, back to the gallery. He could hear Valend grunting with the strain. The harness and its rope, looped over a firm section of railing, had saved Candens' life.

What good was that, though? He had killed his brother. His life was at an end, surely.

Valend helped Candens back onto the gallery through the gap left by the broken railing. For some reason Candens couldn't at first comprehend, Valend was counting aloud softly. A moment later, Ardens appeared, face mottled with anger. Having run up the steps, his breath came hard as he strode forward and slapped Candens hard in the face: once, twice; three times. Then he grabbed Candens' right hand and pulled something from it. With his head ringing from his father's blows, Candens realised it was the knife, which he was still unconsciously gripping tightly.

He had killed his brother... but he had done something else, which was probably far worse as far as Ardens was concerned.

He had stopped the pendulum.

Lambent was not dead. But he was badly injured and unconscious. Both of his hands had been ripped raw by the pendulum rope and one leg was broken.

Nitens and Valend carried Lambent away, out of the chamber. Valend was still counting softly and finally Candens was able to understand why. He was demonstrating that he had maintained the count since the last peal, keeping the time. Candens had no doubt that

144

despite his fury, Ardens was doing the same. Ardens always knew the correct count. Candens himself barely knew what peal was due next, such was his anguish.

Now he stood on the floor of the chamber, shaking with emotion, pain running through him. His father paced back and forth, like some remorseless pendulum himself, saying nothing. Both of the real pendulums hung limp, barely moving, a shockingly unnatural state of affairs. Candens had never known a time when there wasn't a pendulum swinging in the tower. It was like a death in the family. Finally his father regained enough control to speak, though his voice was tight with fury.

"You—you—you have dishonoured our clan. I heard some of your argument with Lambent, towards the end, as I came up the stairs. I've spoken to your mother and to Hermia when I went outside just now to tell them of Lambent's injuries. Hermia says that you told her you loved her and that you wanted her to help you kill Lambent, so you would become the heir in his place and could marry her. She of course rejected your advances. Despite her rejection, now we see your attempt to carry out that evil plan regardless."

Candens was appalled. "That's not true. It wasn't like that."

"Shut up. The servants confirm that they saw an altercation between you two evenings ago. Apparently they've all been gossiping about it. Hermia has no reason to lie and I believe her. She says that she struggled with her conscience about whether to tell Lambent what you had said, unable to believe that you were serious. But at last she did. Lambent was right to be outraged, though I wish he had come to me first before confronting you. You chose to fight him and seeing an opportunity, like a coward, pulled out a knife to try to kill him."

"No, I…"

"Be quiet. There is no excuse. Worst of all, worst of all…"

145

Unable to continue, Ardens waved his hand at the barely moving bob of the active pendulum.

"Those of us still able are maintaining the count. We shall have to restart the pendulum soon based on our agreement to the count. That's bad, that's very bad. It's not accurate. Despite our best efforts, we may lose or gain some time and we won't know which. From now on, the whole of Sunfall may be working on inaccurate time. It's never happened in the memory of the clan. And it's all your fault. You... the Pendulum Master, whom I trusted."

"I'll go away," Candens said in a dull voice. "I'll re-join the Militia."

Ardens flushed. "Damn you, you will not. They won't have you once I tell them. No. No, I can't tell them the details, not without spreading our dishonour. But trust me, I'll make sure they don't take you back."

"Then what..."

What will I do? Candens thought in despair.

"I don't give a damn what you do. But you'll leave here. I disown you. I cast you out. I swear that you are now clanless and no son of mine. Get out. Take your horse and equipment and go."

Clanless. Without a family. It made Candens little better than a Dim.

It was, indeed, the end of his life.

28

Candens

The worst thing about the accusation against him was that so much of it was true, or close to being true. He could only blame himself. He *had* told Hermia that he wanted her. He *had* thought, more than once in his life, of what would happen if Lambent died, though he would never have lifted a finger to bring that about. He *had* drawn a knife during the fight at the top of the Pendulum Chamber. All of this filled him with guilt. But at the same time, there was a part of him screaming *It's not fair! It wasn't like that! I never meant...* But it was too late.

Candens packed a few things into his saddle bags, heart heavy with misery. He encountered his mother waiting for him in the entrance hall. She had been crying, he saw, with good cause. He stopped, uncertain of her feelings. Would she, too, hate him for what he had done to Lambent?

"Oh, Candens," she sobbed. "What happened? I can't believe what your father is saying."

"Thank you for that, Mother. It *isn't* true, at least not the way he's shaping it. I didn't try to kill Lambent, I swear. How is he, do you know? Will he live?"

Eccua nodded.

"I think so, though he's badly hurt. We sent for a healer from the nearest chapel. He's with Lambent now. I should get back to them, but I wanted..." She stopped and stifled a sob. "God and His Sun go with you," she managed.

Candens hugged her.

"Goodbye, Mother. I'll try to find a way to let you know what's happening with me. I don't know yet, myself."

Candens turned away, unable to bear her tears, and ran towards the stables. The servants seemed to be avoiding him; there was no one on hand to help him saddle up Raya and mount her. But he had been used to managing by himself in the Militia and soon they were riding away from the manor and out of the gates of the estate. He didn't look back.

Candens had absolutely no idea where he was going. He felt utterly numb in both mind and body, in a daze. He had no idea what he would do. Not that it mattered. Nothing mattered any more.

For a long, long while, a time lost to him, a time without measure, disregarding the occasional sound of the bells, Candens rode at a fast canter with his back to the Sun. That direction fitted his darkening mood only too well. Raya's shadow and his own stretched out before him towards the distant snowy peaks. After a little while, he allowed her to drop back to a walking pace, but he pushed her on toward the darkness.

Finally, he began to rouse himself. As he continued to head away from the Sun and on into the cold hills, the sound of the bell-towers long faded behind him, he was having to skirt larger and larger patches of shadow and the sunlight which remained was feeble and without warmth. Now Raya was becoming restive beneath him, shaking her head against the bit, her nostrils flaring, breath steaming.

Candens hadn't realised quite how far he had ridden in his daze. Frost lay over every piece of ground here and up ahead it started to merge into solid banks of snow. Candens pulled his mare to a halt. This was ridiculous and unfair to the horse. Perhaps he should let her loose, trusting she would find her own way back to the manor and safety. He could keep on walking away from the Sun until he froze to death in the snowfields. Plenty of others had done that. It was said that when your body became cold enough, you started to feel warm again, before you fell into a deep sleep and didn't wake up. There were surely worse ways to die.

Did Candens really want to die, though? When he had started riding, he had certainly been considering it, trying to find a way to end his feeling of shame, which felt like some great gnawing beast he had somehow swallowed and which was now eating him from the inside.

Yet his body still insisted on its own demands. He still breathed in and out, he still needed to empty his bladder and bowels and eventually he would no doubt feel hunger and thirst again.

He couldn't stop thinking about Hermia and how she had encouraged, or at least, not rejected, his passion for her and then how cruelly and abruptly she had turned on him once he denied her requests. What did it all mean?

Being clanless was a curse and the shame would be terrible; but surely Ardens would not tell any of the other clans why Candens had been disinherited and expelled? Such matters were traditionally kept very private. There would be surprise and certainly no warm welcome given to a clanless man. But no one would be told of his professed desire for Hermia, unless Lambent talked while in some drunken or drugged stupor. Even then, Candens felt that Lambent wouldn't want it widely known, even less the fact that he had fought with his brother and lost. No that secret, like so many other secrets in this world, would be kept close within the clan.

Candens turned away from the darkness and sat unmoving on Raya's back, gazing across the land of Sunfall, his eyes shaded against the everlasting Sun above the waters of the bay. From here, the Sun was just a sharp, brilliant point, with drifts of glorious mist swirling around it and streaming away out towards the distant gap in the hills which led out onto the frozen sea beyond.

Where could he go? Perhaps he might still scratch a living doing some menial task or other. One of the clans might take pity on him to that extent, at least. Or there was the Militia. Perhaps his father wouldn't be able to prevent Commander Fervens from allowing Candens to re-join as an officer. He should at least try.

Before that, though... Candens realised, somewhat belatedly, that there was at least one person who ought, by all duty and obligation, to be told of his change in status. That person might even welcome it.

He stroked Raya's neck and spoke a few soothing words. Then he set off back towards the light and the warmth, towards the manor of the Mirrormasters.

"The first thing to do is to get the other two kidnapped girls involved."

"Who are they?" Campana asked, bending closer to hear Adura's whisper. "Is one of them Maryam?"

"No, she was released early, my clan paid her ransom. I think Raven deliberately made it easy because she was afraid that Maryam might work out that I was one of the Daughters. The girls still here are Sola of the Carpenters and Vivia of the Metalworkers. Do you know them?"

"I've met Vivia. I don't know Sola."

"A great-niece of the clan head, I believe."

"Well, you have the key; why can't you just let them out and we'll all talk together in here?"

"They mustn't learn who I am, so I can't let them hear me speak. And when you escape, Raven mustn't suspect that I helped you on purpose, or she'll tell my clan. You have to make it look as though I was just careless."

Campana suppressed a feeling of impatience and frustration. Still, Adura *was* trying to help, even though she was terrified of being exposed.

"All right. What's the plan? How much time do we have?"

"Raven always returns here just after the eighth peal. That gives me just enough time to ride back home before the Shuttering. The seventh peal has just rung. You can hear the bells from the room above."

Campana felt a sudden stab of trepidation. "So soon?"

"Yes. Be calm, now. This will work. Just listen." Adura sounded exasperated as she went on. "I'm going to give you the key now. Then I will go upstairs. You let yourself into the other girls' rooms and tell them what's going on. You'll say you stole the key without my knowing. See, it's on a cord here at my waist. It could easily have come undone..."

"No, I'll say I cut it off. See, I have this sharp piece of broken pottery. It went under the bed when I knocked the lamp off the drawers. I've been keeping it here under the mattress in case it proved useful. Now it has."

As she spoke, Campana lifted the key and easily cut it from the cord with two swift strokes of the shard. She held the key in her hand. It felt like the most valuable thing she had ever held, more precious than any of her mother's jewellery.

"Good." Adura nodded her approval. "You unlock their doors while I'm upstairs waiting for Raven. Then, when you hear me leave—I'll make sure to slam the door hard so you know—you use the lamp to start another fire here in your room. I got the idea from the way you trapped me. Pile up the bedding and spill some oil on it and make sure it makes a lot of smoke. Then all three of you go into one of the other rooms and start screaming. Raven will have to come down to investigate and she'll go first into the room with the fire. When she does that, run upstairs and let yourselves out. She always leaves the key in the lock of the outer door. She can't stop all three of you."

"Easy," Campana bluffed, not meaning it in the slightest.

"No, but it's the best I could come up with."

Campana took a deep breath. "All right, you go upstairs now, then. The longer I have to explain matters to the other girls the better."

It seemed like a reasonable plan. But would it work?

30
Candens

Half dazed, his body still chilled and a block of ice where his heart should be, Candens followed a meandering path back towards the Sun, stopping now and then to let Raya crop some grass and gulp water from the icy streams that ran down from the hills towards the bay. Eventually he returned to within earshot of the bell towers and was startled to hear the fifth peal sound. The *fifth* peal? It had been after the seventh peal when he had set out from home...

Candens was bewildered. It took him a long time to work out that he had been riding all through the shuttered period and well into the next waking. No wonder he felt so tired. He felt a stab of pity for his uncomplaining horse. Had there been times when they had both stopped and he had slept in the saddle, unknowing? It didn't seem likely, but perhaps it was possible. In any case, there was no arguing with the bells. He pushed on and reached the Mirrormaster's estate some time after the seventh peal.

The estate looked as though they were trying to banish every vestige of the dark. Every dip in the fields which would normally have created permanent shade had its own huge mirror reflecting down the rays of the Sun. Candens noted with some interest that some of these mirrors had curved surfaces, apparently to spread the light to as wide an area as possible. He hadn't seen that before. The manor buildings also sported mirrors on their roofs, reflecting light down into the courtyard. They could afford the expense, Candens reflected. No clan held back from flaunting the products of their own knowledge.

Raya was weary now, doing little more than plodding along. He was ashamed at how he had treated her. She had always served him well and taken him wherever he asked, yet he had abused her trust in him. He dismounted and walked the rest of the way, stroking her mane affectionately and whispering to her comfortingly as he led her to the stables. He handed her over to the care of the stable hands, asking them to feed her and rub her down for him, a task he would have been glad to do himself if he had been at his own manor.

He was unsure of his welcome here at the Mirrormasters and wondered whether he wasn't already taking undue advantage of the clan's hospitality by asking for fodder and care for Raya. Would they already know of his disgrace? Would Ardens already have sent out signals to each of the other clans, telling them? Or would he prefer to keep matters quiet, at least for a while? Candens was banking on it being the latter. Somewhere within him he nursed a hope that his father might reconsider after he had had time to cool down, especially if Lambent recovered. If not... who knew what would happen?

He reached the doors to the main manor building and asked the servant there if he could see Adura. The servant bowed and led him in to a small drawing room. It featured, of course, a huge mirror. Candens stood and stared, barely recognising himself. He certainly didn't make an impressive figure: travel-stained, hair awry, unshaven and wearing an expression of weary grief on his face, but there was nothing he could do about any of that.

In the mirror, he saw the door opening behind him and turned, preparing himself to speak to Adura. But she didn't enter. Instead, it was Adura's father Ignis, head of Clan Mirrormaster. Candens had met him before, of course, most recently after the Pledging, but he didn't know him well. He was a portly man, a little overweight, but dignified.

"Candens? You are here to see Adura?" A degree of puzzlement showed on the man's face. Understandable, perhaps, since Candens had never come here to see his pledge since the ceremony.

"Yes," he said. "There's... something that I have to tell her. Well, I need to tell you both, but I thought to speak to her first."

"She's not here at present. She's with a friend at the neighbouring manor, taking lessons on the lute. If it's urgent I could send a servant, or you could ride over there yourself. Or you could wait here. She'll be back before the Shuttering, of course."

Ignis' face betrayed his obvious curiosity.

"Oh." Candens was at a loss. He had been keyed up, ready to pass on the news of his change of status to Adura. But he could hardly now fail to give Magister Ignis an explanation. "Well, I came to tell her—to tell you both—that our pledge, between Clan Bellringer and Clan Mirror-master is now null and cannot be fulfilled."

Ignis stood looking at Candens, silent, his head tilted slightly to one side as he thought.

"I see," he said at last. "You had better explain the reason."

Candens dropped his gaze.

"I am no longer a member of Clan Bellringer. I am in disgrace and have been cast out. I beg you not to ask me why. I can say no more than that."

To his own horror and shame, Candens began to sob. He put his face in his hands and tried to stifle the ugly noises coming out of his throat.

"Sit down." Ignis was surprisingly gentle. "Come on, now. There's a chair behind you."

Candens sat, or more truthfully, collapsed into the chair. Ignis remained standing, his hands clasped behind his back, waiting for Candens to recover himself.

"I'm sorry," Candens managed eventually. "I am ashamed."

He began to wipe his face with his kerchief.

"No need to be ashamed of genuine tears," Ignis assured him. "I can see that you have had a terrible blow and that you are exhausted. How long have you been riding?"

Candens waved a hand vaguely. "Since before the last Shuttering. It doesn't matter. I had better go."

He tried to get back to his feet, but his legs refused to co-operate.

"Stay where you are," Ignis commanded. "I'll get the servants to make you up a bed."

"No, I can't..."

"You can't ride, that's for certain," the older man observed. "And if your horse is as tired as you, then you're not going anywhere. Does anyone else know of your disgrace?"

Candens shook his head. "My family, of course." *And Hermia...* The pain there went too deep and tears almost returned. "I... I don't know if my father is broadcasting the news, but I think not. Not yet, at least."

"Then we'll say no more about it. Rest here and you can speak to Adura nextwake. I won't say anything to her before then." Ignis sighed. "God knows I've been trying hard for a long time to get her to agree to a date for your marriage. I don't understand her objections at all. But now it seems that my efforts were futile in any case."

"I shouldn't stay. My father will..."

"Enough. Stay and be welcome, for one sleep at least. If your father hears of it I shall not be concerned in the least. I never much liked Ardens Bellringer, to be perfectly honest. Your father is a rigid and unyielding man and I don't believe he has treated your mother particularly well. She never seems happy, poor lady."

"No."

"Very well. It's settled."

Ignis left and a little later one of the servants led Candens into a small bedroom, helped him undress and wash and closed the shutters prematurely. Candens had barely put his head on the pillow when sleep swallowed him whole, like a frog gulping down a fly.

31

Campana

She sat on a bed with Vivia and Sola, the two other girls who had been kidnapped, in the room next to her own. The explanation had gone much better than Campana had expected and they were now all listening intently, waiting for the signal for them to begin their escape attempt.

At last, Campana heard three bangs on the floor above. That was the signal Adura had agreed so that Campana would know that the eighth peal was beginning.

"Not long now," Campana said.

Sola gave a whimper. Campana was worried about her. She had been very reluctant to try this attempt, claiming that she was prepared to wait until her ransom was paid. But Campana and Vivia had combined to persuade her that she should, at the very least, not get in the way. Campana felt certain that when the door above had been opened to the street then Sola would seize her freedom gratefully enough.

Every moment now seemed to last forever. Would Raven come at all? What if something had happened, some accident and Raven never came, leaving Adura and the prisoners to die of starvation?

Then these worrying speculations were swept away. They heard the creak of the outer door and Raven's voice speaking to Adura, who replied inaudibly. The conversation seemed to go on for an absurd length of time, but finally they heard the hard slam of the door as Adura left.

"Now!"

Campana quickly went back into her own room. On the floor was a heap of bedding, already soaked with lamp oil.

158

Campana picked up the little flickering lamp from beside the now-stripped bed and threw it onto the pile.

That was when things started to go wrong. Rather than a small but very smoky fire, the oil in the bedding caught immediately. A huge billow of flame erupted in Campana's face. She stumbled back with an exclamation of fright, knocked over the table and then fell back over it, hitting her arm painfully on its edge.

"What was that?"

Raven's voice came from above. Before Campana could get up and run back to the room with the other girls, she heard the older woman hurrying down the spiral stair.

Campana was unable to untangle herself from the table before Raven reached the entrance to her room, which was now lit up with orange light. The fire was growing with every moment and a pillar of flame was now licking over the wooden ceiling.

"You stupid girl!" Raven screamed and thrust Campana back down as she tried to get up. Another voice came.

"No, no, no!"

It was Sola, standing in the corridor behind Raven and looking in at the fire in horror. Raven turned in surprise, taking a step away from Campana as she also spotted Vivia, standing well back behind Sola. As she moved towards them, Raven turned her back fully on Campana.

It was enough. Campana scrambled to her feet, ran to the doorway and leapt out at Raven, throwing her arms around the woman's neck and clinging on with her legs. Raven staggered forward at the impact, but kept her feet, cursing and whirling, trying to throw Campana off.

"Run!" Campana gasped out to Sola and Vivia. "Get upstairs! Out of the door! Fetch someone to help! Go! Go!"

Sola, though, did not move, standing gaping at Campana and Raven as they struggled. Raven crashed back against the stone wall, crushing Campana.

"Go!" Campana screamed again. Vivia, she saw with relief, was heeding the call at last and was running up the stairs.

"You little bitch!" Raven was still trying to claw Campana's arms away from her neck and swinging back and forth to smash Campana against the walls again and again. On one such gyration, Campana's head hit against the stone and she cried out in pain. Tiny points of light sprang up in the near-darkness and floated about her head disconcertingly. Another crash and her head connected yet again. She felt her grip on Raven loosening. A moment later and she was forced to let go and slump to the floor, her head shooting through with pain and her vision blurring.

Sola had finally come to her senses and she, too, was now running up the stairs. Now free from Campana, cursing loudly, Raven set off after her.

Left alone, Campana sat loosely with her back against the wall. From the doorway of her room, bright flames licked greedily out and she had to pull her arm back in sudden searing pain as the flames reached her. She thought she heard a roaring sound. Smoke was beginning to pour out, too and was filling the space. Campana began to cough: hard, hacking coughs and she couldn't draw a clean breath. Struggling to breathe she found herself sliding over to lie with her cheek against the cold stone floor. The coolness was so welcome and there was a tiny sliver of clean air...

That was her last thought before everything dissolved into overwhelming blackness.

32

Adura

She stood just outside Candens' room, watching his sleeping form reflected in the mirror at the end of the room.

Adura hadn't seen her pledge since Lambent's wedding to Hermia and that meeting had been clouded with her own fierce determination to reject him, to tell him that she could never marry and that she would not be a slave. She had hardly paid him any attention except as a symbol of her future imprisonment and had hardly considered him as a person, or as a man.

Now, as Candens lay on the bed, his face relaxed, his mouth a little open, his light brown hair in disarray on the pillow, he looked utterly vulnerable, like a child. He wasn't handsome in the flashy way that his brother was, but it was a strong face; a good face. Adura began to consider and regret the wrong that she had done him.

She had come here with a purpose, however, not to stand gawking. She'd slipped away from her maid in order to speak to Candens alone. There were things which she had to say to him privately, no matter the consequences. Gathering herself, she knocked on the open door.

"Candens?"

It took him a moment or two to stir at the sound of his name, but then he sat bolt upright in a moment, startling her and making her take a step back. She supposed that he had been trained in the Militia to come awake in an instant at any warning.

"Adura?"

"Yes."

"Could you open the shutters, please?"

Adura did so and bright sunlight spread in. Candens rubbed his face and scratched the stubble on his chin.

"What time is it? Did I sleep through the Unshuttering peal?"

"Yes, it sounded two bells ago. I would have let you sleep longer, but there are things you need to know. Things I have to tell you."

Candens' face grew serious and intent. Adura could see a wince of distress flash over it, as though he had remembered something very painful.

"You have things you have to tell *me*? I came here with news of my own. Did your father tell you?"

"When I got home last evening, he told me that you were here and that you had something you needed to discuss with me. But he wouldn't say what it was. He said that you had been riding for a long time and were very tired. I'm glad you stayed."

Candens did indeed look weary, despite his long sleep. He started to speak, hesitated and then stopped. He took a deep breath and began again.

"What I have to say to you will please you, I imagine, Adura. The fact is that we are no longer pledged. You don't have to marry me after all."

Adura sat down quickly in the nearest chair, feeling that her legs had been cut off from beneath her. Did she feel joy at this news? No, it was more a sense of bewilderment.

"Why? What has happened?"

Candens sighed unhappily.

"I'm no longer a member of my... of the Bellringer clan. I had an argument, a fight, with my brother Lambent. I hurt him badly. He almost died. I still don't know whether he will recover. My father blames me. I have been disinherited and cast out. So the pledge between us is no longer valid, it is cancelled."

Adura sat quietly for a long moment, thinking about this news and trying to work out her own feelings. There was something Candens was not telling her, she realised eventually.

"What was this argument about? What was so bad that you had to fight over it?"

Candens shook his head, looking wearier than ever. "I can't tell you."

"Yes you can." Adura spoke with a touch of irritation. "You're just not saying. Is it something shameful?"

"I… yes. Yes, it's shameful. It's all my fault. But what does the reason matter? The main thing is that you're free now. You're not pledged to me any more. Isn't that what you wanted?"

Adura ignored this question.

"The reason matters to *me*. I want to know why you were cast out," Adura insisted. Suddenly she had a flash of insight. "Was it about Lambent's wife, Hermia?"

There hadn't been many occasions when all four of them—she, Lambent, Hermia and Candens—had been together, but when they had, Adura had noticed the occasional furtive glances Candens made towards the other woman. She felt a fleeting pang of anger and jealousy but Candens could only nod, his face downcast with shame.

"I see." Adura accepted this with surprising calm. "I'm not really surprised. I suppose in a way it's my fault. I never gave you any reason to believe that you would be happily married to me."

Candens fired up instantly. "No, no, it's *not* your fault. It's mine. I was stupid, that's all. Very, very stupid."

Adura sighed. "You're not the only one who has been stupid. We make a pair. That's what I came to tell you. Only… my parents mustn't know what I've done. I'll have to tell them eventually, I suppose, but not yet."

Candens frowned, unable to follow her with such little information. "Tell them what?"

"I know where Campana is. At least, I know where she was lastwake. With luck, she'll be free by now."

"Campana! My God, I've been so caught up with my own troubles, I've barely given her a thought for the last two Shutterings. But how do *you* know where she is?"

Candens sat forward, body language quite different now as puzzlement creased his face. Adura bowed her head so low she could no longer look directly at him.

"How do I know?" Her voice was soft with something... shame? "I know because I was one of the women who took her and the other pledgees. I am... I *was* one of the Daughters of the Dark. Does that astonish you?"

A moment's pause followed and Adura looked up into Candens' grey eyes, which to her surprise showed sympathy rather than condemnation.

"Not really," Candens realised. "I know your views. When the Pledging Ceremony was disrupted I couldn't help but wonder if you were one of them."

"Yes, but I was wrong, though. Not about our cause, but about The Daughters. I found that out too late, though."

Adura began to explain. She had taken a stand, because she had felt a need to show the people around her what their expectations meant for her. But it had become increasingly clear that she had been betrayed by someone with an ulterior motive.

"Once I understood that someone was using us for her own purposes," Adura went on, a bit brighter now, "I tried to do what I could to help Campana and the other two remaining kidnapped girls, to help them escape. If it's all worked out, they should be free by now."

"So where...?"

"Hush!" Adura reacted with alarm. She had heard the tread of feet down the corridor and the slight wheezy breath of her father. A moment later and Ignis was at the door.

"Awake, are you?" Ignis addressed Candens. "Good. Listen, there's been some disturbing news just arrived from the city. I thought you should know as soon as possible."

He came into the room and sat down heavily in the only free chair. "Hmph. I practically ran up the stairs. Should have sent a servant to get you, I suppose. I'm not the man I used to be."

"What news, Father?" Adura felt the beginnings of alarm tightening her abdomen.

"There's been a big fire in the city, so the signal says. Several buildings have been burnt down and it nearly brought down the city's signal tower. But the Militia finally got it out."

An ice-cold blade ran through Adura and she put her hand to her mouth.

"A fire..." She could not finish her sentence.

"Yes, but here's the interesting part and why I felt Candens ought to know at once. While the fire was in full blaze, one of the militiamen was approached by a girl: distraught, with filthy clothes. She turned out to be Vivia of the Metalworkers. You'll remember she was one of the girls who were abducted at the Pledging. Most of them have been freed, their clans paid their ransoms, as we did Maryam's, but Vivia's clan was still negotiating. Those Metalworkers are careful with their money, you know."

"Father!" Adura cried. "What did Vivia *say*?"

"She claims that she had been imprisoned in a room underground near the place where the fire started. And here's the thing, Candens. She says that she had been kept there with your sister and another girl, Sola of the Carpenters. Apparently they had a plan to escape which involved lighting a small fire. And neither Sola nor your sister Campana have been seen since the blaze. I'm afraid... well, you might have to prepare for the worst."

Adura gave a cry of anguish, put her face in her hands and began to sob; great heartbreaking sobs which shook her body. A plan... it had been *her* plan; a stupid and dangerous plan. What had she done? Ignis was puzzled by his daughter's reaction.

"I didn't realise you would be so upset, my dear, or I would have spoken to Candens alone. I didn't think you knew Campana so well. I expect Maryam will be very upset when I tell her; she was Campana's good friend. But you..."

Ignis' voice trailed off as Adura shook her head, unable to speak for despair. What good was all of her subterfuge, all of the things she had done to conceal her involvement with the Daughters of the Dark? All it had done was lead poor Campana into a terrible trap.

After a long while, during which she fought to regain her breath and to be able to speak, she looked up at her father and Candens, her eyes still streaming tears.

"It's my fault. I have to tell you what I've done. If they are dead, *I* am responsible."

And so her story began.

33
Candens

Soft tendrils of fog were beginning to reach over the Mirrormaster estate as the wind shifted. Candens and Adura were standing outside, he by the side of his newly-saddled horse.

"What will you do?" Adura looked up at him, her face still pale and her eyes red from recent weeping.

"I have to go to the city to see if there's any more news, first-hand. Perhaps Campana has been found by now. If not, I want to talk to the militiamen involved in putting out the fire, perhaps speak to Commander Fervens himself. I want to have a look at the damage and the place they say the girls were confined. I'm guessing that there was a lot of confusion. Maybe there are places they haven't yet looked." Candens sighed. "It's probably futile, but I need to try."

"Won't your father and brother be doing the same?"

"You forget that Lambent was badly injured in our fight. I don't know how well he's recovering and of course I can no longer ask. My father will probably send one of my cousins. I plan to see if the Militia will help me find this woman Raven. Even if she is sincere in her beliefs, we can't risk another kidnapping incident like this, or worse. Don't worry, I won't tell the Militia how I know about her."

"I wish I could come with you," Adura said. "But you heard what my father said. I'm forbidden to leave the estate for any reason, unless I'm accompanied at all times by someone he really trusts. I think what hurts him and my mother most is how I lied to them about where I was going.

I'll have to work hard at regaining their trust. It will be a while before they can forgive me, I'm sure. And in any case, if..."

"If?"

Adura fought to control her emotions. "If Campana and Sola are dead, I don't think I'll ever be able to forgive myself."

Candens gently laid a hand on her shoulder.

"You did what you thought was best," he counselled. "At least you tried to help them. Sometimes—often—things don't work out the way they should, despite our best intentions."

Adura nodded a little, but was not much comforted. For a while they stood looking at each other in silence.

"I had best be going," Candens announced at last. "I... I don't suppose that we're likely to meet again, now that we're no longer pledged."

"No," Adura said in a soft voice. Then, as if on an impulse, she leaned forward quickly and kissed him on the cheek. "Fare well, Candens."

"You too."

Candens mounted Raya, who was bright-eyed and clearly well-rested now. He rode off, down the road to the boundary of the estate. From there, he would make his way to the city. Even at a brisk pace it would take him most of the rest of the waking to get there, or if he took it easy, he'd need to find somewhere to sleep along the road.

When he looked back over his shoulder, he saw that Adura was still standing outside the manor, a small lonely figure, watching him go.

34
Campana

Campana did not so much wake up as drift slowly through a cloud of bewilderment and pain towards the light. She remembered fire and smoke and brief, confusing moments of consciousness. There were memories of being lifted and carried, but then it all blurred and she was drifting again.

A little more awake now, she whimpered with pain. Her head was held gently, something was pushed into her mouth and then came the bitter taste of a liquid she had to swallow to avoid choking. She did and gradually the pain eased and blessed sleep returned, followed by more drifting. Finally, after an imperceptible time, at last she was fully aware of herself... and of the pain. The pain was most of all. It ran all the way down her right arm and there was a smaller area on her right thigh, continual and constant and very hard to bear.

Campana wanted to cry, but some instinct warned her to be quiet so she set her teeth against the pain and kept her eyes closed. Someone was here in the room with her, talking to someone else. That meant there were at least two people with her in the room. What room? Which room was she in? It was dim but not pitch dark; she could tell that even with her eyelids closed. It was brighter than the complete darkness she had been kept in for so many Shutterings. Now she focused on the voices, listening to them. They were soft, but she could hear them well enough.

"I've done what I can for her." This was a man's voice; an old man, Campana thought, judging by the timbre and pitch. "I've applied a healing salve and dressed the burns.

She'll be in considerable pain when she wakes. Here is some more *papavera*. Give her a little when she needs it. It is a marvellous aid in masking pain."

Yes, yes, Campana thought. *Now, please!* But she forced herself to remain still and silent. That way she could hear better as the man's voice went on.

"Don't give her too much of it. You know the consequences, of course, should she become dependent on it."

Now answered a woman's voice, a voice Campana recognised. It wasn't quite the same as the last time she had heard it—it had a different quality—but it was familiar enough. It was Raven's voice.

"Very well. You'll keep quiet about this, of course."

It wasn't a question, but a confident command.

"Of course." The man spoke with sad resignation.

"No one must know she is here. Nor can she learn where she is," Raven insisted.

Campana opened her eyes the barest fraction. The room she was in, she saw now, was dim because its shutters were almost completely closed. But at least there *were* shutters. She was no longer underground in the old shadow house. Of course not. She had burned it down, hadn't she?

Over in a dark corner some distance from the bed, two people were standing. Campana opened her eyes a little more, trying to make out the faces, but it was all a blur, her eyes not yet working properly. It was hard to think straight through the pain in any case. Where was she? What was happening? The old man must be a Healer, if he knew about salves and potions. It was hard to join any of it together to make sense. Campana moved her injured arm just a little and despite her best efforts, let out a soft groan as it flared with renewed pain.

"You had better go," Raven whispered. "She's starting to wake. Leave her to me."

Campana quickly closed her eyes again, not wanting Raven to know that she had overheard the previous conversation. A door opened and closed. Campana stirred some more, groaning purposefully this time as she slowly opened her eyes. A few steps away, the woman was adjusting the familiar and hated red mask over her face. She wore an elegant deep-burgundy gown. Ah, here came the loose black cloak, hurriedly thrown around her shoulders with its hood adjusted to cover her hair. Raven was back and turned to face Campana.

"Oh, it *hurts*." Campana whimpered, with considerable truth, but strived to seem only half-awake. "It hurts. Please stop it hurting."

She almost added "Mummy," but thought that might be pushing the subterfuge a little far. And Raven was definitely not her mother.

"Very well. Drink a little of this."

Raven offered Campana a small bottle containing a yellowish liquid and held it to Campana's lips. Campana took a small sip gratefully, forcing herself not to grab the bottle from Raven's hand and gulp down its entire contents. The taste was bitter, with a slight cloying sweetness, as though honey had been added to mask the bitterness. Campana took another sip. Raven withdrew the bottle and stood over her in silence, watching. Very gradually the throbbing, burning pain in Campana's arm and leg started to ease.

"Where am I?" Campana deliberately slurred her voice, trying to seem only half-conscious.

"Somewhere you have no right to be. Keep quiet. You were very foolish and have caused me considerable trouble. I should have left you to burn. I wish I had. We have to work out what we are going to do with you now."

"I want to go home," Campana said. "Please let me go home."

The response was slow in coming.

"Yes." Raven spoke quietly, almost to herself. "That may be the best, once you are well enough. Things have changed back at your manor. You'll find out."

What did that mean? Campana felt a tremor of anxiety at the possible threat in that statement.

"Here now," Raven said, in a peremptory voice. "I'm sure you're still in pain. Have some more of this." She proffered the little bottle again. "Here, drink it all down."

A few moments before, Campana had wanted to do just that. But something about the intensity of Raven's voice gave her warning and she remembered what the old man had cautioned.

"No, I'm all right now."

"I said drink it." Raven's voice was firm. "You'll feel much better afterwards."

"Leave it with me, then." Campana tried to sound as submissive as she could. "I don't like the taste. But I'll keep on sipping at it, I promise. Right now..."

"Right now?"

"I need to use the privy."

Raven made a sound of annoyance. "There's a chamber pot here. You'll have to use that. I suppose I shall have to help you up to it."

Raven put her arm around Campana, avoiding putting pressure on her burned arm and lifted her up. Campana found that her legs were weak and wanted to give way, so Raven had to support her for the few steps which were required. Campana saw that she was now wearing only a white shift. Her once-lovely Pledging dress was gone.

As Campana relieved herself, Raven looked away in disgust. The woman didn't make the slightest move to touch or empty the pot once Campana was done, but simply left it where it was. She wasn't used to doing this sort of thing, Campana learnt. She was used to having servants.

Raven left the room when Campana was back in bed. The lock turned in the door with a loud click. Campana was a prisoner once more.

Alone at last, Campana looked around more closely at her surroundings. She was in a room with a bed, a small table and wooden chair, with a chest of drawers by the bed. The walls were neatly plastered and painted white. A window was covered by shutters, almost completely closed. Campana got out of bed and went over to the shutters. They were locked or tied somehow above her reach so that she couldn't force them open and slanted so that her only glimpse out was of the sky with a few birds wheeling around. If she bent a little lower there was a tiny glimpse of the blinding Sun. It was impossible to guess where she was from that, except that it wasn't a long way from the Sun. She contemplated dragging the table over to the window and standing on it to see if she could untie the shutters to see out. But she felt too weak. Besides, it would make a great deal of noise.

She returned to the bed and picked up the bottle of yellow fluid. She took a final small sip. It took a great effort of will not to drink more. Then, not without a feeling of regret, she went over to the chamber pot and tipped the bottle up so that its contents drained into the pot. No one would be able to tell.

Feeling more and more fatigued with every passing moment, Campana went back to the bed, put down the empty bottle on the chest of drawers and lay down. She slept for a while, but was awoken again by the renewed pain of her burns. She wished sincerely that she hadn't emptied the bottle.

Soon afterwards, she heard a key turn in the lock and closed her eyes again, feigning sleep. Someone came close to the bed and Campana heard the empty bottle being picked up.

"Good," Raven said quietly. Campana heard her go back to the door and after a puzzling delay, the door opened again and Raven said to someone, "Come in now. She's sound asleep, but be quiet. Empty the chamber pot and bring it back. Be quick about it."

It must be a servant, then. Campana opened her eyes the tiniest fraction. Though the room was still dim, she could make out a young woman dressed as a maid coming into the room. Behind her Raven was no longer wearing the disguising cloak and mask.

As the maid went out carrying the pot carefully so as not to splash its contents, Raven moved a little closer to the window. As she moved, a thin stripe of light coming through the shutters briefly ran over her face. Then she was in the dimness again. But it had been enough. Campana had captured that transient, moving glimpse in her mind's eye and was putting it together like some child's puzzle. She *knew* she had seen that face before.

It wasn't a face she had seen often, but certainly it had been more than once. But *where*? Her thoughts were all in confusion and to her frustration she couldn't connect the face with anyone she knew.

The maid hurried back into the room with the cleaned pot and put it down. At a gesture from Raven, she curtseyed and went out of the room again. Raven came over to the bed and Campana hurriedly shut her eyes tight. She heard the chink of a bottle being placed on the chest of drawers. More of the yellow liquid, no doubt. What had the old man called it? *Papavera?* Yes, that was it.

After a pause, the door opened and closed again, the lock was turned and Campana was alone again. She sat up and took another small sip from the full bottle Raven had brought. *Just a little*, she thought, *just enough to take the edge off*. Then she lay back down, her mind replaying over and over that image of a face traversed by a thin line of light.

Gradually, the pain retreated, but so did her mental sharpness. Campana dozed again.

She woke with a sudden start and a gasp of shock. In her sleep her unconscious mind had put the puzzle together. She *knew* who Raven was. The last time she had seen that face was at Lambent's wedding. Raven's real name was Calora: Magistra Calora of the Signaller clan.

Raven was Hermia's mother.

35
Candens

"You can see for yourself, there's not much left of half this block of buildings. The Signallers were damn lucky we stopped it before it took their tower."

Candens looked at the rubble with a twisting knot of grief inside him. Commander Fervens was right: it was hard now to even work out where the boundaries had been between the original buildings, which were now reduced to a shambles of blackened stone and charred timber sticking up at every angle, like the broken bones of an over-roasted fowl. The air was filled with a sour, biting odour and thin trails of smoke still drifted up here and there from the wreckage, even though the fire had been put out over two Shutterings earlier. Militiamen were directing workmen to pick apart the rubble stone by stone, beam by beam, making it slow, tedious work.

"What do the girls who escaped have to say? I understand that Sola of the Carpenters was found wandering?"

"Yes, poor girl." Fervens nodded. "She has obviously been badly shocked and her mind thrown out of balance. She didn't know who she was for many peals and even now can't remember anything more recent than the start of the Pledging. She hasn't been of any real help and we daren't question her too hard, even if her clan would allow it. But Vivia of the Metalworkers is a bright young woman and has helped us as much as she can."

"So what have you learned?"

Fervens shrugged. "Not much which is useful, alas. We're still trying to make sense of it all. However, you can

176

be proud of your sister, Candens. It seems that she helped the others escape. Her plan was to start a small fire to distract their jailor. I'm afraid, though..."

He waved his hand at the smoking rubble and left it to Candens to continue his unspoken thought.

"The fire got out of hand and she didn't get out. Yes, I see."

The grief twisted again, an almost physical pain inside Candens' heart. He'd loved Campana, but it seemed there was nothing he could do for her now except mourn.

"Do you have any idea yet about who these women are, The Daughters of the Dark?" he asked after a moment.

He had, of course, said nothing about Adura's involvement to Fervens, who didn't seem to find the question out of the ordinary.

"It's complicated. The Daughters started up more than four millends ago. They started out as a small, peaceful group, contenting themselves with the occasional protest outside Clan Council meetings. In those early days, some didn't even bother to hide their identities. I've talked to some of them. Most were young women from wealthy clans with too much time on their hands, though one was a widow in middle age who thought she should take her husband's place on the Council. I won't name names. I suppose they have some legitimate grievances and there's no reason they shouldn't air them, so long as they are peaceful about it."

Candens nodded his agreement and Fervens went on. "But we've heard nothing from them in recent centends and I thought the group had disbanded, until the last Pledging. So I went back to talk to those I knew. They deny all knowledge of what happened at the Pledging and I'm inclined to believe what they say. That act of terror and the kidnapping seem to have been carried out by a new extremist group which has taken over the name of the old organisation. We haven't yet had much success in finding out who is leading this radical group. But we'll keep looking, of course, as far as our resources permit."

Candens sighed and looked over the ruins again, his heart heavy. "You'll let me know if your men find Campana's body?"

Fervens nodded. "Of course."

"Commander, there is one other issue. I need to ask whether you have had a signal about me from my father."

Fervens made a grimace.

"Oh yes, Ardens wrote to me." He looked around at the militiamen and the Dim workers swarming nearby. "Let's go somewhere more private and we can talk about it."

Fervens led the way to a nearby tavern, where it seemed he was well-known. A private room was quickly prepared for them and they sat down with a tall beaker of ale in front of each of them. As the door closed, Fervens took a gulp of the ale, swallowed it down with satisfaction and then sat back in his chair, looking at Candens.

"Yes, your father wrote to me. He told me that you have been banished from the clan and disinherited. He gave me some instructions about what to do if you turned up on my doorstep. What he didn't tell me was why. I was hoping that you could give me more information."

Candens looked down at his beaker of ale, as yet untouched.

"I can't tell you all of it, just that my brother and I fought and that I hurt him, badly, though I think he'll recover."

Fervens reached over a hand and firmly pushed Candens' chin upwards so they were eye to eye again. "That doesn't tell me much. What was the fight *about?* See, I don't take well to being given commands by any particular clan head. My loyalty is primarily to the city and I answer to the Clan Council. When your father instructs me not to take you back into the Militia I get annoyed. That's not his prerogative. But at the same time I have to judge the merits of such a demand and you're not helping much by keeping quiet, Candens."

Candens paused only briefly. He knew that he shouldn't insult Fervens by asking him to keep their discussion confidential; he knew the Commander well enough for that. "The fight with Lambent was about a few different things. But the main one is that he found out that I had fallen in love with his wife. I'm ashamed to say that is true. But he also accused me of plotting to kill him and take his place as heir and that isn't true at all. "

Fervens grunted. "How did he find out about you and his wife? Did he catch you in bed together?"

"No, no. That never happened. It's just that one evening when we were alone, she made... No, that's not right. When we were alone I stupidly told her that I wanted her. Eventually she told Lambent about that and he was blind with jealousy, impossible to reason with. He attacked me. We were... we were standing somewhere dangerous, where we could both fall. I tried to stop him, but we fought and he fell. Oh, the dark with it!"

Candens finished in misery, looking away from Fervens in shame.

"You're a damn fool, Candens. Having your head turned by a pretty face like that. I'm surprised at you. Unless your father relents, you've ruined your life. Wasn't your pledge good enough for you? The Mirrormasters' daughter, isn't that right? She's not a bad looking girl, no beauty perhaps, but pleasant. She'll make you a good wife."

Candens shook his head. "You forget, Commander, I'm clanless now. The pledge is cancelled. I went to the Mirrormaster manor lastwake and told them so. In any case, Adura was never happy with her pledging to me. She's free now, though perhaps her father will try to pledge her again."

"She won't be happy with that. Late pledgings are usually poor affairs, there's little choice of pledgees."

That was true. Perhaps Adura would be able to resist her

clan's urgings to pledge again, as she had resisted their pressure to name a date for her marriage to Candens. She was certainly strong-willed, though he knew that the affair with The Daughters and her likely involvement in Campana's death had greatly shaken her.

"As for you," Fervens continued. "I'd certainly like to take you back. You were a damn good officer, but although I hate being given instructions by your father, I can't reject them outright. The Militia answers only to the Clan Council as a whole. It has to be that way so we can mediate disputes between clans. However, in practice your father could make life difficult for me. Worse, if he wanted to he could bring Solus of the Signallers onto his side, because of the connection through Hermia. You know that Magister Solus is now likely to become Council President?"

"Yes. Hermia told me so." Candens put his elbows on the table and his face in his hands. "Oh, it's all such a mess. I don't know what I'm going to do." After a moment, he looked back up at Fervens. "Isn't there any kind of work you can give me?"

Fervens was silent, thinking. At any moment Candens thought that the Commander might simply shake his head and go. But finally, Fervens seemed to make a decision.

"It can't be official. But I do have some discretionary funds, money I can use for particular purposes as I decide."

"So..."

"Understand, I'm talking very small amounts of money. It's usually only to pay for the labour of a few Dims."

"I don't care about money so long as I don't starve."

"Hmm. You might change your tune when you have to do it. But I can pay you—unofficially—to help out in a special investigation. Your name wouldn't appear on our books."

Candens leaned forward, a spark of hope beginning to catch. "What investigation?"

"There's an illicit trade going on in the stronger medicines made by the Healers. They've had some major thefts, as you know. Small quantities are going missing all the time, probably filched by their workers. There have always been a few Brights using these substances and there's not much I can do to stop that. But the stuff has recently become more widespread and abundant. I've even had reports of Dims using it. It's starting to cause real problems."

"Blaze of the Signallers..."

"Trades in the stuff. I know, but he's not the only Bright doing that. I don't know who Blaze gets it from and of course he refuses to speak to me. Our powers of coercion are very limited when it comes to the powerful clans, you understand. And now Blaze's father is about to become Council President."

"Then what...?"

"There's too much of the stuff around to be explained by the thefts from the Healers than we know of. As I understand it, these substances are all made from various plants. Perhaps someone has found out how to grow these plants and prepare the medicines outside of the Healer's control. There could be a hidden plantation we haven't been able to spot, though we've been looking. I don't have the men spare to spend a lot of time on it."

Candens sat back, thinking. "What do you want me to do?"

"I want you to find out as much as you can about the plantation, if it exists. And tell me who is behind it."

"All right," Candens said. "I'll do it. I'm not sure how to begin, but I'll do it."

"Good man. Where are you sleeping this Shuttering, by the way?"

Candens gave a mirthless laugh. "I have no idea. Last Shuttering I slept in the shadow of a rock on the road."

"This tavern is as good as any. I'll put a word in for you with the landlord; make sure you get a newly aired bed

181

without fleas. Mind you, the money I'll be paying you won't be enough for you to stay here long."

"Thank you. I have a little money with me. I can manage for a while."

And when that's gone, Candens thought, *what then? Take up the life of a Dim?*

That fate seemed all too likely.

36

Campana

Campana lay on her bed and listened to yet another Unshuttering peal begin. The bell tower wasn't far away. She had been listening and paying attention to bells all her life and she could distinguish one tower's bells from another by subtle differences in the sound. The bells she heard were those of the Bellringer's tower in the centre of the city. Now that she knew who Raven really was, it wasn't difficult to work out where she was being kept: she had to be in a room high in the Signaller's tower.

Several Shutterings had come and gone since Campana had first glimpsed Raven's face. Each waking, Raven returned, the black cloak over her body, the red mask on her face. Each time, Raven replenished the bottle of *papavera* beside Campana's bed.

Each waking, once she was alone, Campana took a small sip from the bottle and emptied the rest into the chamber pot again, its pale yellow colour making it easy to conceal there. This meant that she had to endure the ongoing pain of her burns almost unaided and she had hardly slept. Each time she tipped the drug into the pot, it became harder to do; the desire to sip just a little more becoming stronger and stronger. Campana wasn't sure how much longer she could keep it up.

To distract herself from such thoughts, Campana spent her time wondering how Raven could engineer Campana's return to her family without exposing Raven's own identity. The more Campana thought about it, the more she thought it unlikely that Raven would let her go. Why wouldn't she just have Campana killed? After all, the Bellringer clan probably thought that she was already dead.

She thought about the fire; how the flames had started to lick up into the ceiling beams. She wasn't sure how serious the fire had been, but there must have been smoke billowing out into the street, at the very least. Someone must have noticed. Even if Vivia and Sola had escaped to tell their tale, it was all too likely that everyone would think Campana had died in the fire.

"I should have left you to burn; I really wish I had."

Raven's bitter remark replayed over and over in Campana's head. Yet Raven had rescued her from the flames (alone? with help?). Perhaps outright murder was a step too far for her. Campana could only hope that was still true.

What was it all about? Raven obviously didn't truly believe in the purported aims of the Daughters of the Dark. That was all just a ruse. Something else was going on; there had to be another reason why Campana and the others had been kidnapped. Was it all down to Raven, or did others in the Signaller clan know about it? Surely they must; at least those clan members living and working in the Signal Tower here?

The thoughts went round and round in Campana's head. She had little else to do but think and try to keep her mind off the pain in her arm and leg.

She heard the door unlock and sat up. The maid came in and gave Campana a nervous glance, before picking up the chamber pot. Campana called out to her, but she just shook her head and left the room, locking the door behind her. The girl was clearly terrified of Raven; Campana had tried several times to talk to her, but always she refused to speak a word.

The maid returned a little later with the empty and cleaned pot. As she turned to leave again, Campana decided to force matters. She jumped quickly out of bed and ran to the girl, grasping both her wrists. The maid, startled, pulled back, but Campana held on, forcing her to listen.

"I know you're not allowed to talk to me. But I want you to listen anyway. My name is Campana, daughter of the Bellringers. If anything happens to me—if I disappear from here suddenly and you don't hear of me again—will you remember me? Will you find a way to let my family know?"

The maid's eyes were wide with fright.

"Let me go, let me go," she whispered. "I can't, I can't..."

"Campana of the Bellringers. Remember it." Campana held on tight, insisting the maid listen to her. Finally the girl gave a tiny nod and Campana let her go, scuttling from the room like a frightened crab. *Click-clack* went the lock. Campana sighed. She didn't hold too much hope. If Raven were prepared to kill Campana, she would hardly hesitate to kill a mere Dim like the maid as well.

Later, after the mid-waking meal had been brought—by a different servant, Campana noted with trepidation—Raven returned, the red mask over her face as usual, carrying the little bottle of *papavera*, also as usual. What wasn't usual was what followed.

"Drink this down, here, now, as I watch," Raven ordered. "Quickly, now."

"I don't like..."

"It doesn't matter what you like. Open your mouth."

"No."

Raven made an angry noise and seized Campana's throat with one hand and pushed her hard into the bedding. It took a moment for Campana to begin to fight back, but Raven was surprisingly strong and Campana was still weak from her injuries and the long period of forced inactivity she had endured. She clawed at Raven's arm, but the older woman squeezed tight and darkness began to swamp Campana's vision. Raven brought up the open bottle and forced it into Campana's mouth. Gagging, Campana was forced to swallow most of the bitter liquid to avoid choking on it.

Raven released her grip and Campana leant over the side of the bed, coughing desperately for breath. Next moment, Raven seized her again and thrust a loose cloth bag over Campana's head. Not again! Campana felt herself rolled over, her arms pulled roughly behind her and rope tied hard around her wrists. By the time Raven rolled her back to face upwards, she was sobbing with ineffective fury. Increasingly dizzy and already feeling the stupefying effects of the *papavera*, Campana heard Raven walk over to open the door.

"Come in," she said to someone. "You can take her now."

Other hands—gentler hands—took hold of her. Two people this time, Campana thought as she felt herself being lifted up.

"My name is Campana," she called out to these unknown people through the bag covering her face. "I'm the daughter of the Bellringer clan. If anything happens to me..."

Her voice trailed off as the pain faded away and the darkness finally welcomed her into its soft embrace.

37

Candens

Magister Percuro of the Healers was nervous and Candens couldn't figure out why. The old man fidgeted behind his desk and kept gazing out the nearby window at the rows of medicinal herbs and vegetables being tended by his fieldworkers. He seemed to pay little attention as Candens spoke.

"...so you see, Magister, I'm looking for work as a guard, perhaps helping keep your deliveries safe. Commander Fervens tells me that you have had a number of thefts recently."

Percuro's wrinkled face looked back at Candens, glanced away again.

"No, nothing serious," he said faintly. "I'm sure it's all under control now. I appreciate your offer, Candens, but I really couldn't see my way..."

"Commander Fervens will vouch for me."

Candens wondered why this wasn't working. It had seemed a good plan, to try and get himself employed by the Healers in a security role, for which his Militia training would be useful and where he might be able to identify how the illicit trade in medicines was happening.

Ferven's idea about a plantation hidden somewhere seemed far-fetched to Candens, but that was something he could investigate when he had exhausted all other lines of inquiry. Trying to locate a small farm somewhere in all of Sunfall, simply by riding around looking for it, would be an exercise in futility. Such a farm would seem innocuous from a distance—how could one distinguish the look of one of the

187

medicinal plants from some ordinary plant or shrub? Indeed, what if the illicit plants were being grown in among the cabbages and onions on a large estate, tended by rogue fieldworkers and unknown to the owners of the estate? Who could tell? For all he knew, such plants were being raised on the Bellringer estate without his father being aware of it. But still, the seeds for such plants would have to come from the Healers in the first place, as would the knowledge of how to tend the plants and prepare the medicines. It seemed sensible to start here, at the source.

Candens acknowledged that hadn't spent the time since he had spoken to Commander Fervens very productively. He'd felt flat and depressed, unable to summon up the energy to take any real action. He had walked about the city, visited a few old friends. At the tavern he had used to frequent he asked after the barmaid Mara, to be told that she was now happily married to a galley captain and expecting her first child. He was glad for her, but it deprived him of a friend at a time when he needed every one he could get.

The bed at the tavern where he was staying might have been free from fleas, as Fervens had promised, but Candens had found it far from comfortable. It sagged in the middle and there were mysterious lumps in the thin mattress. Still, he was no longer a spoiled child and he had grown used to bearing discomfort while he was in the Militia. Even so it had taken him this long to summon up the mental strength to make the long ride out to the Healer's manor and start his investigation.

It wasn't beginning well. Magister Percuro had kept him waiting for several bells and it had only been after Candens had made a noisy fuss with Percuro's manservant that he had finally been admitted. Even now that he was speaking to Percuro he was sensing great resistance and discomfort in the old man.

"The Commander will tell you that my archery and hand-fighting skills are first-class." Candens persisted, determined not to be dismissed. "I'm not looking to be paid a great deal."

Magister Percuro shuffled uncomfortably in his chair, frowning. "Yes, yes, but your father... I wouldn't want to offend an important clan like the Bellringers. You say you've had a serious disagreement with him and that you can't live on your own estate any more." He raised his hands as if he found himself in a difficult position. "Ardens may be unhappy with me if I give you work."

"My father wouldn't want me to starve!" Candens was impatient now. "I'm sure, despite our disagreement, he would be pleased for me to take on any honest labour, whoever it might come from."

In fact Candens wasn't at all sure of this when he remembered his father's fury, but it sounded good.

"Well..."

The old man fell silent. Candens was equally silent. He remained standing, hands clasped before him, looking the part of a reliable guardsman, he hoped. His clothes were neat, his unstrung bow strapped securely to his back. He'd even polished his boots for the meeting. Percuro stared out of the window again. Was he looking for something? Was he expecting someone? Suddenly the old man stood up; clearly he had seen whatever he had been waiting for.

"Forgive me, Master Candens, I see a courier riding up. I'm expecting an important signal—ah—from one of our chapels. I'm afraid we'll have to..."

"That's all right." Candens was quick to insist. "I'm happy to wait here, Magister. Take your time."

Percuro was taken aback. Clearly, he had been hoping that Candens would give up and leave, but Candens squared his shoulders and fixed his gaze forward. Magister Percuro would have to think of a good reason to refuse Candens, or he would stand there until the Sun went dark.

"Ah… very well then, I'll be back as soon as I can."

He wasn't quick. Candens' legs and feet ached from standing in the same position long before the old man returned. Stubbornly, Candens refused to sit or even move about much, wanting Percuro to see he was determined and unchanging.

When the old man did return, his mood had changed markedly for the better. Some burden had lifted. Magister Percuro's worried frown was gone and there was even a slight smile on his face. He cleared his throat.

"Perhaps we could give you a trial after all. There's a consignment leaving nextwake for our sanatorium at Glimmer Peak. You could ride with them and keep an eye out for trouble. One of my great-nephews is riding guard, but someone like yourself might be able to give him the benefit of your Militia experience. I can't pay you very much. Nothing, really, until you've seen the delivery safe and brought the wagon back."

And that got him out of the Magister's study and well away from the manor. Candens suppressed a cynical smile. Glimmer Peak was on the far side of the Sun from here, the very last outpost of civilisation before the bay opened out into the great frozen sea. But it would suffice; it was a start, at least. Whatever Percuro paid him would be a supplement to the meagre allowance Commander Fervens had given him three Shutterings ago. Either way, he now had useful employment, which he could use to gain some impression of how secure the Healer deliveries were. He didn't expect that the consignment he would guard would come under any attack, but he could talk with the man he travelled with and see if he could winkle out any useful information. And at least he would be doing something to pass the time.

Having made a decision which seemed to relieve his mind, Percuro brightened up considerably.

"Well Candens, the wagon leaves early nextwake, immediately after the Unshuttering. You'll need to sleep here. I don't have a guest room free for you, but there's a spare servant's room, if you don't mind that."

And that said everything about Candens' change in status. In a manor the size of this, there were bound to be many rooms available for honoured guests. He was probably lucky to be offered any accommodation at all. He was no longer to be treated as a Bright, but hadn't yet fallen as far to be treated as a Dim yet; a very odd position to be in.

"Thank you. that will be fine."

At least it would probably be better than the bed at the tavern.

~

Indeed Candens did sleep well. Rising at the Unshuttering peal, he went to the yard where the delivery for Glimmer Peak was being prepared and introduced himself to the two men loading the wagon, whose names, he discovered, were Bann and Jens. They greeted him without either enthusiasm or obvious rancour and said little else. They directed him to the servants' refectory, where they ate a simple breakfast together. He heard loud banter among the servants at other tables, but it was obvious that Candens' presence was quelling any such talk at his table.

Outside they were joined by Doriens, who was the great-nephew Percuro had mentioned. Though the Magister had described him as 'young', he appeared to be somewhat older than Candens. Doriens shook hands warmly enough, but didn't seem keen to talk. Candens wondered if he resented his great-uncle imposing Candens on the expedition.

Candens saddled Raya and they set off on the long journey, which would circle the bay to Sun-right, by-passing the city but stopping at a number of chapels on the way out to Glimmer Peak to deliver medicines and check on conditions. It would take several Shutterings to reach there and the same to return.

Glimmer Peak was the tallest hill at the tip of a peninsula across the bay from the city. It was surrounded by deep pools of shadow so that it was like a bright island, catching the last useful glimmers of light from the Sun, hence its name. The peninsula was bounded on one side by the Sun-lit bay, its waters largely free from ice. On the other side, the peak cast its long shadow far out over the frozen sea.

They set off, Candens riding easily beside the lumbering wagon. He tried to start up a conversation with Doriens, but Doriens answered only in monosyllables. Candens hoped that Doriens would relax and become more talkative as the voyage went on, or he would be unable to learn anything of use to Fervens' investigation.

Two bells had sounded during this so-far profitless ride before Doriens leaned over to Candens and said, "There's someone following us. A rider, see?"

Candens looked back. Along the road from the Healer's manor he saw someone galloping. Doriens called a halt to the men on the wagon and they waited for the rider to catch up with them. It turned out to be Percuro's manservant, a little out of breath from his ride. He took a moment to gather himself and deliver his message, which was for Candens.

"Master, Magister Percuro was anxious for you to be told the news we heard this morning. A signal came from the chapel in the Council Lodge."

Candens frowned "What news?"

"Good news. Your sister Campana has been found."

"My sister! Is she...?"

"Alive? Yes. Unconscious or deeply asleep, the healers say. A little injured; some burns, I understand, but otherwise she seems well. They found her lying at the door of the chapel when they opened up this morning. Her captors must have left her there some time after last evening's Shuttering."

Good news indeed. Candens felt a weight lift from him that he had barely been aware of carrying.

"Should I go to her?"

If he rode fast from here, he could reach the city before the next Shuttering. The manservant shook his head.

"I don't think so, Master Candens. The signal said that she was being returned home as soon as could be managed, back to your manor."

Despite his delight at the news of his sister, Candens couldn't help the stab of pain that came with this news. He was no longer welcome at the Bellringer's manor.

38

Campana

Campana fought for wakefulness, which was a slow, frustrating battle. She felt as though she were mired in some thick mud. Every movement was a dragging, slow struggle, while oblivion tried to suck her back down. Opening her eyes at long last involved a deliberate, difficult effort.

The result was unrewarding. All she saw was a ceiling, with bright, striped light patterned across it. So bright! She hadn't seen such brightness for... how long? She couldn't remember.

She tried to sit up, but her body refused to obey, though she could feel no physical restraints. Her burns hurt horribly, but the ropes were gone, as was the hood over her head.

"Where...?" She spoke aloud, unsure if she was alone. "Where am I...?"

Instantly, a calming hand was laid on her arm.

"Hush, hush, my dear. It's all right. You're safe. You're back home now. Don't try to talk."

Her mother Eccua's voice was close to her ear, very soft, almost a whisper. She was home! She was free! Campana gratefully sank back into sleep again; sleep that was restful this time.

When she awoke an unknown time later, it was a more natural process. There was another voice in the room, a touch strident.

"Hasn't she woken yet? Don't you think we should wake her?"

It was Hermia's voice. Hermia... what was it Campana

needed to remember about Hermia? There *was* something, something important. But her mind felt sluggish and confused.

"I *am* awake!" she insisted, but her sleepy voice contradicted her.

The pull of sleep was still strong and her eyes closed again, though she managed not to lose all consciousness this time so she could hear what else was happening around her. Her mother Eccua spoke first. "I'll go fetch Ardens, he'll want to know."

Hermia responded. "Yes. I'll look after dear Campana while you're gone, don't worry."

With that Campana came fully awake and opened her eyes wide. *Hermia!* Hermia was Raven's daughter. Calora's daughter, really. But Calora was Raven and Raven was Calora. What did it all mean?

"Now, my dear, are you in pain?" Hermia asked. "Take some of this, it will stop it hurting."

Hermia stood beside the bed, holding out a small bottle containing a yellow fluid. Campana stared. It was as though she were back again in the Signal Tower, with Raven, unmasked, holding out the bottle.

"No." Campana forced herself to say it, though her body craved for the relief of the drug; craved its blessed blanket of sleep and warm feeling. "Not right now. The pain isn't so bad. Thank you."

Hermia's face showed surprise and perhaps annoyance? Campana couldn't tell. Before Hermia could react further to Campana's refusal of *papavera*, Ardens and Eccua entered the room together.

Campana was surprised by her father's appearance. He looked much older than when she had seen him last. It hadn't been all that long, had it? Or was she just seeing him through new eyes? She noticed more white in his hair and beard and his face had sagged, somehow, as though weighed down at every point.

"Campana. How are you feeling?"

Though the words were kind, Campana felt that they were asked more out of a sense of weary obligation than genuine affection. But perhaps she was being unfair.

"My arm hurts a little," she reported, not wanting to alert Hermia to the true extent of her pain. "And my leg, too. I was burned in a fire, did you know? How... how did I get here? Back home, I mean?"

"You were found outside the doors of the chapel in the Council Lodge, deeply asleep," Ardens explained. "The Healers say you were drugged. Someone—the women who kidnapped you, I presume—left you there after lastwake's Shuttering."

Campana remembered only too well being forced to swallow almost the whole bottle of *papavera*. Perhaps it had been a stronger dose than usual, too.

"No one saw them? The people who left me?"

"No. It was during the sleep period, of course, and none of the after-Shuttering Militia patrols were near the area at the time. Can you tell us anything about where you were kept?"

I could tell you almost everything, Campana thought, but Hermia was standing right there, smiling at her father's side and she held her tongue. She would have to speak to her mother or father alone.

"Not much, I'm afraid," Campana lied. "Underground somewhere. After the fire I was taken somewhere else, above ground, in a room with closed shutters. I don't know where that was, either. The women who captured me always had their faces covered. I don't know who they were."

Did Hermia's smile deepen? Campana thought that it did and was pleased. For now, Hermia mustn't suspect that Campana knew more than she had said.

"Where are Candens and Lambent?" Campana asked. "Do they know I'm free?"

Ardens' face darkened and flashed a warning glance at Hermia and Eccua that Campana didn't understand.

"Lambent is ill. He was badly injured by... in an accident."

"And Candens?"

Ardens hesitated, seemingly unwilling to speak. Eccua spoke up instead.

"He's not here, my love. He's had to go away."

"Where to?"

Ardens regained his speech and spoke in anger. "You must forget him. He is no longer a member of our family. He has been sent away."

Campana was astonished. "But *why*?"

"He behaved in a shameful way, that's why," Ardens said. "Your brother Lambent was badly injured in a fight with him, that's why he's now lying in bed with a broken leg and injured arm and hands. The healer says it will be decants before he's well again."

"But Candens is—"

"Enough!" Ardens' face was flushed. "We do not speak that person's name any more in this manor. You are to forget that you ever had him as a brother."

Campana was silent. It was clear that she wasn't going to get the full story from her father. Her mother might be able to tell her more, or perhaps Campana's maid Libeth or the other servants. They were bound to be gossiping about whatever had happened.

In the meantime, she grieved. She loved both of her brothers, but she had always felt closer to the sober Candens than to the rather wilder Lambent. She couldn't forget Candens, no matter what her father commanded.

Campana stared again at Hermia, pondering it all as she remembered something Raven had said, several Shutterings ago: "Things have changed back at your manor. You'll find out soon enough."

She was right. Something terrible had happened here in this house, but how did Raven know of it? Surely Hermia must have been involved in whatever had caused Candens to be banished. Did it have something to do with her kidnapping? Somehow it all had to be connected, but she couldn't think how. She just knew in her bones that she couldn't trust Hermia. But how could Campana convince her parents of this? She had no real proof, just her glimpse of Raven's face in the slanting light and a long-standing dislike of Hermia that might be nothing but a difference in personality.

Campana looked at her father. Hermia's hand lay lightly on his shoulder as though comforting him for the loss of one of his sons. As Campana watched, her father reached up and patted Hermia's hand in acknowledgement of that comfort. Seeing the same movement, a brief flicker of annoyance flitted across Eccua's face. She said nothing, but her shoulders sagged a little.

It seemed impossible but somehow, Campana vowed, she would find a way to return Candens to his rightful place in the clan. Somehow…

~

The following morning, Campana insisted on getting out of bed and going to see Lambent. She had had more than enough of being in bed and being confined to a single room.

Hermia grudgingly allowed Campana to rise, although she tried to make her wait for a visit from a Healer. Hermia seemed to have taken up the role of Campana's nurse. Or was she a prison guard? Campana really couldn't be sure. Either way, Hermia insisted on staying by Campana's side, to "help manage her injuries," despite the presence of Libeth fussing ineffectively in the background. Hermia had proffered the bottle of *papavera* several times. Despite temptation, Campana refused more than a rare sip of it. In truth, her burns were beginning to heal.

Campana froze in shock when she saw Lambent. He lay on his bed with dark patches under his eyes and had obviously lost weight. His leg was splinted and wrapped in tight bandages. He managed only a half-smile when he saw his sister, though he greeted her warmly enough.

"Campana!" His voice was weaker than normal. "They told me you were safe. I'm so glad..."

At Lambent's side was a young man Campana didn't know, but there was an emblem of the Healers on his jerkin. He was wrapping white bandages around Lambent's left hand. The other hand, too, was similarly wrapped. The Healer looked up and nodded politely to Campana and Hermia, then returned to his work.

Hermia went forward and kissed her husband's cheek.

"Campana, dear," Hermia turned to her young sister-in-law, who was beginning to loathe that word 'dear'. "You must let Radians here look at your burns now. He was coming to see you anyway, of course, but then you insisted on coming here to see Lambent."

Radians of the Healers. Wasn't he...? The young man nodded to her, seeming a little shy.

"Campana, I am glad to see you free at last. I.. ah... I don't know if... that is, I was told..."

"We are to be pledged?" Campana offered. "Yes, I know."

His face wasn't all that spotty, Campana thought. In fact, he was a pleasant enough boy, taller than her, with dark, curly hair. He was nearly a millend older than herself, she thought. Old enough it seemed to be doing the full work of a Healer.

"Perhaps, when you are well enough..." He actually *blushed*, Campana saw with amusement. "I... I imagine we'll still be pledged, even if there isn't a public ceremony."

"Yes, yes, of course," Hermia said briskly.

And do I get a say in this? Campana wondered. *It seems not. Well, we'll see.* She hadn't been at all convinced by

Raven's lectures while she'd been imprisoned and she wasn't going to reject the idea of pledging and marriage outright. But her recent experience *had* changed the way she thought about the world and her place in it. She wasn't simply going to accept what was expected of her in the future. Not if she could help it. So she simply smiled and didn't respond directly to Radians, turning instead to her brother.

"Lambent, why did you and Candens fight? What was it all about?"

She might as well tackle the subject directly. Lambent winced, turning his face away from the subject.

"Campana dear, remember what your father said," Hermia said sharply. "That person's name is no longer to be mentioned in this house."

"But where has he gone? What will he do? I can't just forget about him."

Campana glanced at Radians, who was trying to appear as though he hadn't heard, busying himself with packing his equipment into a large white bag.

"Enough!" Hermia was angry now. "No more. We'll go back to your room. Radians, you'll come and attend to her?"

Radians nodded. Campana reflected that this wasn't the kind of romantic introduction to her pledge that she had dreamed of when she was young. *Come and look at my burns...* No, that was in exactly none of the books she'd read.

As Campana and Radians reached the doorway, Lambent called out to Hermia, who turned back to him. Campana could barely make out the urgent whisper, but she was quite sure he said, "Hermia, I need *more*. Now."

Hermia turned to Campana. "You two go on. I'll join you shortly."

Radians moved on, but Campana lingered a step behind. Just before she was out of the line of sight, she glanced back. At the bed, Hermia was passing something to Lambent. It was mostly concealed by her hand, but Campana recognised it only too well: a little bottle filled with yellow fluid.

39

Candens

A cold wind was blowing sunward as they approached Glimmer Peak along a peninsula which curved further and further away from the warming Sun at the centre of the bay. Candens shivered. The other men accompanying the wagon were better prepared for the conditions, with woollen-lined jackets, but Candens did not have one and he wasn't prepared to squander some of his precious store of money on buying one. Perhaps once the Healers paid him he could afford it, perhaps not.

This waking's riding had been hard. They had begun by skirting along the long edge of the huge umbra—a pool of deep shadow—cast by Moulders' Arm, a long ridge of hills which lay closer to the Sun than their path. People called it simply the Great Umbra: it was the largest region of deep shadow within the boundaries of Sunfall. The land fell away into a deep valley, where the Sun could never reach. Many thousands of strides wide, it was a dark, frozen place where no one ever went and no plants grew.

The wind had been cold enough by itself, but it was somehow made more biting by the proximity of the shadowed land, which seemed to suck up any warmth there might have been in the surrounding territory.

The sound of bells here was very feeble and far away, only heard by chance if the creaking of the wagon's wheels had ceased for a moment. The repeater towers were on the sunward side of Moulder's Arm. The faintness of their call made Candens feel further away from his past life than ever.

Finally, late in the waking, they had moved past the Great Umbra and followed the road down to an inlet of the sea. This far from the warmth of the Sun, the water was dotted everywhere with white chunks of floating ice. Here and there Candens had spotted the elongated black shapes of seals and a fisher-boat stalking them with its harpoons to the ready.

"A hard life," he had said to Doriens, pointing out the boat. "Out amongst the ice all of the time."

Doriens had just grunted. That was the way it had been the whole, long journey. On the first waking's ride, Candens had attempted conversation but received no encouragement. He hadn't learnt anything useful from his companions, despite his best efforts. The two Dims Bann and Jens talked only between themselves, out of the hearing of the others whenever they could manage it. If Candens spoke to either of them, they simply turned their gaze to the ground in apparent deference, but remained silent unless asked a direct question and even then responded only in monosyllables.

Doriens of the Healers had, on the surface, been a little friendlier, but also avoided engagement. It became very clear that he was determined to tell Candens nothing useful about the Healers' operations or the thefts of their drugs. Candens understood that a clan's important secrets needed to be preserved, but this complete refusal to discuss even minor matters struck him as suspicious. Matters of security, such as the prevalence of thefts and quantities which might have gone missing were not core secrets of the Healers' clan and it would only be common sense to discuss them with someone appointed to guard the supply wagons. A more intelligent man than Doriens would have deflected Candens' questions with distracting chatter about other matters, or made a joke, but instead he would just shrug or grunt.

Doriens, Bann and Jens had obviously all been instructed not to tell Candens anything. But *why*? Obviously something was being concealed. Did the Healers *know* about what was happening with the illicit supply of their drugs?

At the first Shuttering after the journey began, they had reached one of the Healers' chapels and delivered a package of goods. Beds were provided in a small dormitory attached to the chapel. Candens had lain awake, listening to Bann snore loudly and thinking it over. Once he was certain that the others were all asleep, Candens had slipped out as if to visit the privy but instead, blinking in the bright light, he had made his way to the shed where the supply wagon was locked away. In his hand was the heavy key he had taken from Doriens' pouch.

Once inside, Candens quickly counted and assessed the size and shape of every package on the wagon and kept a careful mental tally. There were one hundred and forty-three packages in total. With that information he had returned to the dormitory and replaced the key. The other men had slept on.

From then on, Candens had kept a careful note of how many packages were passed over to the priests at the chapels they visited and of the goods remaining on the wagon. After the third Shuttering of the journey, he was certain that the tally did not match. There were fewer packages on the wagon than could be accounted for by the deliveries to the chapels. It was a small enough quantity not to be obvious to a casual observer, but he was certain that somewhere on the voyage five packages of various sizes had gone missing. And Doriens, who was in charge of the wagon's written manifest and the deliveries, must know about it.

Where had those missing packages gone and how? Candens reflected that it wouldn't have been too hard to drop them off while he was otherwise distracted. Doriens had frequently asked him to ride ahead a little way along the road to scout for dangers. On such an occasion, the missing packages could have been left at a pre-arranged location, under a particular tree, perhaps, or in the shadow of a particular rock.

As Candens considered what this meant, they approached Glimmer Peak, which wasn't far away now. The road was passing through a small estate. The light was much dimmer here than on the Bellringers' estate and the shadows were long. The clans whose estates lay here on the peninsula were poor. Their fieldworkers had to toil hard to enable their plants to grow well in the limited light and Candens was interested to see how they were making every use of vertical or steeply sloping surfaces to have as much light as possible fall on their crops.

Up ahead lay a small township on the sunlit slopes of the peak. As in many similar towns, the buildings were mostly two storey affairs, only one room deep from front to back. The exceptional buildings taller than the rest were a signal tower, its mirrors flashing now with an active message, a bell-tower and the Healer's chapel. Part of the chapel building would be the hospice, which was their destination.

The road wound its way back and forth up the steep slope. The ninth peal sounded from the bell-tower as they were plodding upward and it took another two bells before they were finally at the top and moving into the township.

From the height of the peak here, Candens could see back across the bay to the distant Sun, now just a small intensely bright point. Nearer to hand, he saw that the sea below was scattered with ice. The further away from the Sun he looked, the more frequent the ice floes became until they merged into an unbroken white expanse that stretched out into the dimness, a dark, frozen ocean reaching, he presumed, to infinity. He shivered again.

They eventually reached the chapel and its hospice. Candens and Doriens dismounted and the two Dims began to unload the wagon. Candens, watching, counted the packages yet again to make sure he had made no mistake. He had not.

What now? He could confront Doriens and demand to know where the missing packages had gone and who had received them. Candens considered this, but decided that it would be best to appear ignorant and continue to work with the Healers for a while longer to gather more evidence. Doriens might just be a rogue player, earning a little extra money by dealing in drugs, unknown to his clan. Candens needed to know if others of the Healers were involved, too.

Once the wagon was fully unloaded, Doriens approached Candens, holding out a small bag which clinked when it moved.

"Here's your pay."

"My pay?" Candens was surprised. "I thought I wouldn't be paid until I returned with the wagon."

"No need." Doriens gave a slight smile. "We won't be carrying back anything of any value. You don't need to come with us. You can make better time riding without needing to keep pace with the wagon. Magister Percuro said to give you this when we reached Glimmer Peak."

The young man looked pleased with himself. Why, because he had managed to tell Candens nothing of value during the journey, or because he had successfully dropped off illicit deliveries right under Canden's watch?

"But what about your next supply trip?"

"Magister Percuro said to tell you that he will make contact with you if your services are needed again."

Doriens' smile made it clear he didn't think that was very likely.

Candens stood silently, weighing the bag of rings in his hand, eyes narrowed, thinking. He had been dismissed... and his dismissal here had been planned from the beginning. The biggest question was *Why?* Why had Percuro agreed to Candens accompanying Doriens on this long trip to Glimmer Peak, only to relieve him of his duties before they returned? Had the real purpose of this trip been to get

Candens away from the city?

"All right." Candens accepted Doriens' news without visible protest. "But it's not long before the Shuttering peal. Is there somewhere here...?"

"There's a tavern, I understand." Doriens' smile was a little stronger now, almost a sneer of contempt. "We would offer you our hospitality, naturally, but there's only one guest room in the hospice here and I need it. You're welcome to stable your horse here for the Shuttering. You can sleep with Bann and Jens in the dormitory, if you like..."

"No that's all right," Candens assured him. "I think I'll try the tavern."

After making sure Raya was being well looked after in the stable, he stalked off along the street and found the small, run-down tavern with a sour-faced landlady. It smelled strongly of boiled cabbage, which unsurprisingly proved to be the evening meal. At least it was inexpensive.

In the tiny room, with the shutters closed, Candens lay on the hard surface of the bed and thought over what had happened over the last decant: dinner with Hermia, where she had encouraged his attention and drawn from him his words of desire; her suggestion that Lambent might meet with a timely accident; the slap when he had rebuffed her advances. Then the awful fight with Lambent in the Pendulum Chamber, but most of all, of his father's harsh words. Candens' heart felt as though it were bleeding inside of him.

He tried to push these thoughts aside, without much success, but eventually they brought him back to Campana and how she had tried to warn him against his attraction to Hermia. He'd dismissed her warnings at the time as foolish talk from an immature young girl. But now... He really wished he could talk with Campana, but she had been released too late for him to be able to do that. If only he'd still been in the city when she was found...

If only he'd still been in the city... instead he had been sent on this fool's journey before he'd had the chance to do anything about Campana. Could that timing have been something other than a coincidence? Was his despatch on this expedition to the furthest corner of civilisation designed to put him out of reach when she was freed, so he couldn't contact her before she was returned to the Bellringer manor, from which he was barred?

He remembered how nervous Magister Percuro had been the evening before the voyage, awaiting some message. And how, only after that message had been received, had Percuro made arrangements for Candens to accompany the expedition to Glimmer Peak. Had the signal been about Campana? Had Percuro been told that she was free, or that she *was about* to be freed? The more Candens thought it through, the more it all fitted together, although he sensed this was just one shape in a bigger pattern. He really had to find a way to talk with Campana when he returned from Glimmer Peak.

40

Campana

"Nonsense, you dreamed it, is all."

Campana had finally managed to slip away from Hermia and seek out her father. She would have preferred to speak to her mother first, but she was out visiting the family of a servant who had recently died. So it had been to her father's study that she had hurried. Ardens dismissed her story impatiently, but Campana held her ground.

"I didn't dream it," she insisted. "It was Hermia's mother, Magistra Calora of the Signallers. She was the one who was in charge of The Daughters who kidnapped us."

Ardens gave a grunt of annoyance. "I don't have time for this. The Signallers are an important clan and Magistra Calora is a respected woman. Why on earth would she be involved in such an affair, denouncing the institution of pledging? Her own daughter Hermia was pledged and is now happily married."

"But..."

His face relaxed for a moment into something like sympathy. He began to speak in the soft, patient tone he used while explaining some matter at the dining table.

"Listen, Campana. You were in severe pain, yes?"

"Yes." And she still was, but Campana refused to admit this to her father.

"And this mysterious masked woman gave you a drug called *papavera* to soften your pain."

"Yes, but..."

"I know of that drug. It's a well-known fact that it can cause disturbing dreams. It can even cause people to see hallucinations—imagine that they are seeing things, while awake, which are not really there. I myself saw some bizarre things while being treated with *papavera* after I broke my arm when I was young. That's all that has happened here. You took *papavera* and you dreamed, or imagined, some faces which you knew."

"No, that's not it."

The impatience returned. "That's enough, Campana. I'm a busy man, as you know. I've given you all the time that I can spare. Let's hear no more of your dreams. I am glad you are safe and well. Count your blessings and go on with your life. Mind now, I don't want you babbling about these foolish notions to anyone else, particularly not the servants. And say nothing to your mother, you'll only upset her. Do you understand me?"

Campana set her face and tried to control the anger which bubbled inside her. She thought again of Hermia's hand laid on her father's shoulder and his obvious regard for her. She knew that she wasn't going to be able to convince him of anything which showed Hermia or her family in a bad light.

"Yes father. I understand."

She understood far too well. Her words and demeanour were deliberately polite and submissive, but she was burning with frustration and could feel her cheeks flushing in response. With luck, her father would see that as simple embarrassment.

"You must be right about the *papavera*, of course," she added. "Please don't mention my foolishness to Hermia. I'd rather she didn't know how silly I've been."

More importantly, she didn't want to tip-off Hermia and Calora to what Campana already knew.

"Very well. I'm glad you are feeling better and that you have seen reason, Campana."

Ardens nodded and picked up his pen to resume his work.

Campana went to leave, but before she reached the door, she turned back.

"One more thing, Father. I would so much like to go and see my friend Maryam. She was one of the kidnapped girls, too, you remember. It would be good to see her again. Can Libeth and I take the carriage nextwake and go over to see her?"

"Not right away. Your mother and I are visiting the Metalworkers nextwake. I have business to discuss and they have kindly invited us to stay over. We'll be back two Shutterings from now. But the waking after that—yes, I suppose that will be all right."

"Thank you, Father."

Campana smiled as she turned away. It would be pleasant to see Maryam, of course. But the person she really wanted to talk to was Adura. As one of her captors, Adura would believe Campana's story about Raven. And it would be *very* interesting to hear what she thought about that.

41

Candens

He slept badly at the tavern. In the morning, as he rose to
the sound of the nearby Unshuttering peal, he wondered if
he wouldn't have been better off, after all, sleeping with the
Dims. There was no mirror in his room, and he decided
against trying to trim his growing beard without one.
Breakfast was a gritty, unpleasant gruel served in a cracked
bowl. Candens pushed it away half-finished. He would buy
a small loaf from the town's bakery. But first, he had work
to do.

Candens returned to his room and sat on the bed,
leaning uncomfortably forward over the set of drawers next
to it so he could compose a signal to Commander Fervens.
He briefly outlined his suspicions of the Healers and the
evidence of the missing packages on the journey. After some
thought, he added that he suspected he had been sent away
from the city for some unknown reason, perhaps associated
with Campana's release.

He read the note through a couple of times. It wasn't a
detailed report. That would have to wait until he spoke
directly to Fervens. Still, it would alert the Commander and
lead to other investigations. He brought out a coding book
from his pack. Fervens had supplied him with a Militia
cipher so that their communications would be secure. Every
important message sent through the Signallers' network was
encoded using a private cipher and an agreed key-phrase.
That way, no one watching the lights flashing from a signal
tower could interpret the message, even if they understood
how the mirror positions on the tower represented the

message being sent. Only a few casual messages were ever sent in the clear.

The process of encoding a message was a tedious one, which is why signals were usually kept short and to the point. Candens' missive to Commander Fervens was as short as he could make it while making his meaning clear, but coding it was still a lengthy process. Three bells rang out while he was working on it. Finally satisfied, he picked up his pack and bow and went downstairs and out to the street, where his first stop was the signal tower.

The Signallers' outpost here was small. When he entered the building to hand over his message, he had to ring a bell for attention. He heard footsteps coming down the stairs, two, three, four turns before the locked door at the back of the room opened and an elderly man emerged, breathing heavily. It appeared that he was the only clan member operating the tower.

The man took the enciphered message with no comment other than to scan its length and name a price. It was a reasonable price, no doubt, but Candens examined the meagre contents of his purse with resignation after he had paid. Fervens had promised him a small stipend on a regular basis. He would just have to learn to manage.

Next stop further down the street was the bell tower, the local repeater. He wasn't sure of his reception there, but felt that he had to at least make the attempt. He waited until another bell sounded out. Now he knew the operators here would be free to speak for at least a little while before they were needed again.

Nevertheless, it took some knocking at the locked door to the street before Candens could attract the attention of the men in the bell chamber above. Unlike the Signallers, there was little need for the Bellringers to communicate with the public. But eventually, a head poked out from the bell-chamber above, belonging to a young man, with light-blonde hair. Candens squinted, trying to see if he recognised the face.

"Cousin Candens!" The man's voice floated down from above. "I'd heard... wait a moment, I'll come down."

A little later, the street door opened. Now Candens recognised the blonde man. It was his second cousin Argent, one of Great-Uncle Tinnio's grandchildren, several centends younger than himself. Candens hadn't spent a lot of time with him, but he remembered their occasional contacts as having been friendly ones.

"Argent. Am I welcome here?"

The young man looked embarrassed. "Well, your father sent us a signal. He didn't say why, but he said that you shouldn't be treated as a clan member any more. So I'm sorry, but I can't—"

"Yes, that's all right. I expected it."

This was why Candens hadn't attempted to seek shelter here last evening.

"Well how can I help you, then? Do you need food, or money?"

"You are kind to offer, but I don't need anything. I just wanted to know if my father had passed the word around to the towers. I see that he has."

"Why are you here at Glimmer Peak?"

Candens explained briefly that he had taken on work as a guard with the Healers, without going in to the secret reason he had done that. "How do you find it, working out here?"

Argent shrugged. "It's a miserable place, really, cold and dim. And it's damn hard to hear the inter-peal bells from the next repeater in the chain. It's only the major peals we can hear unless the wind is in the right direction. Jovens and I depend on our counting most of the time."

Candens laughed. "Do you know, despite being cast out of the clan, I still count in between peals. You'd better go up, I think, for the next bell."

"Oh, Jovens can handle it. I was on the Unshuttering watch so I'm going to my room to have a sleep now in any case."

"Still I'd better go." Candens smiled. "Give my regards to our cousin."

"Are you going back to the Healers' manor?"

"No, not straight away. I'm on my way back to the city to do some business there."

Argent stepped forward and hugged him, an unexpected move which brought sudden tears to Candens' eyes. He blinked them away rapidly.

"I don't know what happened between you and your father," Argent said as he released him. "But it's a damned shame."

"Yes, well. I hope that eventually he'll forgive me and let me back in, perhaps."

Unable to say any more lest his voice break with emotion, Candens turned abruptly away and went down to retrieve Raya from the stables of the hospice. He was anticipating a long ride to the city, but it turned out to be a much longer journey than he could ever have imagined.

Candens rode back around the bay from Glimmer Peak through many small estates, the homes of various minor clans: the Woodcarvers; the Locksmiths; the Pipers. However small the clan was, he knew each had its own collection of secrets. However trivial those secrets might be in the scheme of things, each family held close whatever it knew, not willing to share its knowledge with its neighbours. And so there was no progress; society was locked in stasis, unlikely ever to change. Depressing thoughts. Candens tried to shake them off, but it wasn't easy.

The road left the coast and started to follow the edge of the Woodminer's estate. Two bells later, he crossed a small stone bridge across a stream running down from the snow-covered slopes above. A little later he reached the edge of the Great Umbra once again and began the dreary ride along its chilly edge. He was in no particular hurry, but it was pleasing to no longer be forced to match the slow pace of the lumbering supply wagon.

He passed a number of other wagons on the road, coming and going, hauling food and other goods out to the remote estates, or taking their products to the markets in the city. Only a few other single horsemen were on the road, though several times he saw the blue-and-gold uniformed couriers of the Signallers, one of them passing him at a gallop on its way bearing an urgent signal to some manor.

A couple more bells passed and he heard the sixth peal sound out just as the road began to descend into a narrow neck of deep shade that couldn't be avoided. The wind seemed to channel through this little dip and its cold cut deeply. He urged Raya into a trot and they soon passed through the shade and rode up the rising slope as the road began to pass along the edge of the Stonemason's estate to his left and the continuing vast darkness of the Great Umbra to his right.

Just as he re-emerged into the welcome light of the Sun, blinking a little in the renewed brightness, he spotted a group of riders heading towards him at a gallop. Their grouping and their speed was unusual enough to attract his attention. Where were they all going at such a speed? They could hardly keep it up all of the way past the Great Umbra and there was nothing much of any interest beyond it which would call for such urgency.

Before too long, Candens could make out the faces of the riders and a thread of unease stitched its way through his abdomen. It was Blaze of the Signallers, with three other men riding behind him. As they got closer, the group of riders pulled to a halt abreast so Candens couldn't pass around them.

"Well, well. If it isn't Candens of Clan... what was it now?" Blaze glanced at his companions as if seeking assistance. "Candens of the Nonesuch Clan?"

Candens examined the group. Blaze he knew well and disliked, but he didn't recognise the others. One was well-dressed and, like Blaze, sported a Signallers' emblem on his tunic. He had a bow strapped to his back, just as Candens did. The other two men were more coarsely attired, probably servants. Those two rode past him a little way, so that in a few moments he was encircled.

"What do you want?" Candens had no love for Blaze, who was at the heart of Lambent's wild lifestyle and the supplier of *marana* and perhaps other substances. "I have important business in the city."

Blaze urged his horse a little closer, a sneer on his handsome face. "That can wait. I want to talk to you. You've been a very naughty boy; been thrown out of your clan. Nearly killed your brother, I hear, and tried to get my sister to help you, she says."

"That's not true," Candens said.

"What part of it isn't true?"

"About your sister. I wasn't the one—"

Blaze gave an unpleasant smile, reached down to his saddle bag and pulled out a hardwood club.

"Are you calling my sister a liar, clanless man?" He turned to the well-dressed man beside him. "Vivens, this turd just called your cousin a liar. What do you think about that?"

"I think it's about time he was taught a lesson in manners," the other man agreed, bringing out a similar club.

David R. Grigg

"Me, too," Blaze said and, without further warning, swung his club at Candens' head.

Candens ducked instinctively, but the club still caught him a glancing blow on the back of the head. He dug his heel into Raya's flanks and tried to force her through the gap between Blaze and Vivens. Another blow fell hard on his back and he lashed out with his fist, striking Vivens on the jaw and making him cry out in pain and sway back in the saddle. Blaze swung again and Candens fended off the blow with his forearm. Then one of the men behind tried to hit Candens, but missed and the blow fell on Raya's rump. That did Candens an unexpected favour, because Raya reared in pain, her hooves menacing Blaze and Vivens and then she bolted free. Candens urged her to her fastest speed and they galloped away from the group.

Glancing back, he saw that the other men were quickly in pursuit. Raya was a fine horse, but Blaze was well-known for his prowess in breeding racing steeds. Candens couldn't hope to stay ahead of them for long. Only one option remained.

To his right was the vast, deeply shadowed area of the Great Umbra. To his left was land belonging to the Stonemasons. Here, though, it wasn't under cultivation and was covered with a scrubby, low brush and small bushes which barely reached his shoulders. It wouldn't provide any cover, but nevertheless he urged Raya off the road to the left and along an ill-defined track through the wiry vegetation, crouching low to her back.

Moments later, he heard the crash of broken branches behind him as Blaze and his cohort followed, yelling loudly with glee at this sport.

42
Campana

The room was too bright. Light streamed into the drawing room through the wide open shutters and was scattered everywhere by the mirrors which seemed to characterise every room in the Mirrormasters' manor. It was a little too ostentatious, too much like boasting.

Campana had to begin this conversation delicately. Her friend Maryam was at her side, while Adura sat on the edge of a lounge opposite, her hands clasped tightly together in her lap. Campana waited until the three women were left alone together as their maids left the room.

She addressed her first question to Adura. "Does Maryam know about the kidnapping?"

Adura glanced at her cousin Maryam, her tight face flushing slightly with embarrassment. "Yes, she knows. I'm not sure that she has quite forgiven me yet."

"It's all right." Maryam waved that away. "I think I understand why you became involved. I was angry at first, but I don't really blame you now that I've been able to think about it. Someone took advantage of you, of your beliefs, but I don't really understand why."

"Neither do I," Adura admitted.

"Nor me, not yet, anyway," Campana said carefully. "But I found out something after the fire, which might help us work it out. My father thinks that I was dreaming, affected by the Healers' drugs. But I wasn't dreaming."

"What was it?" Adura frowned.

"I found out who Raven really is."

Adura's eyes widened in shock . "Who?"

"Before I tell you, I want to ask something which might confirm it. Adura, how did you come and go from the city to your friend's manor so many times without anyone noticing? A young Bright woman riding into or out of the city alone would attract attention. People would talk if you were seen doing that several times. The same would be true of the other Daughters who were helping Raven keep us prisoner. Why weren't you seen?"

"That's easy. We were each given a disguise to wear when we rode there. It was—"

"Stop! Let me guess and tell me if I am right. You were given a uniform, to disguise yourself as a man, a servant. As a courier."

"Yes." Adura's confusion was obvious on her face. "We were given clothes made up to look like the uniform that the Signaller couriers wear. Raven told us that no one ever pays them any attention, because they come and go all the time. And it's true. No one ever gave me a second glance while I was wearing it."

"I don't think those clothes were made to *look* like the couriers' uniforms," Campana said. "I'm sure that they *were* couriers uniforms."

"Stolen, do you think? But how did you guess?"

"No, they weren't stolen. And I guessed..." Campana paused to draw out the suspense, which she was rather enjoying, "...because Raven is Magistra Calora of the Signallers."

Adura fell back in surprise and Maryam gave a little gasp.

"You're sure?" Adura's face was aghast with disbelief. "I've never met her, only ever seen her from a distance. But she seems so elegant, so proud. Are you *sure* it was her?"

"Do you think I was dreaming, as my father says? No. I wasn't drugged, I made sure of that. I saw her face, even if only for a moment. And she has the right height and build.

I'm sure. After the fire, I'm certain I was kept in the city's Signal Tower: somewhere high, well above the noises of the street. I could hear our own Bell Tower not far away. Nowhere else but the Signal Tower makes sense."

Two deep lines of concentration marked Adura's face. "But that can't be right. Why would Calora be involved with The Daughters at all, let alone leading them? Besides, Calora's daughter Hermia—"

"Is my brother's wife, but I've never trusted her. I think she betrayed her own real feelings—probably her clan's real feelings—when we first met, more than a millend ago. That was a mistake on her part, but she was young then. To be honest, I don't think she's all that clever. Not as clever as she thinks she is, anyway."

Just far too clever for poor Lambent, Campana didn't add.

Adura was silent for a long time, her gaze distant, thinking through the implications. "Candens came to see me, to tell me that he had been cast out from his clan and that our pledge was therefore void. He had fallen out with Lambent over Hermia. Do you think…?"

Campana felt another piece of the puzzle fitting into place. She could almost hear the snap it made. "Of course. She deliberately led Candens on so she could create a dispute between them. Somehow it was part of their plan."

"The *Signallers* plan? What plan?" Maryam seemed bewildered by the whole situation.

"I'm not sure yet," Campana said. "I'm hoping that you can help me find out. Somehow we have to stop them. It can't be anything good."

The three young women continued to talk, but they made little progress in understanding what was going on, or working out what to do about it. Campana felt frustrated and powerless, but at least now she had two confidants and in Adura, someone a little older and more mature than herself.

Finally, the sixth peal rang and Campana's maid Libeth came in to remind her that it was time to set off back to their manor if they were to be home before the Shuttering peal.

Adura stood up to see her guest out. At the door to the manor, she said, "I'm going to try to contact the other Daughters and find out if they know anything useful."

Campana was surprised. "Do you know who they are?"

"Not directly," Adura admitted. "We were always told to keep our masks on and speak as little as possible, if at all. Only Raven ever saw our faces, though we were never allowed to see hers. Even so, I'm pretty sure that I know who one of them is. I think I recognised her voice when she asked for more light, just after we brought you all to the shadow house. Do you remember? I think I know who that was. I'm going to contact her and see if she can lead me to the others. Besides, all of The Daughters should know how we were tricked by Calora."

Campana grasped Adura's arm in alarm. "Don't tell them who Raven really is, not yet. We can use that knowledge against Calora if she doesn't know that we know her real identity."

"All right, but I can tell them that we were misled, fooled by Raven? I'm sure most of the others started to feel as I did by the end, that the kidnapping was all wrong."

"Yes, do that. Wait a moment. I have something for you and I nearly forgot." Campana fumbled in her shoulder bag and pulled out a folded piece of paper. "This is a copy of our family's commercial cipher, which Father uses to write to his suppliers. I've written my own key phrase underneath. If you send a signal to me, use the cipher and the key and I'll use the same when I signal back to you. We don't want the Signallers of all people to know what we're saying to each other."

"No!"

"And you will keep in touch? Let me know if you think of anything, or find out anything which might make sense of all this."

"Yes. I'll use the cipher, just as you say. That way we'll be safe."

43

Candens

He drove Raya hard towards a small hill he had spotted beyond the scrub. At his back, Blaze and his men followed, yelling their joy at the pursuit.

Candens urged Raya on, dodging and swerving as best he could to avoid her being scratched badly by the thickest of the scrub. He wasn't aiming for the hill, but the umbra that would lie darkwards of it. It wouldn't be completely dark there, but at least it would be dim and there would be a few precious moments when he would be in the dark and Blaze's people in full sun and unable to see into the shadow.

He rounded the hill and plunged towards the shade. Much less scrub grew here and the going was much easier. Well before he reached the hill's umbra, he deliberately closed his eyes tight, trusting to the horse's instincts to avoid hazards without his guidance. When he felt the sudden change of temperature, he opened his eyes once more. They had adjusted a little, and he scanned frantically about, looking for some shelter. At first, there was nothing, but then he spotted a half-ruined stone hut, its roof long gone. He had hoped for something of the kind—a resting place for a shepherd once he had led his flock into the shadow of the hill for the Shuttering.

Reaching the hut, he leapt off Raya and grabbed his bundle of arrows from her side, then ran for the doorway. The place obviously hadn't been used in millends. A few shreds of rotten wood hanging from the frame were all that remained of a door. Nevertheless, it would have to do.

Inside, he lay down the bundle of arrows, quickly unstrapped his bow from his back, bent it and strung the cord. He stuck three of the arrows into the ground point-first and had a fourth notched in the bow just as he heard Blaze call out from outside. Candens crouched back behind the stone wall.

"So is the clanless man also a coward? Come out and get what you deserve!"

"I'm no coward. Dismiss your cousin and your men. Face me yourself. Give me a club and we'll settle this between the two of us."

"And have you beat me with some underhand trick you learned in the Militia? I'm not so stupid."

"All right." Candens stepped into the doorway. Though it was very dim, there was enough diffused light from the sky to let him take quick aim at Blaze's chest. "I can only be certain of killing one man with my bow, but I swear that it will be you."

Blaze made an involuntary step backward and laughed. But it was an uneasy laugh. During the brief pause which followed Candens saw Vivens unstrapping his own bow and making it ready. Then Blaze gave orders to a servant "Yonn, take his horse's reins."

The servant moved, but Candens said, "Stop! Or I kill your master." The man stopped moving and looked back to Blaze.

"You'd really kill me for the sake of an animal?" Blaze shook his head in disbelief. "You're bluffing, Candens. Vivens and my men will kill you very slowly if you harm me."

"True. But you won't get to see it and at least I'll have the pleasure of knowing that you're dead."

"You're a fool. We can wait you out if we have to. Take turns sleeping. Give it up, Candens. We won't hurt you... much."

"No. Go back to the road and leave me alone. What does any of this have to do with you?"

"A man who plots to kill his brother and tries to involve my sister *is* my business. You lusted after her, isn't that right? Wanted to kill Lambent and marry her yourself? Not that she'd have you. Why should she, when he's a good-looking fellow, not like you."

Candens ignored these claims, though they stung with a degree of truth. "He would be better-looking if you left him alone and stopped selling him your poisons. Where do you get those, by the way?"

Blaze glanced across at Vivens, who was now standing with his own bow aimed directly at Candens. The glance seemed to say *I told you so.* Then he looked back at Candens. "That's a matter of business. My business. A business you've been poking your nose into far too much, from what I hear. Fervens' little lackey, aren't you? Hurrying off to see your master, weren't you, just like some dirty Dim?"

Blaze's loose comment sparked Candens' suspicions.

"From what you hear? *How* did you hear?"

He was certain that Commander Fervens wouldn't have let Blaze of all people know that Candens was carrying on an investigation into the illicit trade in drugs.

Blaze just smiled. "Oh, we Signallers have ways of knowing things."

Vivens made a noise at this. Not a laugh, as Candens first thought, but a half-suppressed exclamation of annoyance. Was Vivens trying to shut Blaze up? Candens narrowed his gaze, forcing himself to concentrate. His arms were beginning to ache with the strain of holding the bow cord at tension for an extended period of time, but this was important.

"How did you know I was heading to the city to talk to the Commander?" He paused, thinking hard. "In fact, you knew which road I was on and where to find me, didn't you?

Your people told you I sent him a signal, I presume. And you must have read it. But it was in the Commander's own private cipher, using a key only he and I know."

Vivens cursed and Blaze's smile vanished. "You think too much, clanless man. Now we're going to have to kill you."

Blaze was right. Candens had been thinking too much. In doing so, he'd lost track of Blaze's men. One of them was missing. At this realisation, he swiftly turned his bow and shot at Vivens, not Blaze. Vivens wasn't expecting it and his own arrow went wild as Candens' shot passed through his upper arm. Then Candens was back behind the cover of the hut's wall, just as the missing servant dropped down through the open roof, his raised club knocking the bow out of Candens' hands. But the man was off-balance as he dropped and Candens was able to swing a fist hard into his jaw before he recovered. He fell backward and struck his head on the hard floor.

"Now!" came Blaze's voice from outside.

Candens snatched up his bow, but there was no time to draw it before Blaze rushed into the hut, a dagger glinting in his hand. Instead, Candens used the bow as a crude staff, stabbing one end towards Blaze's eyes. Blaze muttered an oath and stumbled back into the other servant, who was trying to follow him through the narrow opening.

Using one of the tricks he had indeed learned in the Militia, Candens kicked Blaze hard in the crotch, then struck him in the face with his elbow and pushed him backwards. Before the servant could drag Blaze out of the way, Candens had plucked up another arrow and had the bow drawn and ready. The man on the ground in the hut was silent and Candens didn't think he would come to for a while.

Vivens had come up now. He must have pulled Candens' arrow from his left arm, which was bleeding freely. In his right hand he had a metal-bladed dagger, a lethal threat. His face was red with fury. He and the servant stood facing Candens, trying to judge whether they could safely rush him. Outside, on the ground, Blaze was screaming curses, both hands clasped over his crotch.

"Get away from the hut or I'll kill you." Candens' voice was grim and determined. "Stand well away from my horse."

Vivens hesitated only for a moment. Then he muttered to the remaining servant and they backed away. Candens flicked a glance down. His bundle of arrows and those he had stuck into the ground had been scattered by Blaze's entry, but were still easy enough to hand.

Drawing a slow breath, Candens aimed carefully and shot the arrow in his bow. Not at Vivens or the servant, or at Blaze, but Blaze's horse. It leapt with pain as the arrow entered its rump and screamed as only a horse can. Vivens spun around to look at it, cursing in surprise. Then it pulled free from its tether and bolted away into the dark.

By then, Candens had another arrow in his bow. Vivens' own horse received that arrow and then those belonging to the other two servants, one after the other. Candens aimed only to injure and frighten the animals. He hated to do it, but it was necessary.

Only Blaze's horse managed to pull entirely free and bolt, but the other three horses were rearing and plunging in pain. Calming them down enough to remount them would take time and the horses would not take well to being ridden with a painful injury. With a new arrow ready and aimed at Vivens, Candens dashed for Raya, who was distressed but still standing ready. She had been well trained to cope with battle during their time in the Militia. He leapt on her back and together they galloped away.

"I'll kill you!" he heard Blaze yell at his back. "I'll bloody kill you, you bastard!"

～

Candens regained the road to the city and urged Raya faster once they were clear of the scrub. His thoughts were swirling in confusion. The one thought which came to the surface time and again was that he needed to talk to Commander Fervens as soon as possible.

If, as it seemed, Blaze had read and understood the coded message he had sent to the Commander, a message he had encoded with the Militia's own secret cipher, using a key phrase the Commander had given him in person... what did that mean? Had Blaze somehow gained access to the cipher? But how would he have known the required key to use?

"We Signallers have ways of knowing these things," Blaze had boasted, to the considerable alarm and annoyance of Vivens.

What if the Signallers had a way of reading *every* message sent through their towers, regardless of how it had been encrypted? After all, the Signallers had introduced the practice of ciphering and supplied most of the common ciphering systems used across Sunfall. The use of private key phrases with those ciphers was meant to keep them safe even from the Signallers' operators. But what if that wasn't true? Even so, Candens had been told the Militia's cipher wasn't derived from the common ones, but had been devised separately. By whom? He didn't know.

If the Signallers knew how to crack *any* cipher... the implications of that were vast and appalling. Almost every communication in Sunfall, apart from some letters carried by hand, was sent through the Signallers' towers. It would mean that there were no secrets any more. The Signallers would know all of the plans other clans were making, perhaps even some of their secret clan knowledge. They would be able to pick up valuable commercial information which they could use to their profit. No wonder they were becoming so wealthy!

Candens began to realise that Blaze's oath to kill him was no idle threat, but all too real. The Signallers couldn't allow this knowledge to get out.

Racing along the dusty road, he risked a glance backwards. To his dismay, he saw two riders emerge from the shadow of the hill and begin to gallop through the brush towards the road. By the colour of the lead rider's tunic, it was Vivens and one of the servants. Blaze was probably too sore in the groin to be able to ride and might be so for some time. Candens couldn't suppress a grin at that.

He turned his attention back to the road ahead and to keeping Raya moving at her best speed, though he feared that she would soon be spent if he kept this up for long. His prospects were grim. Vivens wasn't the expert rider that Blaze was and his horse was injured, but the horse would have been bred for racing, while Raya had been bred and trained for combat, which meant courage and stamina rather than speed.

They rode down through a dip and then up a small slope. To his right still lay the vast dark shadow of the Great Umbra. As Candens crested the rise, he saw something which made his heart sink. High on a hill not far from the road ahead, he saw a tall tower, its top glinting with reflected light: a signal tower. That must have been where Blaze and Vivens had ridden from to intercept him.

There's nothing to fear, he thought. *The men in the tower don't yet know what happened to Blaze's party.*

Then he saw that there was something purposeful to a light flashing from mid-way up the tower. It was flashing directly towards him. Were they trying to temporarily blind him or his horse? That didn't make sense. He glanced back again.

Vivens had pulled his horse to a halt and was standing up in the stirrups. Something glittered in his hand, held high over his head. With a shock, Candens realised that he was sending a message to the tower with a hand-held mirror.

Sure enough, as Candens drew closer to the tower, he saw men in couriers' uniforms riding out from the gates. If he stayed on the road to the city, he was going to be trapped between Vivens at his rear and the Signallers ahead.

He looked to his left. No chance of any shelter there. To his right... He had only one chance, to try to hide within the Great Umbra itself. But the edge of its deep shadow was a considerable distance from the road and the slope down was steep and stony. Nevertheless, he turned Raya's head in that direction and his long-suffering steed obeyed. She skittered down the slope, every moment threatening to topple, but expertly keeping her balance. At last she found her feet on a bare, narrow trail which ran along the contours of the slope. Candens glanced up. There were riders there already, following. Hating to to it, he forced Raya off the secure trail and down the steep incline again, closer to the welcoming darkness. Finally, they reached a level area of ground where he could give her her head and they raced towards the edge of the umbra.

The transition between bright sunlight and the dimness of the shadow was a sudden one, only a couple of Raya's strides across. For a long moment he was blind and Raya faltered. But he dare not let her stop. Behind, he could hear the yells of the Signallers following. He needed to reach the deepest levels of the valley, where the light was least and the cold was the most bitter. Yet he couldn't follow any easy trail, or the Signallers would be sure to follow.

His eyes—and his horse's eyes—adjusted to the relative darkness slowly, too slowly. He had to haul back on the reins just before they both plunged over the sharp edge of a gorge. Raya swerved aside at the last moment. They turned to the right and began to canter along the cliff edge. Barely enough light came from the sunward sky for Candens to make out that it was four or five man-heights deep here; deep enough to break both his and Raya's bones if they crashed down into it. Down at the bottom he caught the faint gleam of running water, probably the continuation of the stream he had crossed earlier in the waking.

He glanced back up the slope in time to see the blue-and-gold of a courier's uniform wink out of sight as the rider left the illumination of the Sun and entered the sharp shadow cast by the sunward hills. Candens had no doubt that the Signallers would be determined to follow him wherever he went.

What to do?

If he *had* fallen into the gorge, he would probably be dead or badly injured. If he was dead, or if the Signallers *thought* he was dead, then the chase would stop. He began to turn over ideas, still riding as fast as he could, keeping Raya as close as possible to the cliff while not risking a sudden crumbling of the edge beneath her feet. They were forced to turn aside from time to time, however, to avoid rocky outcrops and boulders. These at least had the benefit of hiding him from the sight of his pursuers until they, too, could round the outcrops.

At his left, the gorge was slowly descending into the valley of the umbra and after a while he could no longer see to its bottom. Either there was less light to see, or the gorge was becoming still deeper.

He rounded a huge boulder, its surface glittering with a thin, twinkling sheen of frost. He pulled Raya to a halt and leapt from her back. How far ahead of his pursuers was he? It was hard to tell, but he thought he might have just enough time for a desperate ploy.

He fumbled frantically with the straps of his two saddle-bags and yanked them both off Raya's back. He ran to the edge of the cliff and dropped the first pack into the gorge, listening carefully. He heard it strike the cliff-face, then again and again, further and further down and finally a soft thud from far below. *Damn!* Moving three strides to the right, he dropped the second pack, with an accompanying silent prayer. A moment of silence and then he heard it bounce once, the sound of a shower of stones it had displaced, then nothing. Both packs were out of sight in the deep darkness of the gorge.

In the renewed silence he heard the sound of approaching hoof-beats.

He stroked Raya's head gently, trying to calm her. Her eyes were wide and faintly gleaming in the dim light, her nostrils flaring and her flanks still heaving with the exertion of their ride. She had served him well and it broke his heart to leave her to the Signallers. But she was a good steed and he hoped they would treat her well and take her into their own stables. In any case, he had no choice now.

He ran to where he had dropped the second pack. He turned his back to the gorge to face Raya again. Then, his heart racing, Candens stepped backwards over the edge of the cliff and into the darkness.

He fell.

After an awful moment which seemed to last an eternity, his feet struck the side of the cliff, then his knees and arms: hard, painful blows. He grasped frantically for a hold, felt stones ripping at his hands, but could not gain a grip. He slid down the cliff, scraping his hands and then was falling free again. Another strike with his boots, lost again. Then a terrible impact jarred through his legs and he felt himself toppling backwards away from the cliff-face. He stifled a cry of despair, sure that he was about to fall deeper into the gorge and to his death.

No. His back thumped onto a solid surface an instant later. Then the back of his head hit something hard. Pain flared and wandering points of light drifted through his sight. But he was down, or at least part-way down. And he wasn't dead. Not yet, anyway.

When his vision cleared a little, he peered upwards. He could see nothing except the sharp edges of the gorge, black silhouettes against the dim sky above. He lay still, listening. Pain from various parts of his body was distracting him, though, demanding attention. His back hurt along a diagonal from his right shoulder down to his lower left— the outline of his unstrung bow. His knees were complaining, his hands felt raw and torn and the back of his head was afire with pain. He tried to ignore all of this and use his ears.

After a moment, he picked out Vivens' voice above. Swearing.

"Damn him, he's left his horse. Where the Dark has he gone? Over the edge here? Or is he hiding somewhere in the scrub?"

Another man's voice. "Can't see a thing down there. Yonn! Get some kindling together. We'll need to get a torch burning, toss it down there." The voice belonged to an older man. It was familiar, but Candens couldn't yet place it.

Vivens again: "Jan! Quick, grab his horse! She's—oh, you idiot!"

Candens smiled. It seemed that Raya hadn't liked the look of the Signallers and had taken to her heels. Good for her.

More discussion followed above and Candens tried to assess his position. Wincing, he sat up slowly, quietly. He felt at his back and was able to unstrap his bow and felt along it, examining it for cracks. It seemed to have survived the impact. But it would be pointless to try to string it here—an arrow aimed upwards would lose almost all of its power before reaching the men above. Regretfully, he set it down.

He looked about him. It was very dark down here. The only light came from the dim ribbon of sky between the sides of the gorge above. He needed to get out of sight. Once the Signallers managed to kindle a fire, he was in danger of being spotted by the light of a burning brand. He didn't think they would risk trying to climb down unless they were certain he was in the gorge.

He rolled onto his hands and knees and crawled slowly about, feeling his way. To one side was the cliff-face. Moving away from it, only a few arms-lengths away in the other direction, his hand swung into empty space. If he concentrated hard, he could just determine that it was a shade darker below. The gorge went deeper still, then. He had landed on a ledge. Lucky. Perhaps.

He kept moving, trying to determine the limits of the ledge and also hunting for the second saddle-bag he had dropped. Surely it was here somewhere, unless it had bounced over the edge and was further down, like the first? But no, he had heard it stop moving.

He glanced up as there came an orange flare of light. The Signallers had their fire going. Not much time left, then. He contemplated dropping deeper into the gorge, but it was impossible to know if he would survive another fall. No point challenging his luck.

Now came a burning brand dropping from above, to his far left. It missed the ledge and fell deeper into the gorge, to be suddenly extinguished with a hiss as it struck the icy stream. Candens heard cursing from the men above and scuttled to be as close to the cliff-face as he could manage. He drew his cloak over his head and hoped to imitate a rock.

Here came another brand and this one struck the ledge and lay burning. But it wasn't emitting much light and Candens kept himself rigid under his cloak until it went out. There were no cries of triumph, just more curses. He hadn't been seen.

They tried a third brand and then a fourth, but they were moving along the edge of the gorge and each one fell further away from where Candens lay.

"The bastard isn't down there," he heard Vivens conclude. "He must be trying to hide up in the scrub somewhere."

"It doesn't matter either way." The older man again. "If he is down there he'll be dead soon. It's too steep to climb out, I'd say. He'll freeze or starve."

The voice was that of someone in command, used to being obeyed. Candens finally recognised it. It was Magister Solus, head of the Signallers.

"But if he's still up here," Vivens argued, "and he catches his horse again... Damn you, Jan, you should have caught the beast."

"She was too quick." A surly voice answered this time. "She was headed up out of the umbra anyway, like any sensible creature. The man we're after won't catch her. And we'll find him easily if he's on foot."

"Blaze won't be happy about this," Vivens said. "He wanted Candens alive if we could catch him, or his dead body if not."

"Blaze should have made sure of him in the first place," Solus said in a waspish tone. "Come on, let's remount and start searching. If he's on foot he can't have gone far."

Candens stayed still for a long while as the noises above diminished and then were finally gone. By now he was shivering. Solus' prediction of his fate seemed likely to be true. Even if he could climb the cliff-face, which was unlikely, what then? Walk out of the dark valley and down the main road into the city? It wouldn't take long for the Signallers to find him, but if he stayed in the Great Umbra, he would most likely die.

There was only one thing for it.

Candens struggled to his feet. He was going to have to climb further down into the gorge and find his other saddle-bag: the one that had his rations in it.

44

Campana

Ardens was clearly agitated. He strode back and forth across his study, his hands clasped behind his back, his face set in a grim expression. Sitting in a small armchair beneath the huge bookcase, Campana watched him, afraid at first that this fury was aimed at her. But Eccua sat calmly beside her and she gave a slight smile as Campana glanced her way for reassurance.

So far Campana knew nothing except that she had been summoned to Ardens' study the morning after her return from visiting Maryam and Adura. Finally Ardens spoke, his voice thick with emotion.

"Campana, we have some bad news, which makes me— both of us—very angry."

"Have I done something wrong, Father?"

"You? No; quite the contrary. In fact, we are angry on your behalf. The thing is, your pledge, or perhaps I should say your promised pledge, has been broken off by the Healers."

"Oh! But why?"

"I wish I knew. This is unprecedented. Magister Percuro and I have had an understanding for more than a millend that you would marry young Radians, his grandson. Do you know him?"

"Yes. He was here a few Shutterings ago, looking after Lambent." Campana felt a stab of regret. He'd been quite a nice young man, really.

"Well, you'll recall that a few centends ago his uncle Medeor was killed in a riding accident. Medeor had no sons,

237

so that made Radians the heir to the clan. That was not long before your Pledging Ceremony, when…"

"She knows what happened then, Ardens," Eccua reminded him mildly.

"Yes. So the pledging didn't go ahead. But the pledge between you and Radians was still promised, that was the arrangement."

"So why…?" Campana asked.

Ardens shook his head, baffled. "It's strange. Not long after you were taken, only a couple of Shutterings afterwards, Magister Percuro send me a signal suggesting that in the light of what had happened, our agreement ought to be put on hold until you were home again. I thought that odd at the time."

Anger surged in Ardens again. He thumped his fist into his open palm and seemed at a loss for how to go on. Eccua continued for him.

"Now that you are home safe, my dear—well, now the Magister says he's had the chance to rethink the matter and does not wish to go ahead with your pledging to Radians."

"Did he say why, Mother?"

Had Radians taken one look at Campana and decided he couldn't face being married to her for the rest of his life?

Her mother shook her head. "Not in any detail. The signal was quite brief."

"I'll have to go talk to him, I think," Ardens said. "He just said that while you were kidnapped he came to another arrangement for Radians which has now been finalised. If you had died, then of course that would have made sense. But this seems very hasty. He could have honourably called off such discussions when you were found alive. All I can imagine is that he fears that while you were imprisoned you might have been infected, as it were, by all of that rubbish the leader of The Daughters was spouting. Abolishing the pledging system, setting up a new role for women in society, all of that nonsense."

Eccua's mouth twitched a little towards a smile and Campana wondered how much of that 'nonsense' her mother secretly agreed with.

Ardens continued, speaking his thoughts aloud as he tried to make sense of what had happened. "He's an old man, very conservative. And of course, it was never expected that Radians would be the heir to the clan. Medeor and his wife might well have had a son in due course. Perhaps that's influenced Percuro. Perhaps he's become even more concerned to keep his clan on the straight and narrow. That's all I can think."

"I see. What will happen to *me*, then?"

"We'll do our best for you, Campana, though I can't hope for such an advantageous union as that with Radians. It might need to be an older man, a widower. Magister Castans of the Ropespinners lost his wife a centend ago, she died in childbirth, poor lady. It would be a useful connection. It's probably too soon to broach the matter with him, but—"

"And do I have any say in the matter, Father?"

Campana couldn't keep the anger from her voice and Ardens looked at her, startled. Eccua placed a calming hand on her arm, but Campana shrugged it off.

"You?" Ardens said, his eyebrows raised.

"Yes, me. I am a person, you know. Not simply a *connection*. I do have feelings. I don't want to be pledged to an old man."

"Oh, Castans isn't old. He's only about my own age..." Ardens' voice trailed off in uncharacteristic uncertainty, in the face of Campana's glare. He turned away, went to his desk and sat down.

"Campana, you mustn't—" Eccua began in a soft voice.

"Yes, I can; I must." Campana was fierce with her reply as she stood up. "Perhaps Magister Percuro is right. Maybe

239

I *have* been infected with new ideas. I want to know who you plan to pledge me to and I want to be able to say 'No' if it's someone I don't like."

Ardens' face flushed red. "Really, Campana..."

"There *is* a change coming," Campana warned him. "And I'm going to be part of it."

Ardens showed a flash of his old fire then. "You're just a girl; you have no idea what's best for your future. You need to leave these matters to me." He paused, then reluctantly, glanced at Eccua, as if realising his mistake. "To me and your mother."

Campana put her hands on his desk and leaned forward towards him, fighting to keep her emotions under control. Anger was her friend. Tears would be fatal.

"I am not *just a girl*." Campana spoke with barely controlled fury. "I'm a girl who has been promised in marriage to a stranger without her consent, then kidnapped, tied up, gagged, imprisoned, threatened, burned in a fire, drugged and delivered like a parcel. I've had more than enough of being forced to do what I don't want to do. I'm no longer a child. I know what is best for my own future."

Ardens leant back away from her vehemence, his face filling with bewilderment. He tried to speak and then stopped himself. As Campana turned away from him, she saw her mother was endeavouring to control her face, obviously suppressing a desire to smile.

Campana stalked to the door. As she opened it, she looked back.

"By the way Father, who is Radians pledged to now, if not to me?"

Ardens looked up at her and she saw for the first time that he was indeed becoming an old man, his face weary and sagging. His voice was distracted. "Radians? Oh, he's now pledged to Lucenta."

"Lucenta?"

"Yes. Of the Signallers. One of Hermia's cousins."

Her brain whirling, Campana stepped out and slammed the study door behind her.

⁓

Coding the message was slow and tedious work, but it was a skill every child in Sunfall was now taught at an early age. The Signallers' towers were by far the quickest way to communicate across distances which would otherwise take several Shutterings for a carrier to travel with a letter written on paper. Still burning with resentment after the conversation with her parents, Campana composed her message to Adura. She had resisted sending a message so far because signals were expensive, but she had a little money saved from her allowance.

Her message had to be brief. Each additional word in a signal cost extra money. Campana longed to speak to Adura and Maryam again face to face, but could hardly expect her father to agree to another such visit so soon after the last, particularly now, when he was angry with her. Her final draft came after much deliberation:

> News. My pledge to Radians cancelled by Healers, will marry Signaller instead. Part of plan? Worried about Lambent. Hermia controls him through papavera. Does anything she says. Any news on Calora? Want to talk to you again, can you visit?

Once it was all coded up, she folded the message over and wrote Adura's name and clan on the outside before giving it to Libeth to hand to the courier along with her father's signals. All she could do now was to wait for a reply. What she wasn't to know, however, is that when the reply did come, it would not come from Adura.

45

Adura

As Adura talked, her mother Lucida continued to draw a bright red thread through the embroidery on her lap, a design which would incorporate a scarlet rose when it was complete. Though she was not yet old, Lucida's hair was prematurely white, a family trait which appeared to accompany the calmness of spirit reflected in her face. Adura wished she had inherited that calmness.

Adura's first impulse after her discussion with Campana had been to conceal her plans from her parents, but then recognised that it had been such secrecy which had ended with her becoming an unwilling participant in a crime.

Yet if she was going to find out what was going on, she needed more freedom of action than her father had been allowing her since what he still insisted on calling her 'disgrace'. Hence this appeal to her mother.

Lucida sat in silence, still stitching, as Adura told her what she had learned from Campana, their suspicions of Magistra Calora and perhaps of the whole Signallers' clan.

"How sure are you of what Campana says?" Lucida asked when Adura drew to the end of her account. "I haven't spoken to her. She's of pledging age, of course, but some young people are still quite childish at that age. Are you sure that this isn't just some fantastic tale that she's made up?"

"Yes, I'm sure," Adura said. "She's remarkably mature for her age and she has been through a lot of suffering. I'm terribly ashamed of my role in that and I want to try to make up for it as best I can."

"What are you proposing?"

"What if we could find proof that the Signallers were involved in the incident at the Pledging, in the kidnapping? Surely the whole clan must have been involved, not just Magistra Calora."

Lucida looked thoughtful as she changed the red thread in her needle for a darker shade to complete the shadowed petals in the design. "You may be right, but it's not certain. I knew Calora when we were children, you know, though we were never friends. She was born into the Weavers Clan. Since then I've met her a few times at balls and weddings and so on. I must say that I never warmed to her. She always seems to be looking for some advantage, hiding some motive behind every question she asks. But I can't see what advantage it would be to her to disrupt the Pledging. It doesn't make sense."

"I suppose that's what we need to work out," Adura said.

Lucida sighed, folded her embroidery and pushed the needle into the bundle still threaded. "I don't see what you can possibly do, Adura. Campana's story of seeing a glimpse of Calora's face won't convince anyone. People will agree with her father... it was just a hallucination caused by the drug she was taking for the pain."

"I have some ideas," Adura ventured. "As a start, I want to go and stay with my friend Alba for a Shuttering or two. She's a niece of the Glassmoulders, you'll recall. I'm almost certain she was one of the others in the Daughters of the Dark. She might know something which is useful. But I'll need Father's permission to leave the manor. I don't want to tell him about our suspicions of the Signallers just yet."

"Leave it to me. So long as your new maid goes with you I don't think he'll complain. You will need to be very cautious about what you say in front of Emm. You can be sure she'll pass anything you say on to your father."

"Thank you so much." Adura looked down at her lap, thinking, then looked up again. "If I *do* find out something, find some evidence which proves that the Signallers were

David R. Grigg

behind the kidnapping, what do you think father would do?"

Lucida's lips twitched in cynical amusement. "He would certainly destroy any such evidence and forbid you ever to speak of it again."

"No!"

"Yes. We really can't afford to offend the Signallers, Adura. They have become one of the most powerful of clans. And they are one of our biggest customers. Every signal tower uses scores of our mirrors."

Adura bowed her head in weary resignation. "It's hopeless, then. I might as well not try."

"I didn't say that. Personally, I would be very interested to know what the Signallers are doing and why. The information could be very useful in our dealings with them. I'll find a way of using it, never fear. In our society, my dear, women can't be seen to act directly, or only in rare circumstances. Instead, we work behind the scenes, use our influence over our husbands and sons. That influence, you will learn, can be very substantial."

"But that's all wrong!" Adura protested. "Women shouldn't have to work by such shadowy means, but openly."

"You are right, of course. In the long run things will change." Lucida paused. "You know that I was born into the Stonemasons. My aunt said to me once that there are two ways of cutting a hole in a large stone. One way is using the hard blows of a hammer on a chisel. That may work, but it creates a lot of noise and may perhaps break the stone in two, making it useless. The other way is the steady drip of water on the stone over many years, which gradually wears away a smooth hole. Our way, women's way, is the way of water."

"Fine words, Mother." Adura stood up suddenly, anger reddening her face. "But it's the counsel of despair. Give me

244

a hammer and a chisel and damn the chance of breaking the stone!"

Lucida was startled. Then after an instant's pause she sat back and laughed. "Oh, I love you, Adura. I admire your spirit. Perhaps our society does need a sharp knock with a hammer after all. Very well. See what you can find out. But for God's sake, be *careful!*"

46

Candens

The climb down to the bottom of the gorge had been very difficult. In fact, it had been less of a climb than a series of controlled falls among showers of stones. The cliff face wasn't solid, but made up of crumbling, soft earth embedded with occasional rocks and stones. Climbing back up, as Solus had predicted, would be all but impossible.

A thin stream of bitterly cold water ran along the floor of the gorge. Where the water pooled and slowed, it was glazed with ice. A little way upstream, he made out a small rocky waterfall, here and there sporting long icicles. It would be treacherous to climb if he tried to go that way.

It was darker down here than he had ever experienced before. His eyes were adjusting as best they could, but it took him a very long time to discover where his first saddle-bag had fallen. He pulled it dripping out of the freezing water.

As best he could in the limited light—just the barest glow at the sunward side of the sky between the edges of the gorge above—he sorted out his possessions and consolidated the essential items into a single pack. He donned most of the extra clothes he had been carrying in the saddle-bags, so that he was swathed in several layers, bulking out his body and probably making him look ridiculous. But that didn't matter here.

After some thought, he did retain his bow and the handful of arrows he still possessed and tied them together onto the outside of the pack. It was unlikely that he would have a need for a weapon down here, but it would be risky to leave it behind. Then he set off along the gorge, following the flow of the stream. In the far distance, barely audible, he heard the sound of bells tolling. The ninth peal of this waking. It felt odd to hear something so familiar in such a desolate, alien place. It must have come from the repeater tower on the Glassmoulders' Estate.

Candens persisted, trying to find his way on rocks and small areas of gravel in order to keep his boots out of the water. But the gorge was narrow and there was more and more ice as the stream descended, making the rocks slippery and treacherous. Still, he forced himself onwards.

He heard another distant bell, just when he expected it. Despite all that had happened, he realised, he had been subconsciously keeping the count since the last peal; accurately, too. His father would have been pleased with him, he thought with a wry smile. More bells sounded, ever so faintly, as he struggled on. Then sounded the unmistakable four notes of the Shuttering Peal. *Time for bed!* Candens was weary enough to lie down, but to lie down and sleep here in the cold would be fatal. He had to get out of this gorge. It must end somewhere. He kept on moving.

It was getting colder the deeper he went into the valley of the Great Umbra. He shivered, despite his exertion and the many layers he was now wearing. Solus had been right. It was all too likely that he would freeze to death down here. All he could do was to keep on moving, trying to warm his body by sheer effort.

He struggled down the gorge, hearing no more bells. The after-Shuttering bells were always muted by the ringers and would be too soft to hear at this distance. The stream was now clogged with ice and was spreading from one side of the cleft to the other. It became harder and harder to find rocks to stand on, but at least there were patches of ice solid enough to bear his weight, though occasionally his boots broke through into the water beneath. They were good Militia-issue, however and so far his feet remained dry.

Finally, he reached a point where solid ice filled the gorge from side to side. It was strong enough to walk on, though slippery. The gorge opened out to a level area of ice stretching wide to each side and far ahead, forming a frozen... lake, perhaps. This wasn't the sea, just a low area between the hills behind and those ahead, which had been filling with frost and water from the stream he had been following, for how long? Hundreds of millends? Thousands? It couldn't have been forever, or surely this valley would be full to the brim with solid ice like this now. These were foolish, unhelpful thoughts, but it gave him something to do and Candens couldn't stop his mind from trying to think out such matters.

He was glad now that he had left Raya behind. Even if there had been some way to get her safely down into the gorge and to reach here without breaking a leg, there was no feed here and no liquid water for her to drink. This was a dreary, desolate place where nothing grew and nothing would ever grow. Nothing could live down here.

He turned left and started walking along the edge of the lake where the going was easier. He was often able to leave the ice and walk along solid ground, though it was frozen hard as rock. It was a little brighter, too, now that he was out of the dark confines of the gorge and there was more of the sky visible. A diffuse glow shone above the far hills, indicating the presence of the hidden Sun.

Candens' plan, such as it was, consisted of heading up the slopes of the sunward hills ahead, crossing over the ridge back into the sunlight and then descending into the estate of the Glassmoulders. Once there, he might be able to seek the help of Magister Nitens. Assuming he made it that far, what then? Would he be able to convince Commander Fervens to take action against the powerful Signaller Clan? *Could* the Commander take action? It seemed a remote hope from here. Like everyone else in Sunfall, the Militia had grown to depend on the swift communications provided by the Signallers.

Giving up these futile thoughts for the moment, he trudged along the icy shore. For a long while, nothing occurred during this trek except that the cold intensified and Candens drifted off into a half-dazed state, his gaze continually cast down to check his footing on the slippery, frozen mud of the lake shore.

He wasn't sure what eventually made him look up. But when he did, he stopped with an oath. Something loomed up ahead, like the silhouette of a giant man with dark arms reaching up to the weak light of the sky. For an instant he felt a surge of panic and stepped back abruptly. Moments later, his heart still racing, he realised that whatever this was, it wasn't moving. Cautiously, he moved on, coming closer. Finally, he realised that it was a huge tree, far, far larger than any of the orchard trees with which he was familiar and one denuded of any foliage. He approached it cautiously and felt its massive trunk with wonder. It was coated with a thin layer of frost, its trunk so wide that he couldn't reach around it with his arms. It was cold and as hard as stone. Indeed, this might well be the statue of a giant tree; but why would someone make such a thing and place it here in the dark? No, it must once have been a real, living tree. But how could it ever have taken root and grown here in the endless dark and cold? He shook his head in amazement.

After a while, he went on again and encountered another such frozen tree, then another and another. There were dozens here, a whole frozen, gigantic orchard. Most of the trees were still standing, but several had fallen, branches shattered over the ground. He wondered what kind of massive fruit such trees would have produced. They would be the size of watermelons, surely. It was a strange mystery.

Then it occurred to him that frozen trees like this might well be the secret source of the prized timber sold by the

Woodminers Clan; hard-grained wood of a length unmatched by any from an orchard. Was there another cluster of such giant trees in the large umbra that lay behind the Woodminers' estate? Yet their clan name suggested that their wood was being excavated rather than cut down. This was pointless speculation. The Woodminers would never tell anyone the answer, of course.

His body gave a violent spasm. It wasn't so much a shiver as an all-over jolt that rattled his teeth. He had been standing still for too long, staring up at the huge trees. He could no longer feel his feet. His gloved hands, paradoxically, felt as though they were being roasted before a fire.

A fire...

Could he build a fire here? It was rarely necessary to start a flame in Sunfall, but it was a skill taught in the Militia so that torches could be lit or cooking fires built when away from an estate and his pack contained a kit with flints and tinder. There had been no fuel during his long trek down the gorge, but here... All around him was scattered wood from the giant trees, but it was all in large pieces, frozen and encased in a layer of frost. They would never take fire from the tiny flame of his tinder. He needed something smaller.

He began to gather some of the smallest pieces of wood he could find, a tiring process which involved him kicking hard with his boots to free pieces of branch from the frozen ground and from each other. After a time, exhausted, he had to stop. He had gathered a bare two handfuls of icy pieces of wood. None could be described as twigs. Most were too thick to catch easily even if they were not frozen. Shuddering as he did so, he pulled open the layers of his clothing and shoved down the pieces of wood against the already cold flesh of his chest and stomach. He stumbled around, desperately trying to keep awake and warm enough for his body to reluctantly thaw the wood. For all he knew, even if he could warm them, they would prove water-sodden. Still, he had to try.

Then, almost in the last moments, he realised that he did have access to a little dry, unfrozen wood. Cursing himself for his stupidity, he took off his pack. His fingers would barely obey him as he struggled to untie his bow and the bundle of arrows. The arrows were easy to break into pieces, though he did so with regret. His only remaining weapon now was his short dagger. But the enemy here was the cold and it was crueller than any human enemy.

The bow was much more difficult to break, as its supple willow-wood had been designed to flex with strain. He had to wedge it in a gap between two frozen lumps of wood and push hard against it until it snapped in two as he gasped in relief. Again. He had to do it again. He wedged the longer of the remaining pieces in the gap and did the same as before. With a shorter length, it was even more difficult. Using all of his remaining strength he pushed at it until it suddenly broke and he felt forward onto the hard ground, sobbing with exertion.

He couldn't go on. It would have to be enough. Choosing a spot nearly circled by large fallen chunks of wood, he used the pieces of arrow and the broken shards of his bow to create the makings of a fire. He pulled out the pieces of wood which had been against his flesh and leaned a few of them against the pile of dry wood. He didn't know if they were warm or dry enough yet and could only pray that the bow-wood would thaw them further and allow them to catch.

He took the tinder-box out of his pack. Again, his cold fingers fought against him, but he managed to hold the flints. Strike. Strike. Strike. *Come on, damn it!* Strike. A spark. Another. *Come on!* The tinder, a small amount of shredded cloth which had been soaked in lamp-oil and then dried, finally caught and showed a tiny flame. He held a piece of arrow against it with a shaking hand. It stubbornly refused to catch for the longest time, as the tinder began to gutter out. Then at last it began to char and finally caught fire. He put it at the base of the prepared stack and fed it with some strips of dry cloth he tore from his undershirt. The flame spread and the arrows were burning. Then the bow began to char and finally to burn. Patiently, step by step, he fed the flames more and more pieces of the wood he had thawed against his flesh. He stacked the larger pieces around, leaning them against the logs of frozen wood.

Eventually, the fire was large enough to warm his hands by. They hurt like the very dark. At last he could sit back, resting against the great trunk of a fallen tree, wearied to the very death but gaining enough warmth from the fire to feel that he wouldn't freeze just yet.

He fell asleep. Then with a jerk, he was awake again. If he slept now and the nascent fire went out, he would die. He struggled to his feet again and looked for a larger piece of wood that might last for several bells before it burned through. He found one such piece sitting up at an angle, propped on another. His energy almost completely spent, he kicked and kicked, despairing, before it finally broke loose.

He stumbled back to the fire with it and balanced it above the flames across the frozen logs. All he could do was hope that the fire beneath would thaw it enough that it would catch fire before it was too late.

That done, he slumped down again, completely spent. He had to sleep. Whether he would freeze and die as he slept or would wake again was a matter in the hands of God.

Surely this was the lowest point of his life? How had it come to this? Would his fortunes ever swing back up again, like the bob on a pendulum?

With these despairing thoughts, sleep finally claimed him.

Candens awoke, shivering violently. But he was alive.

The fire was still alight, now reduced to a small pile of glowing coals. His bow and arrows had long since been consumed. The branch he had bridged over the flames had fallen into the fire and the three frozen logs he had chosen to be a hearth had also thawed and were partially charred through.

Candens forced himself to his feet, though every muscle was stiff and painful. He kicked the remaining loose pieces of wood into the coals then stepped well away from the fire and relieved his bladder.

How long had he been asleep? It was impossible to tell. He had long since lost track of the subconscious count in his head and until he caught the faint sound of another peal he would have no idea of the time. Had the Unshuttering peal sounded? Would he have heard it if it had? And what did it matter anyway? Here in the dark shadow of the valley, all time was alike.

Candens found himself wondering about his clan's obsession with time, the whole meaning of their business and their trade. What did it matter what time it was? Why did everyone need to close their shutters at the same time, open them at the same time? Did humanity really need such regulation?

However, madness lay that way. If he had ever expressed such doubts back at the manor, his father Ardens might have cast him out of the clan on that basis alone.

In the corner of his eye, something caught his attention in the sky, in the extreme darkwards direction. Little faint points of light, scattered here and there. He'd never noticed those before. If he tried to look directly at them, they faded from sight. Only if he looked slightly away could he catch them at the edges of his vision. He briefly wondered what they were, before he realised that he had no time for such idle speculations. If he was to live, he needed to begin moving before he froze.

David R. Grigg

He ate a little of his rations as he squatted by the fire. He stared at the coals, wishing there was an easy way to carry them with him. He contented himself by gathering together a bundle of warm, dry pieces of wood from the outskirts of the fire to act as kindling for another. He still had his tinder box and enough tinder to start another flame. He was hoping, though, that if he pushed himself hard enough to keep walking he would not need to light another fire.

He gazed longingly at the faint glow above the hills ahead of him. If he could only reach the warmth of the Sun again... After that? It didn't matter. He needed to focus on one goal at a time.

He packed his things together and set off, still following the edge of the lake of ice past the orchard of giant trees. As he trudged along, he caught the faint sound of a peal of bells and made out *DON! DIN! DUM! DAN!* It was the mid-waking peal! His sense of time had been completely thrown off.

A long while later, he saw a thin outline beginning to appear against the sky in the sunward direction as he approached. At first he thought it might just be another giant tree. No, this outline was not branched but straight. Puzzled, Candens made a slight change of direction to head towards it.

Soon, he realised what it was. A skeleton tower, its black bones framed against the sky's faint glow. Candens suppressed a superstitious shudder. Who would have thought that one of the strange towers would have been built here, down in the Great Umbra, far from the warmth of the Sun? No one knew why the twisted constructions had been made long ago, or by whom, but surely they must have been built for some purpose. Perhaps by human beings who craved light and warmth? He discounted the tales of gods or inhuman monsters passed around by the Dims.

254

Something was strange, though, about *this* skeleton tower. For one thing, as he walked closer, he could see that it wasn't all twisted about like the towers he had seen before. Instead of bars of godsteel bent into strange, curved shapes, as though melted in a forge, the bones of this tower appeared to be straight and level, making a neat frame. And there was something more. Although the upper levels of this tower were empty and bare like every other skeleton tower he had seen, as he moved closer he saw that the lower levels were enclosed by walls of some solid material. Seeing it like this and ignoring its impossible height, it could almost be taken for a manor building.

At last, he came right up to the tower. The walls seemed to be made of solid sheets of some substance, each several man-heights tall and broad, coated with a thick layer of white frost. Candens reached out and felt the nearest surface. Even through his glove, he could feel its deep cold. Was the base of the tower embedded in ice? He rubbed at it and to his surprise, the frost showered away, revealing a clear, smooth surface which he couldn't scratch, even with his dagger. Was it very hard ice? Or was this glass? He looked up at the size of the panel, doubting it. Surely the Glassmoulders had never in the whole history of their clan made a continuous piece of glass this large?

Candens peered through the gap in the frost. It was too dark inside to see much. If this was a manor, then it was a manor of ghosts. Then, just for an instant, he thought he saw something within, something moving rapidly, as though startled. But then it was gone. Just a trick of his eyes or of his mind, perhaps, as he strained to see anything. Whatever it had been, it didn't happen again.

Giving it up, he walked slowly all the way around the tower, trying to find some kind of door. He couldn't find any way in.

From beyond the ridge ahead came the weak sound of another peal. The eighth peal of the waking. Still greatly puzzled by this peculiar building, Candens recognised that he was wasting time and energy again. He had to push on, or die.

Nevertheless, the mystery of the strange skeleton tower nagged at him as he trudged on. If it was some kind of dwelling—a manor for humans, not ghosts—why had it been built here in the dark and cold? And when had it been built? A very long time ago, he guessed.

Like the giant trees, the ghost manor suggested that there had been a time when this valley hadn't been dark and cold. But that was impossible, wasn't it? The Sun could not move. Well, that wasn't quite true, if the Holy Book of the Sun was to be believed. Candens had always considered its words to be more inspirational and poetic than literally true. Yet the Book said that the Sun had once been distant from the Earth, but had shone too little light to sustain life, so that God had made it fall from the sky. But the Book was silent on what kind of life might have existed before that. Had there been people, plants and animals in the world back then, shivering in what little light and heat had been provided by the distant Sun? Could the giant trees have grown then? Could the skeleton towers and the ghost manor have been built in that far remote time?

Candens, absorbed in these thoughts, tripped over a rock and sprawled on his face. *Stupid!* Candens pushed himself wearily back to his feet. *Must keep on walking.*

He forced himself on. Eventually, he heard the Shuttering Peal, the bells a little louder now. A little after that, he was rewarded for his perseverance by a slow but continual rise in the slope of the ground. He had reached the beginnings of the hills which made up Moulders' Arm. Ahead, up a long, wearying climb, would be the top of the ridge, sunlight and warmth. Life!

And a society at the mercy of the Signallers.

47

Adura

The easiest way for Adura to reach the Glassmoulders' estate from her own was to take a carriage down to the coast past the Boatbuilders' estate and take the ferry there. Ships like the ferry always hugged the edge of the coast; a direct route straight across the bay would take them too close to the Sun and its overwhelming heat.

Adura was accompanied on the journey by Emm, the new maid her father Ignis had insisted on appointing to keep an eye on her. Emm was a humourless, middle-aged woman and Adura found her a dispiriting companion. Still, she reflected, perhaps Emm was a punishment she had deserved and in any case there was nothing she could do about it.

During the long journey there was not much to do except sit under the shade and think about what Campana had told her at their meeting and in the surprising signal she had sent two Shutterings ago. Why had the Healers broken off Campana's promised pledge to Radians? Was it because he was now the heir? It was surely significant that he was instead now to be pledged to a member of the Signallers' clan. But *what* did it signify? It was all a puzzle.

At last, the ferry approached the port and they drew up and disembarked. Alba was waiting for them in a coach and the two young women embraced, exchanging pleasantries and a little gossip. But their maids were with them and it was not until they were alone at Alba's manor that Adura could explain the real reason for her visit.

David R. Grigg

Alba, after a moment's alarm, admitted readily enough that she had been one of the Daughters involved in the kidnapping, but she was reluctant to go further.

"I don't want to talk about it." Alba shivered and slid far back into her chair as though to distance herself from Adura's words. "Commander Fervens was here only two Shutterings ago. He kept asking me and asking me about The Daughters: where I was during the Pledging, who could vouch for me, where I had gone since, what I knew; it was awful."

"Did you tell him anything?"

"Not really. But he *knew*; I could tell I wasn't fooling him. He knew that I was one of The Daughters. One of the *bad* ones."

"We weren't *bad*," Adura objected with a degree of impatience. "We had good intentions. We thought we were working for a worthwhile cause, but we were misled by Raven."

"Ugh, that woman..."

"What would you say if I told you that we know who she is?"

"What would I say?" Alba's face showed her puzzlement. "I would say that I already know. She's Magistra Calora of the Signallers."

"What?" Adura was startled by this response. "How do you know that?"

"Oh, it was easy to tell. All sorts of things: her height and how she walks, for example; the shape of her shoulders and back. I'm an artist, don't forget. I spend a lot of time looking at peoples' shapes and how they move. I already knew that *you* were one of us, the same way. Calora has been here with Magister Solus many times to talk to my uncle and aunt, so I know her pretty well. And then there's her voice. The mask disguised it and she tried to make it sound different, but

258

because I was already sure about who she was, it was still recognisable as hers."

"But why didn't you say anything?"

"Who would I have told? We weren't supposed to talk to each other. Besides, I've always been a bit afraid of Calora. She's very spiteful. I just wanted to keep quiet and not attract attention."

"Didn't you ever wonder why she was leading the Daughters, carrying out the kidnapping?"

Alba looked down at her hands, a slight flush in her face. "She's such a strong, forceful woman. I imagined that she was unhappy in her marriage to Magister Solus. I thought that she must genuinely feel that women are being treated unfairly and that pledging is wrong. But after a while, I... oh, I don't know Adura. I really want to forget all about it; put it all behind me."

Adura pondered all this. While it was good to have this confirmation of Raven's identity, there was still no actual proof they could use even to accuse Calora; only the word of Campana, who claimed to have seen Calora's face; and that of Alba, who said her artistic skills had enabled her to identify Raven by the way she stood and moved. None of that would hold water at a Grand Council Court—the forum where clan members could be put on trial and be judged by their peers—particularly when the Council President was now soon likely to be Magister Solus.

And *why* was Solus acting as Council President? Because the previous President, old Magister Neptus of the Boat-builders, had been so traumatised by the events of the Pledging that he couldn't continue in the role. Might that have been at least part of the reason for Calora's actions? Did Solus know about what Calora was doing? Was the whole Signallers clan behind what was going on? Adura felt sick and helpless. How could the other clans be warned of the danger posed by the Signallers? How could the plot be exposed?

David R. Grigg

She had absolutely no idea.

48
Candens

His head bowed, he staggered up the steep slope, barely able to stay upright. Exhaustion dragged at every limb and numbed his mind. He had lost all track of time, of where he was, even of who he was. All he was able to do was to keep on moving, placing one foot in front of another, the ground so shadowed and dim that he could barely even see his feet. Despite the cold, sweat continually trickled down from his scalp and into his eyes.

Something changed in an instant and he looked up. Bright light. He cried out in shock as his eyes reacted with pain. He stumbled, lost his footing and fell onto his back, sliding down the slope a short distance. A burning after-image filled his vision and took long, long moments to fade enough so that he could see again.

In his weariness, Candens took a long while to recognise what had happened. Then, on hands and knees, he crept back up the slope again, into the light, towards the Sun.

He was at the top of a ridge, looking down over a grassy slope dotted with sheep. Before him was the bay and in the centre of its waters, wreathed in blazing swirls of cloud, was the glorious, life-restoring Sun. Candens put his face into his hands and wept with relief. He had traversed the Great Umbra and was still alive.

The moment of relief was short-lived, however, as a rough voice hailed him from nearby.

"Hoy! You!"

A little way down the sunward slope, a bulky man dressed in the rough woollen clothes of a shepherd was running up towards him, brandishing his sturdy crook. Candens tried to get to his feet, but his legs refused to obey. It was all he could do to raise his arm as the man swung the crook towards him. It smacked painfully into Candens' forearm and he cried out in pain.

"Away! Shadow thief! We've had enough of your kind!" the shepherd roared as he raised the crook for another blow.

"Stop!" Candens croaked out, his voice as frozen as his body had been. "Not thief. Need help! Please!"

The shepherd paused, the crook still raised over his head.

"Who are you then?" he demanded. "What are you doing here, creeping up from the umbra among the Magister's flock?"

Candens slumped back and lay on his side in the grass, overcome with exhaustion. "Walked," he forced out. "All the way, across the umbra."

"Across the—" The shepherd's tanned face showed his doubt. Then he took a few moments to examine Candens in more detail: his tunic; his pack; his boots; before asking his next question. "You a militiaman?"

"Was," Candens gasped. "Please help."

Darkness was creeping in at the edges of his vision despite the brightness of the Sun. How could that be? But it went on and the bright sky shrank until it was at the end of a long dark tunnel. The last thing he saw at the end of the tunnel was the shepherd's puzzled face. Then Candens' own personal umbra swallowed him and for a long while he knew nothing.

⌒

He awoke to the tantalising smell of something cooking. A considerable amount of wood smoke, too, which made him want to sneeze. He opened his eyes and tried to sit upright, but for the moment it was beyond his strength.

He was in a small round hut, its walls made from interlaced wicker sealed with mud. Light spilled in from an open doorway. He turned his head away from its brightness and saw the muscular shepherd squatting next to a small fire, a terracotta pot hung over it.

The man turned and grunted when he saw that Candens was awake. He picked up a small steep-sided bowl and dipped it into the pot. It came up dripping and he shook it lightly before bringing it across to where Candens lay.

"Mutton stew," he said. "Have some."

Candens sipped at the hot stew, tentatively at first and then greedily. Chunks of sheep meat, carrots and parsnips with a lacing of some herb he didn't recognise. It was delicious—the first hot food he had had for many Shutterings—and it was all gone quickly. The shepherd took the bowl and refilled it.

"Thank you," Candens said. "Thank you...?" He left the sentence hanging, a question.

"Han. My name's Han. Who the hell are you and what the dark were you doing down in the umbra?"

"I'm Candens of the..." He stopped, remembering his new status with regret. "Just Candens. And I was in the Great Umbra because I was running away from someone."

Han grunted. "You must have been pretty damned scared of them to go down into the umbra."

"Yes. I was. They were trying to kill me."

Han squatted on the ground. There didn't seem to be any furniture in the hut other than the bed, or much in the way of other possessions. Candens couldn't see another bowl, for example. Han was dressed in sheepskin, clasped at the waist with a thick leather belt. In the belt was a wooden-handled knife, the blade sharpened flint.

"Who were they?" Han asked, reasonably enough.

Candens paused. "I'd rather not tell you just now. They were members of a certain clan."

"Brights? You're a Bright. I can tell by the pretty way you talk."

It was clear that "pretty" was not intended as a compliment.

"I used to be a member of a clan. But I did something wrong and they cast me out. I'm clanless now."

"No better than me, then," said Han with an amused look.

Candens paused for a moment, thinking over his privileged life until his expulsion and his reduced circumstances now. "I don't know that I ever was better than you. Luckier, perhaps."

Han scowled at that, his face darkening. "Those are fine words, but they're full of air. All the Brights I ever knew treated me like an insect they were too proud to step on."

"You're right. I know many people who behave like that towards Dims. People I don't like very much. Maybe I was once like that, too. But I was in the Militia with a Dim called Jud. He was a damn good man and a friend. I don't think badly of Dims now."

Han's scowl did not lessen. "One thing you obviously didn't learn, young Bright, is that we don't like being called *Dims*. We're shepherds, or field-workers, or servants, or miners, or whatever. There's a better word for the lot of us than Dims. You could try using it in future."

Candens frowned. "What word?"

"*People.*"

Candens flushed with embarrassment. "I'm sorry," he said. "I'll remember that."

A long silence followed while Han stirred the pot again and served himself some stew in the same bowl he had given Candens.

"You say you were part of a clan. Which one?"

That seemed harmless enough. "The Bellringers."

"A Bellringer?" Han gazed out of the doorway, pondering. When he went on, his voice was a trace more friendly. "There's a bell-tower two peals walk away from here. I could show you the way."

Candens shook his head. "Thank you, but no. I don't think they'd be prepared to help me now that I've been cast out."

He tried to remember which of his relatives was currently posted to the repeater tower on Moulders' Arm. Someone less accommodating than his cousin Argent, he was sure.

"No," he went on, "it's Magister Nitens who I want to speak to."

Han examined Candens sceptically. "He'll not see you. You won't even get in past the manor gates. You may talk like a Bright, but you look like a bog-cutter the way your clothes are now."

Candens looked down at himself. It was true. He had discarded his cloak somewhere on the long climb up the dark slope of Moulder's Arm, its weight not rewarded by the extra warmth it had given him. His tunic was filthy and torn, his pants muddied. To one side of the bed were his boots, which Han must have removed for him. They too were muddy and scuffed. His pack was in a similar disreputable state. He could clean off the mud and some of the dirt, perhaps even get Han's help to sew up the worst of the rips, but at best he would still look like a vagabond.

And he had to keep reminding himself that he was in fact now clanless, his social status little better than that of a Dim—than a field-worker, he corrected himself. Magister Nitens of the Glassmoulders had been close to his father Ardens. Surely he would have been told by now of Candens' expulsion. If Candens turned up at the manor, filthy and ragged, babbling some fantastical tale about the Signallers, with no proof other than what he claimed to have heard... No, it was hopeless.

"I'll have to get back to the city, then," Candens decided with a sigh. "What's the best way from here? The ferry, I suppose?"

"Yes. You'll have to pay for your passage, though, which means that you might need this."

Han reached over and picked up a purse from the ground. It was Candens' purse. He tossed it in his hand as the rings inside jingled, looking thoughtful. Candens was silent for a long moment, sensing that how he reacted to this was critical to what happened next.

"You could keep that, of course," he acknowledged.

Han was far bigger and more powerful than Candens, even if Candens wasn't feeling as weak as he did now.

"I could." Han stared at Candens without blinking.

"I would be grateful if you didn't, though. I thank you for the help you've given me. I would be pleased if you would let me pay for the stew I have eaten."

"My very best," Han said. "I charge two silvers a bowl. Do you want another?"

It was an outrageous price. Paying for the two bowls he had already eaten would take almost half the meagre amount of money he had left in the purse. Candens thought that Han must know that, had already counted the contents of the purse.

Still, Han was being honourable enough, in his own way. He could easily have killed Candens, or simply thrown him down into the darkness of the umbra stripped of his clothing and taken the whole contents of the purse, plus Candens' dagger, whose metal blade was valuable in its own right. No one would have known.

"I won't have another bowl, I thank you," Candens said. "But I'm happy to pay for what I've eaten already." *Happy* wasn't his true feeling, but he had no option.

"Done."

Han opened the purse and deftly removed four silver rings before tossing it back to Candens.

"I'd better set off, then," Candens said, trying to struggle back to his feet.

"Stay there. The Shuttering is only two bells away. You can sleep here and leave nextwake. It's a good three peal walk from here to the port; you'll need your strength back. Rest up. I have to go and round up the sheep to go into the Shuttering pen over the ridge." Han grinned. "You can even have another bowl of stew, if you like, on the house."

49

Adura

Adura had slept at the Glassmoulders' manor. She and her friend Alba had spent a long time the previous waking talking through their shared time in the Daughters of the Dark and doing their best to make up a list of the other young women they thought had been involved with them. Now Adura and her maid Emm were going home, heading for the ferry port in the Glassmoulders' carriage. Just as the carriage wound its way around a corner of the hill leading down to the port, Adura heard the driver curse.

"Get off the road, you filthy oaf!"

She heard the driver's whip crack. An answering, angry curse came back up from whoever had been blocking the road. Adura frowned as the carriage rolled past. Through the window she saw a disheveled, dusty figure with a ragged beard standing beside the road. It was only a brief glimpse and then the man was behind them...

"Wait!" she cried out and then hammered hard on the partition dividing her from where the driver sat. "Stop!" The carriage slowed and she hammered again. "Stop, I say!"

The driver slid open a grill and she saw his rough, red face peering down. "Mistress? Is something wrong?"

"Yes! I want to talk to that man we just passed. Wait for him, make some sort of sign. Oh, forget it. I'll get out."

"What is it, Adura?"

Emm looked alarmed, but Adura ignored her. She opened the carriage door, pushed out the folding step and used it to clamber down onto the dusty road. She looked back up the hill. The man had resumed walking and she waved urgently at him.

She had recognised him at the first glance, though his hair was whitened from the dust of the road and his equally dusty beard was unkempt and longer than she had ever seen it before. He looked like an old man, slouched over and weary in every step.

As he came closer, he saw who it was who had hailed him. His face brightened and he made an effort to straighten up.

"Adura?"

"Candens, why are you here? And why are you on foot?" In a surge of pity, she asked, "Did you... did you have to sell your horse?"

He smiled, which gladdened Adura's heart as he shook his head slightly, releasing a shower of dust. "No. I didn't sell Raya. But I had to let her go. It's a long story. I think... I think I'm too tired to tell it right now."

"Get in the carriage. Come on."

"No, no, I can't. You shouldn't be seen with me."

She frowned. "Why ever not?"

He gestured down at his ragged, dirt-covered clothes. "For one thing, look at me. And for another... I seem to have made some powerful enemies. You shouldn't put yourself in danger."

Adura's hands landed on her hips. "I don't care how you look, or about your enemies, for that matter. Get in. I need to talk to you. I'm not leaving you here by the side of the road."

Candens laughed for the first time in a long while.

"You always knew your mind, Adura. All right. Let me try and dust myself off a little first."

Candens stepped away from her and began to beat at his pants and tunic. Clouds of dust arose. He ran his fingers through his hair and beard and shook himself once more before coming back to the carriage.

Emm stared at Candens in disbelief as Adura gestured for him to climb up. "Adura! You can't bring this man with us! Your father..."

"Can't I just?" Adura said. "I tell you I can. My father will understand when I explain it to him. He knows Master Candens here."

Emm sat back, her mouth taking on a disapproving shape, as Candens sat himself down opposite her in the carriage. Adura sat beside him, with a little space left between them so that her dress did not brush up against his dirty clothes. She knocked on the partition.

"Drive on!" she commanded.

They moved on for a while in silence before Candens spoke.

"There's a signal tower at the port, isn't there?"

"Yes, of course," Adura said. "Why, do you need to send someone a signal?"

"No! Just the opposite. I'd rather the Signallers there didn't know about me, that's all. I'd rather not be seen by them. They might not recognise me in this state. But I can't take the risk."

At the mention of the Signallers, Adura's heart gave an unpleasant leap. "Are the Signallers the enemies you mentioned?"

"Yes. As I say, it's a long story."

"We'll be at the ferry in a short while," she said. "We'll go straight to the dock and not stop in the town. You can come with us and pretend to be our servant. Keep your story until we're on board and at sea. Then I'll tell you mine."

"All right," he said and sat back in a more relaxed manner. Even so, he turned his head away from the carriage window as they drove into the town and hid his face behind his hand as they passed by the signal tower. Then they were past and drawing up to the quay.

270

The galley was just coming in to port and they waited quietly in the carriage while it discharged its passengers and readied itself for the return voyage to the city.

"I can pay for my passage."

Candens reached for his purse.

Adura was sad to see how few rings appeared to be inside it. She was tempted to offer to pay for his voyage herself, but she looked at his firm, proud face and knew that it would be the wrong thing to do.

"All right, but give me the money. If you're supposed to be my servant then they'll expect me to pay for my whole party."

Candens nodded and doled out the money. It left a mere four rings to chink against each other as he put the purse away.

Adura told the driver to pull the carriage around so that they could descend and board the ferry while shielded from the view of anyone in the town. Then they moved aboard, Adura's maid Emm still frowning with disapproval and annoyance as Candens walked ahead of her onto the galley's deck.

"Come to the sunward side," Adura said as the oars began to splash. "There'll be fewer people there. It will be hot, but I'll cope. Emm, stay here in the shade." Emm began to protest, but Adura was firm. "I can't get lost or get up to any mischief on a galley, Emm. You stay here. You'll be more comfortable in the shade."

Adura knew only too well that this would be retold in much complaining detail to her father, but at this stage she didn't much care. She and Candens moved to the sunlit side of the galley. She had been right. Few people preferred the glare and the heat here and they easily found a spot to be alone.

Candens sat back and gave a sigh of contentment. "It feels so good to be warm again. I've spent far too long recently in shadow, nearly freezing. The cold seems to have become soaked into my bones. Thank you so much for picking me up on the road. I wasn't sure that I could sneak past the signal tower on my own. You may well have saved my life."

"You're not joking, are you?" Adura watched him shake his head. "Tell me why the Signallers are after you."

"I found out something about them that they don't want generally known. Well, two things, really. The first is that they have some kind of secret arrangement with the Healers to provide them with drugs. The second... no, I'd rather not tell you. I don't want to put you in danger, too."

"But what happened? Tell me everything that you can."

Candens gave another sigh, this one much sadder than the last and began his tale.

He told the story well, with few hesitations. Adura was sure he played down some of the drama and violence of his encounter with Blaze and his men. She was open-mouthed with wonder as he described his long, desperate walk across the Great Umbra, describing the giant frozen trees and the skeleton tower whose lower walls were clad in vast sheets of glass. He finished with a brief account of his dealings with the shepherd Han.

"Now," Candens said. "What about you?"

Adura did not respond at once. She was still thinking through Candens' story and trying to bring it together with what she had found out from Campana and Alba. When she did speak, it was with obvious concern in her voice.

"Candens, I don't think you are the only one at danger from the Signallers. We all are. There's something going on, something they are trying to do and we have to work together to stop them. But before I tell you what I know, I need to ask you a personal question."

"What is it?"

"After all that has happened to you, after what you have found out about the Signallers—Well, what I'm trying to ask is this: are you still in love with Hermia?"

Candens' face dropped and his brows knit in concentration. "I suppose... Darkness claim me, I haven't thought about her for a long while. It's been such a battle to stay alive."

"Well?"

His face cleared as he thought it through. "No. I see everything differently now. It seems so long ago, after all I've been through, but of course it's not long at all. Thinking about it now, I don't think I ever was 'in love' with her. Just infatuated, bedazzled; stupid. She played me for a fool, didn't she? It was all deliberate, trying to set me and Lambent against each other. And it worked. But *why*? What was it all for?"

"I don't understand that either, not yet, not all of it, anyway," Adura said. "But now we know for certain that it was the Signallers who were behind the disruption at the last Pledging Ceremony."

"What? How?"

"During her kidnapping, Campana caught a glimpse of the face of Raven, the woman who was leading us. She's certain that it was Magistra Calora of the Signallers. And I've just been speaking to my friend Alba of the Glassmoulders. She says she came to that conclusion on her own."

"My God—"

"There's something else. You won't have heard that Campana's promised pledge to the Healers clan was broken off. The heir of the Healers clan, Radians, is now to be pledged to a Signaller. She suggested that perhaps one reason for the kidnapping was to prevent her own pledge to Radians going ahead. Given what you've told me about some kind of connection between the Healers and the Signallers that must mean something."

Candens gazed into the distance, stroking his beard. "I must get this cut," he muttered, his thoughts obviously elsewhere.

"What if..." he began and then stopped for a moment, gathering his tumbled thoughts. "What if that's one of the ways the Signallers work? They marry one of their girls into another clan, as everyone does. The custom, of course, is that once married a young woman becomes a full part of her husband's clan and renounces her old loyalties. But what if, against all custom, a Signaller girl has been raised to understand that her secret role will be the opposite: to find a way to weaken or undermine her husband's clan, or else to find out its secrets if she can and pass them back to her birth clan? My God, Hermia had Lambent as tame as a lap-dog begging for crumbs. If she asks him about our clan's secrets when he is drunk, or after smoking *marana* or any of those drugs, he'll probably tell her anything she wants to know."

He struck his forehead with his palm. "Of course! That was what triggered it. I was trying to get Lambent to stop drinking so much, tried to warn him off using illicit drugs—drugs he bought from Blaze of the Signallers. They needed to stop me doing that; to get rid of me. So Hermia..."

"You're right," Adura agreed. "It all fits. They must already have some powerful influence over the Healers; must be able to force them to do whatever they want, such as supplying them with drugs."

"That would explain why old Magister Percuro was so reluctant to take me on at first, before he decided that the easiest way of getting rid of me was to send me on a pointless expedition to Glimmer Peak."

"But what hold could they have over the Healers already? From what you've said, I can understand that having the Healer's heir married to one of their own women could give them great power. But how is it that they *already* have such influence?"

"I don't know. Perhaps they read—" Candens stopped suddenly, realising he had said too much.

Adura placed her hand gently on his arm. "You said that there were two things you found out about the Signallers. Tell me what the other thing was. Don't be afraid for me. I can look after myself. And I want to work with you, to help you." As she took breath, tears started in her eyes. "Don't you see, Candens? All I ever wanted was to be treated as an equal partner; to work alongside you."

Candens looked at her for a long moment, a long steady gaze from his dove-grey eyes. Then he smiled and placed his hand on hers. "Yes, I do see. I've been such a fool, Adura. I'm so sorry."

Unexpected joy flooded through Adura and her tears fell freely. "I was foolish too," she said, her tears drying as fast as they had appeared. "Now, tell me."

"Blaze and his men knew exactly where to find me. And he made a mistake. He mentioned something he could only have known by reading a coded message I had sent to Commander Fervens. That message was encrypted with the Militia's own secure cipher, with a key phrase only Fervens and I knew. Yet the Signallers *must* have decoded it. And if they could decode such a message, then..."

Adura was quick to see the implication and reacted with alarm. "Do you mean that you think the Signallers can read any message they send, even if it's encrypted?"

"Yes. I can't prove it... and they can't read *every* message; there are far too many being sent. But if they want to find something out about a particular clan, or about a particular person, they can keep an eye out for a message which appears to be important and decode it."

"Candens!" Adura gripped his arm tightly. "This morning, before we left the Glassmoulders, I sent a coded message to Campana, telling her that Alba confirmed what she had said about Magistra Calora being behind the

Daughters of the Dark and the kidnapping. If the Signallers read that..."

A grim silence fell, filled only with the splashing of the galley's oars, as they stared into each other's eyes, thinking of the implications.

50

Campana

Campana had been looking out for the courier from the signal tower ever since breakfast. There had been a brief message from Adura three Shutterings ago, saying that she was going to visit her friend Alba of the Glassmoulders. That message had been sent in the clear without any encoding, just an innocent message between friends about a social occasion.

Now Campana was anxiously awaiting any new information Adura might have discovered.

When she glimpsed the blue and gold of the courier riding along the drive, she ran quickly down the stairs and to the door. It was normally Parr's job to collect and distribute the mail, but she was too impatient for that. She reached the door before the manservant. The courier was just dismounting and opening his satchel.

She took the proffered bundle of papers and scanned through them quickly. Several signals were for her father, of course, business matters. One was for Hermia. Another was for Lambent. And there was one for her! She pulled it out and handed the rest to Parr, now standing frowning behind her. Still, however much he frowned he was only a servant and couldn't say anything to her.

Signal in hand, Campana ran lightly up the stairs to her room, dismissed her maid Libeth and went to her dressing table. She broke the wax seal bearing the Mirrormaster's sigil and began the decoding.

She was only a little way through the laborious process when she heard a sound behind her. She turned in her chair.

Hermia was at the door, her face dark and hostile, a paper of her own in her hand. "You needn't bother with what you are doing. This will save you the trouble."

Hermia crumpled the paper into a ball and threw it at Campana like a child petulantly throwing a toy. Campana put up an arm to shield her face and the ball bounced off, hit the floor and ran under the bed.

Hermia stood staring at Campana, her chest rising and falling rapidly as though she had run up the stairs.

"Well, Campana," Hermia said, all the false friendliness in her voice now gone. "You've been a nosy, interfering little bitch yet again. I'm going to have to do something about that."

With that, Hermia slammed the door shut behind her and turned the key in the lock.

Alarmed by Hermia's obvious fury, Campana stood up from her dresser. As Hermia took a step towards her, Campana swiftly picked up the chair by its back and held it in front of her as an awkward shield.

Hermia laughed. "You fool! Do you think you'd stop me with that? If I should ever decide to kill you, I can assure you that I would succeed. It will be a sad accident, everyone will think so. But not here, not now."

Campana shrank back from Hermia's callous certainty. "My—my father—" she began.

Hermia showed her amusement. "Your father already believes that the kidnapping has affected your mind. You've become afraid of shadows, jumping at invisible threats. That's what he thinks, you know. He tells me so."

"He tells..."

"Of course he does. You don't think your little chats with him have been *private*, do you? He sees me as a confidant. Your mother is too fond of you to be impartial. I know everything you've said to him. I've tolerated it all so far. But now that you have tangled that pathetic creature

Adura in your nonsense, it has to stop."

Campana stood up straighter, trying to control the trembling in her legs. "We know that your mother Calora was behind my kidnapping."

"Don't make me laugh. You can't prove anything. No one would believe you. Your own father doesn't believe you. If it ever came before the Council, he would testify about your disturbed state of mind."

"I..." Campana stopped, helpless and trapped. What *could* she do? The Signallers were so powerful. They controlled almost all communication in Sunfall. And Hermia's father Solus was now President of the Clan Council.

"This is just a warning, Campana. Forget all about this nonsense. Stop making a fuss. Stop dealing with Adura and anyone else you've tried to get involved. If you don't, I *will* kill you and get rid of your annoying interference for good. My mother was an idiot to save you from the fire you started yourself and a bigger idiot to be persuaded to let you go after that."

"Why, then? Why did she save me? Why did she let me go?"

Campana was genuinely curious, but she also wanted to keep Hermia talking.

"Why?" Hermia was contemptuous and Campana shivered, thankful that it hadn't been Hermia controlling her fate during the kidnapping. "She had you carried out of the fire because she thought she could still extract a ransom. And as for letting you go... let's just say that a third party became involved and insisted that you be released unharmed. He was bluffing, he would never have spoken out, but my mother couldn't see that, it seems. More fool her."

A third party? Who? That raised more questions than it answered.

David R. Grigg

"But what's the point of all of this?" Campana demanded. "What is it all about? What are you trying to do?"

Hermia laughed again. "I'm not telling you any more. You'll have to wait and find out. If you're still here, that is, and haven't had a sad little accident. Don't tempt me, Campana. You've been an annoyance for far too long. Keep quiet and we'll get you married off to someone who'll quickly fill your belly with a baby to occupy your tiny little mind. Your pledge might be someone who lives across the bay on the other side of the Sun, perhaps. Too far for you to visit back here. So sad, but at least you'll be alive."

"I won't marry—"

"Oh yes, you will. Your father told me about your little tantrum on that subject. I'm surprised that he didn't put you in your place right then and there. But it doesn't matter. Ardens will do as I suggest. He doesn't pay any attention to what your mother says. I can control him almost as easily as I control your brother." Hermia turned and unlocked the bedroom door, watched by a spellbound captive. "Goodbye, Campana. You'll be a good little girl now, *won't you?*"

Campana could only nod, but as Hermia went out and closed the door behind her, Campana's legs gave way. She slumped down onto the floor, put her face in her hands and began to sob.

A long time passed before she brushed away her tears with savage swipes of her hands, chastising herself. *Enough self-pity! Focus on what comes next.*

She knew she was in terrible danger, but she couldn't just give up and let Hermia win.

As she tried to gain the emotional strength to get back to her feet, she caught sight of something white underneath her bed. She stared at it for several uncomprehending moments before she understood what it was. She reached over and pulled it out.

51

Candens

The galley was drawing in to the harbour. Candens and Adura returned to the darkward side of the ferry and re-joined Emm in the shade. Adura's maid flicked Candens an annoyed look, to which he returned only an apologetic shrug. Then he turned to look out at the city.

The signal tower and bell tower dominated the city's profile. They were the only really tall buildings, both brightly lit from this angle, their shadows out of sight. Anyone at the top of either tower would be able to see across the whole of the city and far out into the bay. Still, Candens felt safe enough from discovery for the moment, standing in the shadow of the canvas. But once he reached the streets, it would be another matter. Right now, the only weapon he had against the Signallers was that they didn't know he was still alive. He couldn't give up that advantage. If he were seen on the street, his life would be worth nothing.

Even though he had kept these thoughts private, Adura addressed them. "Come with me. My father will have sent our carriage to pick me up. We can go back to my manor and we can talk to him and ask his advice." Then she hesitated. "Although…"

"Although?"

"My mother says that he won't want to hear anything affecting our business with the Signallers. She says he would stop us releasing any evidence. We can try, though. If you are right about the Signallers being able to decode any message, he would be very alarmed, just from a business point of view. That could force him to help."

Candens thought about it for a while, but then shook his head. "Thank you, but no. I really need to speak to Commander Fervens. That has to be the priority. He ought to know what we have found out, even if he can't take any action. Our biggest problem is that, no matter how strongly convinced we are, we don't have any real proof of anything."

The galley's oars lifted high, dripping, as the ferry was edged in sideways to the quay. There was a series of small bumps before the ropes were tossed over and made fast. A short wooden gangplank was dropped down and almost before it touched the quay, feet were on it and passengers were leaving the ferry. Candens, however, was in no hurry. He scanned the open plaza beyond the quay, looking for the Mirrormaster's carriage. The dock was a busy place, full of people on foot coming and going, together with many carts bringing goods to the galleys for delivery to distant parts of Sunfall around the bay, or else fetching goods from them for delivery into the city or out to the clan manors. A hubbub of noise filled the plaza; a hundred different conversations and shouted orders, overlaid by the rumbling of cartwheels and the creaking of the boats.

Candens finally spotted the carriage painted with the Mirrormaster livery, but it was well away from the quayside, at the other side of the cobbled plaza. To reach it, he would have to cross a wide open area and risk being spotted. He was less concerned about being seen from the heights of the signal tower, much more about being seen by someone he knew who might innocently mention that they had seen him. Would he be recognised, in his worn and dirty clothes, with an untrimmed beard? Perhaps not, but he couldn't take the risk. There had been no-one on the ferry who he knew other than Adura, but that had been simple luck. In the busy plaza, there were many more people.

Adura looked up at him and he saw that she understood his plight. He felt almost light-headed with joy to have someone like her on his side as an ally and friend. She was clever and resourceful and he knew that he could trust her. He put his hand on her shoulder and then lightly touched her face. How could he ever have thought her plain? Her face was full of character and quiet strength. Impulsively, disregarding the scandalised expression of the maid, he leaned over and kissed Adura lightly on the lips. She was startled and stepped back away from him, but then she smiled.

"Careful," she said. "You're supposed to be my servant. And we're no longer pledged, remember?"

"I remember only too well. You haven't been re-pledged, have you?"

"Me? Not yet. My father's looking for someone, though. I don't care. He won't be able to force me into anything this time."

"That's good. When all of this is over... well, let's wait and see. When all of this is over I might be dead."

"Don't say that! Not ever, not even in jest."

"All right. Well, how are we going to manage this business? I need to stay hidden."

"Yes, I know. Don't worry. You stay here, or if they make you get off the ferry, stand on the quay looking out to sea. Emm and I will go to the coach and I'll get the driver to pull in as close to the quayside as he can. He needs to come closer anyway to pick up our luggage. It won't be as easy as at Moulder's Arm, but if you're quick, no-one should see you. Once you're safely in the carriage, we can decide where to go."

"Good. I'll wait."

It looked to be a simple enough plan. He did as Adura suggested and when the ferry captain came down the deck looking to see that the ferry was fully unloaded of passengers, he walked off and stood at the edge of the quay, looking out in the direction of the blazing Sun, his hand raised to shade his eyes from its glare, as though looking out to see if a hoped-for ship was coming.

Time passed. He waited for the sound of approaching coach wheels but they did not come. Puzzled, he remained as he was, fighting the urge to turn around and see what was delaying Adura.

Just as he was about to give in to this impulse, a hand fell on his shoulder. He turned and saw Adura's maid. Emm was panting for breath and her face carried a desperate expression, her earlier antagonism towards him apparently vanished.

"Master Candens," she gasped out. "Mistress Adura... oh, please come, they are trying to take her away!"

He spun around and saw that the coach was not far away from where he had first seen it. But now it was surrounded by a group of armed men, one of whom was holding the reins of the carriages' horses. Adura was being pulled out of the carriage, struggling, her arm held firmly by one of the men.

Candens ran towards the group, disregarding his earlier concerns.

It was only when he was half-way across the plaza that he saw that several of the armed men wore the uniforms of active militiamen. He stopped abruptly and ducked behind a tall pile of crates full of melons. Militia. Why would the Militia want to take Adura away? They must have been waiting for her, watching the carriage.

Emm caught up with him. "What are you doing? Why don't you stop them?"

Though he was itching to do just that, common sense prevailed. "There are too many of them and I don't have any weapons. Besides, they are from the Militia. They won't harm her. Perhaps they just want to talk to her."

Emm's face was full of contempt. "You coward!"

Candens let out a slow breath, trying to contain his anger. "I'm not a coward. But I can't help Adura if I get caught too. I'm going to follow them and see where they take her."

He peered out from behind the crates. Adura was still arguing with the men trying to take her away. A mounted man was with the militiamen, apparently directing them. With a shock of horror, he saw that it was Magister Solus of the Signallers. And now that he was close enough, he saw that four of the group of men were not in Militia uniform but instead bore the Signaller's emblem on their tunics; Solus' bodyguards, perhaps. Strong, rough-looking men, anyway, armed with heavy clubs and daggers.

What was going on? Technically, as President of the Clan Council, Solus had the power to direct the Militia. But it was unusual for the President to be in control of specific Militia operations. Why was he here? Was it just a coincidence that he and his men had been to hand right now, or had he been tipped off that Adura was to be arrested?

Adura, perhaps realising that it was pointless, ceased her resistance, though she was clearly furious. With her arms held by a militiaman on either side, the group began to march her off, the Signaller men at the rear. Magister Solus followed, a smile of satisfaction on his face.

Candens turned to Emm. "I promise you that if I think she's in any danger I'll do everything I can to save her. In any case, if they are going to the Militia headquarters, that's where I want to be myself. I need to talk to Commander Fervens."

Emm clenched her fists and glared at him. "Go on, then. Go after them. Talk to those men and tell them you want to see the Commander. What's stopping you?"

He sighed. "I can't allow myself to be seen. There's no time to explain. It's vital, Emm. I don't know who I can or can't trust. But I'm going to trust you. If you want to help Adura, you need to help me first."

She gave a shudder of anger and frustration, but then forced herself to calm down. "You need to follow them, but not be seen?"

"Yes."

She looked around the plaza and then, leaving Candens still hiding behind the crates, strode a little distance away to where a cart was being loaded by two men. She spoke to the older man, whose beard was streaked with grey. Candens saw her pointing back towards him. Then she held out her hand to the man and he saw the glint of metal as she passed over a few rings. The man shrugged and nodded and Emm beckoned to Candens. He strode across, moving quickly to the sunward side of the cart and then squatted down, out of sight of the signal tower.

"Get into the back of the cart, behind the boxes and lie down," Emm said. "Sed here will follow the Militiamen and call back to tell you where they are going. You can trust him, he's my father's cousin and I've paid him well. Just let him know when you jump off the cart so he knows he can go on with his delivery."

"All right. Thank you. I'll repay you as soon as I can."

"Repay me by making sure my mistress is safe. I'll take the carriage back to the manor to tell Magister Ignis what has happened."

"Yes. Please don't mention me, however."

She snorted. "It's my duty to let him know everything that Adura does and about everyone she speaks to. That's what I'm paid to do. And you—" She broke off, voice rough with derision. "I hardly know what to think about you."

"Please?" Candens forced himself to try again. "I was pledged to Adura once. Your Master took me in and offered me a bed when I needed it. He knows me well. At least wait a little before you tell him that you saw me."

"Very well. But if anything happens to her—"

"I understand."

"Now go! Sed is ready and if you're not quick he'll lose sight of those men."

Candens nodded and leapt up onto the back of the cart and crouched down behind the boxes of pots stacked there. "Go!" he called to the old man. With a jerk, the cart moved off.

The cart rumbled along the cobbled streets at a slow walking pace. It was a very uncomfortable ride. Candens lay in a narrow space between two crates, his face itching from the jutting stalks of straw packed around the pots.

He was only able to catch an occasional glimpse between the crates to see where they were going. They seemed to be following the narrower, shaded lanes behind the buildings rather than the brightly-lit streets on the sunward side. The direction seemed right for reaching the Militia headquarters.

Candens risked sitting up for a brief moment and looked forward. Magister Solus was still riding ahead of the armed group, as though in charge of them. Candens suspected that Commander Fervens would be irritated by the man's presumption. He ducked back down again to lie on the floor of the cart.

At least travelling down the darkwards lanes meant that Candens was highly unlikely to be seen and recognised by anyone he knew and there was no chance he could be identified from the heights of the signal tower. He would just seem like some drunken Dim who had had too much to drink and was now being carted home.

The cart took a turn and then another. They entered the service lane running behind the Militia headquarters and approached its rear entrance, to their left. Candens risked another quick peek and saw that Adura was being escorted through the doors, her arms still held by the militiamen, like any common criminal. Two of Solus' guards went in, too, though Solus himself remained on his horse. Candens lay flat again and turned his face away as the cart passed the doorway, his heart beating wildly. He mustn't let Solus recognise him! Then they were past.

It was frustrating. The Militia Headquarters was where he most wanted to be, not only to find out why Adura had been brought there, but so that he could tell Fervens everything he knew or suspected. But there was no help for it. With Solus and his guards in the lane, he couldn't approach the doorway. He would have to loop around and go in by the main entrance from the street and take the risk of being seen by someone he knew.

When Candens judged the cart was far enough ahead that it might be safe, he raised his head a little and looked back over his boots. All of the Signaller guards had come out again and were gathered in the street, laughing. Solus was giving them some command, pointing up the lane in Canden's direction. Had he been seen? Surely not. There seemed no sense of urgency in the men's behaviour. But if Solus began to ride this way he could hardly fail to overtake the cart, see Candens lying there and be close enough, perhaps, to identify him.

Still lying flat, Candens turned his head towards the driver.

"Sed!" he called softly, but there was no response. The old man might be deaf, or the rumbling of the cart too loud. Candens spoke again, more loudly. "Sed! I'm getting off the cart. Do you hear me?"

Still there was no response and no slackening in the speed of the cart. Candens cursed, but had to take the risk. He shuffled down the cart to the point where his legs were hanging over the end. Just as they passed a narrow alley between buildings to his right, he pushed himself off the cart and in two swift strides was into the alley.

Had he been seen? There were no shouts from the lane behind him. But Solus and his men would soon be passing the entrance to the alley. He had to find somewhere to hide.

The alley he was in was very narrow and dark, just a means of access to the backs of a row of commercial buildings. There were open access doors high above, each with a beam jutting out carrying a hook. The hooks would be used to carry ropes so that goods could be hauled up from below. Right now, though, all was quiet and no ropes dangled. Barrels and crates were stacked here and there in the alley, making it even narrower. At the far end there was a brightly-lit intersecting street. It would take him the wrong way, away from the Militia building, but there was no help for that. He started down the alley, but as he did he heard the sound of hooves clattering on cobbles in the lane behind him.

Candens had been through a great deal recently. He was weary and dispirited. Had he been in a better mental state, he might not have made the foolish mistake he did then.

Hearing the approach of Solus and his men, he panicked. Thinking to better disguise himself as an ordinary workman going about his everyday job, he lifted up one of the barrels in the alley and put it on his shoulder. It was heavy, but not unmanageable. He began to carry it onwards.

That was when a bulky workman stepped out of a doorway which had been out of sight behind a pile of crates, grabbed Candens by his shoulder and slammed him into the wall of the alley.

"Thief!"

Candens' head cracked against the stone and a flare of red and white light filled his vision. He dropped the barrel and sank to his knees, crying out in agony.

"Here, you!" he heard the man call out. "You men! Come and help me with this thief!"

Candens lay dazed for a moment on the muddy surface of the alley. Then came a savage blow to his chest, as the man kicked him with a boot which felt to be made of lead.

Damn this! Candens thought. As the big man swung again, Candens grabbed his boot and heaved, throwing him

289

backwards to sprawl into the pile of crates, which toppled over in front of the Signaller guards now running towards the fight.

Candens forced himself to his knees and then his feet. Blood ran down his face and was running into his right eye, together with a cataract of pain. Ignoring the shouts behind him, he began to run, half-staggering, down the alley towards the brightly-lit street ahead.

52

Adura

By the time she reached the Militia headquarters, her earlier fear had now been replaced with utter fury, stoked by the sight of Magister Solus riding ahead of the group as if in command of them. She had considered calling out to him, or denouncing Magistra Calora in front of the men, but had thought better of it. Better not to expose the precious cards she held in this strange game. There would be a time and place to play them, but not until she understood all the rules and she didn't yet.

At the door of the building, she bridled as the men forced her forward with her arms held on each side. They could just as easily have let her go and she would have gone in of her own accord. Instead, she was being treated as any common criminal. She started to kick at the shins of the man on her right. He reddened, but simply tightened his grip. The two men dragged her in. Two of the Signaller men followed as if to ensure that she wouldn't escape the militia. Waiting to receive her in the hallway stood Commander Fervens.

"Commander! This is outrageous!" Adura said. "How dare your men treat me this way? My father will lodge a complaint with the Council. He will—"

Fervens interrupted her tirade. "That's enough, Mistress Adura. Let go of her, men."

Her arms were released and Adura stood panting with exertion and anger. "Why have I been seized this way in public? In front of my servants!"

David R. Grigg

Fervens looked sharply at the man whose shins Adura had been kicking.

"Well, Dynens? I told you to bring the lady here to talk with me and to insist if she refused. But you were meant to use tact, not to humiliate her and bring her here by main force. It seems as if it took a whole squad of armed men to apprehend one young woman. That's not what I had in mind and you should have known it."

Dynens was abashed. "Magister Solus met us on the way there," he explained. "He told us that her servants might have weapons and might fight to stop us. So he came along and loaned us some of his men. He's outside if you want to talk to him."

Fervens was impatient. "I will indeed, but not now. Magister Solus may be President of the Clan Council, but last time I checked I was still in charge of the Militia. You should have used your common sense, if only you had any."

He waved his hand at the men bearing Signaller ensigns. "Get out and go back to your duties. Dynens, we'll discuss this later. Mistress Adura, I apologise. But I did want to see you."

Adura was still angry. "Well, I don't want to see you, Commander. May I go?"

Fervens sighed and indicated a stairway leading, she assumed, to offices on the floor above. "I'm afraid not. Will you come this way?"

"No."

Fervens sighed again.

"Mistress Adura, I'm trying to make this as easy as I can for you. But you really don't have any choice, I'm afraid. You are being arrested for involvement in the outrage at the Pledging Ceremony and the subsequent kidnapping of eight young women. *Now* will you come?"

"Arrested?" Adura whispered, in shock. It seemed unreal. She had spent so long blaming herself, regretting

292

what she had done, but she had worked hard to put those incidents behind her and had begun to excuse herself for her foolishness. And no one other than her parents and Candens knew of her confession. Well, there was Alba, but she wouldn't incriminate herself. It felt completely unfair to be brought here now to face the consequences of her past actions.

"Please?" Fervens indicated the stairway again.

With feet that felt like stones and legs even heavier, Adura began to climb the stairs. On the next floor, Fervens indicated that she should continue up the next flight of stairs. As they reached the top floor of the building, Adura felt as though she had been climbing a mountain and these were the last few steps to the peak.

Fervens led her into a small room with a desk and two chairs. Like most upper rooms in the city this close to the Sun, its shutters were angled sharply to restrict the glare. Wide bright lines of light patterned the ceiling and rear wall. As Adura sat down, Fervens adjusted the shutters to make sure that the light was not directly in her eyes. She wondered if a real criminal—she still didn't think of herself as such—would be afforded this courtesy. She doubted it.

"Now." Fervens sat behind the desk and leaned forward, hands clasped before him. "Will you tell me about the Daughters of the Dark?"

"I don't know anything about them," Adura said firmly.

Fervens gazed at her in silence for a while.

"There's no point in you trying to deny it, Mistress. I have solid evidence that you were part of the group. Perhaps an important part. I've had a list for some time of those I was sure were involved. It wasn't too hard to put together. Young women, mostly, about your age. Women who couldn't give a reliable account of their movements during the Pledging and for the decant following. You were already high on that list, Adura. We've had people speak to your servants. Just casually, one Dim worker to another, just gossiping. It wasn't hard to discover that you were leaving your manor at times when we know the Daughters were active."

"I was taking music lessons with a friend."

"And did you think we wouldn't speak to your friend, put a little pressure on her? She told us you have a secret lover. But it wasn't a lover, was it? You were active on the business of The Daughters."

"I..." Adura couldn't find any more words.

"And below, when I told you why you were being arrested, you didn't for a moment protest your innocence. You were shocked, no doubt and now you've had time to calm down. But that doesn't change matters. I know that you are one of the Daughters of the Dark."

Adura was silent as Fervens watched her. Finally, in resignation, she nodded, her eyes cast down.

"I *was*. But no longer. I'm not part of it now."

"Do you tell me so? What if I put it to you that, far from having left the movement, you are its leader? Have been its leader from the beginning?"

"*What?* No, no, that's nonsense." Adura was staggered by this new accusation and she gaped for a moment before recovering a little of her spirit. Now seemed like the time to play her trump card. "I can tell you who really was the leader. Who misled us, used us. It was Magistra Calora of the Signallers!"

His face did not change in the least. "Is that so? She told me that you might make some such absurd accusation."

"What?" Adura felt as though a blade of ice had been plunged into her breast.

"It was Magistra Calora who provided us with the definitive evidence against you."

"Evidence? What evidence?"

"Testimony which demonstrates that you were the leader of the group at the Pledging. That you were in charge and actively recruiting like-minded young women, your friends, perhaps, to join the cause. You were in control of them and it was your own plan to disrupt the Pledging and kidnap the girls." Fervens leaned forward, raising his voice. "What have you done with the ransom money, Adura?"

"Nothing! It's not true," Adura said weakly. "It's a lie. What evidence, what testimony?"

"The testimony of Magistra Calora's daughter Hermia, whom you tried to recruit. Despite declining your solicitation, Hermia says that she agreed to your demand that she stay silent about the matter. Only recently, seeing the mental distress that the kidnapping has caused Campana of the Bellringers, did Hermia confess to her mother that you asked her to join you and that therefore she knew who was leading The Daughters."

"Is that all? Just Hermia's word against mine? She's lying. It was she who—"

Adura's voice caught in her throat.

"No. There are these." Commander Fervens brought a sheaf of papers out from a drawer and tossed them across the desk to Adura. They were each folded into three with an address written on the outer fold of each. Signals. Hands shaking, Adura picked up the one on top. It was addressed to her friend Clara of the Metalworkers. She unfolded it to see a message set out in neat rows of code. At the bottom was attached a note in clear language, indicating who the sender was, when the message had been sent and the fee charged... a note which would have been added by the Signaller's clerk.

"These are all signals sent by you to various young women. Almost all of them were already on my list of suspects. The date they were sent was a few centends before the most recent Pledging Ceremony. Perhaps you weren't aware that the Signallers keep all of the messages sent through their towers, keep them for at least a millend? Magister Solus was extremely helpful when I asked him to have his records searched for messages which you had sent.

David R. Grigg

We can't read the coded messages themselves, of course. But it's clear that you sent many nearly identical messages to the group of women who I'm sure are in the Daughters. It's no coincidence, is it? You may as well confess."

Adura sat back with an unhappy laugh, speechless for the moment. It was all so pat. The Signallers held all the trump cards. Feeling as though her previous life had been swept away like a leaf in a storm, she could only shake her head.

"Very well, then," Commander Fervens said. "I'm sorry, Adura, but you will be brought before a Grand Council Court, four Shutterings from now. I warn you, these charges are very serious and the punishment will be severe if the Court finds against you. You may mitigate that punishment if you make a full confession before the trial. No? Very well. I will send a signal to your father to advise him. He may wish to appoint an advocate to defend you. Until then, you will remain in our custody."

He called out and the man Dynens came in.

"Take her away. Treat her well, but lock her up."

Job done, Fervens turned to the window and opened the shutters to gaze out into the distance.

53

Candens

Gasping for breath, he burst out from the dark alley into a busy street whose far side was brightly lit by the Sun. The glare struck into his eyes and redoubled the terrible pain in his head. Brushing aside the blood which was blinding him on his right side, he ran across the roadway, dodging between the carriages and narrowly avoiding being struck by the hooves of a horse. Across the street and a little way to his left there was another alley, just a gap between buildings, narrower even than the one he had been in. He dashed into it, hoping to avoid being seen by his pursuers. No light lay ahead, only shadow.

Candens ran mechanically, his legs protesting and his balance almost lost. Behind him, to his despair, came a shout from one of the Signaller guards.

"There he goes!"

Candens reached the end of the alley and found a solid stone wall. It was a dead end. He looked up, trying to see if he could climb the wall, but it was too dark to see whether there were any useful footholds. Even if there were, he knew that he didn't have the strength to climb even an arm's length. It was hopeless. From behind the voice came again.

"Stop, thief!"

Out of the darkness a barely-seen hand emerged and clamped itself on his right arm.

"This way, brother," came a hoarse voice. Candens was pulled hard, sideways, stumbling. Another hand landed on his head. "Down, down! Duck now or you'll get a crack on your skull." Candens obeyed. A deeper darkness lay ahead.

297

He felt a shove on his back and stumbled forwards, missed his footing and fell, saving himself with outstretched hands. There was a thud behind him and the sound of a bolt sliding shut. "Now be quiet, brother. Wait!"

The darkness was complete. Not even in the depths of the Great Umbra had it been so dark. With a soft groan that he couldn't repress, Candens let himself down and lay his face onto a stone floor. Pain flooded his head. He was only barely aware of the warmth of another body close by and a rough, earthy smell.

Muffled sounds from beyond the door indicated that the guards had reached the end of the alley and were debating what to do. A loud rattle came as they tried the low door or hatch that Candens had come through; softer rattles showed that they were trying several similar doors in the alley. There was more talking, a curse and a couple of laughs. Then silence. Still Candens and his unseen companion waited quietly.

"Gone," said the hoarse voice in the darkness. "They think you climbed the wall, brother. Now, fair's fair. What did you steal?"

Candens was about to protest his innocence, but stopped himself. He felt at his belt. It was still there.

"A purse," he said, trying hard to keep his voice rough to match that of his saviour. "A few rings in it, not many."

The hoarse voice grunted.

"You're a damned poor pickpocket, then, to be caught for so little. Still, hand it over, brother."

Candens sat up with difficulty, pulled off his purse and held it out. He could still see nothing. An unseen arm swept across and found his own, then his hand was grasped and the purse taken from it. He heard the jingle of rings. Candens sighed inwardly. All of his money was now gone. But he was surprised to find the purse thrust back into his hand after a moment.

"Poor pickings, friend. Two rings I've taken," the man said. "Might be silver, might be brass. That's my chance. I'm a big believer in luck, brother. Let's have a light and see what it's dealt me."

The sound of a flint being struck, sparks flying. Candens glimpsed the face of an old man. Then a small flame began and a taper was thrust into it and the flame transferred to a small oil lamp. An orange glow lit up the space in which Candens now found himself. He swiped away again at his face to get the blood out of his right eye.

The other man had a grizzled beard and an ugly scar across his forehead, ending in an eye which showed a blank, blind white. The other eye looked at Candens in curiosity.

"Haven't seen you around here before?"

"No," Candens said. "I'm new here. I ran away from one of the estates." Candens was trying hard to sound like a common labourer and not like the Bright he was, or had been. "My name is... Lonn. Call me Lonn."

The old man laughed. "And that's a poor lie, if I ever heard one. But that's all right. I tells a lot of lies myself. I'm called Denn. Denn of the Delvers. Head of the clan, in fact."

He tapped his chest and laughed again.

"The Delvers?"

"Yeah. Dare say you've never heard of us, brother, if you've been living out on an estate. They won't let us in to the Clan Council. Can't think why." Denn slapped his thigh and laughed yet again. He peered at Candens. "That's a nasty blow you've had, Brother Call-Me-Lonn. A mace, was it?"

"No. Just a wall. Cracked my head against it."

"Or had it cracked for you. Yes, I see. You're new to the game, I can tell. Well, this is your lucky waking, young Lonn. The things I could teach you! We Delvers ain't like your big clans, brother. We don't believe in keeping our secrets all to ourselves, oh no. We likes training up young ones like you. Provided, of course, we gets our fair cut, brother, you see?"

"Yes," Candens said. "Thank you for..."

Denn held up a hand, grimy palm towards Candens. "No, no. We don't deal in thanks, brother. I took my fair pay from that purse. Now, let's see..." He held up the rings he had taken to the light of the lamp and examined them with his good eye. "Two bronze rings. Ah, well. Good luck to you. One man's bad luck is another's good, as they say."

"Yes. Do you think the Sig... Do you think the men chasing me have gone?"

"Hard to say. If they're any good at their job they'll set a man to watch the alley for a while, just in case. Or they'll fetch the Militia to do it. But it don't matter. You aren't going back out that door."

"No?"

Denn laughed again. He obviously enjoyed laughing. "Not if you've got any sense. If you have any sense you'll let me show you a better way. The Delver's way. But the way we goes depends on where you wants to get to, that stands to reason, don't it?"

Where *did* he want to go? Candens could hardly tell Denn that he wanted to be taken to the Militia Headquarters.

"Is there somewhere I can get this cut seen to?" He a hand to his bleeding head. "A Healer?"

Denn chuckled. "You don't have enough in that purse to pay a Healer, brother. They may have tended to you on your estate, with your master paying. But they're not for the likes of us here in the city, unless you have more money stashed somewhere on you?"

Denn gave Candens a speculative look.

"No that's all I have."

"Then you needs to forget the ways of the Sun, brother. You're in the realm of the Delvers now. In the Delver's Domain, you might say. Here, you have to do things the Delvers' way. Come with me. I'll take you to someone who'll bind your wound. Can you walk?"

"Yes..." Candens started to get up.

Denn's hand grabbed him. "Not so fast, Brother Call-Me-Lonn. You'll crack your head again. The ceiling's low here. Crouch and keep a hand raised over your head." Denn raised himself and demonstrated by example. Then he picked up the lamp. "Follow me."

His way barely illuminated by the flickering lamp, Denn headed into the darkness away from the hatch. Candens followed.

54

Campana

Sitting at dinner that evening was a serious challenge to Campana's mental strength. She spent the whole meal picking at her food and trying to control the expression on her face. It was vital that Hermia continue to think that Campana was helpless and afraid of her. In truth that wasn't very hard to manage. Campana was indeed terrified of Hermia and what she might do, but she certainly wasn't helpless.

It was astonishing to see how easily Hermia slipped into her role of loving, thoughtless wife, chatting cheerfully to her husband sitting next to her. On the last few evenings, Lambent had been able to get up and with the aid of a crutch come to the dining hall for the meals. But his face had grown thinner, the bones beneath his flesh more prominent. His eyes had dark circles under them and Campana noticed that his hands trembled as he cut his meat. He seemed to have little interest in Clan matters. When asked a direct question, it was often Hermia who answered for him, to Ardens' obvious annoyance.

Hermia, however, acted as though nothing had changed. She was cheerful and as full of conversation as ever. Campana felt an intense loathing for her, but forced herself to show nothing.

Ardens was in a bad mood this evening and began to talk about how busy he was being kept by the affairs of the clan.

"Lambent," he said after a while, "I know you are still recovering and you can't ride with that leg of yours. But you could still help me greatly by taking on some of the administration. You can work perfectly well behind my desk. That would free me to look after other matters. Now that your brother—now that the person whose name we don't mention is no longer with us, we're badly stretched. I've been doing my best to cope while you regain your strength, but I need your help as soon as you can give it. What do you say?"

Lambent smiled, but it was a thin smile. "I don't know, Father. I'm finding it very hard to concentrate. The medicine I'm taking to control the pain makes my head very fuzzy. You wouldn't want me to make a mistake and double-pay one of our suppliers, now would you?"

Ardens was irritated. "No. I'll double-check what you do. Any help you can give me would assist."

Hermia beamed. "I could help Lambent out, Ardens. I know I'm not allowed to know any of the clan's secrets. We weak women aren't capable of handling such important knowledge, of course."

Campana flashed a sharp glance at her at that. Surely her father could see how false she was? But Hermia's cheerful face, which she put on so easily, showed only an expression of perfect innocence.

"However," Hermia went on, "I'm sure there can be no harm in my seeing how many onions we buy, or what you get paid for our barley. You could choose what correspondence you are happy for me to see."

No! Campana wanted to scream. *Don't trust her!* But she could say nothing as Hermia looked directly at Campana, a warning clear in her eyes.

Ardens simply shrugged.

"It's possible, I suppose. But I really think Lambent needs to try a little harder. It will be all his responsibility soon enough, when I am gone."

Hermia exclaimed. "Oh, Ardens, no. I'm sure you will be with us for many millends to come. Won't he, Eccua?"

Campana's mother made the faintest of smiles and then looked down at her food again.

"Lambent is in no hurry to take over, are you, Lambent, dear?" Hermia glanced at Lambent, who seemed about to say something, but Hermia put a firm hand on his arm and he closed his mouth and just shook his head.

And that was it. Campana felt sick to her stomach. When Ardens died, Lambent would be in charge of the clan, but Hermia would be in charge of Lambent, just as she was now. If Lambent tried to block anything she wanted, she would just hold back the *papavera* until he agreed. Hermia and the Signallers would effectively control the Bellringers.

It was an awful prospect.

Campana couldn't take her eyes away from Hermia's lovely, smiling face. Would Hermia do anything to speed Ardens' demise? Why would she not, if she could find a way to do it without being detected? She had a heart of stone and veins of ice.

Campana looked back at her plate, with half the food uneaten. She pushed it away from her, feeling nauseous. She had to find a way to contact someone outside of the manor, sometime very soon. Sending a signal, of course, was now out of the question. Campana stood up and excused herself. As she left the table, she could feel Hermia's eyes following her closely.

Campana slept badly that Shuttering, her thoughts tumbling over and over with plans and rejected plans, futile, hopeless. At breakfast next waking, she felt downcast, with her spirits at a low ebb. The mirror that morning had shown her the dark circles beneath her own eyes. Her father was oblivious, but her mother considered her anxiously.

"Are you all right, Campana?"

Campana hesitated, wanting to tell her mother all. But in that moment, Hermia came in, helping Lambent to the table. Campana closed her mouth and answered her mother with a simple nod.

Lambent was more cheerful this waking, though his hands still had a fine tremble as he cut up his food.

"I received a surprising signal first thing this morning."

Ardens addressed this to Eccua, who made an obvious effort to seem interested. "Yes?"

"You'll remember Adura of the Mirrormasters? Candens' pledge?" He hesitated, perhaps realising that this was the first time in a long while that he had spoken Candens' name.

Campana looked up with a tremor of fear running through her. "Yes, Father? What about her?"

"Well, it seems that *she* was the leader of the group of women who disrupted the Pledging and kidnapped you and the others, Campana. Who would have thought it? But she's been found out and arrested. There's a Grand Council Court arranged to charge and punish her in three Shutterings' time. All the clan heads are requested to attend."

Campana looked at Hermia, who smiled a terrible smile.

"Oh dear." Hermia's gaze met and held Campana's. "What a surprise. But, on the other hand, I do recall her speaking out strongly against the Pledging. She tried to get me to join some group she was organising. Of course I refused, though I did agree to keep it secret. Perhaps that was foolish of me, but now of course there's no longer any need to keep it quiet. I will be happy to give evidence, Ardens, if it is needed."

Campana stood, overcome with fury. "You're a liar!"

She picked up her plate and threw it, contents and all, at Hermia, who ducked. Though it spilled food as it flew, the plate missed Hermia and shattered on the floor beyond.

"Campana!" Ardens stood up too, his face dark. "Control yourself! Your kidnapping seems to have upset the balance of your mind. Really, I think we need to have you seen by a Healer again. "

Hermia, her face suffused, angrily brushed pieces of food from her dress. Glaring at Campana, she said coldly. "That, or she needs to be put away somewhere. The Healers have such places, I'm told."

It was Eccua's turn to be outraged, her natural timidity forgotten. "She is our daughter, Ardens. She will *not* be put away somewhere." She took a deep, shuddering breath. "Campana is *not* mad. But she has been put under terrible stress. If you send her away, you'll need to send me as well."

Ardens clenched his fists and for an instant looked as though he was seriously considering doing just that. Then he made a gesture discarding the thought and turned back to Campana. "I want you to apologise to Hermia. Now."

Campana remained silent.

"Come now." Ardens softened his voice a little. "I know that you are fond of Adura's cousin Maryam. Perhaps you feel betrayed, knowing that it was Adura who was behind your kidnapping. I can understand that. Now apologise and we'll say no more about it."

Campana looked at Hermia with hatred. In a flat voice, she said, "I apologise. Now can I go?"

Ardens, frowning, nodded. Campana turned from the table, glancing at her mother's anxious face for an instant and then walked briskly out of the room. She had to get away from here... and it had to be very soon.

55
Candens

Candens moved along in an uncomfortable crouch, following Denn. This space was a storage cellar. Barrels and kegs of various sizes were everywhere. As they moved further away from the hatchway, Candens started to hear noises from overhead: the thump of boots and a gabble of talk. What he had thought was the wooden ceiling of this cellar was actually the floor of the room above. A tavern, no doubt.

Denn stopped, raising a finger to his lips to tell Candens to be quiet. He set his lamp down next to a group of small kegs, examined them and then lifted one up.

"A little present for me lady wife," Denn whispered, chuckling. He tucked it under one arm and picked up the lamp with his free hand. He shuffled along, Candens doing his best to keep up in the low, awkward space.

They squeezed around a narrow corner, Denn juggling the lamp to keep it upright and aflame.

"Now down here, brother," Denn whispered. "Have to put out my lamp here. You'll need to crawl for a bit. Watch that head of yours. Don't go too fast. There's a drop at the end."

Denn set down the keg and pinched out the flame of the lamp. All was darkness. Candens heard the scrape of cloth on stone as the old man apparently squeezed through some narrow opening. Then came the sound of the keg being rolled along.

Candens hesitated. Should he trust Denn? Where was he being taken? He had no doubt that Denn had saved him from his pursuers, though he was pretty sure that the Signaller guards had no idea who they had been chasing. Even if some of those men had seen Candens before, say at Lambent's wedding, they would be unlikely to associate that formal image with the fleeting glimpse they had had of a ragged, dirty man with a heavy beard.

"Where are you, brother?" A whisper crept out of the dark towards him.

Candens put aside his futile thoughts and felt in front of him. A square opening, lined with stone. It was narrow and a powerful farmyard smell was wafting out of it. That gave him a pretty good idea of where Denn was leading him. Sighing, he squeezed through the opening and crawled forward on his knees, keeping his head low.

After a short distance, perhaps six arm-lengths, one hand sank into empty space. Unbalanced, he dropped forward onto his chest and let out a curse.

"Careful, careful, young Call-Me-Lonn," Denn said with a chuckle. "Don't want to fall into the shit below, now do you?"

Candens could heard the movement of water below. The stench of excrement was almost overpowering. Still blind, he could only assume that this was the main sewer of the city. The smaller tunnel he had ventured into while on patrol with the Militia must feed into this one.

"Pretty, ain't it?" Denn asked. "That's the reason we don't want no lamp lit down here."

"Why? So we can't see it?"

Denn laughed at that, a deep chortle which ended in a bout of coughing. "See it? No, that's not the reason. All that shit, it makes a kind of gas. A flame can set it all off burning. Might make a big bang. Happened to my brother, killed him stone dead."

"I'm sorry."

"Long ago, long ago. Now, there's a ledge here, feel it? We can stand up here, but you got to be careful of your feet. Gaps, broken stones. Make sure there's something solid beneath you every time you puts a foot down, right?"

"Right."

Candens could hear Denn shuffling along the ledge and began to follow slowly. As Denn had warned, there were many places where the going was treacherous and Candens had to feel about carefully to find the next safe place to stand. They continued this way for what seemed like an eternity. The awful smell from the stream below made Candens dizzy and nauseous. His head ached terribly, but at least the blood had stopped running into his eyes.

Finally, the old man said, "We goes to the left here, through the archway. Then we'll squeeze past the door and be at the ramp. It goes down."

"*Down?*" Candens had been expecting to be led back upwards towards the world of light.

"Down, brother. Just a little way, around a few turns. Then we're home, into the easy tunnels and we can have a lamp again."

Puzzled, Candens felt along the wall as he followed the sound of Denn's movement in the darkness. Sure enough, after a couple more paces the wall opened into some kind of archway. A few steps further and Denn said "Here's the door. It's made of that old godsteel no one can cut. Someone long ago tried to get the door out, maybe to use it for something. They broke away all the stone around the lock, but they couldn't move it much even then. But there's enough room to squeeze past."

Candens heard the old man grunting with effort as he did so. Putting out his hand, Candens could feel the sucking cold of the flat, ancient steel. To the left was a hole, surrounded by ragged, broken stone. Hoping he wasn't being led astray, he pushed his body through the gap.

"Put your right hand on the wall, brother. Feel it and you won't lose your footing as we turn. No steps here, just a ramp, down."

Candens obeyed, increasingly puzzled. The wall he was touching was surprisingly smooth, as though the stone here had been ground flat. He couldn't even feel any breaks between the blocks of stone which must surely line the passage.

Round and round, down and down. After what felt like three turns of a spiral, Denn called out, "We're down, brother!"

A few steps later, Candens felt his feet reach a solid, level surface. He heard Denn put down the keg. A moment later there came the sound of flint being struck and he saw sparks again. Another moment and Denn had his lamp lit once more.

As the flame lit up their surroundings, Candens frowned, baffled. They were in a long straight passageway, unremarkable enough in itself. But it was lined with... what? Its surface was a flat, light grey, with a few speckles of black here and there. But there were no divisions between blocks of stone. It was all one continuous material, or so it appeared.

"Where *are* we?"

Denn chuckled.

"Home. In my domain, brother. The Delver's Domain, just like I told you. Not many knows about these deep tunnels and fewer still want to come down here. Too dark and too cold, they says. Quite a few who has come down here have gotten themselves lost. We find their bones sometimes. But Clan Delver knows where the tunnels lead—all over the city, that's where. There's ways into them and ways out of them, but only for them that knows." He peered at Candens. "How's that head of yours?"

"Hurts like the very dark. But I'm all right."

"Good. Not far now. These are the easy ways, like I told you. Come on."

Denn set off down the tunnel at a surprisingly fast pace, toting the stolen keg under one arm and carrying the flickering oil lamp in the other. Candens, bewildered, followed.

~

Without Denn as his guide, Candens would have swiftly become lost in the labyrinth of smooth-walled tunnels deep under the city. Despite Denn's repeated assurance that they didn't have far to go, the old man made turn after turn as each tunnel met another, or branched into two.

There were slight markings on the walls of the tunnels at the intersections, faded patches of colour, as though there might once have been painted signs. But all that now remained were tiny flecks of coloured dust. Denn seemed to pay these markings only the slightest of attention, apparently navigating mostly by memory. Perhaps with long familiarity the layout of these tunnels would be as clear as a map, but to a stranger like Candens they remained a maze.

Right, left, right, right again. Candens was soon dizzy and feeling increasingly unsteady on his legs. His head wound started to bleed again and he could feel a lump on his head the size of an egg.

Finally, there was one last turn and they passed through a dark opening and stopped. They were inside a great black void, flecked here and there with little lights. It took Candens a long moment for his brain to sort out what he was seeing. Then it came into focus. A vast open space, mostly dark, but lit up here and there with the tiny flickering of lamps and the larger flames of camp fires. Judging from the furthest such fire, the space must be at least a hundred strides long. Above, he could see no roof, but it must be high, as Candens was unable to see any of the lights reflected back from its surface. Somewhere in the space came the sound of water running. There was a strong smell of wood smoke.

Denn waved a hand. "Welcome to my Council Hall, young Lonn."

"It's... amazing."

As Candens' eyes adjusted and he could see a little more readily, he could pick out the tenuous outlines of the space: longer than it was wide, with a darker channel running along its entire length. That was where the sound of water was coming from. But it didn't appear to be a sewer, as there was no obvious stench. Here and there groups of people were camped. Already some of the closer groups were calling out greetings to Denn and he cheerfully called back, before leading Candens further in. He could see that the old man was held in great respect. Perhaps he *was* a kind of clan head after all.

They went down to the central channel, where children were hauling up water in open barrels suspended on ropes. "You wants to use the privy, you go downstream yonder, understand?" Denn said as they crossed the stream via an obviously makeshift wooden bridge. Candens nodded.

Up a slight slope on the other side, they reached a group of people camped up against one wall of the space. Several oil lamps and a campfire lit the area and by their light, Candens saw three people. Make that four. One was a baby suckling the breast of a young woman reclining on a straw mattress laid on the floor.

"Denn!" A gray-haired woman called out from a wicker chair. "You've been long enough gone! And who's this? Another mouth to feed?"

This last was added while she glared at Candens.

The final member of the group was a man of indeterminate age, his hair and beard cropped very short, leaning against the wall. He was so lean that he could have been put together out of canvas and rope, thin but taut. He, too, glared at Candens, his eyes narrowed. An ugly red scar showed on his forearm.

Candens' heart skipped a beat. He had seen this man before. In the sewer, when he had been chasing the thieves with the Militia patrol. Candens felt certain that this was the man who had mysteriously escaped. The question was, would he recognise Candens and denounce him? On a second thought, it seemed unlikely. Candens had only been lit from behind in the darkened sewer and the man had been intent on getting away. And, of course, Candens now looked very different than he had then. But still, the man's eyes were full of suspicion.

"Now, now, my dear," Denn was saying to the older woman. "Let's be welcoming. This is Brother Lonn, a fellow in the trade. Running from a bunch of ugly men with clubs, he was, with a purse he'd stolen. I brought him here to have his head bound up. Don't you see the crack he's had on his head? And besides, Ella, here's some brandy for you, just like you wanted."

He handed her the cask and her face changed from disapproval to glee.

"Well that's all right then." She set the keg down, struggled up out of her chair and came over to Candens. "Bend down a little, Brother Lonn, so's I can see."

Obediently, Candens inclined his head. Instantly, though, a wave of weakness washed over him and he had to put out a hand against her to stop himself from falling.

"Sit down, sit down," Ella said. "I'll get you some salve and a clean cloth to wrap around your poor head."

The lean man still glared at Candens. He was carving a short length of wood with a knife. The blade glinted and judging by its sharpness its blade must be metal. An expensive item to be found among such people as these, hiding like rats beneath the city streets. After a moment, Candens realised that the man was shaping a wooden dart like the one hurled at him during the chase in the sewer. Not much doubt, then, that this was the man who had escaped him. And now he knew where the man had gone.

Ella returned and applied a fragrant-smelling compound to Candens' wound. He winced as it began to sting. She tied a long strip of cloth around his head and tied it as tightly as she could. Standing nearby as if supervising, Denn rubbed his hands together.

"Now we'll have a little bite to eat. But Ella here was right, we don't have enough to feed extra mouths for long. We finds what we can in the cellars we can get into, but we has to be careful. Too easy to get caught."

"That's all right." Candens waved them away politely. "I don't need any food. Thank you for helping me, I'm sure you saved my life."

The lean man flicked a large chunk off the wood he was holding and sneered at Candens. "Seems to me, this ain't no ordinary thief, Denn. I don't reckon he's one of us. Talks almost like a Bright. Has he any money on him? Take it and kill him, I says."

Denn was alarmed. "Now, Rinn, don't be like that, son. Lonn here is our guest."

Candens returned Rinn's glare. "I have one bronze and one silver ring left in all the world. I used to work on an estate, that's true. But I don't belong to any clan."

"But you did once, didn't you? You sure ain't no Dim."

Rinn held Candens' eyes for a long moment and Candens' heart began to race. If this man denounced him as ex-Militia, that would be an end of him down here. Candens remained silent and did not shift his gaze. After a few tense moments, Rinn shrugged and looked away.

Ella meanwhile was tending a small fire in a makeshift hearth. Smoke drifted up and out of view. On the fire she placed a pot and shortly an enticing smell began to waft up. Despite his earlier protestation, Ella insisted on bringing him a bowl full of a thick stew. He ate it gratefully with the wooden spoon she supplied. He wasn't sure what animal the small pieces of meat in the stew had come from and right at that moment he didn't want to know.

As she served food to the others, Denn looked around. "Gem not here?"

Ella gave a laugh. "Out wandering again, as usual. You know what she's like. She can forage for herself these days." Denn shrugged but looked unhappy. Some straying child, Candens assumed.

As they ate the food, Rinn's face remained hostile, but he said nothing. After the meal was over, Candens said, "I'll be going now. Can you tell me where we are underneath the city? How do I get out?"

"Don't worry, brother, I'll guide you out. You won't find the way yourself. Where do you want to get to?"

Candens had been thinking about this as he ate. He was certainly not going to declare in front of the angry, dangerous Rinn that he really wanted to go to the Militia Headquarters. But at the same time he didn't want to emerge somewhere where he had to walk a long way through the streets and risk being spotted, either by someone he knew, or worse by the Signallers.

"There's a tavern I stayed in, close to where that big fire was a couple of decants ago. A man called Todd was the owner, I think. Do you know it? A friend of mine often stays there; he might lend me some money."

It sounded reasonable, but in truth, he wanted to get to the tavern because it was only a short block away from the Militia building.

Denn chuckled. "Todd's Tavern? Oh, I knows it well. There's a tunnel runs near it and we broke our way up into his cold store. Sometimes there's good pickings there."

"Well, if you could take me there, I'd be grateful. But wait... what time is it? Can you hear the bells down here? Is it after the Shuttering?"

Rinn gave a grunt of disgust. "We don't listen to no bells. We don't need no bells."

Candens was offended and puzzled by Rinn's easy dismissal of the whole business of the Bellringer clan. "But how do you know when to sleep and when to wake?"

"Listen, pretty boy. We sleep when we're tired and we wakes up when we're not. Is that simple enough for you? We don't need shutters down here where the Sun never shines."

"All right, I understand." Although it seemed a very odd way of living to Candens. "But I can't be out in the streets between Shuttering and Unshuttering. The Militia patrols might catch me."

"It's long after the Shuttering now." Denn glared at Rinn. "I heard the late bells while I was having a piss in that alley before you came along, young Lonn, bringing a pack of guards on your tail. So rest up; take a nap. You're safe here, brother."

Glancing at Rinn again, Candens wasn't so sure, but he was bone-weary and there was little he could do until the Unshuttering peal sounded in the city above. He lay down on the smooth, hard floor and used his arm for a pillow. Despite the discomfort, within a few heartbeats he was asleep. He dreamed of being lost in a dark maze, with something terrible hunting him, invisible and evil, hiding in the shadows.

56
Adura

Sleep came fitfully at the Militia Headquarters.

Adura had been comfortable enough, however. Rather than place Adura in one of the dank cells in the cellar of the building, Commander Fervens had arranged for a cot to be brought in to one of the rooms on the same floor as his office. The room was small and the door was locked, but it was at least warm and dry. Still, it wasn't her own bed or her own room and she was under arrest, charged with serious crimes of which she was not guilty. It took her a long time to fall asleep, only to be awoken, seemingly moments later, by the Unshuttering peal.

She heard the key turn in the lock. A middle-aged woman with an unsmiling face came in, followed by Commander Fervens. He stood watch while the servant opened the shutters and took away the privy pot.

"Are you ready to talk again?" Fervens asked. "I'll have breakfast brought in, but I need to speak with you immediately after that. Trust me, it will go far better for you if you cooperate and tell me what you know."

Adura had spent much time thinking about this. She now realised that she had played her cards poorly during her previous interrogation. She had been too shocked, too humiliated by her arrest and bewildered by the false evidence given against her. But she had now had time to think.

"I'm happy to tell you the truth," she said. "But can you tell me whether my parents know where I am?"

"Yes. They are coming in to see you, I understand."

"Good. There's a great deal I have to tell them."

The servant-woman brought in a simple breakfast of bread and cheese and a hot, spiced fruit tea. Adura sipped at it, still thinking. When she was taken to the Commander's office, she was ready.

"Now. What do you have to tell me?"

Adura clasped her hands before her. She had to choose her words carefully.

"Firstly," she said, "I am not—was not—the leader of the Daughters of the Dark. That was someone else, calling herself Raven, who contacted us and gathered us together in secret, all of us wearing masks so that we didn't know who the others were. I have told you who I believe that person was."

Fervens appeared about to interrupt her, but she went on determinedly.

"Secondly, I never sent any of those signals you showed me lastwake, the ones sent before the Pledging."

She looked into his sceptical eyes and went on as calmly as she could manage. "I know that you don't believe me, but it's true. I didn't send those messages. I swear that I did not. *Think*, Commander. All of this so-called evidence comes from the Signaller Clan. They have done a good job, I grant you, a very good job, in trying to throw the blame on me. But it won't stick. There's a reason that they are trying to make me out as the villain—to deflect suspicion from themselves."

She stopped herself from raising her voice, though it was hard. She mustn't appear to be hysterical. "I tell you again that Magistra Calora was the one in charge of the Daughters. They are trying to cover that up. Why should I make that particular accusation—why of all people would it be Magistra Calora who I would choose to accuse—if it were not true? You said yourself that you couldn't believe it. Why wouldn't I choose to accuse one of my friends, or some other lady? Why Calora? I tell you that I have evidence that Calora was behind it."

Fervens frowned, deep lines coming together in his forehead. It was clear that he hadn't expected such a spirited defence from Adura.

"What evidence?"

"Nothing on paper, but testimony of two people who have no reason to lie. The first is Mistress Campana of the Bellringers, who you'll recall was the last of the kidnapped girls to be released. She was imprisoned somewhere above ground after the fire and she claims to have seen the face of Raven while there. It was the face of Magistra Calora. Secondly, Alba of the Glassmoulders, another of The Daughters, says she is certain that Calora was Raven. She's an artist and could tell by all sorts of visual clues."

Fervens pursed his lips and shrugged. "Such testimony is hardly convincing. In the Council Court it will carry little weight. The Signallers are a powerful clan; and even more so now that Magister Solus is head of the Council."

"It's true, I know it. But there's something else. I've spoken to Master Candens of the Bellringers. He was chased and left for dead in the Great Umbra by a group of men led by Blaze, the Signallers' heir. But he survived by crossing the umbra to Moulder's Arm."

Fervens sat forward, suddenly attentive. "Do you tell me so? I haven't heard from Candens since he went off to try to find work with the Healers. I understand he was appointed to guard a delivery to Glimmer Peak. After they arrived there, he seemed to disappear. His horse was found wandering on the road near the Stonemason's estate. I've sent out agents looking for him, but there was no word. But you tell me you've spoken with him?"

"Yes. I rode with him on the ferry back from Moulder's Arm. But he told me that he sent you a signal from Glimmer Peak. Did you not receive it?"

Fervens shook his head, a sceptical expression still on his face.

"Candens told me that... oh, of course." Adura felt as though she were falling into a deep hole. Of course the Signallers hadn't passed on Candens' message to the Commander. "They intercepted it. They read it and stopped it."

"They?"

"The Signallers. Candens discovered that the Signallers *read* his encoded message to you. They read it even though it was encoded with the Militia cipher and a key-phrase you had given him. I know he was secretly working for you, you see. They wouldn't send on his message once they knew that it threatened them."

Fervens' frown deepened even further and now showed on his weather-tanned face like deep, dark grooves etched in mined wood.

"I find that very hard to believe. Our ciphers have always been perfectly secure. What do you claim that this mysterious, lost message said?"

"I don't know the details, but Candens said that it was about how Blaze was getting hold of illicit medicines from the Healers."

"Hmmm, so you say. And where is Candens now?"

"I—I don't know."

"Do you know how to get in contact with him?"

"No, but—"

Fervens turned and stared out of the window for a while, obviously deep in thought. But then he turned back and shook his head slowly. "No. It won't do, Adura. If what you suggest were true, it would shake society to its roots. It's preposterous."

"Candens said—"

"Without being able to speak to Candens himself, I can only think that this is an elaborate story which you have made up to try to save yourself. In any case, it's too late to try to persuade me. A Grand Council Court has already been arranged three Shutterings from now. You can present what defence you have to the Court. The clans will decide."

Adura clenched her fists. She had been so sure that she could convince Fervens. It was hard to accept the fact that he was unmoved by her story.

"Is there anything more you wish to say?" he asked. "You persist in denying that you led the Daughters of the Dark? You won't confirm which of the women you wrote to joined the organisation?"

Adura could tell that these were just formal questions which Fervens felt he had to ask. He barely seemed interested in her answers.

"I was *not* their leader," she repeated. "I've already told you that Alba of the Glassmoulders was one of us. The others I don't know. I've been telling you the truth, Commander."

He gave a small nod of acknowledgement, but it was obvious that he didn't believe her. He called one of his officers to take her back to the locked room.

57

Campana

She made what little preparations she could for leaving the manor, though it was difficult. Hermia's eye was all too often on her. Never before had she felt so confined and restrained by her life, and understood what a useless and futile life it was. All of the occupations she had enjoyed in the past now seemed like so much time-filling. And so many of them—reading, sewing, playing music—were expected to be carried out in the common room shared with her mother, Hermia and other female members of the household.

Pleading a headache, she retired to her own room. The key to her door was missing. She hunted for it for a while, but soon realised that Hermia must have taken it to ensure that Campana could not lock her out.

Indeed, Hermia quickly came visiting, "to check on how poor Campana is feeling". Though Hermia did not renew her threats, they hung there like an invisible sword dangling over Campana's head. She took a long time to leave.

Finally, it was dinner-time again. Campana tried to keep herself calm as she sat down to the table. Ardens nodded to his daughter and resumed reading a paper he had placed next to his plate. Her mother was tending to the needs of her Aunt Nola, who was now failing of memory and was more like a child every waking. Lambent was unusually quiet during the meal. Indeed, her brother appeared to be in a daze. Perhaps, Campana thought, he had recently been given a dose of his 'medicine'.

"You still seem unwell, my dear." Hermia stood and brought a cup across to Campana. "Here, take some of this. It's a herbal medicine. I'm sure you'll feel better once you've had some."

"Thank you." Campana pretended to sip at the liquid. Did Hermia think she was stupid?

She continued to pretend to drink from the cup as she ate a little of the meal set before her. The third time she set the cup down she placed it at the very edge of the table and contrived to knock it over the next time she reached for her knife.

"Oh! I'm so sorry!" She watched the cup fall to the floor and smash, spilling liquid everywhere. One of the maids hurried forward to tidy up the mess. "Never mind," Campana said, "it was nearly all gone anyway."

Hermia gave her a sharp look, but said nothing.

At last, the meal was over. Hermia helped Lambent up and with the aid of his crutch he began to hobble off towards their room. As soon as they were out of sight, Campana wished her parents and Great-Aunt Nola a good sleep and then ran up the stairs to her room.

Her maid Libeth was there. Earlier that waking, in one of the brief moments they had alone together, Campana had asked her to be on hand immediately after the evening meal.

"Libeth," she asked now, "do you love me?"

Libeth smiled and tilted her head to one side. "Love you, mistress? I like you very much, but you are my mistress and I am your servant."

"Would you be my friend, then?" Campana asked. "Don't be my servant. Be my friend."

Libeth's face grew serious. "Yes, Campana, of course I will. What is it?"

"I'm going away from the manor. This Shuttering. I have to get away and no one must know of it before the Unshuttering. Will you help me?"

"But why—?"

"I can't tell you why, just yet. But it has to do with Hermia."

Libeth's lips firmed into a line. She detested Hermia. "Yes, then. What do you need me to do?"

"Would you sleep here this Shuttering? In my bed, pretending to be me? I think Hermia may come after the Shuttering to check that I'm here. I can't lock my door, I'm sure she's taken the key. I... I don't *think* she'll try to do you any harm." Campana's voice caught and it took an effort for her to control herself before she went on. "But Libeth, I can't be sure. I'm so afraid of her. I wouldn't forgive myself if..."

Libeth smiled. "Don't worry. I'm a light sleeper. And I'll take one of the carving knives to bed with me. But where will you go? How will you go?"

"I don't want to tell you. Then you don't need to lie if they ask you. As for how, I'm going to ride. I know how to get into the stables after the doors are barred. You know how you used to scold me about sneaking out after the Shuttering? I used to do it so I could pet my pony. I climbed up the wall on the darkwards side of the stables and squeezed in through a gap under the eaves. I can get in that way again."

"No, my dear. You're a lot bigger now and that's too risky. Give me a few moments. There's still a little time before the Shuttering. I'll talk to one of the stable-men, he's sweet on me. I'll tell him to saddle your horse and leave the darkwards doors closed but unbarred. Then I'll fetch a knife from the kitchen. Wait here."

"Oh! Thank you so much."

Tears started in Campana's eyes and she brushed them away as Libeth quickly went out.

Campana changed into a dark blue dress and drew on a black cape. Then she went to a green dress hanging in the wardrobe. It had long sleeves and was now a little small for her. She felt inside one of the sleeves. Yes, what she had hidden was still there. She drew it out and placed it inside the small pack she had prepared. Now she was ready.

The Shuttering peal was just beginning to sound when Libeth came back, a little out of breath. She showed Campana the knife she had taken from the kitchen, its precious metal blade long ago worn into a curve by innumerable sharpenings.

"It's all organised," Libeth said. "Wait for a little, while everyone settles down to sleep. And Campana, my dear, please be careful."

"You, too. If you're discovered in my bed, blame it all on me. They think I'm crazy anyway, so I don't mind."

"All right." Libeth put her arms around Campana and hugged her tightly. "The answer is yes, my dear. I do love you."

They were silent in each others' arms for a while. Then Campana sighed.

"I'm going now. If all goes well I'll see you again in a few Shutterings' time. Pray for me."

"I will. God speed."

Outside, in the deep shadow of the buildings, Campana made her way to the stables. The darkwards door, as Libeth had promised, moved easily when she pushed against it.

As she went in, she was greeted by the warmth of the animals, the stink of their dung and the sound of the horses shifting in their sleep. The front shutters, of course, were closed tight. A little light crept in through the inevitable gaps in the wooden boards.

Campana found her way to the stall of her favourite mount Gram, a gentle gelding who she knew to be capable of a fast gallop when called upon. Gram was already awake and saddled, his eyes wide as though with equine curiosity.

She took his reins and led him out of the darkwards door. She closed the door, mounted the horse with the aid of a step and started off. The horse had clearly been expecting to be led out of the manor's shadow and into the sunlight, but Campana turned him away instead, deeper into shadow and over the ridge on which the manor stood. Only once she was out of sight of the buildings in the umbra darkwards of the ridge did she turn Gram's head. Riding just below the ridge out of sight of the Sun, she urged him to a canter.

It was a strange feeling. She was a curfew-breaker, a shadow rider! Excitement alternated with fear. *Please let me get far enough away before they find I'm missing! And, please God, don't let Libeth come to any harm.*

She rode on. Soon enough, she would be forced to leave the shadows and re-enter the sunlight, still within sight of the manor's bell-tower. Would anyone on duty up there see her and sound the alarm? Unlikely, but it was possible. With luck, no one would know she was gone until the Unshuttering. Libeth would need to sound the alarm then, or it would be obvious that she was complicit in Campana's escape.

She needed to be far away by then. She bent her head against the chill air streaming past her and rode on.

58

Candens

Candens awoke sore and stiff. His head still throbbed a little, though the lump on it had gone down considerably. To his relief, Rinn had gone, as had the young mother and her baby, leaving only Ella and Denn in the group of people near the wall. The fire had been allowed to go out, but three oil lamps still burned.

Ella gave Candens a crust of bread and a cup of water for his breakfast. She staggered a little as she handed over the cup, splashing some of the water. Candens suspected that she had been sampling the stolen brandy more than a little while he had been asleep.

Denn was pacing about as though he found it difficult to stay still.

"Come on, brother, let's be up and about. I'll lead you to Todd's Tavern. Not far."

Candens suppressed a smile. He knew now that Denn's 'not far' could mean a long walk. He prepared himself to leave. Short work, as he now had few possessions.

Denn led the way and soon they were again following the twists and turns of the maze of tunnels. At rare intervals, Candens saw another of the spiral ramps leading upwards.

"Where does that lead?" he asked Denn the next time he saw a ramp.

"Nowhere, brother. Most of them are blocked at the top, filled with dirt and rubble, or a godsteel door we can't get past. There's only a few ways in and out of the Delvers' Domain, like I told you, and only we knows them."

They went on, Candens thinking hard about his future. The first priority was to talk to Commander Fervens. After that, who could tell? Even if he could avert the revenge of Blaze and the Signallers, his prospects were bleak. He thought bitterly of how Hermia had led him into a trap, driven by his own foolish desire. Forcing his thoughts away from her, he thought instead of Adura, wondering why she had been taken by the Militia and how she was faring. It was true that she had been involved in the kidnapping, but...

Suddenly something occurred to him. It was like being blinded by the Sun on the sudden opening of a shutter. Giving an oath, he stopped short. He put out a hand and brought Denn, too, to a halt.

The old man turned to him, puzzled. "What is it, young Lonn? Am I going too fast for you?"

"No, it's not that. Tell me, the buildings that burned down two decants ago. Was there one of the ramps leading up into them?"

Denn rubbed his grizzled chin. "Used to be. Came out into an old shadow house. But that's all crashed down with the fire and you can't get through now. I can't take you up there, brother."

"The tunnel that leads up to it: where does it go in the other direction?"

Denn shrugged. "There's cross tunnels all along it, but if you keep straight, you'd end up going towards the sea and it keeps on going under the water. Don't know how far though; nothing there for us."

"Does it run under the Council Lodge, do you think?"

"The Council Lodge? Could do, I suppose. It must go somewhere nearby. There's a ramp down that way, but it's blocked, like most of them. Why do you want to know, brother?"

"Blocked by rubble?"

"No, it's a godsteel door. Steel frame, too, can't get past it, though I tried once."

It was obvious now to Candens. Someone had known about the tunnels beneath the city, or at least about one of them, the one leading from the Lodge to the old shadow house. That was the way that Raven had led the Daughters of the Dark with their captives. The entrance to the ramp from the Council Lodge must be well hidden, or the Militia would have found it during their search. But Raven—Magistra Calora—had somehow known how to get past the steel door.

"Could you take me there, instead of Todd's Tavern? Take me to that ramp. You can leave me there and I'll find a way through that door."

Denn was silent for a long while, rubbing his chin again, his eyes searching Candens' face. "Rinn was right, young Call-Me-Lonn. You ain't one of us, are you?"

Candens sighed. "I'm down on my luck, Denn. I've had bad times recently. Will you help me? You can have what's left in the purse."

Another lengthy pause, Denn finally shrugged. "All right, brother. You might not be one of us, but you're a decent sort. I'll take your purse and lead you there. Purse now, though, brother, not later."

Candens brought out the purse and the last of his money, which chinked forlornly as he passed it to Denn. Denn nodded and grinned. "Will you tell me one more thing, Brother Call-Me-Lonn?"

Anticipating the question, Candens smiled. "My real name is Candens. Once of the Bellringers. Not any longer, though, as you can see." He indicated his filthy, ragged clothing.

"Well, then, Brother Candens, let's go. Bit of a stretch."

Denn turned back on the path they had been taking and started to lope off, Candens following. A little later, Denn took a sharp left turn at an intersection, then another to the right. One more turn, back again to the left.

"Shadow house was that way," he said, pointing. "The other ramp is this way. Come on."

It was a long walk. Candens couldn't help but think about his poor sister stumbling along this distance, terrified about what might lie ahead. He set his mouth. The Signallers would pay. He would see to it personally.

Finally, they saw the spiral ramp ahead. The tunnel they were in ran onwards beyond the ramp and was beginning to slope slightly downwards. Candens pointed to it.

"You say that goes on under the sea?"

Denn shrugged. "I've been down it a little way, brother, but it just keeps on going and going, too far for me. It must run under the water; might go out as far as the Sun. Would be a nice cool way to get there, eh?"

"Yes..." Candens was baffled. This whole underground world was so new to him, yet it must be extremely ancient. There were too many mysteries. And no spare time to think about them.

Together, they started up the ramp and climbed around three full turns. The smooth grey walls came to an end and before them was a dark metallic door, set in a frame of the same material.

"Godsteel," Denn said. "You won't get through that, young Candens."

"I think I will. Someone I know came through it not so very long ago. That means there must be a way to open it."

Candens went forward and pushed at the door. It was cold and hard and moved not a fraction even when he put all of his weight against it. He could feel no handle or any other grip by which he could pull at it. He tried sliding it, first one way and then the other. Nothing. Still, he kept trying. There must be some trick to it.

After a while, Denn started to make agitated sounds and Candens looked back at him. Denn held up his flickering oil lamp.

"Running short of oil, brother. Not much left. I might be able to find my way back in the dark, maybe, but maybe not. Even us Delvers sometimes gets lost down here. So we has to start back now, brother, to be sure. Come on, quick."

"No, you take the lamp and go." Candens sounded more convinced than he felt. "I'm certain I'll find a way through, even in the dark. If not, well, I've done my best in this world and we'll see what the next has in store."

Denn hesitated. "But, brother…"

"Go! And thank you for all you've done for me, Denn of the Delvers." Candens slapped the old man on the back appreciatively. "You saved my life and you've helped me greatly by bringing me here."

"Farewell, then, Brother Candens."

Denn headed back down, but not without several glances back to see if Candens had changed his mind. Candens shook his head and waved. Soon the old man was out of sight and Candens was plunged into utter darkness. For a moment, his resolution faltered and he almost ran after Denn. But he steeled himself and turned back to the door. He had no choice now. He had to pass through this door or die. He would never find his way to the Delvers' Domain by himself, in the dark.

He spent a long time feeling around the frame to see if there was some hidden catch or lever which might open the door, but there was nothing. Or was that a sound? He paused and put his ear to the cold steel. It was just at the very edge of hearing, but he thought he could detect a noise. Was that someone moving?

His decision was made. He began to thump on the door with his fist. Bang! Bang! Bang! He paused and put his ear to the door again. The sounds beyond had definitely changed. He started to hammer again. Bang! Bang! Bang!

With his ear to the door once more, he heard a muffled, tremulous voice: "Who's there?"

Bang! Bang! Bang! "Candens of the Bellringers!" he bellowed. "Let me through!" Bang! Bang! Bang!

With a kind of sigh, the door shifted and began to slide to one side, letting in a blaze of light which blinded Candens for the moment.

Candens found himself looking into the pale, frightened face of old Magister Percuro of the Healers.

Percuro was white and shaking as he sat opposite Candens. Not merely his hands, but his whole body was shaking, as though he were extremely cold, cast into the outer darkness. And perhaps, in a way, he had been. Candens himself had been severely shaken by where he had found himself when the steel door opened, behind the altar in the Healer's Chapel, adjacent to the Great Hall. The door which had slid aside so magically was covered with a religious mosaic on its other side. When Percuro had closed it again, no one would ever have suspected that there was an opening there.

Now Candens was in Percuro's adjoining study, into which the old man had hurried Candens. Sitting in a soft, upholstered chair covered in delicate brocade, he felt utterly out of place. No doubt his filthy clothing was soiling the fine material. He didn't much care.

Percuro had said almost nothing since Candens had emerged from behind the hidden door. Just sat and shook. After a long silence, he said, "Candens, please. There's a flask over there on my desk. I must have some, or I might die. Please?"

Candens brought over the flask, filled with a reddish liquid. Percuro sipped desperately at it and after a few moments, some colour returned to the old man's face. "Better," he whispered.

Candens sat back down, waiting. He was full of questions, but he wanted Percuro to take the lead. Finally, Percuro asked, in a cracked voice, "Candens—how did you get there, beyond the door? Did you find the control when the chapel was empty, sneak in there?"

The last question sounded as though Percuro was hoping against hope that it was true.

"I didn't get into that place from the chapel, Magister. I think you must know the way I came. I came from the tunnel."

Percuro bobbed his head. "Yes. Yes, I knew that had to be it. I'm sorry, you gave me such a shock, I can't—"

Candens, impatient now, leaned forward. "Magister, you must know that when the girls were abducted from the Pledging Ceremony, they were led into the chapel under cover of the smoke and taken through that door and down the ramp into the tunnel. And from there, along it and up into an old shadow house, where they were kept prisoner."

Percuro said nothing, but his face grew pale again. He sipped again from the flask. "Yes," he whispered at last.

"Why, Magister? You must have known all about it. You must have told the kidnappers about the door and the tunnel and the shadow house. All the time the Militia was hunting the girls, you *knew* where they were. Why did you say nothing?"

"They were safe," the old man said. "I insisted upon it. Your sister—I insisted that they let her go after she had been burned in the fire."

"You insisted!" Candens's anger surged suddenly. "But only after she nearly lost her life. And who, Percuro, are 'they'?"

Percuro covered his face with his hands. "I can't tell you, Master Candens, I simply can't. Please…"

Candens felt a scrap of pity for the old man, but only a scrap. "Was it the Signallers? Was it Magistra Calora? Tell me!"

His hands still over his face, Percuro shook his head slightly, but his whole body was shaking again, so much so that Candens couldn't be sure that he had actually received an answer.

Sighing, Candens tried a different tack and asked in a less accusing voice, "How long have you known about the tunnels, Magister? And about the secret door in the chapel?"

Percuro lifted his hands from his face, which was streaked with tears. He couldn't meet Candens' gaze, but looked away towards the chapel. "We've always known."

"We?" Candens was startled.

"The Healers clan has known since the very beginning, perhaps; long, long ago anyway." Percuro turned his head back to Candens. "The tunnels aren't a complete secret, you know. Sometimes when workmen are digging the foundations for a new building they will break through into a tunnel. But no one is much interested. The tunnels are dark and cold and empty. There's nothing of value in them. The holes just get filled in."

Not quite empty, Candens thought. *They are the domain of the Delvers.*

"But your own way into them? The door in the chapel?" he persisted.

"It's always been there, so far as I know. Only we—the Healers—know of it. And then only a few of us; just the clan heads and our heirs."

"And you used it to get to the shadow house unseen." Candens was disgusted.

Percuro, however, shook his head firmly.

"No, not to the shadow house. That's not where—" He stopped himself. "We didn't use it to go to the shadow house. Not myself, anyway. My grandfather, sometimes—yes, I fear so. Perhaps my father also. But not myself, I swear."

"What hold do the Signallers have over you?" Candens asked. "You've been supplying them with drugs. You provided the information and the means which allowed the kidnapping to take place. Why are you so beholden to them?"

Percuro only closed his mouth and shook his head.

Candens persisted in his questioning for some time, but it was clear that short of threatening to physically harm the frail old man, he wasn't going to learn any more. Yet if he were to hurt Percuro like that, Candens didn't think he could face himself in the mirror.

Eventually, he gave it up. But to his surprise, after a long silence, Percuro seemed to come to a decision. He laid a hand on Candens' arm and volunteered some information.

"Have you heard that there's to be a trial here? A Grand Council Court in two Shutterings?"

"Who is on trial?" Candens had a sinking feeling in his stomach that he could already guess the answer.

"Your one-time pledge, Adura of the Mirrormasters. She's accused of leading the Daughters of the Dark."

"But Percuro, you know that isn't true."

"Yes. I do know it, God help me."

The trembling had begun again.

"Will you remain silent, then, and let her be punished? She may be locked away in shadow for millends."

Percuro started to speak, stopped, bit his lip. "I promise you that I will do everything that I can. It may not be enough. But I will try. Please, Candens, I've said as much as I am able to."

And Candens had to be content with that.

59
Adura

"It's time."

Commander Fervens stood in the doorway to make his announcement. As a special dispensation, Adura had been allowed to move into the Mirrormasters' private quarters in the Council Lodge in the company of her parents, to await her trial. Militiamen stood guard on the door to ensure she didn't escape.

Where would she even go?

Her father Ignis had been strident in asking for this dispensation, but Adura knew that there had been an ulterior motive which had helped win Fervens' agreement. Her hastily-arranged trial had created a sensation among both Brights and the general population of Dims. Bringing her here discreetly before word had spread had avoided the problems of trying to bring her into the Council Lodge through a crowd of unruly spectators.

There had been an uncomfortable reunion with her parents. Her father had stridden about, filled with angry condemnations, until her mother had calmed him down and they had both listened patiently to her account. In the end, Ignis had agreed to support his daughter even with the near-certainty of losing the business of the Signallers. He had even agreed to act as her advocate at the trial.

She looked up at her mother Lucida.

"I'm ready." She stood up and turned to Commander Fervens. "Let's go."

Fervens smiled a very slight smile, an expression which his face clearly experienced only rarely.

336

"Come, then."

With her parents at her side, Adura was led down the stairs and into the Great Hall, already packed with the representatives of clans both minor and major. A low level of conversation erupted into a busy babble as she was led in and on to the stage. The side shutters of the hall were partially closed to restrict the full light of the Sun and the ceiling mirror had been arranged so as to beam its light around a chair at the front of the platform. There she was led. She kissed her mother and father and they left her there, illuminated by light and the focus of every eye. Lit up in that manner, it was difficult for her to make out faces in the comparatively dark hall.

Lustris, Healer of Souls, stepped forward to bless the trial and ask God to ensure that truth would be revealed. His words were clumsy and hesitant. Clearly he was still not yet accustomed to the role he had taken on after the death of his nephew Medeor. The great shutter doors were slid open fully for a moment to allow the light of God's Sun to pervade the hearts of those present. Adura, however, experienced only a moment of dread as her shadow briefly appeared, stretching out towards the audience of her peers.

Then the shutter doors were part-closed again and the Arbiter came forward to address the audience.

There had been furious negotiations leading up to the trial. Normal protocol would have had the Council President acting as the Arbiter for the trial. However, as Magister Solus was currently President, Adura's father Ignis had argued strongly before the Council that normal protocol should be set aside because his daughter's defence involved accusations against the Signaller Clan, a clear conflict of interest for Solus. In the end, Solus had to give way, with bad grace. Instead, he insisted on taking on the role of Accusing Advocate. Ignis had tried to resist this, too, but had been unable to gain a consensus from the Council.

David R. Grigg

Magister Nolans, head of the Metalworkers, had been selected by ballot as Arbiter for the trial. It wasn't a bad choice, Adura thought, as she watched him come forward. A strongly-built man in late middle-age, he was clean-shaven and greying at the temples. She had only met him once or twice, but he appeared to be direct and honest, essential traits for someone dealing in precious materials. She could only hope that he would deal with her as carefully as he did his bronze, silver and steel.

"Magisters and Magistras, Masters and Mistresses and clan members all. We are here to decide on a very serious matter. Many of you were present in this very hall when the Council President, Magister Neptus of the Boatbuilders, was attacked and injured; when the sacred ceremony of Pledging was interrupted and prevented from continuing; when eight young women were abducted and removed from here to be confined for many Shutterings, in fear for their lives."

Adura was surprised. The man spoke so well that he could be an orator. She only wished that he were not so eloquent about the crimes in which she had taken part.

"You have before you Adura, daughter of Clan Mirrormaster," Nolans went on. "She is accused of planning the outrage you recall so well, of gathering together a group of like-minded young women and leading them here to this hall, of detonating an incendiary device, of holding hostages and of profiting by their ransom."

He paused. "But although Adura is here accused of these grave charges, remember that they are not yet proven. You must hear the evidence that has been brought against her, listen to her defence and then make your judgement. If you find the charges proven, you must then determine an appropriate punishment."

Nolans fell silent, then, looking around the hall.

"I yield to Magister Solus of the Signallers, the Accusing Advocate, to detail the evidence against Adura and to question her on your behalf."

He stepped to one side and sat down.

Solus strode onto the stage, full of confidence and power. Somewhere in the audience, Adura knew, would be his wife Calora looking on, perhaps with a smile on her face, waiting to deny with contempt any counter-accusation from Adura or her advocate.

Deny it all you will, Adura thought. *But at the very least we will raise some doubt which remains in people's minds after the trial. Perhaps in future people will no longer be so trusting of the Signallers.*

It was a slim hope, but it was all that she had.

⁓

Solus stepped forward to stand in the pool of light centred on Adura's chair and faced the audience of his peers. Adura, for her part, refused to look up at him and continued to gaze out into the hall, her hands quiet in her lap.

"Members of the assembled clans of Sunfall," Solus began. "I accuse Adura, daughter of Clan Mirrormaster, of the long list of crimes you have heard described. Long as that list may be, there is however a yet further crime committed by this wicked young woman which Arbiter Nolans failed to mention."

A murmur of comment wafted through the crowd. Adura wondered what approach Solus was taking. She didn't have to wait for long.

"That further crime is the vile slander which Adura has raised against Magistra Calora, my own wife, in a desperate attempt to deflect the accusation. You will hear Adura claim that Magistra Calora was somehow involved in the outrageous acts which occurred here. She has no proof of this wild charge, of course. You will agree with me that even to hear such a slander is to recognise it immediately as

339

absurd and to dismiss it outright. I will therefore give it no more attention, but focus on the major charges."

So it was to be a frontal assault on Adura's defence, trying to weaken it before it was even put forward. *Patience*, Adura thought. *Your time will come.*

"Let me begin," Solus said, though Adura was under the impression he already had. "Let me begin by asking the accused a simple question. Mistress Adura, are you a member of the group known as the Daughters of the Dark? A simple 'yes' or 'no' will suffice."

Adura raised her voice. "No."

That seemed to puzzle him. Solus knew that she had already admitted her involvement to Commander Fervens.

"You deny it? On your oath, again, are you a member of that group?"

"No. I *was* once a member. Now I am not."

He was irritated. "Don't play word games with me. You *were* a member, you admit. And you were part of the group which carried out the outrage at the Pledging Ceremony?"

Adura clasped her hands tightly together, forcing herself to remain controlled. She spoke loudly but without strain. "Yes. And for that I deserve and expect due punishment. But I was *not* the leader of—"

"That was not my question," Solus interrupted.

She was determined to be heard. "I was *not* the leader of the group. I now know that the woman who directed us was Magistra Calora of the Signallers."

A hubbub of muttering came from the audience. Solus feigned outrage. "You repeat your slander even here, even on your oath? Clan members, do you need to hear any more?"

Ignis, Adura's father, stepped into the light. "Arbiter, slander is not slander if it can be shown to be the truth. We will bring proof of my daughter's claim during her defence."

Proof was a big claim, Adura thought even as she

welcomed her father's intervention. If only Campana was here to tell her story, but despite an official order from the Council, the Bellringers had claimed their daughter too ill and mentally distressed to appear before the Court. Adura worried about that. What was wrong with her young friend?

"Nonsense!" Solus said. "Arbiter, may I continue?"

Permission granted, he turned back to the audience.

"Clan members, you have heard Adura admit her involvement in the crimes of which she is accused. Her only slim hope of reprieve is to convince you that she was not the organiser and leader of the group. But here I bring proof that she was at the very centre of the Daughters of the Dark."

He pulled out a sheaf of papers from a pouch at his waist. Adura knew those papers well.

"Here are the signals Adura sent to twelve young women—the very women who Commander Fervens now suspects formed the Daughters of the Dark. Signals sent a centend before the Pledging. Signals bearing identical messages, clearly designed to recruit and organise the group."

Ignis of the Mirrormasters stepped forward again. "Arbiter, may I ask Magister Solus a question about these signals?" Arbiter Nolans was out of Adura's line of sight, but he must have consented, because her father went on. "Magister, were these signals all encoded?"

"Yes, of course," Solus snapped.

"So you are unable to say what the messages are actually about?"

"Certainly not. But the coded text is identical on each signal. You have been allowed to examine the papers, I believe."

"And these messages were all sent on the same waking?"

"Yes, from the signal tower closest to your own manor, Magister Ignis."

David R. Grigg

"Magister Solus. I know only too well how expensive it is to send encoded messages." A ripple of amused agreement came from the audience. "Twelve such messages, all sent in the same waking, some to distant manors, would represent a significant sum. I assure you that my daughter did not borrow such a sum from me. I keep detailed accounts, which I can tender here."

Solus shrugged. "She is clearly capable of any crime. Perhaps she stole the money."

"From where, I wonder? But put that aside," Ignis continued. "If these messages are in code, then how did the young women to whom they were sent decode them?"

That gave Solus a moment's pause. "Obviously they had agreed the appropriate cipher and a pass phrase before-hand."

"So, if you are claiming that this was an attempt by my daughter to *recruit* members of the group, then she must have contacted these young women previously in some other way to arrange the cipher and the key phrase."

Solus was obviously now uncertain of the line that Ignis was taking. After a pause, he said, "Yes, that must have been so."

"In which case, why would Adura not pass on all of the information she needed to at that prior time? Why go to the expense of twelve encoded signals and the risk of attracting attention? As it happens, I visited the signal tower myself on the following waking to despatch a particularly important signal. You will have that in your records. It is surprising that your clerk did not mention to me the flurry of signals supposedly sent so recently by my daughter."

Angry now, Solus waved the papers high. "Yet here those signals are! Do you deny their existence?"

"No," Ignis said. "I merely question whether they were in fact sent by my daughter."

"Are you calling me a liar, you—"

Arbiter Nolans called out, "Gentlemen, enough! Magister Solus, do you have any further evidence?"

Solus, breathing deeply, was trying to control his anger and not quite succeeding. "Yes. I had hoped not to expose my daughter to this, but I call on Hermia, now a wife of Clan Bellringer."

She noticed a disturbance in the audience as Hermia stood and came towards the stage. Though it was still difficult to see, now that she knew where to look Adura could make out Lambent and his parents.

Hermia came into the light and without so much as a glance at Adura, faced the audience. Solus indicated to her that she should begin.

"I wish so much that I had spoken out earlier, when she first tried to get me to join her and those other women. But I was afraid." Hermia pointed to Adura. "She threatened to tell people that I *was* involved, even though I had refused; that *I* had tried to recruit *her*. Then, after the Pledging, when I could prove I was at home in our manor the whole time, she threatened to accuse my mother of being the leader of the group. Just as she has done here."

Candens had warned Adura that Hermia was easily able to present a false face and portray herself as someone she really was not. Adura saw it quite clearly now. Hermia was convincing as a shy, fearful woman, uncertain of her place in the world.

Ignis came forward again. "Mistress Hermia, with the greatest respect, how could she threaten you before the kidnapping? If you had told someone that Adura had tried to recruit you to some mysterious group, what possible threat would stop you from saying so?"

Hermia contrived to look embarrassed. "It's foolish, I know, but I thought that people might believe her. I was newly married, I didn't want any scandal."

"And after the Pledging? How could she threaten you? When and where did you meet so she could threaten to expose your mother?"

"No..." Hermia hesitated, for the first time seemingly uncertain what to say. "She sent me a signal. I'm sure my father could find the paper if he were to have our people look for it."

"I'm sure he could," Ignis said drily. "Was this message sent in the clear or encoded? You had better let your father know what to prepare."

"Arbiter!" Solus shouted, furious.

Nolans spoke from somewhere behind Adura. "Magister Ignis, you go too far. You are close to being accused of slander yourself."

Ignis bowed. "I apologise, Arbiter. Consider my remark withdrawn."

Yet it had already been said and Adura hoped it might make people think.

"Very well, I will forget the matter." Solus raised his voice and turned to the audience. "Arbiter, Magisters and Magistras, Masters and Mistresses, you have heard my accusation and have seen my evidence. It is for you to judge."

He bowed, then he and Hermia left the platform together.

60

Candens

Candens stood in the shadows at the back of the Hall, anxious and finding it difficult to keep still. Beside him stood Commander Fervens, who put a consoling hand on his shoulder. "Your time will come; just wait."

Candens nodded, but was still ill at ease. Physically, he felt himself to be a completely different man than the filthy wanderer clothed in rags who had terrified Magister Percuro two Shutterings ago. Now he was well-fed and rested, neatly dressed once more, his hair and beard well trimmed.

Adura knew that he was here. They had had a quiet reunion in her clan's quarters the previous waking. He had cleaned himself up with Percuro's help so that he was again presentable. Adura had been shocked but greatly relieved to see him safe. He had spent a long time describing to her and her parents his adventures in the Delvers' Domain. After that, they had sent a trusted servant to fetch Commander Fervens, warning the man to say nothing of Candens' presence in the Mirromaster quarters.

Now, Candens fretted as he watched the proceedings and heard Adura accused, with apparently unassailable evidence brought against her.

Her father, Magister Ignis, was doing an excellent job in creating at least some doubt about the Signaller's evidence. Now he was presenting the defence, leading Adura through a description of how she had become involved with the Daughters. Candens was shocked to hear her declare that it had been Hermia who had first put Adura in contact with the mysterious woman 'Raven'. But of course that all made sense. It had all been part of the overall machinations of the Signallers.

Adura was describing the meetings of the Daughters of the Dark, with all of the participants masked and unknown to each other.

"So at that stage you had no idea who this woman 'Raven' could be?" Ignis asked.

"No," Adura replied.

"What leads you to claim now that Raven is in fact Magistra Calora of the Signallers?"

"It was Campana, from Clan Bellringers. She had discovered who *I* was—she pulled off my mask when I brought her food while she was imprisoned. I agreed to help her escape. By then I was disillusioned with Raven and realised that the kidnapping of the pledgees was all wrong. But my plan went wrong, terribly wrong, and Campana was burned. She was taken somewhere above ground after that. While she was being treated she pretended to be asleep and she saw Raven's face without the mask. It was Magistra Calora."

Solus called out from the audience. "Arbiter, I protest!" He hurried back onto the stage and stalked into the light again. "We only have Adura's word of this fanciful claim by Campana. Even if the girl were here—"

"She *is* here. I *am* here!"

A voice rose from the audience and a slim figure stood up. Candens was stunned. He had seen Radians of the Healers come in earlier, accompanied by a slim young man who Candens had assumed to be a cousin. Both had taken seats next to old Magister Percuro. Now that young person stood up and had thrown off a hood. It was Campana.

Campana, in truth, was hardly recognisable as the young sister he had last seen wearing a lovely dress at her Pledging. Now she was dressed as a boy, her auburn hair cropped

346

short. And she seemed far, far older. As the hubbub of surprise from the audience quieted down, Campana spoke in a clear, carrying voice.

"I am Campana of the Bellringers. And what Adura says is true."

Candens saw a disturbance over where Hermia and Lambent had been sitting with his parents. Hermia was on her feet and Lambent was rising, too, speaking softly to her, his hand on her arm. On stage, Solus was taken aback, but persisted.

"Arbiter, we cannot hear testimony from this person. Her mind, I understand, has been disturbed by her unfortunate experiences. She has been babbling fantasies ever since her release. We have no time for this nonsense."

Campana remained standing, resolute. "Arbiter, will you hear me? It is for you and the clan members here assembled to hear what I have to say and judge whether I am mad or sane."

Arbiter Nolans spoke. "We will hear you. Come to the stage, Mistress Campana."

Campana began to weave her way down to the floor of the hall even as Solus renewed his complaints, to which Nolans turned a deaf ear.

"Did you know she would be here?" Candens whispered to Fervens.

Fervens gave a short laugh. "No. We've been trying to find her. Your family claimed she was unwell and in bed, but the servants told a different story, that she had gone missing. Interesting that she came in with young Radians."

61
Campana

Campana's heart was racing as she reached the stage and stepped into the light. For a moment, she was unable to speak. She opened her mouth but nothing came out. She had never in her life been the centre of attention of so large an audience, not had she ever had to speak to more than a few people at a time.

My God, she thought in a panic. *I'm going to stand here gaping and they'll all be sure that I am in truth mad.*

Seeing her distress, Magister Ignis, Adura's father, came over and whispered in her ear.

"Are you all right, my dear? Do you want to speak out directly, or shall I ask you a series of questions to guide you? Would that help?"

Campana nodded, grateful. Magister Ignis went back to his place and started his questions.

"Mistress Campana, we have already heard the story of the kidnapping. Adura has told us how you discovered that she was one of those keeping you prisoner. What happened after that?"

After a momentary stumble, Campana found her voice and went ahead, refusing to look at anyone except Magister Ignis for the time being.

"Adura was kind. She told me how unhappy she was to have been involved. And she tried to help me escape. It wasn't her fault that it didn't work out."

"I see. Now, did you ever see the woman calling herself Raven and the person you had discovered to be Adura

348

standing side by side? Did you ever see them both at the same time?"

"Oh!" Campana hadn't thought of that. Magister Ignis was very sharp. "Yes, of course I did. Several times; they were often in my room together."

"So they could not possibly be the same person?"

"No."

A murmur of comment swept across the assembled clan members. Solus protested again, but the Arbiter commanded him to be silent. Ignoring Solus, Magister Ignis continued.

"Mistress Campana, we are told that you caught sight of the face of the woman calling herself Raven. How did that happen?"

"After the fire, I was unconscious. When I woke up I found myself somewhere different from where we had been kept before. It was somewhere high above ground. I had been burned and I think a Healer had been tending my burns while I was asleep. I didn't see who it was, though."

"A Healer?" Ignis showed his surprise.

Solus jumped in again. "Arbiter! This clearly demonstrates that this young person is delusional. What Healer would tend to her, knowing her to be a prisoner and yet keep quiet?"

Solus couldn't prevent himself from glancing in the direction of Radians and Percuro.

Campana could not think what to say, but Ignis came to her assistance. "Setting that aside, Mistress, how did you come to see Raven's face?"

Campana described how Raven had tried to make her drink the yellowish fluid she now knew to be called *papavera* and how she had contrived not to consume too much of it. Then, pretending to be in a drugged sleep, she had seen Raven unmasked, but her mind was clear enough to recognize her.

349

Solus was again scornful. "You were in great pain, you had a medicine at hand to stop the pain, but you want us to believe that you did not drink it?"

Campana felt a great calmness on her now. "I drank enough to dull the pain, but not enough to dull my brain. I saw what I saw. Magistra Calora is the woman calling herself Raven, the leader of the group who kidnapped us."

Arbiter Nolans finally allowed Solus time to speak. The head of the Signallers Clan spoke for a considerable time trying to discredit Campana's testimony, pointing out, as had Campana's father, that *papavera* is well-known for causing hallucinations.

"In conclusion." Solus strode about the stage, confident in his assumptions. "This whole confabulation makes no sense. *Why* should my dear wife Calora be involved with this vicious organisation? What possible motive could she have for disrupting the pledging and kidnapping the girls? It is so obviously absurd!"

"As to that," Ignis interjected, "I believe that we can supply an answer." He looked towards the back of the hall. "I call on Candens, once of the Bellringers, now clanless."

Campana gave a gasp of surprise at the announcement of Candens' name. She hadn't seen her brother for so long. Now she watched him stride forward out of the shadows and begin to walk down the central aisle towards the stage. Then, unable to help herself, she looked across at where the members of the Signallers clan were seated. Shouts of anger were beginning to come from a group of young men there. Sitting amongst them Campana then spotted an older woman glaring at her, her face livid with hate. It was Calora. Campana shuddered and forced herself to look away, focusing instead on her brother.

62

Candens

On the stage, Solus was red-faced and furious, arguing with Nolans.

"Arbiter, these proceedings have descended into a farce. You cannot hear testimony from this man. He attempted to seduce my daughter and tried to persuade her to help him kill his own brother. He did indeed gravely injure Lambent. He was justifiably cast out of his clan in consequence and since then has been living the life of a ringless rogue. Whatever he has to say cannot be given any credit."

Nolans turned to Candens, who was now on the stage.

"What do you say to these charges, Master Candens? What Magister Solus says has weight. Why should we hear you?"

"Arbiter," Candens began, "clan members all. What I have to tell you is of the greatest importance to the whole of Sunfall. The charges Magister Solus makes against me— which I deny—arose entirely as the result of the schemes of Clan Signaller, schemes to greatly increase their power and influence. That poses a grave threat to the whole of our society. The whole of the proceedings here are the consequence of the unbridled ambition of the Signallers."

Solus had gone white and for a moment was at a loss for words but not for long.

"Arbiter, this young man, like his poor sister, appears to have lost his reason. My clan is being slandered and denigrated. The purpose of these proceedings is to charge one wicked young woman and see her punished. Instead, we have these absurd claims continually being made against my own honour, my wife's honour and the honour of our clan. I say again, this person has no credibility."

While he had been speaking, another figure had been walking down the length of the hall. It was Commander Fervens.

"Arbiter," he said, "will you hear me?"

Nolans looked from one person to another on the stage, clearly bewildered by now, and then back to Fervens.

"Speak, Commander," he said in a resigned voice.

"I can vouch for the character of Master Candens, once of the Bellringers. He was an excellent officer during his time with me in the Militia. Since his expulsion from his clan, rather than being a 'ringless rogue', he has in fact been acting secretly as my agent in investigating the source and distribution of illicit drugs."

As Fervens spoke, Candens saw that Solus had stepped out of the light on stage and was making a series of gestures towards his son Blaze in the audience. After a moment, Blaze and someone else—it was Vivens, Candens saw—stood up and started moving quickly towards the exit doors. They would be up to no good, Candens knew. They had already threatened to kill him and no doubt would, given the chance. But he could pay no more attention to them. The Arbiter was speaking.

"Magister Ignis, Commander Fervens," Nolan was saying. "I fail to see the relevance of any testimony to these proceedings which Candens can make. These alarmist claims and accusations against the noble Clan Signaller seem gratuitous and unnecessary."

Ignis was ready for this. "Arbiter, we have shown evidence that Magistra Calora, rather than my daughter, was the woman who gathered together the Daughters of the Dark. Magister Solus asks us why she should have done so. Candens has important evidence to address that question. If you believe his testimony, as we are sure that you will, you will understand that the consequences for our society are profound."

Nolans was silent, shifting in his seat as though uncomfortable.

"These grandiose claims seem overblown, Magister Ignis. I cannot decide." He stood and addressed the audience. "Clan members! I ask you to decide whether or not to hear this testimony. Will the head of each clan raise his hand if he wishes to hear what Candens, once of the Bellringers, has to say?"

Candens looked about the audience, full of anxiety. Several hands were raised and more were being lifted tentatively. He looked directly towards where his father was sitting. Ardens' hand was raised high. *That* was interesting, Candens thought, surprised but pleased.

"Those against?"

Only a scattering of hands rose. The Signallers, it appeared, did not have too many friends. Either that or most of the clan heads were more intrigued by the prospect of hearing some juicy gossip than protecting their relationship with the Signallers.

"Very well." Nolans resumed his seat, clearly irritated that his hand had been forced. "By the majority decision of this assembly, we will hear Candens."

Solus said nothing, but the pallor of his face told everything. He was afraid, with good reason. Ignis indicated that Candens should begin.

For a moment, Candens was silent as he gathered his thoughts, but he, Ignis and Adura had spent several bells' time during the previous waking planning out what he should say and the words came easily enough once he got started.

"Magisters and Magistras, Masters and Mistresses, clan members all. Thank you for your attention. I must begin by admitting that both Adura and I have acted foolishly. Adura was led astray by hoping that a radical group could effect change in society. She joined that group under the influence of a masked woman who called herself Raven. You have heard my sister identify that woman as Magistra Calora of the Signallers and her conviction cannot be shaken. Adura obtained further evidence of that identification in speaking to a friend who admits also to being a member of The Daughters and who can also identify Magistra Calora as Raven. We can bring her forward if necessary."

He paused and then went on.

"Magister Solus asks what motive there could be for his clan to control the Daughters of the Dark. I believe that at first the reason was to give them the opportunity to blackmail the young women who joined the group, to influence them by threatening to expose their involvement with such a radical association.

"Then came the accidental death of Magister Percuro's son and heir Medeor. He died without leaving any male children, unexpectedly placing Percuro's grandson Radians in line to become clan head. That was the trigger. Radians had been promised as pledge to my sister Campana well before Medeor's death. Now he was a very valuable catch. The Signallers set out to prevent his pledge to Campana ever being made so that Radians could instead be married to one of their own young women, whose existing pledge-promise also needed to be broken. The disruption of the Pledging Ceremony gave them time to achieve both ends."

He stopped and looked around. The audience was completely silent, waiting for his next words.

"My own foolishness was to be distracted by a pretty face, that of Hermia of the Signallers, now my brother's wife." He glanced across at Hermia, whose face was set and unreadable, but Lambent was showing his anger.

"Clan members, you know that it is our settled custom that once a woman is married, she takes on her husband's clan as her own and puts her original clan behind her. It is the strongest of customs that she never use her new role as a means of advantage to her old family, that she not pass back to them any secret information she may accidentally learn from her husband. But what if one clan—an ambitious clan—decided to break that custom as a matter of policy? To strategically pledge its daughters and nieces in important clans and through them influence and even control them? I believe that this is what the Signallers have been attempting to do with my own clan, the Bellringers, through the marriage of Hermia to my brother."

Solus couldn't restrain himself. "Lies!" he yelled. "Arbiter, we have heard enough!"

Candens did not wait to see if Nolans would try to stop him, but went on. "Even well before the marriage, Blaze of the Signallers was dealing in drugs, ensnaring my brother and leading to his addiction. After the wedding, Hermia made no effort to restrain Lambent's indulgence in drugs and wine, perhaps even encouraging it. According to what my sister wrote to Adura, she continues to supply him with an excess of the drug *papavera*, threatening to withhold it if he is not compliant. He has become her puppet. If I had been still living in the manor, I would have stepped in to prevent that. That is why I had to be banished. My foolish infatuation with Hermia made that all too easy."

Hermia, he saw, was on her feet, her hands clenched into fists at her side. Lambent was staring up at her, open-mouthed.

"I admit my fault," Candens continued. "I am truly sorry for it. More, I am sorry that in the ensuing argument with my brother, which Hermia engineered, he was grievously injured. I ask his forgiveness."

"Lies!" Solus shouted again. "What evidence is there for any of this?"

Candens faced him. "My sister, I am sure, will testify as to Hermia's behaviour in the manor once I was gone. As for Blaze trading in drugs, Commander Fervens is well aware of it. And while I was acting as a guard for the Healers, I discovered evidence which showed that the Healers are complicit in providing these drugs to the Signallers."

"More slander!" Solus turned to the audience. "Magister Percuro! Speak and deny these mad claims!"

This was the crucial moment. Candens stared across at the old man, his heart almost stopped. Would the Healer yield to Solus' command? Slowly, with face ashen and grim, Magister Percuro shook his head. Solus was both astonished and infuriated.

"Percuro! Speak, or I shall do what I threatened!" he yelled in anger, realising too late he had given himself away. Clearly he had engineered some influence over the old Healer and had now admitted it in public.

"Leave him alone," Candens interrupted. "We now come to the crux of the matter. Clan members, your attention please. Every waking you send hundreds of signals through the Signallers' towers. Every waking you trust that important, confidential messages which you send remain secret, both through the ciphers you use and through your trust in the Signallers. I am here to tell you that your trust is misplaced. The Signallers can and regularly do, decode and read your secret messages."

A roar of astonishment and dismay burst up from the clans in the audience. Almost speechless with fury, Solus strutted to the front of the stage.

"Clan members, these are outrageous lies! We have no way of reading your coded messages, nor would we ever do so." He had to repeat his denial several times over the clamour in the hall. When some quiet had returned he resumed, panting for self-control. "Arbiter, I appeal to you. I demand a stop to this."

Arbiter Nolans addressed Candens with a deeply sceptical expression. "Such a scandalous claim demands irrefutable proof, Candens. So far all we have heard are your

356

speculations and opinions. Unless there is real evidence, you must stand down and I will let Magister Solus respond."

Candens drew a breath, about to launch into his tale of how his message to Commander Fervens from Glimmer Peak had been intercepted and read. But to his surprise, before he could do so, his sister Campana spoke up.

"Arbiter, *I* have proof."

"Mistress Campana?"

"I have written evidence which proves that the Signallers are able to decode encrypted signals. May I show it to you?"

Frowning, Nolans indicated that she should come forward. Out of an inside pocket of her jacket she produced a bundle of papers. She unfolded them.

"There are three papers here." Campana explained as she passed them one by one to the Arbiter. "The first is an encoded signal sent to me by Adura from the Glassmoulders' manor a few Shutterings ago. She will confirm that she sent it. It's encoded in my father's commercial cipher, using a unique key phrase we had previously agreed between us. The second paper is the beginning of my own deciphering of the message. You can see that I translated several lines. While I was in the process of doing that, Hermia came into my room, very angry. She was carrying this third paper, which she balled up and threw at me. I retrieved it later and uncrumpled it. You will see that it is a signal addressed to her from the staff of the signal tower. There are a few coded lines at the start, but the rest of it, *in the clear* is the full message which Adura had sent."

She turned to the audience. "The third paper shows that Adura's message to me had been completely decoded. Not by me, but by the Signallers themselves. They sent it to Hermia to warn her of what Adura and I had found out about her mother Calora. Hermia then came in and threatened my life. It was in fear of her that I left my manor two Shutterings ago."

Abruptly, Solus moved. Not towards Campana or Candens, but to Nolans. He grabbed the Arbiter's tunic, hauled him out of his chair and threw him to the floor, scattering Campana's papers.

"Enough!" Solus roared. "This assembly is at an end. I end it now by my authority as Council President." He looked down the length of the hall. "Men! Seize these people and take them away!"

A large group of armed men, clad in the Signallers' blue and gold livery, burst into the hall from the rear entrance. They ran towards the stage, maces and clubs raised, bows strung and arrows notched.

63

Campana

The hall was in an uproar, almost every person on their feet and shouting. Campana dropped to her knees and scrabbled for her papers, which had fallen from Arbiter Nolans' hand when Solus had thrown him from his chair.

Solus was still shouting, trying to be heard. On stage, men in the blue-and-gold livery of Signaller couriers and guards were taking hold of everyone there: Ignis, Adura, Candens, Arbiter Nolans; even Commander Fervens. One of the men bent down to Campana and took her arm. He was a well-muscled man with a large black beard.

"It's all right, Mistress," he whispered. "Don't be afraid. Be patient, I won't hurt you. My name is Jud. Stand up if you will, but please say nothing."

Greatly puzzled, Campana stood.

Solus had managed to achieve enough quiet to at last be heard in the hall. His voice, though, was hoarse.

"Clan members, attend to me!" The noise level dropped again. "Clan members! You see that my men have taken charge here. I caution you all not to resist them. In view of these ridiculous charges against my clan, which have apparently been taken seriously by some of you, I now declare a state of civil emergency."

He stood up straighter, proud, imperious. "Across all of Sunfall, my signal has gone out, calling on my family, my servants and my couriers. All of them are well-armed. They are even now moving to your manors and taking hostages. No one will be harmed, provided you comply with my instructions."

A renewed angry buzz started up again in the hall.

"Without the services of my clan, you have no effective means of communication. Consider that. You cannot organise against us. All of Sunfall is dependent on Clan Signaller and has been for many millends. It is time now to make that dependency explicit."

This must have been their plan all along, Campana thought, her heart sinking. *All we've done is to make them carry out their plan immediately rather than taking their time about it as they gained influence over one clan after another.*

Complete quiet now reigned in the hall. Solus went on, a triumphant tone in his voice. "I hereby appoint myself President for life; my son Blaze will inherit the title. The Clan Council is hereby dismissed and will be replaced by administrators who I will appoint directly."

Furious shouts came from the clan heads currently making up the council, but Solus went on, ignoring them, his head held high.

"The Signallers shall lead Sunfall from now on and we will tolerate no dissent."

Campana felt an awful despair fall upon her. After all her efforts and her desperate flight from Hermia's threats, it had come to this. It was all over.

~

As Solus was making his triumphant declaration, Campana was surprised to see Commander Fervens move without struggle away from the man in blue and gold who had been holding him.

Stealthily he moved across the stage behind Solus and quietly came up to his back. At the end of the Signaller's proud speech, Fervens raised a dagger and placed the point of it at Solus' throat.

"That's enough, Solus," the Commander said.

Solus stood open-mouthed. His eyes flickered wildly from side to side.

"Men!" he croaked out. "Blaze? Vivens?"

The only response was that the men on the stage drew off their blue and gold tunics and threw them to the floor, revealing their Militia uniforms beneath. Campana gave an astonished shout of joy. In the audience, she saw, other militiamen were moving towards where Calora and Hermia still sat.

"These are *my* men and not yours, Solus," Fervens said. "On behalf of the Clan Council, I arrest you. Your peers are already present here. I see no reason that we cannot try you here and now."

Solus was bewildered. "Blaze..." he repeated, a pathetic tone creeping into his voice.

"Blaze and Vivens were arrested by my militiamen the moment they left the hall," Fervens said. "I have more than enough evidence against them for trading in illicit drugs. Do you understand, Solus? They never reached the signal tower. The message to your men never went out. We were expecting some such reaction from you should Adura's trial go against you, as we hoped it would. Now you are condemned by your own words."

Solus sagged, unsteady on his feet. "But the livery..."

"Some of the tunics are the disguises supplied by Magistra Calora to Adura and the other Daughters of the Dark. The others have been sewn together over the last two Shutterings."

For a moment, Solus looked as though he might topple. But then he rallied and turned towards old Magister Percuro sitting in the audience. "Percuro, you old fool! I told you not to cross me, or you would regret it. Shall I tell them what I know? Shall I?"

"That's enough."

Fervens dug in the point of his dagger so that a trickle of blood started, but Magister Percuro was now rising to his feet.

"You don't need to tell them, Solus. I shall do that. I should have done it long ago rather than be subject to your continual, wicked demands. But I was weak and foolish."

"You—!" Solus began, but Fervens twisted the dagger a trifle and he stopped. With a gesture of his head, Fervens called Jud across and the two men began to march Solus away.

The old Healer looked around at the audience.

"I would not be speaking now unless I had been forced to do so. Our society has already suffered many shocks this waking. What I have to tell you will, perhaps, be the greatest shock of all. All I can hope is that our community will ultimately be the better for the knowledge that I have to pass on."

~

The ceiling mirror was redirected towards where Magister Percuro stood at his place in the ranks of seating, surrounding him with a bright pool of light. Every eye was upon him. Percuro looked old beyond his already considerable years as he looked miserably about.

"Let me begin by saying that all of what Master Candens has told you is true. The Healers *have* been supplying drugs to the Signallers. Much against our will, I assure you. Mistress Campana was also telling the truth. A Healer did attend to her burns while she was kidnapped. It was I myself, visiting her in the city signal tower to where she had been carried after the fire. I was summoned there by Magistra Calora. All this is true.

"And now you must ask, why was Percuro forced to do as the Signallers demanded? Why has he not spoken out before? Why indeed. The reason is that I was blackmailed. They discovered a secret which I felt it was my sacred duty to preserve at all costs. Now, however, if I do not reveal that secret to you, Magister Solus will do so. It is better that you hear it on my terms.

"Several millends ago, the Signallers intercepted and read an encoded message that I had sent to my son Medeor. Yes, that also is true. The Signallers can read any message. You have no secrets. It is likely that the Signallers know them all."

A renewed burst of chatter came from the audience. It took a moment to quiet down again. Slowly, people were resuming their seats.

The brightest light in the hall now fell around where Percuro was speaking, but by shading her eyes with a hand, it was possible for Campana to see the audience in the dimmer light. Magistra Calora, her face like carved stone, had a militiaman at her side, dragging her away.

Over where the Bellringer Clan was located, she saw that Hermia, too, was standing with a militiaman next to her. Eccua was still seated, looking up at Ardens who was on his feet, his face florid. Lambent had propped himself up on his crutches and was arguing—with who? Hermia? The militiaman? His father? It was impossible to tell.

"In my message to my son," Percuro went on, "I described in detail a secret which until now has only ever been known to the clan head of the Healers. This secret has been kept for hundreds of millends, perhaps thousands. Normally it is passed on when the heir reaches the age of maturity at seven millends old. It is never written down. But as it happened, at the time Medeor reached that age, I had fallen gravely ill and feared for my life. He was away from our manor, several Shutterings ride away. I felt it was vital to pass on the information to him before I died. And fool that I was, I trusted to my secret code and to the Signallers' honour. That trust, as I have said, was betrayed.

"Having read and understood my message, Magister Solus knew that I would be desperate to keep it secret. Solus used the threat of revealing it to force me to do a great deal against my will. Perhaps it should never have been kept a secret at all; but I imagine that my clan felt that the

David R. Grigg

knowledge would shake people's faith and perhaps cause panic. That is still a danger, but now I have no choice.

"The secret is simply this. The Sun did not fall from the heavens to the Earth by God's command. No. The truth is that the Sun was *made* and placed where it stands in the bay, not by God but by man. It is a mechanism."

The hall was once again in an uproar.

Campana, though astonished at what she had just heard, had nevertheless been keeping a nervous eye on Hermia. Now she saw that Hermia was involved in some kind of struggle. The militiaman holding her unexpectedly fell back, right into her mother's lap. Now Lambent was grasping at Hermia, shouting something. Then he fell over, his crutches flying. Ardens grasped at Hermia and then jumped back, as though he had touched something hot. Eccua, half-rising, began to scream. Hermia squirmed past the others in an instant and began running down the steps between the seats.

Percuro, oblivious, continued, raising his voice a little.

"I beg of you, do not lose your faith in God, who surely created the Earth and the heavens, created mankind and all the creatures and plants which dwell upon the Earth. But we who lead the Healers know that the Sun which lights and warms us is not part of the natural world; not part of God's creation. The Sun was built, we believe, by human hands, thousands of millends ago. We see traces everywhere, do we not, of the great, lost civilisation of the ancients? See it in the godsteel artifacts, unworkable by our poor tools; see it in the skeleton towers. And beneath our feet runs a grid of tunnels lined with a smooth material no one today can make. It is clear that the ancients built the Sun with unimaginably powerful technology we have long since forgotten. We may thank God that they did, for without it all would be freezing darkness."

Hermia reached the floor of the hall and was now running full-tilt towards the stage. Campana cried out in
364

alarm, but the attention of everyone was on old Magister Percuro. Staring in horror at Hermia, Campana thought *I'm the one she blames. Not Candens, not Adura. Me.* She felt numb, unable to move, like a mouse cornered by a cat.

Hermia was up the steps and onto the stage in a flash. Candens, seeing the movement at last, turned and shouted. But it was too late. Hermia held a knife and it dripped with something dark. In the last moments before Hermia reached her, Campana recognised the carving knife Libeth had taken to bed to defend herself.

Hermia's eyes were wild with madness and fury. "I said," she gasped out, "that when you died, people would think it a sad accident. I was wrong."

Then Hermia evaded the hands Campana was raising to protect herself and plunged the knife into Campana's chest, just beneath the breast. Campana felt the knife stick for an instant between her ribs and then slide deeply within.

Candens and Ignis were there now, hauling Hermia away as she struggled and screamed curses. In the ranks of seats, Magister Percuro, finally realising something was wrong, stopped speaking.

Campana looked down. The knife was still sticking into her, a little blood now beginning to stain her tunic around its shaft. *How strange*, she thought, as her knees began to give way. *It doesn't hurt at all.*

Then somehow she found that she was lying on the floor, staring up towards the ceiling. She was finding it difficult to breathe and dark shadows began to cluster at the edges of her vision.

64

Adura

Adura's mind was whirling with all she had heard and experienced during the trial. Now, she leapt from her seat and ran to where Campana lay, with red blood beginning to stain her borrowed clothes. Adura knelt and reached a tentative hand to the knife handle protruding from Campana's chest, until a voice stopped her short.

"Leave it alone! The blade might be all that's keeping her alive."

It was Radians the Healer, who squatted down beside Campana.

"Can you save her?" Adura's voice broke with emotion.

"I'm going to do my very best. Just don't touch that knife." He looked upwards and shouted. "You there, shift the mirror so we have the light back down here. Grandfather!" The latter was a call to Magister Percuro, still standing forlornly in the audience. "Grandfather, we need your advice!"

The old man left his place and hurried down towards the stage. Radians turned back to Adura.

"She hasn't yet lost enough blood for her to lose consciousness. I think she simply fainted. That's hardly surprising."

As if to confirm Radians' diagnosis, Campana's eyes flickered open for an instant.

"What's... what...?"

"Don't move," Radians ordered gently. "You've been badly wounded. Don't try to speak."

"Radians..." Campana whispered. "This is... becoming a habit."

Adura was distressed to see that Campana's lips were taking on a slightly blue tinge.

"Quiet! Save your breath."

Radians pulled clean white strips of cloth from a bag at his side. A moment later and Magister Percuro was kneeling down too beside the fallen girl and the two Healers were consulting in quiet but urgent tones.

"The lung is punctured," Adura heard the old man say. "We'll need to—"

Then Adura's attention became distracted. The Great Hall was in uproar, full of shocked and distressed people. Arbiter Nolans stood at the front of the stage, bellowing as loudly as he could, urging the clan members in the audience to disperse, either to their private quarters or to leave the Hall entirely and go back to their manors. Slowly, people were beginning to obey and their numbers thin.

Eccua came running up the stage to be by her daughter's side, tears running down her face. Then came Lambent, lurching up on his crutches. His face was as gray as wood ash, his handsome features distorted and blurred. Adura intercepted him, fearing that he might blunder into the group of those tending to his sister. He seemed bewildered, unable to comprehend what was happening around him.

"Master Lambent. I'm Adura of the Mirrormasters, once Candens' pledge. Do you remember me?"

Lambent looked at her with a vacant expression. Was it just shock, or was he still under the influence of the drugs he had been encouraged to become dependent upon? Both, probably.

"She *pushed* me." Lambent's voice was pathetic, like a little boy bullied in a playground and his toy stolen. "She pushed me over. And she— Hermia said she was going to kill Campana. She was mad, insane. She had a knife, pulled it out of her sleeve and stabbed the militiaman. I tried to hold her but she pushed me over. Then my father tried to stop her, but she stabbed him, too. He— He's *dead*. And then..." He looked over to where Campana lay. "Hermia, my wife! I can't believe..."

His voice trailed into silence.

"Lambent, listen," Adura said gently. "Is a Healer looking after Magister Ardens and the militiaman? Your father may not be wounded as badly as you think."

"Doriens." Lambent nodded. "A Healer... Doriens came. The militiaman is just wounded, but my father... he said... too late. Too much blood!"

Lambent was obviously in no fit state to be left alone. Adura looked towards where Campana lay, hoping that she could gain assistance from Eccua, but she was still intent on her daughter. Adura turned back to Lambent.

"Please come with me, Lambent. You should go back to your quarters and rest. Come."

She put her arm around his shoulders and began to guide him towards the short flight of steps which led down from the stage. After a moment's resistance, he moved with her compliantly enough.

Just as they descended the steps, Candens came up along the floor of the hall. His face bore two long scratches, still bleeding. He stopped when he saw Lambent and Adura.

"Lambent?" Candens was clearly unsure how his brother would react to seeing him again.

"Candens... Is it true that Hermia lied to me and fed me *papavera*? I... I can't do without it now. I can't, Candens, I can't." Lambent face screwed up as though he was about to cry. "You weren't trying to kill me?"

"No. It was all part of the Signaller's plot. I'm sorry that we fought and that I hurt you. Believe me, it was the last thing I wanted. And I'm very much to blame for being taken in by Hermia. I was so stupid. Can you forgive me?"

"Forgive?" Lambent's face was still full of confusion. "I hated you, you know. *Hated* you."

"And now?"

"I... don't know. I'll try."

"Candens." Adura spoke quietly. "It seems Hermia stabbed your father, too, before she ran down to the stage. Lambent says that he's dead."

Candens closed his eyes for a long moment as he absorbed this new information and this new grief. The most immediate thought he had and hated himself for having, was that Lambent was now head of Clan Bellringer. *God help us all.* But there was no time to process that thought. He pushed it aside.

"And Campana? How is Campana?"

"Still alive. Radians and Percuro are doing what they can for her. But the knife has gone through a lung."

He shook his head, lips pressed firmly together, despair hanging over him like a shroud.

"I'm taking your brother back to his quarters," Adura said. "He's had a very bad shock. Your mother is with Campana, you should go see how she's bearing up."

"Yes. But then I must go and help the Commander. We stopped Blaze from sending out the signal to rally the Signaller troops, but the men in the signal tower could tell something had gone wrong and they've sent out some kind of message on their own initiative. We have a fight on our hands. Solus was right; they can communicate easily among themselves, but for us it's going to be a difficult struggle. Fervens is calling on all able-bodied men to join the Militia for the duration of the emergency."

Adura grimaced and then said with some of her old bitterness, "If only I had been taught to use a bow and a mace, I would join you myself. Think how much stronger you'd be if all of the women from all of the clans could take arms alongside you."

"Well, that's a longer battle. But we'll fight it together and win, Adura, I promise you."

She smiled. "I'll hold you to that. Now I must take your brother and settle him down."

Before she could lead him away, Lambent roused and spoke again to his brother.

"Candens? Our father is dead. That means it all falls on me, doesn't it? But I can't... I can't run the clan. Not by myself. Not like this."

"You'll get better, Lambent. I'll do what I can to help, I promise you."

"Then... if I'm head, I can do things, can't I? I can revoke father's banishment? Of you, I mean?"

"If you want to," Candens said slowly, not wanting to take advantage of his brother's currently limited presence of mind.

"Then I do. Do you hear me, Adura? You can be witness. I need Candens back in the clan."

"Thank you," Candens said. "But I can't take much joy in it, I'm afraid. I may well not return from this war we're going to have with the Signallers. Until you have children of your own, you should appoint Valend as your heir if I'm killed."

Left unsaid was the issue of the status of Lambent's marriage to Hermia. That bond would need to be annulled if Lambent was to marry again.

Candens turned to Adura.

"I have to go. I'll see you again as soon as I can."

"God speed," she said and kissed him on the cheek.

65

Candens

The remaining members of the Clan Council met on the following waking. After a little discussion, they unanimously appointed Nolans of the Metalworkers as their new President. They put plans in place for another session of the Grand Council Court. Its purpose would be to formally condemn and proscribe the whole of the Signallers Clan and dispossess them of their lands and property. That was going to be easier to declare than achieve, Candens knew.

Solus, Calora, Hermia and Blaze were all confined in the Shadow Prison awaiting the decision of the court. To Candens' dismay, however, Vivens had apparently escaped the militiamen sent to arrest him and was now leading the forces of Clan Signaller. It was obvious that the Signallers weren't going to give up easily.

Furious battles were raging with the remaining Signallers and their allies. Though mostly minor clans, there were more of them backing the Signallers than Candens would have imagined. In almost every such case, though, the clan head or heir turned out to be married to a Signaller. The loyal servants of the Signallers and these other clans fought fiercely alongside their masters.

Vivens developed a highly effective tactic of surprise ambush. Using their towers, it was easy for him to coordinate the movement of their forces. That was why Commander Fervens' strategy was to try to take and hold each signal tower in turn, slowly depriving the Signallers of their most powerful weapon. Even so, every waking saw hand-held mirrors flashing from hill-top to hill-top, sending undecipherable messages.

Commander Fervens formally re-appointed Candens as an officer in the Militia. In this role, he had already been instrumental in fighting off an assault by Vivens' men on the Shadow Prison, attempting to free Solus and the other Signallers imprisoned there. It seemed likely they would try again. It could be a long and bloody war.

Adura, too, had taken on an active role in the conflict. Together with other young women who had been tricked by Raven, she had formed a new organisation: The Daughters of the Wind. Mounted and speeding across the countryside, they were carrying vital messages back and forth between the Militia's forces. "We may not have been taught how to fight," she said to Candens, "but we know how to ride." Although slower than the messages flashed between the Signallers, they were a very necessary, indeed a vital component in the fight against them.

Because of the distractions of his role in the Militia, it took Candens far longer than it should have for him to realise that they had access to a powerful communications medium of their own. While they couldn't as yet send very detailed messages like those the Daughters of the Wind could carry, the bell towers of his own clan could readily sound out alarms and spread them throughout the land. He began to work out a system of coded bell-peals which could convey other useful information to the troops in the field.

⁓

A few decants later, during a short lull in the fighting, Candens took the opportunity to return to his manor to see his family.

Lambent was now almost fully recovered from his injuries, but he was still struggling against his dependence on *papavera*. Old Magister Percuro was taking a personal interest, blaming himself for the quantities of the drug he had provided to the Signallers. Slowly, very slowly, he was helping Lambent reduce his intake, but it would be a long process. Lambent himself now seemed a mere shell of his former carefree self. Without Hermia he was adrift and according to his mother, often spent long periods wandering aimlessly around the manor. Formally, of course, he was now Magister Lambent of the Bellringers, but everyone including himself agreed that he was not yet ready to take over control of the clan. Valend was effectively clan head and Nitens was Pendulum Master. Old Sonor still worked on as Book Master, now with much more than usual to record, filling page after page in his volumes of history.

Campana was not there, but under close care at the Healer's manor. She was alive, but still engaged in a struggle with infection just as fierce as the conflict against the Signallers, each breath its own battle. She drifted in and out of consciousness. Radians was by her side at every moment he could spare. As time went by, he began to express more confidence in her eventual recovery. He told Candens the tale of how, several Shutterings before the trial, he had been asleep in the Healer's Chapel where he worked, to be woken by his servant well after the Shuttering peal. A young woman was at the door, demanding to see him. It had been Campana. After she had convinced him of her story, together they devised a strategy of smuggling her in to the Council Court, disguised as a boy, to retain the advantage of surprise over the Signallers.

Libeth, Campana's maid, had gone missing from the manor at the same time as Campana and for a long time it had been thought that she had travelled with her mistress. It was now clear that she had not. A search had begun for her body. The Healers strongly advised against passing this news on to Campana until she was fully recovered.

Candens found that his mother Eccua had changed in ways he had not expected. She stood straighter somehow, and her face had gained strength. Her white hair was like a crown. At Ardens' funeral, she had stood by the pyre shedding copious tears, her grief obvious. Candens had found that a touch surprising, given how unhappy she had always seemed, always in Ardens' shadow. He had thought she might find his death a kind of release. As tactfully as he could, he now asked about her feelings. Eccua didn't answer for a while and then not directly.

"I did grow to love him, in a way, at least, as best I could. He was a hard man, but that was just the way he was, the way he had been raised. I suppose I'm sad for what might have been rather than what was. Does that make sense?"

"Yes." Candens hugged her. "I think it does."

66

Adura

She sat to one side of the stage in the Great Hall, feeling weary. Her legs and arms were aching from the constant riding to and fro she had been doing, carrying important messages as one of the Daughters of the Wind. Beside her, Eccua sat fidgeting nervously. Adura laid a hand on the older woman's arm to calm her and she responded with a weak smile.

The assembled clans in the Hall had just completed the major purpose of this gathering—the proscription of the Signallers, by now a mere formality. Solus and Hermia would spend the rest of their lives in the Shadow Prison. Calora and Blaze were each sentenced to spend at least two millends there. Adura thought that sentence far too light. But the sentence also specified that neither would be released until the war with the Signallers was over, something not yet in prospect.

Now, Council President Nolans addressed the audience.

"Magisters and Magistras, Masters and Mistresses. Much has now changed in our world. Our commerce and our social lives are now greatly constrained by the loss of the messages previously transmitted by the Signallers. We must learn to live without signals until we can find a way to replace that service once the war is over. How we can do that and retain trust in those operating the signal towers will be no easy matter to resolve. In this regard, I have been interested in the proposals put forward to the Council by Master Candens of the Bellringers. I ask you now to give him leave to speak to this assembly."

There was no dissent.

Adura watched Candens walk to the centre of the pool of light cast by the mirror above. He stood silent for a long moment. She understood his hesitation. What he had to say was so important and yet so perilous. But it was very necessary. He glanced back at her for reassurance. She nodded and smiled at him and he appeared to take strength from that and began.

"Clan members all, thank you for hearing me. As President Nolans has said, much has changed in our world over the last centend. We uncovered the plot of one clan to take control over all of Sunfall. We learned that many messages which we sent in the past were not secret, as we thought them, but were easily read by the Signallers. And yet our whole society has been built upon secrets, each clan keeping what it knows from every other clan. Any knowledge that we discover, any technology which we develop, has been kept closely by the clan that found it. There has been almost no progress in our society for many hundreds of millends, perhaps for thousands. Progress which would have come if clan knowledge could be shared equally between us all, with each clan able to build upon what another clan has found out.

"Magister Percuro told us that we have no secrets. That is both true and not true. The Signallers, between them, probably know many of your closest-kept secrets. And even though I am confident that we will win the battle against them, this remains a dangerous situation. The clan head and his closest family are in prison. Vivens will follow when we finally win this war. But what are we to do then with the many other clan members, their servants and their couriers? We cannot imprison them all. We cannot claw back our secrets from them. Would it not be better to open all of the shutters and let light in on our knowledge? Isn't it better to let everyone know what we have kept secret for so long, rather than allow the Signallers to regain power by using what they have already discovered? I say that it is. Let each clan retain its speciality—that clan will always be best at what it has practised for so long. But it can share what it knows with its neighbour and learn what its neighbour knows which might improve what it does."

Candens took a deep breath.

"In this regard, Clan Bellringer is prepared to open its doors and reveal how we keep track of time and what we know of bell-making." It had taken some strong persuasion to get Valend to agree to this, but he had won. Lambent had agreed too, but as yet seemed to care little about the future. "The Healers, too, will reveal what they know of medicine, information which should be in everyone's hands. We now ask the other clans to join us and begin to share their knowledge."

Candens was met with complete silence from the audience. Adura felt a pang of unease.

"I see that you doubt the need for such a change," Candens continued. "Then think about this. At the Grand Court several decants ago, Magister Percuro was forced to reveal a secret about the very nature of our world. I'm sure that few of us have yet made sense of what he told us, let alone considered what it means for our future. Magister Percuro revealed to us that the Sun is not a natural object. It was made, constructed, presumably by human hands. It is like a campfire lit in deep shadow, lighting up and warming only a small circle around it. But, of course, on a vastly greater scale."

He paused, letting that sink in.

"What is difficult to understand is how incredibly advanced the knowledge of the Sun's creators must have been. If mankind once possessed such knowledge, such technical power, how did we come to lose it? Why was the Sun created? What was the world like before it was made?"

David R. Grigg

He hesitated, seemingly unsure whether to go on, but with the audience silent, he continued. "I have had a nightmare. Perhaps a few of you have shared it. It is this: if the Sun is simply a device, however complex, something built by human hands and therefore fallible... what if it should break? What if, one waking, the Sun were to stop working?"

Cries of horror, a few screams. Some people jumped to their feet as though they wanted to run in panic. Few, it appeared, had shared Candens' fears until now. *But surely,* Adura thought, *any intelligent person thinking about it would eventually come to that conclusion?*

"Please! Calm yourselves!" Candens shouted. It took a while, but quiet returned. "The Sun has been working for thousands of millends at least, perhaps for many thousands. There is no immediate prospect of it failing. Perhaps it may last for many thousands of millends yet. But I put it to you that this fear is the strongest reason of all for our society and our culture to change. If we ever have a need to repair or replace the Sun, we will need to have a technology as advanced as that of the Ancients. We will never get there if we continue to keep all of our secrets to ourselves."

He looked towards where Adura and Eccua stood at the side of the stage. "Nor will we get there if we continue to waste half our resources by refusing the help of our women. There is no doubt that our society has been greatly distorted by the keeping of clan secrets. I ask you now to hear my mother, Magistra Eccua of the Bellringers; and Mistress Adura, daughter of Clan Mirrormaster."

Eccua was breathing quickly as she and Adura went up on the stage. Eccua was holding Adura's hand so tightly that it hurt, but Adura did not complain. Such a public appearance was a great challenge for the older woman. But such was its importance that she was forcing herself to step

378

forward. They stood together before the audience and Eccua opened her mouth, but only gaped like a fish.

"It's all right," Adura encouraged her. "Take a deep breath and go on."

Eccua looked into the audience and spoke out, at first hesistatingly, but her voice eventually gaining strength.

"What my son Candens says is true. I am becoming old now and I feel, as I'm sure many older women do, that my life has been largely wasted. Women in our society, Bright women, that is, are deprived of truly useful work. Clans are obliged to keep their deepest secrets from their daughters and nieces, knowing that they will eventually be married into other clans. Even when married, men have kept their wives in a similar state of ignorance and subjected them to sometimes brutal control." Eccua paused, before adding quietly, "I know that only too well."

Eccua gulped and stepped back to make way for Adura as a wave of muttering spread in the audience. Adura waited for their full attention, before speaking boldly.

"What a waste of women's potential!" she said. "What a loss to society!

"You know of my trial, how I joined the secret organisation the Daughters of the Dark and how my desire to see change was cruelly exploited by the Signallers. But that desire has not faltered. The pledging system must be abandoned. Don't forget that it was through that system that Clan Signaller strategically placed its daughters and nieces into other clans, to spy and sabotage for their own advantage. The Signallers may have failed. But if the pledging system remains, what is to stop some other unscrupulous clan trying to do the same in future?"

Renewed muttering came, louder this time.

"We urge you to join us, men and women both, to work towards positive change. Even if you will not actively work with us towards that end, at the very least, I beg you, teach your women about the work of your clans and let them help you with it. Do not pledge your daughters and sons, but from now on let young people follow their hearts in choosing whom to marry."

A burst of agitated chatter swelled in the audience. The proposal to change the way pledging worked was far more controversial than the change to the keeping of clan secrets, it seemed.

Candens rejoined Adura and his mother on the stage. He had told Adura that he would find occasion to speak here again, when he planned to speak out against the artificial and damaging division in society which existed between the Brights and the Dims. But not this waking.

"Thank you for hearing us," he said. "Please think carefully on what we have said."

The audience was silent for a long moment as the three began to leave the stage, but one person began to clap and the applause quickly spread, strengthening into a full-scale barrage of sound.

"Well done," Candens whispered to Adura. "Well done," he repeated to his mother.

"You, too," Eccua said. "Let's hope that it does some good."

67

Candens

Candens was filled with a nervous excitement unlike anything he had ever felt before.

With Adura at his side, he walked down a smooth-lined tunnel sloping beneath the sea. A seeming eternity ago, she had walked in the opposite direction, towards the shadow house, leading a group of frightened young women with hoods over their heads. He knew that she deeply regretted that now. Yet it had led to important, world-changing events and they had to be content with that.

With them walked Old Magister Percuro, limping a little with age, and young Radians, his heir. Radians held a lamp high to ward off the dark and the cold and carried a back-pack which made slight chinking noises as they walked.

Campana had begged to be allowed to accompany them, but he and Radians had quietly persuaded her that she was still too weak to make the journey. Candens knew that he would have to remember every detail so that on his return he could tell her everything that her eager mind wanted to know.

They had been walking for perhaps the duration of one bell, a fifth of the time between peals. When they had first begun, Candens had feared that they would need to walk all the way to the Sun, which would surely have taken them two Shutterings or more; too far for old Magister Percuro, surely. He had assured them that the voyage would not be so long, but would not elaborate. The reluctance to let go of old secrets was still strong. On the other hand, bringing

David R. Grigg

Candens and Adura along was a ground-breaking shift away from secrecy in itself.

"We come here several times each millend," Percuro had said, "the clan head and his heir. It has always been this way. That, of course, is the reason for the secret door in the chapel which leads down to this tunnel. To gain access to the Sun. I don't know which of my ancestors was the first to go in the *other* direction and find a way into the shadow house. Or perhaps he set up the shadow house, I don't know."

Something changed in Candens' view ahead. Was the tunnel coming to an end? As they drew nearer, he could see that they were approaching a steel door. He tried to avoid thinking of the weight of the sea which must surely now be over their heads. It was impossible to know how deep they were now beneath its waters.

Percuro limped up to the tunnel wall next to the door. A shallow alcove there held seven circular shapes like the wheels of a child's toy. Candens now could see that the shapes were faintly glowing with their own light, illuminating a set of markings around them.

"Radians!" Percuro called. "Come. You must see and understand this, it is vital."

Radians obediently came closer and watched as Percuro spun the wheels, one after the other in a complex sequence.

"Do you see? Will you remember?" Percuro asked.

Radians nodded.

"Show me," the old man insisted and watched as Radians repeated the operation.

"Good," Percuro said. "Now once more, but much faster this time. The lock will only open if you complete the sequence quickly."

Radians obeyed, his hands moving rapidly between the various wheels. The steel door gave a loud sigh before it broke into seven segments, which retracted into the tunnel walls, revealing a clear bright light, against which everyone

382

stood blinking for a moment. Ahead the tunnel continued, with overhead bars of light illuminating its length.

"Come." Percuro turned to Candens and Adura and walked forward.

As he set his foot past the doorway, the floor of the tunnel came alive and started to move of its own accord. Wonderingly, the others followed. Behind them, Candens heard a soft sigh. He glanced back and saw that the seven-segmented door had closed again.

Once they were all on the moving floor, it began to speed up and the walls slipped by in a blur. Only a short while later, the floor slowed and stopped. Another steel door stood before them. Again, with Radians watching, Magister Percuro operated a set of wheels embedded into the wall. The second door sighed open and they emerged into a room which was blazing with light.

Some of the light fell down from a circular window overhead, some from windows to left and right. Each was fitted with a pane of thick, dense and very dark glass, which must be greatly reducing the light passing through. Looking up in awe, Candens saw that they were now at the very foot of the impossibly tall tower which those in Sunfall called the Pillar of Fire. At its top the Sun poured forth its furious incandescence. To each side, he saw details he had never been able to make out before because of the brightness of the Sun: the shore of the small island in the middle of the bay on which the tower stood and great pipes passing between the tower and the sea.

Other light in the room came from curious glowing glass portals set around a semi-circular wall. There were seven such portals and beneath each were painted ranks of little pictures.

"You see..." Magister Percuro pointed at the pictures. "The Builders of the Sun must have feared—or maybe they knew—that their descendants would forget their knowledge. They did not know what language we might speak long after they were gone. So they made these simple pictures, which tell a story of what needs to be done to keep the Sun operating. You will see a few levers here and here and this bin here, see how it opens? These strange glass plates show us signs if something needs attention. That is all. I fear that the Sun-builders did not trust us. They felt that we would be very ignorant." He sighed. "As indeed we are."

A question came to Candens. "Why was it, do you think, that Clan Healer was given this grave responsibility, Magister?"

Percuro gave a slight shrug. "That is a good question and I do not truly know the answer. Family legend has it that much of our medical knowledge, written down in books which have been copied and recopied countless times over the millends, originally came from the Builders. The health and perhaps the spiritual welfare of those who live in Sunfall must have been of great importance to the Builders."

"But why does the Sun need our attention at all?" Adura was puzzled.

"That's another good question, to which I don't really know the answer. I imagine that there are some materials that it requires that it cannot obtain itself. See here, where this orange symbol flashes on this panel? That tells us that it needs to be supplied with metal. It is usually metal, but at other times it calls for certain kinds of rock, identified by colour and hardness. But now it is metal. Radians, show us your pack."

Radians took off the heavy pack and opened it to reveal various items of bronze such as small statues and a broken scythe-blade, together with a few pieces of silver jewellery and a handful of rings, bronze, silver and steel.

"Empty it here."

Percuro opened the bin and Radians did as instructed. The metal rattled into the bin and down a chute. Gradually the orange symbol changed colour to green and stopped flashing.

"It needs very little," Percuro said. "It must be designed to do everything it can to repair itself. But perhaps there are small losses over time. Perhaps there are moving parts which rub against each other, wearing each other away? That may be too crude an understanding. We know so little. Metal is so expensive now, however. It strains our resources to provide even this. I do wonder..."

Candens frowned as Percuro's voice drifted off. "What do you wonder?"

"Whether there was once far more metal available in Sunfall. Perhaps once it might even have been common. But over thousands of millends, providing this regular... what shall we say? This regular *tribute* to the Sun, perhaps much of it has been consumed."

"That's not a pleasant thought. What happens if we run out of metal?"

For a long moment the only answer was silence.

"Without metal..." Candens finally expressed the unspoken dread in the room. "Eventually the Sun may die."

"Yes." Percuro spoke sadly.

"Then we must find another source of metal." Adura spoke as if this was obvious. "Even if it means going beyond the light of the Sun."

"Yes," Candens said. "Once the war is done, we must travel out. We must venture into the outer darkness."

He could not have imagined at that moment how long the war would last, nor what it would cost. Still less could he imagine what they would eventually discover outside the oasis of light that was Sunfall.

Acknowledgements

I would like to thank the very many friends and family who helped me work on this novel over several years. Without their encouragement, support and expertise, I would never have completed it.

These people include:

- My dear wife Sue, who supports me in every way.
- My wife, my daughter Kathryn and my mother Nellie. Each read early drafts of the book and had many useful things to say about it.
- My beta readers Becky Raymond/Becket Morgan, Ian Buchanan, LynC and Robert Brunton, whose generally positive reactions kept me going and whose occasionally negative reactions made me rethink matters.
- In particular I want to thank Jyoti Q Dahiya, whose detailed criticisms and suggestions were extremely helpful (and led me to dropping one or more scenes I'm now glad I lost).
- Bruce Gillespie, who inspired me with his early enthusiasm for the book and who supported me in many ways.
- My oldest friend Carey Handfield, who has been nagging for me for decades to write and keep on writing.
- My structural and copy editor Suzanne Lucadou-Wells, from whose professional skills I have learned a great deal, and who significantly tightened up and improved every page of the manuscript.

What Next?

Thank you so much for reading this book. I hope you enjoyed it! I'm planning to write more. The next book in this series is already in progress.

Here are some things you can do next:

- If you liked it, please let your friends know, and consider leaving a nice review on Amazon or Goodreads (or both!).

- Email me at *fallen.sun@rightword.com.au* and let me know what you thought about the book, good or bad.

- Follow me on Twitter: *@david_r_grigg*.

- Visit my website at *rightword.com.au* for the latest news.

- Visit and follow my Amazon Author Page via *bit.ly/davidrgrigg*

- Buy my books from Amazon, Kobo, CreateSpace, Gumroad, or from *rightword.com.au/books*.

—DAVID GRIGG
August 2018